PATHWAYS

Also by Katie Ward

Girl Reading

PATHWAYS

KATIE WARD

FLEET

2024

FLEET

First published in Great Britain in 2024 by Fleet

1 3 5 7 9 10 8 6 4 2

A CIP catalogue record for this book
is available from the British Library.

Hardback ISBN 978-0-349-00418-1
Trade paperback ISBN 978-1-84408-905-5

Typeset in Electra by M Rules
Printed and bound in Great Britain by
Clays Ltd, Elcograf S.p.A.

Papers used by Fleet are from well-managed forests
and other responsible sources.

Fleet
An imprint of
Little, Brown Book Group
Carmelite House
50 Victoria Embankment
London EC4Y 0DZ

An Hachette UK Company
www.hachette.co.uk

www.littlebrown.co.uk

This is a book for Emma.

Contents

What reads books is the whole person.

MARY MIDGLEY
Science and Poetry

1

Nociceptors

pain

Heather

A shred of light. Gone, and back, and gone again.

Heather chops with her arms, fingers splayed. Not together like oars, although she's been told to enough times. Fringe stuck over her eyes as she lifts out her face to take a breath, and is swept back when she dips down. This is for babies, she thinks.

Exhales below the surface making bubbles of interference, chlorine up her nose.

Inhales above it, eyes scrunched against the splashes, stinging, and playground noise of the municipal pool. Scissor kicks.

It's quiet underwater, where Heather aims for the lower half of a woman in a black swimsuit. The locker key lit and unlit on her wrist as she beckons her.

Cara

She needs to know. Turns off the ignition, and the radio chatter continues, a discussion about the wage gap conflated as usual with maternity rights.

Welcome to Eglantine Manor.

The care home is an eighties build with a pattern of red and yellow bricks like an Aran jumper. The website has pictures of hanging baskets bulging with geraniums, tomato plants at waist height, and sunflowers taller than residents. Today nothing grows in the borders except weeds.

She sees a visitor speak into an entry system to gain access.

Cara would ask outright, but Paul doesn't like to be reasoned with. He doesn't like hearing the legal advantages of getting married either; that for instance it's in his interests to do so because if something happened to her – her, Cara – then he'd be all right. She has offered to pay for a solicitor to get things moving. Once they even got as far as booking an appointment; then the duty manager called to report an accident with a hoist that resulted in three stitches. It was unfortunate timing.

The two incidents were unconnected, and Cara told him so. Yet he took it as a sign, and they didn't rearrange.

Her plait is coming undone, and she presses wisps behind her ears. Dithers over her sunglasses, which will be conspicuous if worn indoors. Swaps them for normal.

She wants to be with him. Not in a *Guardian*-reading, Ed Sheeran-listening kind of way – where the woman likes football and the man likes romantic comedies. She's okay with them being together in a real way. The rough with the smooth. As long as she knows what she's dealing with.

She enters Eglantine Manor with a flourish: she is buzzed in.

'I'm Dr Brenner,' she says, reaching for a pen to sign in as if she's done it a hundred times. 'To see Mrs Wycliffe.'

The care worker is an Eastern European with sharp cheekbones. 'To see Ruth?'

'That's right, Ruth Wycliffe.' She writes *Dr* then her surname illegibly and scrambles the registration details of her vehicle.

'You're her doctor? You have been before?'

'I'm from the Neuroscience Centre. I'm here to assess her. I'm surprised you weren't expecting me.' She offers her photo ID.

'From the university?'

Cara sanitises her hands in a businesslike fashion. And she has done enough to be shown through. 'How is Mrs Wycliffe?'

'She is no trouble, takes her medication like a good girl. Appears happy.'

'I assume she cannot feed herself? Bathe, um, bathroom herself?'

'None in her wing do, they are very limited mobility, unless we move them. She is having a duvet day.'

They go down a corridor with a lino floor and handrails along the walls. Faded prints of countryside cottages and teddy bears hang crookedly. Doors and doors: a few open to functional, magnolia bedrooms, a cross between a hospital and a Travelodge.

The residents are in pyjamas and tracksuits. There's a lounge area where armchairs have plastic covers and a repeat of *Poirot* on a communal TV. They watch, nap or fret. A carer, also wearing a plastic cover, dispenses drugs from a trolley.

The noticeboard is covered with announcements including *Smile, You're on CCTV!*

Cara doesn't. 'Can Ruth, Mrs Wycliffe, can she speak?'

The carer taps a security code on another door. 'She should not be in here.'

'What makes you say that?' If Ruth's too lucid, she must find a way to leave.

'Too young. She shouldn't be with the old people. Her husband is strong. He should take care.'

An assistant offers Cara tea from an urn, which she refuses, not wanting to touch any part of this place with her mouth. The smells of urine and bleach.

A frail resident in a red dressing gown chants, 'I want a biscuit, I want a biscuit, I want a biscuit,' without pausing for breath.

'No, naughty, this is not your visitor.'

The whine of an alarm calls the carer away, and Cara is left alone.

Room 19, Mrs Ruth Wycliffe.

Ruth is raised in bed. Her head is propped with pillows and she clutches foam rolls to stop her nails digging into her palms.

Yes, she is young compared to the rest, her expression fixed with her mouth open and bushy eyebrows raised. The sheets are bunched, her torso bolstered with more pillows along one side, and on the other there's a guard rail to prevent her falling. Her feet almost fold back on themselves, and her tiny frame is contorted. Her fair hair is cropped short. Her skin, dry and flaky. Grey eyes. The print on her nightie is of seashells.

'Hello, Mrs Wycliffe. I'm a friend, here to visit. I'd like to know how you're getting on.' Cara leans closer to get her attention. 'How do you feel? Are you well today?'

Ruth's stare goes right through her.

'My name is Cara Brenner. Has anyone mentioned me to you before? Would you remember if they did?'

Ruth sounds like she has a cold.

Cara takes out her iPad as though it were a genuine assessment after all, mainly because if someone comes in she ought to look busy.

Ruth is smirking. Or was it a flash of pain?

If Cara had her in an fMRI scanner, things might go differently.

'I'm going to ask you a few simple questions,' she'd say. 'To answer *yes*, I want you to imagine playing tennis ... And for *no*, imagine you're walking around the rooms of your house. Got that? *Tennis for yes* – pretend you're chasing a ball around the court, and you send it flying over the net with a good swing – and being in *your own home for no*. All right, let's begin. First, are you in physical pain?' Cara visualises the parahippocampal gyrus lighting up, which shows the subject accessing spatial memories. 'Very well then. Let's see if you know what month it is. Is this February? Is February the month we're in ... ? And what about the future; will you agree to a divorce so that your husband can get on with his life?' She'd look for a response in the supplementary motor area at this point. 'Am I a joke to you?'

'Wuh.' Is she laughing at her? Perhaps Ruth understands more than she lets on.

Cara puts the iPad away. Prefers looking at brains as data sets; that's where the substance is.

There are photos around the room: Ruth in a wetsuit hugging a surfboard with beach hair. Ruth in a halter neck drinking a milkshake. Ruth caught off guard in some ruins in a hot country: she is wearing a hamsa pendant and pouting in a familiar way.

Cara tries guessing where it is: the Acropolis, or Ephesus maybe. Paul hasn't mentioned a holiday abroad like that.

Ruth in fancy dress with four friends in a pub: she is Cyndi Lauper, and they're the girls who just want to have fun. In the next picture they're her bridesmaids, and Ruth's wedding dress is shocking. (Cara couldn't come up with four female friends, but at least she has taste.) Paul looks slimmer and has thicker hair, although he never looks comfortable in a suit. He isn't in many of Ruth's photos. Come to think of it, he isn't in many of Cara's either.

Then a ginger newborn in Ruth's arms, which gives her a pang. A ginger toddler by the swings. A ginger child petting a ginger cat called Nugget.

And a gap of years like a redacted document.

It is unclear why Ruth has a bookshelf. *Moby-Dick, Frankenstein, 1984.* Anne Rice, V. C. Andrews, Stephen King. Hannah Arendt, Michel Foucault, Susan Sontag. They're mostly paperbacks, and it's hard to imagine who might be reading them to her.

Cara opens the only mint-condition hardback, *Claribel of Tunis* by Reginald Ely. She glances at an inscription in the author's handwriting:

Ru,

Be gentle, keep hopeful and stay free.

Yours ever,

Reg

A Cambridge snow globe is on the windowsill. Cara shakes it in front of Ruth's face, to see if she'll react. Storm static covers King's College Chapel, then dissipates. Ruth doesn't seem to notice.

There's a CD player and FM radio with buttons missing.

'You ought to listen to music,' Cara says, tuning to a classical station. 'Studies show how well it works, better than drugs. Don't they go in for digital here? Do the immigrants steal whatever they can sell on?'

She flicks through a wallet of CDs, like the one she used to keep in her glove compartment. Etta James, James Brown, Carole King; Bob Marley, Leonard Cohen, Patti Smith; Kate Bush, Siouxsie and the Banshees, The Cure.

'I'm jealous of your CD player, I rather miss mine. CDs get a bad rap, don't they?' She slides one out of the sleeve and turns it over. It's scratched on the back.

Paul calls it a well-spouse affair, but she is sure that's a term he read online and uses incorrectly. For one thing, Cara doesn't have an ill spouse, so their relationship isn't based on a shared experience and bitter-sweet mutual support. For another, an affair suggests adultery committed in secret, but they live together openly and have for a while now.

On her way out Cara can still hear, 'I want a biscuit, I want a biscuit, I want a fucking biscuit,' echoing through the hallway.

She pours gel on her hands till they sting and smell of isopropanol. Shoulders her way into the fresh air.

At least we're moving in the right direction, she thinks. Consciousness will be explained sooner or later. When enough neural correlates have been discovered and understood, and once the data issues – sharing, massiveness and complexity – are overcome. When that happens, borderline cases can be resolved. Ruth hasn't done anything wrong, except go on too long.

She gets in the car and has a piece of chewing gum in lieu of lunch. Needs to get back. As she turns the ignition, Cara catches a glimpse of red in the rear-view mirror. And there's the pang again.

Heather

She opens her dad's white van – can't see what she's looking for. Hand tools, power tools, drill bits are stored haphazardly with cables, alarm systems and replacement parts.

She looks in his toolboxes. In a hardcase. In a bucket, where she finds rolls of gaffer tape and takes one. Pulls out black plastic sheeting from under a stepladder, knocking around fast-food containers. Pockets a Stanley knife.

Rescues cardboard from the recycling. Liberates the kitchen scissors. Tries to make everything fit in her rucksack.

At Eglantine she finds a trolley with clean towels and bedding. Heather grabs some of these too, before going into her mum's room and locking the door behind her.

Heather takes a selfie: her dimpled smile, and Ruth's grimace and half-closed eyes.

'Good one. Your hair looks pretty today. Smells appley, very feminine.'

Ruth spasms.

Heather starts by laying towels along the crack under the door, and covers the hinges by taping plastic over them.

'I'm not especially interested in boys. Girls aren't much better really, not as mature as they say. Those bitches are ignoring me now, which I prefer. I'm hanging out more with Betty Willis? I don't know why she likes me because she's quite cool and I – I like her because she's thoughtful. She sends me messages and answers mine, you don't need to worry about that, and ... She does these amazing faces like a real make-up artist? I'll see if I can find you any.'

Heather looks for pictures on her phone, holds it in front of Ruth's nose and swipes.

'And this is us eating ice cream we bought at a stand. I had strawberry and Betty had ... Can't remember, there were bits in it. We walked in the grounds of one of the colleges – just strolled in through the gates and sat on a bench. The porter man said we were trespassing and made us leave, which was mean, we were only sitting there, we weren't spoiling anything. We were almost finished, so, quite funny really? It's pretty with the bridges and boats and the grass all flat and the same length, but you're not allowed to walk on it, it's just for looking at.'

The view from Ruth's window is of evergreen trees, a bird table and fence, and the rear entrance of Purple Patch soft play centre. Heather blacks it out like wartime. Uses gaffer tape and sheeting to obscure every chink of light.

'Betty said he noticed us because of her, and I could've got away with it if I was by myself. And I said, I'd rather be kicked out with her than taken for one of them. But I don't think it helped, she seemed upset. You can't tell what's going on with people, I guess. We don't do anything stupid, I mean, dangerous. I wanted to ask you what you did when you left school? What countries you went to? Dad doesn't seem to know and he gets funny if I ask too much. Were you a waitress or have I made that up? Shall I be a waitress?'

Heather strokes her mum's hand and imagines working in a

posh restaurant. Imagines weaving between tables with white tablecloths on a busy evening. Knowing her customers' names and the menu by heart. Carrying large plates with fancy little portions. She'd have a black dress, hoop earrings, and her hair done up in an elegant knot with a pen tucked in. There'd be candlelight, and then dawn.

She moves a chair against the door and stands on it to block out the transom windowpane above.

On the other side, a member of staff supporting a resident looks up at her.

'A waitress can work anywhere she likes,' Heather says, taping along the frame. 'It hardly matters what city you end up in. I bet you know a lot, more than *she* does. I wish I paid you more attention when I was younger. I should've asked questions when I had the chance, shouldn't I?'

She turns off the light switch. The room darkens.

'Dad thinks he can keep secrets from you. It's stupid, because you know everything. He's not as strong as you are. Please be patient with him?'

She takes the knife and makes a cut in the centre of the black plastic on the window: a peephole to the garden. Even as she's doing it she realises it's too large. It gapes from the glass, daylight leaking in.

She tries cutting a hole in a piece of cardboard instead, the size of a five-pence.

While she's taping it snug over the first hole, there is a knock at the door.

'Is everything all right?'

'Don't come in,' Heather calls back.

'Why did you cover the small glass? What are you doing? It is not safe.' The care assistant tries the door. 'Unlock this, please?'

Heather works faster to make the room black with a dot of light.

There are raised voices from the hall and they're trying the door again. 'What's happening? Open it, now.'

'Go away!'

In the seconds it takes for her eyes to adjust – and Ruth to emerge floating in the sky – they find a key and force their way in, ripping through the materials.

The bedroom is saturated with light.

And there is Heather standing with a blade in her hand.

She is made to wait in the manager's office for Paul to collect her.

Sits in the passenger seat of the van with his old issues of *Coast* magazine and *Classic Boat*. Fanta bottles at her feet, and a tree air freshener dangling from the mirror.

'Explain what you were doing?' he says as he drives.

She doesn't reply.

'Skiving. Not for the first time, was it. Stealing. Carrying a knife. What else don't I know about? Druggies?'

Heather rolls her eyes.

'The damage you've done to the paintwork,' he says, 'they'll bill me for. They'll move her out to redecorate and won't bother moving her back in. She'll get a worse room because of this. That was a nice one she had, where she could watch the birds, and near the nurses' station in case there was a problem? You've ruined it. You aren't allowed to visit her by yourself any more.'

The ring road is at a standstill. Cyclists weave around roadworks. It rains thinly, the windscreen wipers making visibility worse.

'I don't want you seeing the end. Cara says you aren't old enough.'

'She said that?' It comes out louder than she intends. Cara is supposed to be on Heather's side. She goes on about 'us girls' sticking together.

'Cara knows more about these things. She said it's too disturbing for young minds. I'm sorry for you.'

'Mum wants me there when it happens. It'll be good for us.'

'Your mother can't have a say in what she doesn't understand.'

The traffic in front of them stop-starts. The light is green, but there's nowhere to go.

Heather sighs. 'Will you be with her? Or will you be in the car park eating Greggs?'

His face settles in a blank as if he hasn't heard.

Cara

Virtual brain slices with blobs of orange and blue, hot and cool like weather systems on grey maps. Data spools across a screen in the control booth.

Behind thick glass, the volunteer lies in an fMRI scanner, like a pharaoh in a magnetic sarcophagus. Trussed up in a head brace, blanket, and trailing wires. He is obeying the instruction to keep still.

He's shown pictures and his answers appear as he presses a keypad in his hand.

[Pyramids of Giza] ... [Green].

[Snowflake symmetry] ... [Green].

[Tiles from the Alhambra] ... [Green].

Silvia, who administrates timeslots in the scanner, is monitoring him.

[Conch] ... [Green].

[Surrealism painting by Miró] ... [Red].

[Rings of Saturn] ... No response.

[Celtic No. 3, from Owen Jones's The Grammar of Ornament] ... [Green].

[Dandelion clock] ... [Red].

[Sculpture by Barbara Hepworth] ... [Red].

End of slideshow.

Cara speaks into the mic. 'And finally, I'm going to show you some more number sequences and I want you to tell me whether you can see a pattern? As soon as you spot a pattern of any kind, I want you to click green for *yes*, as in, *yes, there is a pattern* – and if you can't see one, if you think the numbers are just a random jumble, then I'd like you to click red for *no*. Same fingers as before, and the length of time will vary. Is that okay with you?' She holds down the talkback, waiting for the reply. 'Can you hear me, Mr Fremont?'

'Yes,' he answers, crackling through the speaker. 'When you ...'

She turns to Silvia. 'The sound quality is awful. I can hardly make out a word.'

Silvia checks the volume and shrugs.

Cara talks into the mic again. 'You're looking for numbers in an order. Click green for *pattern* – and red for *random*. Can you manage that for me?'

'Index finger if I can see a pattern like ... what ...'

'What?' (Several tonnes of magnet costing millions. Intercom that costs shit.) 'Splendid, Mr Fremont. Let's see how we get on, shall we?' Cara runs the program.

The slideshow starts, appearing simultaneously in the booth and for the volunteer inside the tube.

22, 25, 28, 31, 34 ... [Green].

He gives a correct response to the first set. He is off to a good start.

7, 17, 27, 37, 47 ... [Green].

96, 108, 120, 132, 144 ... [Green].

As his mind works, his vascular system sends glucose and oxygen to his hungry brain. Blood rushes to the neurons

16

demanding it most. What the scanner isolates are pumped ions active in his blood flow: they light up like a flare in the night sky. *That's* where the thought is with near-millimetre precision. Which is impressive—

291, 57, 529, 62, 16 ... [Red].

—until you realise that a single cubic millimetre of human brain contains a billion or so connections, and no existent computer is able to map it.

101, 103, 107, 109, 113 ... The scanner howls like an aircraft.

Cara expects activity in the horizontal segment of the intraparietal sulcus. That's not news. Also in the left angular gyrus, if he's wording towards the solutions. But what she's really interested in is Mr Fremont's orbitofrontal cortex in the frontal lobes, a so-called hedonic hotspot.

It's not just whether he sees patterns, and how quickly he answers, and his rate of accuracy. Are they satisfying answers? Are they *attractive*? Cara is curious as to whether, as it were, they're pretty patterns.

9, 16, 25, 36, 49 ... [Green].

888, 777, 666, 555, 444 ... [Red].

The experiment is out of her hands now.

She looks sidewise at Silvia and says, 'You need a trip to Maplin to fix that thing. A job for you in the morning, perhaps, before I come back next week.'

200, 14, 783, 94, 0 ...

1, 10, 11, 100, 101 ... There's a noise like a fire alarm.

The program freezes and a warning flashes on the screen.

Silvia jumps to attention and turns on the main lights. 'Panic button.'

'No, no, I don't think so.' Cara presses the intercom. 'Don't be silly, Mr Fremont, you only have four minutes left in there.'

Mumbling on the speaker.

Her colleague snatches the microphone away. 'Relax, sir, everything is all right, I'm coming for you now.'

'We're practically finished—'

The doors are thrown open, and the table he's on slides out.

Silvia holds his hand like an angel of mercy. She unpacks him, setting him free from wires and equipment.

After a moment it's clear he's perfectly fine. Probably just bored.

A single booking takes four hours, from prep to sign-out. It costs nine-hundred pounds, which comes out of Cara's budget, no matter what the outcome is. And this entire session has to be junked.

She scoops up her folder and laptop, and a pen she threw on the floor.

He says, 'I never thought of myself as claustrophobic before. It was like being in a drawer in the mortuary.'

'More like a sleeper train,' Cara says. 'Not remotely scary when you think about it.'

'You did very well.' Silvia pats him on the arm. 'We're extremely grateful to you for giving up your time to help the university with our research. Would you like a cup of tea? I can sit with you until you feel better.'

He says, 'I should be getting home. What an adventure; I can't wait to tell the missis.'

'I hope you enjoyed yourself,' Cara says. 'The invoice will arrive by post.'

Silvia glares at her.

'*Cheque*, I mean.'

When Cara first told her parents that Paul was a security systems engineer, what they heard was 'locksmith'. They had this idea that locksmiths earn a fortune, because when someone's locked out of their house, they'll pay anything to get back in. The reality is that Paul installs burglar alarms for little old ladies, and had a two a.m. callout to reset a warehouse unit in Chelmsford last night.

He is dozing on the sofa with a quiz on TV. Next to him on the coffee table is a KitKat wrapper, a tube of crisps and his Canaries mug. Stirs when Cara sits near him. Finds the remote, lowers the volume. 'How did it go?' he asks anxiously, because he thinks every day involves lecturing to a packed auditorium and at least one major scientific breakthrough.

'My volunteer pressed the panic button in the scanner. He ruined my experiment. It wouldn't have happened if we weren't using tin cans on a piece of string.' She leans in for a kiss. Offers him a drink.

Paul shifts his weight. 'I can do it?'

'I will. And I'll open a jar of sauce if that's okay. I'll make it veggie so I don't have to use a separate pan for Heather.'

'Whatever you think,' he replies, adding, 'Yangtze River,' for the benefit of the quiz show host. 'Hang on, she needs to talk to you. Sounded, um . . .'

Cara waits.

'It might be female-related? Better if she comes to you, rather than looking at websites, which can be confusing for a girl her age.'

Cara softens because she's had an effect on him after all.

The wine rack is the most used part of the new kitchen, which Cara chose because it reminds her of Scandinavian television dramas. She's spread the cost over several credit cards, chasing down 0 per cent interest deals, but it was worth it.

Gives Paul his wine and leaves him to a sudden-death tiebreaker.

Heather is doing her homework. At least, her books, notes and laptop are spread about on the bed, which is a start.

Her bedroom looks as though it belongs to a younger child. Stuffed toys hugged until they're falling apart. Crystals with spurious powers. Mermaids. Under the bed is a pair of customised Converse sneakers that Cara gave her, and an imitation pair from Primani that she obviously prefers. She hoards fast fashion, tote bags with inspirational quotes, crusting cosmetics. Flavoured lip balms. Cutesy body sprays. She is a true redhead: pale, freckles, and acne.

Thumbs her phone as if Cara isn't there.

Cara perches with her wineglass: the silence runs on until she says, 'Glimpses of the whole world. No wonder you can't help yourself.'

Heather wipes her nose on her sleeve. 'Were you still a virgin when you were my age?'

Officially, Cara is offended, but is also quite impressed by her gumption. 'That's very personal. Whatever makes you ask?'

They've had the talk, such as it was. She was mindful that Heather must have looked up anything she was curious about, and that Cara's role was more of a reality check. (Which is more than Cara had to go on. Apart from sex ed with Miss Kowalik, she had to make do with magazines passed around at break times. She used to get one with a drawing called *position of the month*. Glenda thought she bought it for the free eyeshadow.)

'Betty told me there was this boy she was dating who didn't know girls grew hair down there; he thought we're all Barbie dolls. And there was this other boy in our year – different school – who was getting sexy with his girlfriend for the first time and started trying to choke her?'

20

'Oh God, did she report him to the police?' And if she hasn't, Cara thinks, does that mean I have to?

'He wasn't into it; it's what he thought you do. He freaked out. Mustn't it be horrible being a boy, worse than being a girl?' She bites a cuticle.

'Is a boyfriend putting pressure on you? Because if he is—'

'When you're a virgin, you're frigid. And when not, you're a slut. Is that right?'

'The difference today is how they shame you for it because the pictures never really go away, but basically it's always been the same . . . You have to be careful what you share and with whom.'

Heather is looking at her phone again. Looks *at* it. Is turning it over like a piece of obsidian. 'When is it okay to have sex?'

'When you're safe and it's right for you,' Cara says. 'The rest is a matter of taste.'

'Does that include other people's feelings?'

Cara sips her wine. Extracts an old paperback *Tempest* from underneath some socks. *Ruth Clark* is written on the inside cover. For a split-second Cara thinks, Who's she? Then takes another slurp. 'I studied this when I was at school, although I didn't see it at the theatre until I was an adult. On a weekend away in Stratford-upon-Avon, a long time ago.'

Heather buries her face in her arms. 'I feel sorry for Caliban.'

'Maybe you're supposed to. Write about him if a question comes up. You can afford to be subjective if you feel strongly.'

'What's subjective?'

'It means people disagreeing over what they see. There aren't any wrong answers as such when your argument is well made.'

Heather taps the book. 'What do you see?'

She considers for a moment. 'Caliban is a creature of the earth who does the manual labour, whereas Ariel is a floating, ephemeral spirit. The two seem incompatible. However, Caliban has dreams, and Ariel can feel pain. Therefore, neither is purely one substance. Both must be both. The tempest is not weather. It is a struggle between physical and mental states.'

'Oh that's clever, but I can't use it because I didn't think of it.'

'Trust me, you'll think of something better. Likewise, Shakespeare loved his books and creations more than his responsibilities at home.'

'You mean Prospero?'

'Didn't I say that?'

'No, you said Shakespeare.'

'Hmm. Sorry, was it gibberish?'

Heather puts the text under her pillow. 'Do you want to help me or not, with what I want help with?'

'Haven't we done that already? All right, go ahead.'

'Will Dad pay for me to take a gap year, do you think?'

Paul doesn't pay for his own petrol half the time. The monthly allowance Cara gives him, he spends on crap. She says, 'A gap year implies that you've got a plan for what to do when you're finished. Have you decided yet?'

She shrugs.

'Study, work or training? I'm afraid you have to do something. Nothing isn't an option.'

'I don't see why I *have to* do anything. Can't I think about the future while I'm off travelling somewhere? Maybe I'll find out what I'm good at when I'm there?'

'Where would you go?'

'I'm not really sure, because what's the point of getting excited if he's just going to say no? Will you ask him for me?'

'So you don't know where you want to go, and you've no idea what you want to do when you come back? Ask him yourself.'

'He's mad at me, Cara.'

'Why? What did you do?'

Heather touches her forehead to Cara's shoulder and makes a puppy noise.

She sighs into her glass. 'You aren't giving me much to go on. But I can see you've got a lot on your mind. And perhaps rushing into a career when you still don't know what your passion is isn't very wise? Perspective could be useful. I admit part of me regrets not taking a gap year when I was your age, I didn't have the chance. It doesn't mean you shouldn't.'

'Yes, and you are brilliant at this kind of problem-solving. Can't you find out if he'll listen a bit, please?'

'Not at the expense of your A levels. If I help you with this, then you have to promise to see them through and try your best in your exams, no matter what else happens. Have we got a pact?'

'Yes, I swear. *Tak.*'

She smiles weakly. 'I'm doing veggie pasta tonight. We're having the same.'

'Good, that's how it's supposed to be. You won't tell Dad what we talked about, will you? The private stuff?'

'Of course not. Girl talk is girl talk.'

Heather's cheeks turn pink. 'Scientists disagree all the time. You're always bitching about how someone else is wrong and you know best. Science is subjective then?'

'Absolutely not.' She finishes her drink, giving her an excuse to go for a refill.

Heather

The offshore wind farm is a mile out. A millennial harvest. Heather can't remember a time it wasn't there. Gusts come in from the North Sea.

Dog walkers are making the most of the wide, empty beach. Day trippers wear coats and carry ice-cream cones in their gloved hands.

It's pre-season in Great Yarmouth, with attractions opening freshly painted shutters. The road train runs up and down the promenade. Chip shops. Amusement arcades din noise and blink lights. Bags of candyfloss hang in kiosks, and claw machines are full of unclaimed prizes. Seagulls spar for scraps.

Cara offers Heather pirate golf, the rifle range and the model village. She refuses them all. The twenty-pound note she gave her stays in Heather's purse.

What's left is scenery, and watching people on the dodgems.

Cara says, 'Shall we do a selfie on the pier?'

'No thanks.' Heather looks back out at the wind turbines.

'Tell me what you'd like to do.'

We both know the answer to that, she thinks. They drove two hours to prevent it.

Cara studies each donut stand and burger bar with interest. Takes her phone out for inspiration.

'We can meet later if you like?' Heather says. 'I'll go for a walk and you can read in a café?'

'There's no need to wander off. If you won't decide, then I will ... Aha, I knew there was a reason we came here.'

When she sees an aquarium of jellyfish at the Sea Life centre, Heather smiles, however briefly. It is like a porthole, and the water cycles the pulsing bodies in alien light, tiny balloons with trailing strings. 'This is for babies.'

Indeed, there are a lot of families here, and Cara isn't best pleased. Her attention switches between the lava lamp tanks throbbing with jellies, and the parents who can't control their offspring.

Heather moves along without her.

The centre is narrow, and the exhibits set in low-lit artificial rocks. The aquariums shimmer with fish – hanging shapes in space. Silver and flecks of electric green. White with spots. Transparent so you can see their needle fishbones.

Some fish are ugly brutes, grubbing on the bottom for food. Toby puffer. Paddletail. And chocolate chip starfish.

Some are comic-characters darting between plants and scenery, usually on a sunken ship theme. Pajama cardinal. Blue tang. Lined sweetlips.

They come and go. Take fright and hide. Eyeballs swivel and mouths gulp. Some look hard at you, holding your gaze, and some won't stay to be examined.

The tanks are multisided prisms, large like coffins. The water heated or cooled to the captives' liking. Continuous bubbles.

Heather circles one, taking in views from its other windows. She cannot see in the top or underneath. Parts are blacked out.

Creatures inside tremble and change. There is a community in there, a vibrating system.

A glow reflects her back in outline.

She likes to think this is how Ruth looked when she was the same age. She should've come here with her mum when she was small enough to appreciate it, instead of being practically an adult with Cara. This is – what's the word? – a travesty.

Heather presses her forehead to the glass. Do they want out as much as she wants in?

Cara is on the other side, shown by some trick of light as far away and shaded. Adjusts her faux-fur hood, flattens her gilet. Takes a picture she has no intention of sharing. Is doing this for something to do, to distract her brain.

An underwater tunnel: the closest Heather will ever get to swimming with the sharks and rays soaring overhead – and to a turtle ancient like a dinosaur. It's primeval in there. You could fit humans in this aquarium, and she wonders if they do.

Heather imagines herself suspended in water. Imagines herself naked, in silence, skin tinged green, mouth and eyes dead open. Hair spreading like seaweed, with gills. Imagines people staring at her and unable to come near. She'd stay in there, another creature, can almost feel the flutter of fins and slip of tails along her body.

Cara is beside her again, staring up at the pale underbelly of an orbiting reef shark. 'You'd be good at conservation work,' she says, not realising that saying it means Heather will never do it. 'When you're a young person, you have this idea that your parents will always be there and will never change; and that the friends you make at school will last for ever; and when you meet someone, romantically, you might truly believe that you are going to stay with him for the rest of your life. It's a trick of the developing brain, these strong feelings. Powerful emotions are normal; the good and the bad. They come and thrive for a while. They seem overwhelming. Then they pass.' She nudges Heather's shoulder with hers. 'Your dad and I are separate to Ruth. Do you understand?'

'Yep. I get it.'

'Blended families, well, show me one that isn't these days. Still, there is no question of me trying to replace Ruth, whatsoever. I wouldn't dream of it.'

'No. You wouldn't.'

'Because you and I are separate too, Heather, so we get to define what *this* is. What being "steps" means to us girls. Our version doesn't have to be the same as anyone else's. And we have fun too, don't we?' She attempts a reassuring smile.

'Do we?'

'Yes. Who else can I binge-watch Nordic Noir with?' (Cara is saying this because of Paul's lifelong hatred of subtitles. Cara drinks wine while Heather eats veggie Haribo, and they have spirited debates about who the murderer is. Heather keeps track of who's been with who; and Cara points out production mistakes. They can polish off a whole season in a weekend.) 'We should watch the American remakes for a laugh, I bet they're terrible.'

'When?'

'I wasn't suggesting – neither of us wants to right now. Sometime.' Cara takes her phone out. Is she checking for texts from Paul? Is he above sending the news that way? Make Cara break it to her, on top of the rest?

'Dad doesn't love you like he loves Mum.'

'I beg your pardon?'

'You deserve to hear it, after everything.'

Cara is jostled by a woman with a buggy trying to pass. 'I have been patient, haven't I? I made room for you.'

'I know that you try.' Heather presses her palm on the aquarium wall. The turtle with its craggy face comes near, every wrinkle and horny scale fills her view. 'Hello, my sister.'

Later, there is a homeless man in a doorway hunched on cardboard. He has holes in his sleeping bag. Heather gives him twenty pounds.

Cara

The funeral is the same day that Cara is interviewed for a documentary, and she wears the same outfit for both.

When it's over, Paul puts his wife's affairs in order as if he's rehearsed it. Her input isn't needed if you don't count his overdraft (and she is willing not to for the time being).

Paul is vacuuming his van. The extension cord runs down the path. His feet stick out of the back and he is sweating through his T-shirt in a manly way.

She brings him squash in a plastic tumbler. 'Is there anything I can do for you?' she asks again.

Inside the van is as neat and tidy as she's ever seen it. He seems to be thinning out his tools and creating space. For new equipment, she thinks. Is he setting up his own business? Wouldn't put it past him.

'Looks great,' she says, because it's important to show him that she's impressed. 'Almost like new, you could sleep in there if you had to.'

'Yeah, been on the cards for a while. Good to get it done at last.' He sighs guiltily.

'It's okay,' she says in a soothing tone. 'Some sense of relief is normal, as much as the loss is. You did your part, seriously, everything that was asked of you, with honour. I admire how well you're coping. I'm saying – it's fine to put yourself first for a change.'

He nods.

'I hope I have been supportive enough.' Then she adds, 'For Heather, too.'

'You're incredible.'

'Am I?'

'I can't believe you stayed with us this long – let us stay here.'

'Silly. This is your home too.'

'I see the two of you together and it's very maternal, I suppose.'

Not the ideal compliment, but she'll take it. Is it pathetic that she wants him to say things like, 'Cara Mia, you make me the happiest man alive'?

He leans into the van to run a cloth through the tie-down rings.

'It's my birthday soon,' she says gently. 'And it's okay with me if we don't do anything special. I'm not expecting a present. In fact, I'd rather postpone it until there is less sadness.'

Did he hear her? Does she need to repeat herself?

'What have you got in mind?'

'Mm, I was thinking a city break – not now – in a few months, when we feel more settled and can talk. A long weekend, just the two of us. I haven't been to Venice and I always wanted to go. Or the three of us, if Heather is too young to be left alone. I don't think she is, though. Trusting her to show some independence could be exactly what she needs.' Cara is afraid she has pushed her luck.

'No harm in checking the flights.'

'Research, yes; good idea. Why didn't I think of that? I'd love to visit Piazza San Marco with you, the Doge's Palace, and

Gallerie dell'Accademia; and there's a bookshop I'm dying to see. We can be tacky tourists and ride in a gondola.'

'Under the Bridge of Sighs.' He squints. 'It's called that because it connected the old court to the prison – and after they were sentenced, prisoners who were led through there saw their last view of Venice from its windows, and they sighed.'

'A made-up story,' she says, muffled by another blast of the vacuum cleaner.

'There are two elliptical arches,' he adds, 'one above another, so it looks soft. Fragile.'

She opens her mouth. 'I might explore the cost of going by train. I'm sure I can find a hotel with a nice terrace bar for when you're bored of sightseeing because that's important too, you relaxing. Lido beach. It'll be the best of both. But it's only an idea. We can book cheapy flights if the train is expensive.'

'I have to check with work. I've had a lot of time off lately.'

'No rush,' she says, looking up at Heather's bedroom window—

Heather

—looks down as her dad goes in with a brush attachment next. Funny, he never vacuums the house.

The Audi is parked next to it. 'Will you do mine, seeing as you've got it out and everything? My car?'

Heather can't hear his reply.

'Don't worry,' Cara continues. 'I'll get it valeted. It's always spotless when the Polish boys have finished with it.'

'No need,' he says. 'The least I can do. I should've offered.'

Heather wishes they'd have a big row. Emotional outbursts can be good, although Cara doesn't believe in them.

Ruth's possessions – what was kept at Eglantine, or stored in the attic for some alternative universe where she still needed them – have crept out of their bags and boxes and taken over Heather's bedroom.

Clothes from the sick years, comfy and over-washed. Brochures, maps and tickets that are flimsy to the touch. Spanish playing cards. A sewing tin. A pretty comb. Costume jewellery in silver and semi-precious stones, including a necklace with a hand-shaped charm. Out-of-date guidebooks, and a stack of novels that Heather has no interest in.

The sum of the parts feels important to hold on to. When she examines each item, however, she can't tell the rubbish from the record.

She gets as far as sticking a few photos on the wall for their slippery, nostalgic feel. The Wycliffe family. Nugget the meow. Ruth the free spirit.

Sits cross-legged on the bed. Opens her laptop. Closes a homework reminder that Cara set up (there're that many she doesn't notice them any more).

Heather's essay is on *civilising the savage*. She is keen to point out that what with all the usurping, slavery, threats and gaslighting going on by the allegedly 'civilised' nobles – not to mention the duke's fixation with his daughter's virginity, and how he keeps knocking her unconscious without asking permission – *they* aren't exactly civilised to begin with.

aside from the exploitation and bullying taking place in front of us the audience there is absolutely no reliable [backspace] impartial witness to confirm what a tyrant said happened years ago in the past we know her as a foul witch because HE calls her it but then he also admits she was strong and powerful and was there before he was and then she died

Heather types three paragraphs without a single punctuation mark because of her feelings on the subject. Is finding her flow when her phone chirps. Urgh, she's sick of scrolling through condolences.

How? she resumes. *We don't know what happened to her or what became of her body? Was she murdered BY HIM? He had the means motive and opportunity unquestionably. We don't hear her side of the story do we. They say nasty things about her till she doesnt even matter anymore and her child is abused because hes different. Different NOT 'misshapen'.*

33

Therefore, to get back to the essay question because Heather has wandered off-topic and it is probably costing her marks, *what is civil about name calling? How can we be sure the 'savage' wasn't brutalised by the 'noble duke' in the first place? He might have been an innocent?*

Heather starts in the middle. Then she'll write a conclusion. Finally, she will do an introduction if she can be arsed.

More notifications. Messages sending thoughts and prayers and *[gif hugs]*. The funeral was the same, filled with people who knew and loved Ruth that Heather had never seen before. They seemed to expect a reaction from her.

. *Ruth Wycliffe, what a stunning and hilarious woman you were, taken in a horrible cruel way. I miss you and you are forever in my thoughts. Keep on dancing. RIP Babe! Tina & the Masons Arms Band XXXxxxoxox*

. *Shocked by this sad news [sad crying face] I will remember your well years with fondness. Raising a beer to you. Clive [thumbs up] [beers]*

. *Heather, We are Devastated to hear what's happened. Stay strong and if there's Anything we can do to help don't hesitate to ask. We are here for You. Best wishes at this tragic time. Lots of love, Aunt Kathy, Uncle Trev and Charleston oxo*

Kind of you! Heather replies to the next post. *Sweet, this'd make Mum happy and mean a lot to her [happy, blushing face].* Running out of ways to say thank you, she resorts to more *xs*, *[rainbow]*s and colourful *[heart]*s.

. *Ruth Clark was careless, argumentative and vain. Reg*

What's this, a troll? Eww.

You can't let them get to you, Heather thinks; you're not supposed to feed them either. It happens all the time, even on tributes for dead people.

She clicks on the active profile of *Reginald Ely, Author of the classic self-actualisation novel* Claribel of Tunis.

Cara enters her room without knocking. 'Aren't you sorting this out yet?'

'Course work,' Heather says, fumbling to swap her phone for her laptop.

'You can't even see the floor,' which is one of her catch-phrases, only today it's true.

'I'll do it later, I swear. Listen, I need to tell you something, I don't think I'm a four-subjects girl any more, you know?'

Cara nods. 'I understand. Three is generally what's required.'

'What?' Heather says, mimicking the reaction she expected to receive. 'I thought you'd be disappointed with me.'

'I was expecting this. I don't think you should spread yourself too thinly.'

She exhales, glad she hasn't caused a scene. And Cara's big on women owning their choices. 'I might drop religious studies?'

'Not tourism? Well, it is your decision. Would you like help with mathematics? You could go up a grade if you put your mind to it.'

'*Use of* maths,' she says.

'I'm sorry, what's *use of* maths?'

She offers up the textbook and Cara steps over the mess to glance through it.

She flattens her mouth. 'I've never heard of this subject before. I thought you were taking—'

'I am. Tools for the real world, Cara, it's handy. Graphs and data, like pie charts? I like pie charts. They give a rounded view. I did tell you.' Heather adds the book to the mess. 'Is it all right to put some of this back in the loft for a while? Please?'

'You'll only have the same problem the next time you try,

except with more dust and mould. Do yourself a favour, and declutter. Paul is. Get rid of anything you don't like or won't use again. Whatever you keep is your responsibility from now on.'

Heather's cheeks grow warm. 'I can feel Mum watching over me sometimes.'

'That's nice.'

'Do you think she is?'

'I think it is fair to say you're going through a process. When my dad died—' She knocks over some aerosols. Makes a bad job of setting them upright between the rose quartz (for love and compassion) and a tiger's eye (for psychic power). 'This is out of control, how can you possibly concentrate?'

'I'll organise, I promise, I'll . . .'

Cara reaches across her to pick the photographs off the wall. Lays them in Heather's palm like wages. 'Blu Tack leaves marks,' she says.

Heather types nonsense on her computer until Cara takes the hint and leaves her alone. Grabs her racerback swimsuit and octopus towel. The essay will have to wait.

Cantabrigians complain about Parkside Pools because it's old-fashioned without being old. There are three, including a competition pool which closes to the public when they host galas, and a kids' pool with water slides. It has a gym in it, diving boards, raked seating, and a waveform roof.

Heather likes the glass walls best, allowing you to see the blue swimming pools from outside, moist and enclosed like a paludarium.

And then when you're swimming *inside* when the weather is freezing – and you're loose, dripping and nearly naked – you can see the pedestrians go by in their overcoats. They make her die.

She isn't a great swimmer as she learned late – was taught by Cara, who was shocked she couldn't already. Cara listed some scenarios where Heather might conceivably drown: river, ocean, the artificial lake at the Botanic Garden. She wouldn't have let Heather play on the stepping stones if she had known; she asked Paul why he hadn't seen to it.

Paul replied it was bad luck for a sailor to learn how to swim.

Heather doesn't do it to compete, to lose weight or to be sociable; none of those are appealing. She isn't exactly fit either. Plenty of wrinklies pass her in the lanes. She swims when her body is tired and her head is crazy. It's good because you haven't made anything, so nobody can tell you you're doing it wrong.

She does sensible breaststroke for a while.

Sculling backstroke.

Likes to hold her breath and watch the blurry bodies from the neck down. She likes to go deep – the bottom of the pool falling away like a valley, then she breaks the surface with splashy drama when it feels uncomfortable.

Climbs out, chilly and wet.

Walks parallel to the window wall: the real world with its uneven grass, bus shelter and skate ramp is less familiar through it.

Paul is out there at the front, waiting by the entrance. He is holding a coil of thin blue rope.

She waves and says, 'Dad,' a few times, but he's not looking this way. Hurries to dry and get dressed, wrapping the wet swimsuit in her towel. Her ponytail makes a damp patch on her denim jacket between her shoulders.

'I can get home by myself,' she says. 'I'll text if I need a lift. What have you got there, is that a noose?' It's reasonable for her to ask, because there's a knot tied in it with a loop at the end.

'No, a bowline.'

'*Bowling?*'

'A loadbearing mariner's knot, easy to tie and undo. Ancient. Very useful. They call it the king of knots.' He attempts to tie it again, one-handed, uses his pinkie to control it. He manipulates the rope to pull the loose end through a hole he's made. Drops it. 'Easy with practice.'

'Yeah, it's good. Are you okay, Dad? Does Cara know you're here?'

'I need to tell you something that she won't understand.' He gathers the rope in his left hand and prepares to retie a knot with his right. 'I saw your mother.'

'Really? Today? When?'

'A few nights ago. It was dark. I was in the back garden having some fresh air. I swear it was her.'

'What did she look like?'

'Full of cheerfulness. Sparkling.'

By the light of his eyes, she can see Ruth too. 'Aren't you lucky,' she whispers.

'You believe me then?'

'I do.' She shrugs.

'I'm glad. Because she spoke to me. She had a message.'

Heather's mouth goes dry. A message from her mum.

'You mustn't worry any more, she said. It's all going to be all right.'

'Whoa. Anything else?'

'The way ahead is clear. She's made sure.'

'Clear? Did she say that?' Heather sniffs behind chlorine-scented fingers.

He shakes his head sadly. 'She faded away then, back to where she came from. I don't know whether you believe in unsolved mysteries – what's unexplained? I didn't want to keep it secret from you, even if I sounded crazy.'

'Thanks. You were right to tell me.'

'We took care of her and now she's helping us too, I reckon.'

'I wish I'd been there.' She presses her head against his arm and squeezes.

'Here, hold this.' He gives her the coil of rope and wraps the end behind his body.

'Smooth,' she says.

'This is dinghy rope. You be the rescue crew . . .' He tucks his left hand in his pocket to show he can't use it.

'Shall I pull you in?'

'No! Not yet.'

He crosses the short end over and winds the line round his knuckle, feeding the end through towards his body. He steps away and Heather pulls: the knot synchs. Paul is tied in a load-bearing loop.

'A bowline can be tied when you're clinging on to rocks or treading water,' he says. 'This could save your life.'

'Right. I'm with you.'

In the evening Heather finds the framed photo of her mum at the ruins in Carthage, and a hammer and picture hooks.

Cara

Cara is led to the kitchen, blindfolded. She touches Paul with the exaggeration of a seeing actor playing a blind character. 'I'm going to scream if people jump out at me.'

'Okay, you can look *now*.'

She takes the blindfold off, hair fluffing up.

Heather gestures grandly to an aquarium on the countertop containing two goldfish – an orange one and a white one – swimming through stringy plants and watery space. 'Aren't they divine?'

Cara says nothing. Then says, 'Why does it have to be so big? I thought goldfish live in bowls.'

'Oh no, that's cruelty, you mustn't keep goldfish in a goldfish bowl, it causes them stress. They can grow to a foot long. I hope these do.'

Paul pecks her on the cheek. 'Happy birthday.'

'They have three-second memories and food drops out the sky,' Cara says. 'What is there to be stressed about?'

'They can remember months at a time,' Heather explains. 'The man at the garden centre told us, which means these can still remember being for sale, poor things. See how shiny they are, and shy.' She stoops to the glass. 'This is much nicer, you'll like it here.'

The fish she is talking to swims away.

'If I had a million guesses …' Cara slips her arm through Paul's. 'What possessed you?'

'Better than jewellery,' Heather mutters.

Cara clenches her teeth. Goes closer to examine her gift. 'Are they males or females? Not one of each, I hope.'

'What do you want them to be?' says Heather.

'Oh God, are we going to be overrun? Do they eat their offspring?'

'Don't you like them?' Heather looks genuinely hurt by the possibility. (Paul wouldn't've come up with this by himself. This is Heather's doing, and she expects it to be received with delight.)

Cara checks her reaction. 'I admit it is original. They'll look good in the lab, I expect.'

'You can't move them, they're traumatised enough as it is. They belong here with us.' She points. 'This one likes you. What d'you want to call it?'

'You can name them, really, you choose.'

'No, they're yours. We meant to get three, only we'd need a larger tank and it wouldn't have fitted. I measured.'

The white goldfish scoots along the glass, eyeing the humans. The orange goldfish stays in the background.

Heather says, 'They love each other.'

(How much did it cost? She won't check his balance in front of him, that's rude.)

'I'll name one and you can name the other,' Cara says. 'What about that?'

A present, a takeaway and a birthday treat. These are the traditions. Cara used to groan her encouragement if Paul did something she liked, except he hasn't got the stamina to keep going, and she fakes so they can stop sooner.

She is ready for new traditions. Venezia. Eating *linguine ai frutti di mare* with a cold Soave. Then she can truly celebrate. Tomorrow she will send Paul links to her shortlisted hotels: her enthusiasm for that is real.

He holds hands with her across the duvet. 'I reckon I took you by surprise.'

She giggles.

'You're a bobby-dazzler,' he says. 'I take it for granted almost. It's a shame we haven't spent more time together being private.'

'What's stopping us?' She strokes his hair. 'How about if we set aside an evening every week for date night, just us grown-ups? I promise I won't do any work. And you and I can talk, and share, and we'll book our weekend away.' She kisses him.

'I wish it was always like this.'

'It is. We can be.'

He looks wistful. 'Can I ask you something?'

She bites her lip.

'I know it's a big step,' he whispers, 'and we shouldn't rush into anything. Only I think, maybe, before anything else happens, we should get you sterilised?'

Downstairs in the not-as-new-as-it-was kitchen, which she kept meaning to take pictures of before it had a big fat fish tank in it, her laptop emits blue light in the dark.

The curry containers weren't washed properly and are smelly in the recycle bin. She won't do it, not while it's still technically her birthday.

She kills a bottle of Petite Sirah. Opens another email.

This is not what we agreed. The Austrian research demonstrates a correlation and I was under the impression we were of the same mind . . .

Cara is with Paul precisely because he's different from the men she used to go for. She doesn't want to come home and carry on the same conversations she had in the lab. Doesn't want to live with a colleague who feels threatened by her success.

So what if he's got a few rough edges? Haven't we all?

You've lost perspective on this occasion, Dr Brenner, and, I say this out of respect, have made an error unworthy of you . . .

In a sense they are both new to this. God knows she's held back plenty over the years. It is, therefore, inevitable that he couldn't discuss certain issues with her while his wife was alive.

Perhaps this is his way of expressing a need for greater intimacy? At least he is thinking long term. That's not nothing.

If you elect to withdraw that will be a blow to us and yet it could be preferable to having involvement with a project in which you have little faith. I await your prompt reply.

There are no ideal relationships. Only real relationships. With compromises we're prepared to make, and those we aren't.

She clicks on social media from habit.

. *'Few Rewards: A lacklustre study by @CaraMBren @StewartBANG adds zero to our understanding of the nucleus accumbens. What next for the #neuroscience of motivation?' [shortened link] #NAcc #neuro #neurobiology*

. *Experiments on animals are pathetic and POINTLESS. EVIL. No excuse. KILL YOURSELF first before hurting another lab beagle. Beg for forgiveness. [frightened animal]*

. *wot long words grandma.*

She gnaws the inside of her cheek.

[Report]

[Block]

[Repeat]

It's not too late to buy herself a present. She could join a wine club that delivers a mixed case each month, then they'd be less likely to run out. Probably work out cheaper.

Supervisions. Babysitting, depending on your point of view.

'The conclusions might suggest that men's neural connectivity is optimised for intrahemispheric communication,' Cara says, 'which favours spatial perception and motor control. While women's wiring is interhemispheric, facilitating analysis and intuition. Front and back, versus left and right. Thus, human male and female connectomes seem to reinforce society's expectations. This could be the neurobiology of gender difference. What are your questions?'

The room she time-shares overlooks a main road and is large enough for a two-person sofa, plus a desk against the wall. The plumbing squeals when a tap runs next door and her whiteboard has the remnants of a pornographic doodle on it (not by her).

The students sit as far apart as the tiny sofa allows.

One dresses like she's running a cake stall at a village fete. Although Naomi has had bad luck with her experiments, they demonstrate an interesting thought process. Naomi says, 'The inclusion of children and young people is peculiar. Given that the upper age limit of participants was twenty-two years old, when synaptic pruning hasn't even finished; given that the brain is still developing into our mid-twenties; given that we're only just starting to understand plasticity, including in diseases and old age – it can be said at best to confirm gender stereotyping among teenage kids and, er, my question is this: is anybody fully formed at that life stage? I certainly hope I wasn't, or I'm fucked.'

'Thank you for your contribution.' Cara turns to Henry. 'And what do the rest of us think?'

Her second student checks his notes.

When Henry introduced himself at the start of Michaelmas term, he said he wanted his own research group by the age of thirty. Hasn't said anything impressive since. His experiments go over safe ground and get positive results accordingly. He says, 'It's a huge sample. Much larger than most MRI studies, you can't deny it.'

'Yeah,' says Naomi, 'in the patriarchy.'

He snorts. 'I have no idea what that even means. It's irrelevant. This is an American study.'

'Where a hundred per cent of available subjects live in a society of white male privilege. The sample is frigging biased. We don't know what we're looking at.' Naomi chews a bitten-down nail as she talks. 'If you were serious about researching how well the sexes fit in their stereotypical roles – and whether there's any bearing in neural maps – I'd prefer to see a study of adults in both traditional and counter-intuitive jobs – jobs perceived as having gendered cognition. Firefighters, taxi drivers and boiler engineers are typically considered as men's roles, agreed? Things like primary school teachers, secretaries and nurses for women. Both sexes are competent in all those careers and … What do male and female firefighters have in common with each other, for example? Male and female nurses? What's the same, and what is different? Put them in scanners, please, in equal numbers.'

'Is this gender studies?' he asks in a sulky voice.

'Furthermore, I'd like to show the researchers some connectomes in a blind test. If their study is as significant as they say it is, they should have no bloody trouble separating them into men and women.'

'They haven't claimed one sex's skills are better,' he says. 'Only that there are differences, *which there are*. If anything, the guys come off worse. They have physical-brains, and the girls have brainy-brains.'

Cara controls the urge to laugh.

Naomi resumes: 'The study might be indicative of how boy children are encouraged to participate in sports and physical exploration of the world. Whereas girl children are encouraged to be passive: they are the observers who take on a greater share of emotional labour. And the more you steer a group towards a type of lived experience, the more likely they are to follow that path. Be competent. Improve. Lo and behold, they are wired for it. This is a study in self-fulfilling prophecy.'

He spreads his arm along the back of the sofa. 'I hear you: you don't like the findings.'

Cara thinks, You ought to be somewhere like Sheffield, you'd do well there. She wills Naomi to respond.

The girl rolls her eyes to the ceiling.

'We shouldn't shy away from controversy,' he says, shaking his pretty head. 'What's wrong with research that creates traction?'

He prattles on, adding nothing that Cara can latch on to and develop. Her mind turns to the patisserie she's brought in, that her colleagues are too virtuous to eat. They're getting dry in the fridge. And she needs energy for the extra emails.

She finds the house quiet where usually there'd be sport on, or a game show, telling her that Paul's home.

The 4K ultra-high-def TV has gone, all 49 inches of it. The sound bar, cables, 3D glasses that he insisted were necessary for a cinematic experience – all gone. The empty stand is like the mouth of a cave.

Her kitchen still smells bad. Heather has left toast crusts on the side, and the breadknife she used for spreading the Nutella. Crumbs and globs on the lid.

Cara retrieves the curry cartons. Gives them a good rinse and wipe, and empties the recycling into the blue bin in the garden.

The buddleia is huge, no matter how she cuts it down to the stalks, it always bounces back like the Hydra. There are a few rollie butts on the ground. Paul thinks she doesn't know, but of course she does.

Goldfish George rests in weed, while Goldfish Oliver chomps on stones and spits them out. They break the surface tension with their pale mouths to find flakes.

As Cara feeds them, a memory comes to her from a time when TVs were boxy, front-heavy and an investment. He's getting it fixed, she thinks, as opposed to, We've been burgled.

She sprays the worktops and puts the Nutella in the fridge.

How she hates those magnets, the sailor penguin and the penguin with a pink bow. Well, sailor penguin is missing. Smashed on the floor tiles hopefully. Perhaps pink penguin will lose heart and throw herself off, then the fridge can be plain, the way Cara likes it.

We'll have plungey coffee after dinner, she thinks. She'll get the cups and cafetière ready. Does it stiffly, as though being filmed. And so to the cupboard for his beloved Canaries mug, which isn't there and must be in the dishwasher – humming to itself – or else it could be stranded upstairs, which she has warned against. Sets out the generics instead.

In the larder there was a twelve-pack of Wotsits with eleven packets left that've disappeared. The cereal bars, Ghost Ship and pickled onions – are nowhere to be seen. Her pink apples. Have they got an ant problem?

Cara swears under her breath.

What kind of ants would steal the Tardis keyring from the spare keys?

The Union Jack dinner tray Paul likes his takeaway on has been taken away; and, she might be wrong about this, the ice cube tray that makes icebergs and Titanics, because regular ice wasn't fun enough for him.

Paul's phone charger hangs out of the wall. She switches the socket off. If he's without his charger, he can't have gone far.

His toothbrush is missing from the bathroom, but it was getting old, that doesn't mean anything. She looks in the waste-basket to see if he's thrown it out, and what she finds is a full bottle of post-shave balm that she bought for his rash and which he insisted was working.

His shower gel and 2-in-1 are left in the shower, but his deo-dorant is gone.

She checks the laundry hamper with (here's the absurd part) a sense of foreboding. This isn't like Cara. How does one check a laundry hamper with a sense of foreboding?

She shrieks.

She has stood barefoot on a Lego admiral adrift in the carpet. Sits down on the bed to rub the pain away.

Opens Paul's side of the wardrobe. She has guessed already there'll be empty hangers and shelves. Perhaps if she looks without panicking, she can work out how long he'll be away for.

He has taken jeans, sweaters, sci-fi shirts. But left his shorts, sandals and euros (he's not on some Balearic revenge tour then). Left behind his smart shoes, shoe brush and polish kit (so he isn't going anywhere nice). He's taken the alarm clock with the radium dial that she has wanted to get rid of for years – and left the Seiko watch with the titanium bracelet they chose together two Christmases ago.

He's taken the big suitcase with the initials *CMB* on it.

He's taken the cat's ashes, for fuck's sake. Nugget, the Wycliffe family pet of old, accompanies him on his voyage.

She catches her reflection in the full-length mirror and this, more than the accumulation of lost objects, gives her pause. She looks as if she never uses sun block and never gets enough sleep. Both true. Her hair is thinner, except for above her lip where new hairs are sprouting. Her arms are flabby. The waistband of her trousers cuts in, and her boobs and belly will soon merge. Cellulite so deep, no amount of cream vanishes it.

Paul doesn't dare answer his phone.

She leaves a voicemail with barely a quiver of accusation. 'Now look here,' she breezes, 'what's going on? Talk to me and we can fix this, okay. Before I send out the search party. I'm worried for you, you git. Don't let me down, please?'

Cara has tried expensive bras to lift her breasts and give them shape. Used bold jewellery to create a diversion. Paired slim-fitting capri pants that draw attention to her legs with floral tops. The spectacles that are supposed to look metropolitan look naff. Style advice is wasted on her.

She stands in the Wonder Woman pose to see if she can increase her testosterone and decrease her cortisol. Gives up after a few seconds because she looks like an Alan Bennett character.

Cara has a headache coming on – and Paul's raided the pharmacy cabinet, hasn't he. Oh why the ibuprofen! she laments. Why the Gaviscon! Why the box of tissues! Doesn't he know she'll have migraines, heartburn and a long cry after this?

The tech in the office is untouched, as are her credit cards from when she did the kitchen.

The magazines and memorabilia are no loss. Good riddance, Mr Potato Head. Also, Trivial Pursuit and, unless she is mistaken, *Rod: The Autobiography.*

Paul's documents are in the filing cabinet, however. That settles it. He definitely needs to come back for his passport, birth certificate and Ruth's death certificate.

Fine. Then they will talk.

She goes to the kitchen to pour herself a drink. It would be horrid of her, she thinks, to jump to conclusions without giving him a chance to explain. He bought her fish, didn't he? That was a sign of commitment.

Maybe he's on a diet, and that's why his snacks are gone ...

Maybe after years of collecting plastic tat, he's finally realised it's a stupid hobby for a grown man ...

Maybe he has donated his ugly clothes so he can change his image, which is precisely what she asked him to do ... Why does Cara presume the worst? Why not think she is worthy of a lover like that?

A goldfish gives her a withering look.

Put down your glass, Cara, pick up your phone, and whatever you do, don't leave a feeble message.

She dials.

Can hear his ringtone. The Bee Gees are singing in her house.

She walks out of the kitchen and they grow quieter. Walks back in and they grow louder again. She can't hear much over the drone of the dishwasher.

Hears it best when she is standing next to it. She has never opened the dishwasher mid-cycle before. What a quiet life she's led.

It's easy, and the sprayers slow down sadly. The water is contained apart from steaming up her glasses.

Paul's phone is in the top rack, ringing 'To Love Somebody', having survived most of the cycle. She takes it out with a rubber glove.

Cara drinks wine on the sofa, fumbling with her mobile like worry beads.

At last she hears the front door, sits up, pushes her hair back from her face. Whatever his excuses are, she'll hear him out. Peace first. Punishment later.

Heather flops on the armchair smelling of fruit liqueur and smoke. Slips out her earbuds and says, 'Where's the telly?'

2

Hair Cells

sound and balance

Cara

Cara's tone changes to *let us know you're okay* scattered across various inboxes.

Believe it or not, Paul still calls it the World Wide Web and thinks the purpose of social media is to find out what people you went to school with are doing now. His accounts were set up under duress. His friends and followers stay in double digits. His status lies dormant. He didn't post unless Heather made him.

I am in a tie. Cara is giving a speech in her gown. H and I prod.

That event was over a year ago. Is logging out all it takes to disappear?

She scrolls vainly. Considers appealing to a celebrity for help. Paul follows Andrew Marr, Richard Osman and Stephen Fry, plus a bunch of sportsmen she's never heard of (and not a single sportswoman). He might come home if Alesha Dixon asks him to.

Remind her what we did when somebody went missing before the internet?

Cambridgeshire Constabulary sends a community support officer. A slip of a thing called Lauren. 'How are you related to Mr Wycliffe?' she asks in a tiny voice.

Cara explains.

'Was there any reason to think Mr Wycliffe planned his departure?'

'He handed in his notice at work without telling us and returned some equipment he borrowed from the company. And, this could be a coincidence, he cleaned his van meticulously.'

'And when did Mrs Wycliffe die . . .? Did the bereavement put a strain on your relationship?'

'Not especially, no.' She flicks her gaze away from Heather, sickly pale. They must look dreadful, the pair of them. 'He was upset. He didn't *not* love his wife. He was dutiful and honoured his vows. Sad as it was, we all knew what was coming, didn't we, Heather?'

Heather tuts.

'Sad.' Cara sighs. 'He had time to prepare, though, and he appeared to be adjusting well. He practically said as much. There is no doubt in my mind that if Paul was at home with us, and feeling like himself, we'd be getting on with our lives. We discussed formalising our, er, commitment to each other. I certainly never gave him ultimatums.'

Heather leans back as though the wall keeps her from falling.

'Were you engaged?' asks Lauren.

'Is this going to find him faster?'

'I'm trying to establish if Mr Wycliffe left of his own accord.'

'Paul is a missing person,' she says, giving in to pressure to make it sound as bad as possible and thus escalate it up the chain. 'He is not good at being alone. He isn't exactly dynamic.' She turns to Heather. 'Not to say he isn't capable, your dad can be organised when it's required of him. He needs support some-times, like we all do. On reality shows they call it a journey – we have been on a journey. We're invested in this relationship. He simply wouldn't run off, it doesn't make any sense. Please,

Heather, will you explain what I'm talking about? Heather can vouch that this is quite out of character. Paul doesn't take the initiative.' She pauses so at least one of them can agree with her. 'Something must've happened because it is beyond unreasonable. There is absolutely no reason for him to piss off like this.'

'Miss Wycliffe, is there any information you can add?'

'Yes, go ahead, tell the officer what you know to be true?' Cara says it with such conviction that when Lauren and Heather leave the room, it's as if it's by her choice, not theirs.

They seem to be gone a while.

Lauren nods serenely when she returns (she is extremely petite under that uniform) and produces a Salvation Army leaflet from her stab vest. 'Mr Wycliffe cannot be considered vulnerable.'

'Vulnerable is exactly what he is. He's being childish.'

'Paul Wycliffe left of his own free will, was in good health, has access to funds, and no history of a diagnosed mental illness. It's a lost contact case, Dr Brenner.'

'As in – a bad break-up?'

Heather folds her arms, stares at the floor.

'I'm afraid Cambridgeshire police cannot get involved with a private matter.'

'Have you asked them? When I find out what's happened, and it transpires he's dead in a ditch, and that you could've prevented it, there is going to be an inquiry. And it will be detailed and expensive, far costlier than if you had done your job properly in the first place and I will – I'll go to the newspapers. There, I said it.'

Lauren leaves the leaflet on the side.

When they're alone she says to Heather, 'What have you done? What did you say in there?'

57

'I'm sure he thought it was for the best, or he wouldn't of?'

Cara has never wanted to hit somebody as much as she wants to hit Heather, now. 'Your father has abandoned you. Aren't you furious?'

'I'm not pleased, since you ask. We can't get too angry, or it'll be harder for him to come home when he's ready.' Heather tries putting an arm around her.

Cara can't bear it. 'Bloody hell, do you know where he is? Has he contacted you?'

'No.'

'You're covering for him.'

'I haven't spoken to him and, no, he hasn't reached out to me, I don't know where he went any more than you do. Check my phone if you don't believe me.' Heather offers it to her.

Cara glares at it for several seconds, turns on the spot, and chucks the Salvation Army leaflet in the recycling. 'Is he seeing someone else?'

'Unlikely.' She runs her fingertip down the aquarium glass. 'I understand why you might think that, given that you were the other woman? Accept what you cannot change, and it'll hurt less.'

She sways. 'I do not accept – this isn't over – not by a long stretch. He is going to explain himself to me.' She tears off sheets of kitchen roll and sobs a single boohoo. 'I'm sorry. This must be ghastly for you. I didn't mean it when I said he might be dead. He isn't. I was only trying to get her to do something. I won't let this rest. I'll force them to investigate. I know someone who's retired from the police, he'll help us. And if that doesn't work, I have contacts in the media. I can hire a private investigator if necessary. There's bound to be CCTV footage and number-plate recognition, all sorts to try if they wanted to. We'll set up a website with an appeal on it. I'll go to our MP.'

Heather says, 'He wants to be with her more.'

When you have a regular table at the supermarket café, when the server remembers how you take your coffee and says, 'Apple Danish today?' is it a sign that things have got out of control?

Are there support groups for people like her?

Yes, Cara thinks, yes, there are. They're called Slimming World.

'Any news?' Heather asks periodically.

Paul is on the databases of several missing person charities. His description is posted on numerous message boards. His photo circulated by email. Cara has pursued every possible lead. (Not posters on lampposts, though; that's a waste of time.)

If Heather finds a site she wants them to register with, Cara explains his case is on there already, or why they shouldn't bother because it duplicates a better one.

What's left is keeping her responses fresh. 'Sorry, H, I'll tell you the moment I hear anything.'

The girl mixes hers up with a nod, a pout, 'Thanks for trying,' and so on.

She occupies herself like a consummate only child. Stays in her room chatting online for hours. Takes an inordinate number of selfies and distorts them with filters. Does homework, apparently. Does laundry, occasionally. Takes responsibility for the goldfish since Cara can no longer hide her dislike of them.

Sometimes, when Cara is on her computer, or doing the dishes, and once when she was flossing, Heather approaches from behind the way she used to, to give her a silent hug. Then apologises.

Never asks for money for Pukka Pads or bath bombs or – whatever teenagers like these days.

He must be struggling by now.

Cara considers putting extra cash in his account. Then she thinks, no, why should she. The smart thing is to cut him off, and when he's desperate he'll ask for it.

She cancels the standing order for his allowance.

The spreadsheet suggests there's less disposable income. But without subsidising his season ticket and quiz night, his subscriptions, consolidated repayments and his schoolboy plastic crap, Cara can afford a cleaner once a week. (Sonja is slightly unhinged, but Cara can live with that if she doesn't have to dust.)

There are no used teabags staining the sink any more. No nearly-empty bottles rattling around in the bathroom. The house smells of furniture polish instead of feet.

She refreshes her bed with new linen and Persian throw pillows. Buys a coffeemaker, suits, and puts a bird of paradise plant on the sunniest windowsill. A Rodin ornament – what a difference it makes compared to Robby the Robot. Reminds herself what a materialist she is, in both senses of the word.

Cara can eat hummus again.

It's silent when she works from home, to the extent that she can't tell whether she's alone or not. Whole weekends go by without them speaking more than a few sentences to each other.

Heather texts when she's staying at a friend's house, makes herself scarce for days on end. Then she reappears in a zigzag maxi dress Cara wouldn't attempt because the print goes widthways.

Heather's hair grows longer, turns deeper red, and if a strand sticks to her lip she leaves it there. She poses with her arms on her head like a dancer while she waits for the microwave to ding. Stands on a chair to catch a daddy-long-legs with her bare hands, careful not to hurt it. She lowers her voice like a Hollywood actress in her first serious role. The acne fades, her complexion turns dewy, and she experiments with Instagram eyebrows.

Cara's stepdaughter-in-waiting is turning into, well, her housemate.

Eating together falls into abeyance. Later, separate shelves are introduced.

Cara throws away the expired veg pots. 'I'm going to stop buying these,' she says.

Heather barely looks up.

'I'm giving extra lectures, and they keep piling on supervisions. Squeezing more out of you is the new normal. I can hardly fit in my research between grant applications. And the marking . . .' She wants to say marking that somebody higher up has palmed off on her, which strictly speaking she isn't qualified to do, but that could be construed as ungrateful. 'I need less stress in my life. You can help by contributing.'

Heather yawns.

'Sorry, am I boring you? Why is it my job to put food on the table as well? Show some of the independence you're clearly capable of.'

'It must be fucking awful being you,' she whispers, taking a cream cheese baguette upstairs.

Cara snaps a pill out the blister pack, as she does twenty-one days out of twenty-eight. The dot rests on her fingertip, the last of a six-month prescription. Cara hates making these appointments. Waiting at the surgery because they're running late. Having the same conversation with the nurse.

'Any problems? Headaches? Spotting? Let me check your blood pressure . . . Yes, you're fine.' Repetition like purgatory.

She's taken several thousand of these, like the sensible

feminist she is, and hasn't read the enclosed leaflet in years. Takes them automatically. Couldn't – this is awkward – name the side-effects.

Because it's the last pill of one hundred and twenty-six, Cara has the urge to take it for the sake of completion. She may yet meet a man who whisks her away to Venice, Prague or Seville, for days of culture and nights of passion. It could theoretically happen. Must happen to some women some of the time, and isn't her turn overdue? She'd have to sort out her body hair first. Wouldn't want to give the guy a shock.

If you aren't renewing your prescription, her rational voice interjects, if you're frantic with work, overweight and basically celibate, there is no point in taking a pill you don't need.

Pill and packaging are dropped in the bin.

The evenings are getting lighter when Cara says, 'Look, I need to talk to you. Are those my sunglasses? I wondered where they were.'

Heather takes them off, holds them out to her.

'It's time to talk about you paying rent. No, you can wear them for now. It's all well and good you being here . . .'

'Whatever you decide is cool with me.' Heather slides the glasses back on.

'Your father's approach to money was, shall we say, uneven. Being self-sufficient gives you choices. It is an expression of female autonomy.'

Heather raises her theatrical eyebrows.

'If you've got a part-time job you haven't mentioned it,' Cara continues, 'nor finances generally. And getting into debt isn't the answer.'

'No-o.'

'Nevertheless, you ought to be treated as an adult. We'll not rush into a new arrangement then. I won't drop it on you out of thin air.'

'I work in an office, if you must know.'

'You have an office job?'

She blinks. 'Cleaning one. They leave leftover cereal in their bowls all day, and it goes rock solid, and they don't include me when they send cards. There, I talked about it. I can clean this place too if you like, to save money? What do you pay Sonja? I'll do it for less.'

When did Cara last exercise? Walking doesn't count – she needs to do the kind of exercise that will make her breathless. She'd have to say since before iPhones were invented. What her undergraduates call 'the olden days'.

She browses for apps and sportswear. Searches for local running groups – then decides they won't want her, because she wouldn't want her if she were them. There are blogs which give conflicting advice, with pictures of athletes who are impossibly toned, tanned and determined. She watches videos of stretching and warm-ups, while eating a cookie.

The clincher is this: it's good for the brain. Cara is terrified of her abilities leaking away, until she's ordinary. Until she is below average. Until she's a helpless mess.

Call to mind a face she recognises and a name that escapes her. Call to mind forgetting where she's parked the car. Call to mind freezing mid-lecture, when she is supposed to be the expert in the room. Call to mind leaving the oven on. Call to mind incontinence pants, being a victim of cold callers, and not remembering who the Prime Minister is. Call to mind a care home, where Cara is on the inside punching a door code, trying to get out. And a published paper that she is not only incapable of reading, but that she doesn't remember having written.

There. Enough to move her.

She wakes with a sense of urgency. Puts on her Team GB T-shirt bought in the fever of London 2012, and tracky bottoms she does gardening in. Starts with sixty seconds of running, alternated with ninety seconds of walking.

The moment she staggers back through the front door, sweaty and wheezing, Heather decides to ambush her.

She stares at Cara like a model in a perfume commercial and says, 'You will say if you hear anything before I do? Promise you won't leave me in the not-knowing, not for this?' After weeks, *months*, of being phlegmatic, she suddenly talks about her dad as if he left yesterday.

'It's sad you have to ask,' says Cara.

Heather turns paler than usual. Her pupils dilate. The last time she looked this way, she nearly fainted. 'Promise you'll tell me yourself,' she whispers. 'Please?'

'Don't worry. I promise I'll be there.'

Breaking up with Heather would be a simple matter if she was a man.

'I could give her a month's notice,' Cara mumbles to the fishes. 'Do it nicely. Then I can flush you.'

Heather

Study and scrubbing. Heather can't afford to give up either.

The office is a hub for third-sector organisations, which has to be explained to her as she's never heard of them. There are private-sector companies: businesses run for profit like banks and retail – this is the first sector. Next, there's the public sector: hospitals, schools, roads, and everything paid for with taxes – that is the second sector. Finally, there's the third sector.

On this floor they help ex-offenders, people contemplating suicide, pensioners who wear emergency pendants on lanyards in case they fall, and a food bank. The office literature shows pictures of delighted clients giving feedback in speech bubbles, but Heather hasn't met any of them to hear their stories firsthand. Neither will she, as it takes place 'in the community'.

Her colleagues must be good at their jobs if the amount of disposable coffee cups is anything to go by.

Initially she thinks the cereal bowls are the worst. Then she thinks skid-mark toilets are the worst. Then she thinks puddles on the floor and overflowing sanitary bins are the worst. Then the eye-watering yogurts when she deep-cleans the fridges. Then she decides the worst of the worst is when they leave her notes.

These mugs are tea stained.

A perk that comes with working alone after everyone else has gone for the day is the photocopier being left unattended. She gets the idea when she sees a ream of canary-yellow paper in the stationery cupboard.

Shoves them, still warm, into her rucksack.

Betty meets her, armed with a staple gun and raspberry vodka in a travel cup. 'I normally put soup in it. It might taste weird.' She smiles from her eyeliner flicks to her labret-pierced mouth. Points to Heather's sunglasses. 'These are sharp. Were they Ruth's?'

'Big C's. I keep expecting her to ask for them back.' Heather shows what she's made because she needs Betty's approval, as silly as it sounds.

'Clear layout, strong font. Are you definitely up for this today? You've got goosebumps on your arm.'

'Only a tickle. The wind from across the Atlantic, my skin saying hello.'

They staple them to tree trunks. Tape them to telegraph poles. Pin them on noticeboards. Stick them in as many windows as they're allowed to, and in a few they're not. In pubs, in news-agents, in churches. In barber shops, Co-ops and a synagogue. The crêpe stand, a burger van, and into the hands of tourists on a ghost walk.

On bus stops. On iron gates by *no trespassing* signs. A home-less shelter.

They pause to listen to a nerdy folk musician and to share Betty's drink.

He finishes his tune and Heather puts a poster in his guitar case, then gives him a thumbs-up. Who knows what'll work?

They retrace the footsteps of other families, careful not to cover theirs.

. LOST CAT – Black F, name of EUREKA. 10-y-o. Chipped w. silver collar. Adored family pet. Reward if found.

. MISSING DAD – Paul Wycliffe. Specialist skills: general knowledge and Barry Gibb impersonations. Enjoys steak bakes, sci-fi and the Shipping Forecast. Please make contact soon. Bring him home!

Heather worries she has unfriended Aunt Kathy by mistake. Reminds herself that Aunt Kathy lives in Lowestoft (not Norwich) with Uncle Trev (not married to him) and their son is an actor who changed his name to Charleston for Equity reasons and is currently working at a festival in Guildford. This is how you stay in touch with the grown-ups and why you can't completely leave.

The sisters-in-law, Ruth and Aunt Kathy, took turns babysitting for a while. Charleston (fka Carl) stayed over at least once, and Heather stayed at theirs – she gags – at least once in childhood.

She remembers a barbeque, back when she still ate meat. There was a long garden with a tyre swing, and they pelted her with foam darts. She remembers singing along to Elvis (British Elvis, with the song about detectives, Aunt Kathy and Uncle Trev called him class).

She remembers the war room with shelves full of Dresden, Stalingrad and the Normandy landings. Pictures of fighting units. Diagrams of tanks.

'Come and see my collection,' Uncle Trev said. 'I'll let you hold my old man's medal.' Heather switched to vegetarian soon after.

'Will I get the train in for class?' she asks Cara.

'We're giving this a try. Nothing is permanent.'

67

'Wouldn't you usually say something along the lines of I've been wasting my time if I quit now?'

Cara doesn't reply.

Heather shakes her head. 'I'm not moving out then?'

'No,' she says. 'Don't think of it like that. You're visiting your family. Most people want to be with their family. Most people feel it's where they belong.'

Heather touches her mouth like she can hear a faint noise and is trying to work out the cause. *What was that?* the gesture goes. Hang on, no, it's gone.

Cara says, 'Of course I want you to study; there's no reason why you shouldn't. Everyone needs to find out what they're good at, it's how we get by in life. Don't you like Kathleen?'

'I like Aunt Kathy just fine.'

'You don't have to stay with her if you don't want to. I won't make you, that wouldn't be fair.'

'Is this respite?' Respite is what her dad had from her mum at first. Half a day here and there, then for a couple of nights, until Eglantine could take her permanently.

'I can cancel the whole thing. Kathleen won't mind, and neither do I.' Cara wields her phone to prove it. 'They're pet people, aren't they? You love animals.'

'How long for?'

'Mm, what do you think's appropriate?'

'You haven't given me a chance to do this how I would choose?'

She looks her in the eye. 'Tell me, what would you choose?'

'You know, when I can ... I was going to ...' Heather folds and unfolds her arms. 'You said I need a plan, and I kind of do, soon.'

'Please don't start crying.'

'I wasn't.' She wants to, but she wants to *not cry* in front of Cara even more, if she's to be taken seriously. 'Have I pissed you off?'

'Did I say that? This is about doing what's right. Suppose you were in an accident.'

Her body jolts. 'What sort of accident? What did I do?'

'I'm being hypothetical. Suppose for a moment you were in intensive care having been knocked over by a car. Now, if you were in hospital, unconscious, and I went in and said, "I'm here to see Heather Wycliffe," the first thing they ask is, "Are you family?" And I would have to say no. They might not even tell me you were there because of patient confidentiality. I'm not next of kin to you. I have no, er, claim on you. Kathleen is your next of kin, and your godmother, by the way.'

Heather thinks, If you were in hospital, I would break the door down. 'What has that got to do with it?'

'When the parents have died—'

'He's not dead.'

Cara checks her fitness tracker on her wrist. 'Traditionally the role of the godmother is to take responsibility for a child's welfare in the event that the birth parents cannot.'

'Is this because I lost your sunglasses?'

'No. It has nothing to do with that.'

'It was annoying, wasn't it? You were right, I should've bought a cheap pair. I'll replace them. I can pay more rent; they're looking for a cleaner in the office upstairs . . .'

'Oh God, I don't want your money. This is absurd, I'm calling it off.'

Heather grabs the phone away. 'No, I don't want you to. Aunt Kathy is expecting me. It's revision left, mostly, I love Norwich, I mean Ipswich, I mean Lowestoft. They're all great. I have to pack.'

*

69

Their pet is a hamster called Cherry, rolling across the carpet in a plastic ball, clunking into a nest of tables. He nips if you try holding him.

Uncle Trev is on an auction site sniping for badges. He rubs his goatee as he watches the bids go up and the seconds count down.

'He knows you can get an app, but he prefers doing it himself,' Aunt Kathy explains. She has straightened hair, a waistcoat over a beige dress, jeggings, and an ever-present vape. Her speech is punctuated with a cough Heather recognises from the funeral. 'Tell me what food you like, and we can go to the Asda?'

'Anything except meat and fish.'

'You're a veggie? Good for you. Maybe having you around will encourage us to eat better. More salads and roughage. Talk to me about my baby brother.'

'I was hoping you might tell me?'

Aunt Kathy drags on her vape, and chemical smoke wafts around her. 'Always on the quiet side, although that doesn't mean there was anything wrong as such. He came out his shell more after he met your mum. Ruth used to tickle him. They'd have tickle fights until one begged the other for mercy, like kinky foreplay, right there in front of you. Sorry, do I shock you? We're very plainspoken.'

Heather giggles.

'I don't know that your Dr Cara is the tickling type?'

'She isn't *mine.*'

'No, not what you'd call warm, is she? Kind of stuck up. She's all right, but she's too, you know, into what she likes.'

Cherry rolls along the skirting board until he's blocked by a pouffe.

'She kills mice in her lab,' Heather says. 'She thinks she hides it, but I know. Worse than that she's done, on monkeys, because they're like humans, but cutting them open is allowed.'

Aunt Kathy mouths: *Vicious.*

'Hounded him out,' Uncle Trev says, without looking up from his screen.

'Hang on, we don't know that, do we? Cara is a career woman, very driven. That's to be admired. You can't argue the fact that Paul was punching above his weight, again, because he certainly was with Ruth. I wish you could've seen her in her prime. What a beautiful girl she was. Cara isn't attractive in a conventional way, but she's younger than he is.' Aunt Kathy narrows her eyes. 'Isn't she? She has one of those old-before-her-time faces that're hard to read. Usually I'm spot on.'

'He was a doormat,' says Uncle Trev.

'It's our mother's fault as much as anybody's. We had to fit in with her. Paul idolised her, couldn't do enough for his mummy, but it didn't earn him any favours. Never a boy to stand up for himself. Hold his own in a fight? Pff, useless. Always had to be told what to do by a strong woman. *Submissive*, if you catch my drift.'

Heather says, 'He's a good dad.'

'Totally. Don't get me wrong, Dr Cara is the one to blame. He'd never have left if she hadn't made his life a misery, nagging and the rest.' She takes a big e-drag. 'What was it then? There must've been something to tip him over the edge.'

'Mum died,' she answers quietly.

'I'm afraid there's more to it than that. I'm sorry, but there is. Something doesn't quite add up. Nobody throws away a cushy arrangement like he had, unless he's been victimised. He must've planned it for years – or d'you think he snapped? What do you think, Trev? Did he plan it for years, down to the last detail – or did he wake up one morning and decide, right, I've had enough of this, I'm off?'

Uncle Trev considers. 'We used to shoot deserters.'

A Chinese takeaway is delivered to the door and Aunt Kathy pours three large glasses of rosé from a box. Puts Cherry back in his house, where he hops on his wheel and keeps going.

Uncle Trev tastes the wine by sucking air between his teeth. It's a sound Heather remembers.

Over what's left of beef in oyster sauce, duck with pineapple, and Kung Po vegetables, Aunt Kathy leans on her shoulder. 'We're going to be okay, because your mum and me were like that.' She crosses her fingers. 'What's it called? Ruth was my bestie.'

'Your bae?' Heather smirks.

'You should've seen her put this stuff away.' Aunt Kathy drinks downs to the dregs. 'A real party girl. Dancing and stumbling all over the place. You and I are going to make it. Paul meant well, right up to the moment he bogged off. Spineless. Men are trash, aren't they?' She vapes. 'Ruth had an aura about her. You've got it too. You look like, what's-she-called, like – I can't remember her name – skinny, with the massive houses. Married to the bloke on that thing . . . Are you into sports?'

'No.'

'Me neither. I tried joining a gym once. What a scam that was.'

Heather feels warm. It must be the spicy food. 'Swimming is my favourite.'

Aunt Kathy croaks with laughter. 'You're in luck; we've got the whole sea for you to swim in!' She boops her on the nose. 'Such a baby face. I can be your mentor. I can teach you everything I wish I'd known when I was your age. We can go shopping together and we'll stay up late and chat. I'll be the sophisticated

72

aunt you talk about sex with. What I should've done with Ruth years ago, we're going to do right, me and my niecey . . . You know there was a time when Trev and I were separated. That was a helluva three months.'

No reaction from Uncle Trev, comparing prices of commemorative coins.

'He was sleeping with that tart from the Marina.' Aunt Kathy refills their glasses generously. 'I was at my lowest ebb. But Ruth was there, soaking me with booze. She kept me from slitting my wrists. "What do you want, Kathleen?" she said. "What's in your heart? When you know how you feel inside, then you'll know what's right."' Her breath is a mix of rosé and vape. 'No one had asked me that before. She was this old soul . . . What happened to her shouldn't be allowed, they should be working day and night to find a cure. Was a wicked thing.'

'The best die young,' says Uncle Trev.

'Not like that, though. Slow and with her dignity gone. Soiling herself, and nothing going on between the ears, except pain. We were devastated, weren't we? We wouldn't even let Cherry suffer that way.'

The hamster is filling his cheeks with food.

'Poor you,' Heather says, 'for feeling devastated. How horrible for you.'

Uncle Trev glances at them. 'Show her where she's sleeping tonight.'

Charleston's bedroom, a shrine to musicals, talent shows and am-dram, is out of bounds.

'This is our room,' Aunt Kathy says, pointing. 'And that's Trev's war room.'

She snorts. 'Yep, he showed it to me when I was a kid.'

'I think it's grown since then. He's forever adding bits and bobs, whatever he can lay his hands on. Parts of his collection are extremely rare, it's practically a museum.'

'He let me hold his medal.'

'Plus scans of documents and hundreds of photos he keeps on disc. Stacks of DVDs. Give him *The Dam Busters* and I don't see him for the rest of the day.'

'Is that really what you think he does in there? Watches *The Dam Busters* or – I don't know any others. Is there a tunnelling one?'

'This is you.'

The guestroom has a tumble drier in it. Washing baskets, boxes marked *eBay*, and a foldout sofa bed. Heather parks her suitcase, sticks her tongue out in the mirror to see how it's discoloured.

'There's a towel, and help yourself to toiletries. We can go to the Asda in the morning for anything we don't have.'

'How long am I staying for, did you and Cara agree?'

'Let's see what happens, shall we? Whatever we don't have ...' The offer vaporises. 'I still can't believe Paul has done this to us. We don't deserve it. I expect you're as frantic as we are.'

'I was at first. I really want to know he's okay. And I try staying calm mainly so he can make contact when he feels up to it? Is ready to. Basically I'm selfish, though, I'm doing it for me. *Before* was when he needed us – and I was a pain in the bum. He made a choice ... Wouldn't be fair to intrude on his, his, his process. People think he's stupid because he's quiet, and he's not, he's just, as I said, quiet. Being a private person who doesn't ask for help is his biggest flaw, which isn't bad as flaws go, is it? There are worse people in the world.'

'A shy boy.'

Heather raises her voice. 'At least he's harmless. He tried to be kind even when he wasn't sure how. I guess you know that, you keep saying how important they both were to you?' She peels off her socks as she's speaking, shrugs out of her top. 'I don't recall you coming over to check . . .? As far as I'm aware you never came to Cara's house or, um, visited Mum at Eglantine. You weren't the only ones, all her mates dropped away. I have memories of her, actually. I remember when she was getting ready for a night out, I helped her choose what shoes to wear with her bad jeans – black boot-cut with rhinestones on the pockets and she held her breath to do them up? Badass jeans I thought she meant. The only person who bothered was Cara, weirdly. Mum wouldn't've had such great care if it weren't for her. You do realise if it had been the other way round, Mum and Dad would have been here for you in a second, you and Trev, and – what does my cousin call himself these days? Charleston. Dad's good at giving lifts, he'd have taken Charleston to auditions, including Guildford, if you asked him to. And Mum would think of ways of having fun, silly stuff like karaoke. Go for walks. She liked ruins, you know, lumpy castles and forts, and temples in foreign countries? Crumbly walls, because she saw something in them, in the gaps. Could sense energies. She wasn't any good at history, not like Uncle Trev is, but it was sweet. And she couldn't cook to save her life, but she'd manage a lasagne for you once a week – and Big Trev – with his big shiny medal. *Spit and polish* . . . I reckon he practised that whole routine. Yeah, he'd definitely done it before. Mum made new friends, in case you were wondering, friends who cared for her after she lost her speech and the rest? Dad ran away from you as well, it's not as if he begged you to talk him out of it.' She curls on the sofa bed, partially dressed. 'I think you know, even if you don't *know* know. You'd snoop around Trev's desk and find some clues pretty quick because that is your style.'

Her aunt turns off the light.

'But to stay with him? Wow, Aunt Kathy.' She sniggers in the dark. 'I thought they were called *medals* for ages. I couldn't watch the Olympics without blushing.'

Heather has sweaty, broken sleep. The minutes go by as if she's pressed snooze and fallen into dreams of uncertain length: Ruth in the doorway of the laundry-slash-box room. To pick her up and take her home because it's what Heather wants. Full of cheerfulness. Sparkling.

Ruth has a message for her. 'Don't argue with me,' she's saying authoritatively. 'Pack your case. We're going.'

The main light stabs her in the eyes.

Cara, in a coatigan over the same clothes she wore earlier, her expression like an emoji without a mouth. Typical.

I didn't ask for you, Heather thinks.

Swish, the blanket is pulled back. *Yawn*, she dresses again quickly. *Trundle*, the suitcase is wheeled to the car, and she doesn't bother with 'thank you for having me'.

Heather opens the passenger-side window a crack. Nods against it, and the sky lightens above the A11.

'You're not going to be sick, are you? If you are, I'll try to pull over.'

'I don't think so.' It acts as a hypnotic suggestion. Her stomach lurches. 'Have you had wine too? You shouldn't be driving.'

'I'm afraid leaving you there wasn't an option, and I can't miss work today.'

'Don't worry, you won't.'

'Why did you sabotage it? What did you do?'

'Wasn't on purpose, it was – what's the thing you say when you've had a lot? I didn't know rosé could come in a box.'

Cara

—'*In vino veritas.*' She squints in the rear-view mirror. 'I don't suppose you found my sunglasses?'

'Wouldn't I be wearing them?' Heather browses for a radio station she likes. Says, 'They have a lady presenter, I thought they only did travel reports.' Closes her eyes for the rest of the journey.

At the house, Cara takes her coatigan off. Heather pulls it on automatically and slumps.

'I daren't sit down. I'll never get going again.' Cara checks her activity stats. Slices a loaf. 'Dr Stewart will wonder why I'm in early. Maybe I should bring a peace offering. Toast? Have peanut butter, or boil an egg. Protein helps a hangover. Here's the paracetamol.' She places it next to her.

Heather shrieks.

'What's the matter?'

Tears come immediately. 'Oh my God. Oh no. Did you kill George Harrison?' She's staring at the aquarium.

The white goldfish is floating motionless on its side.

'Oh dear, that's a shame.'

'Did you do this?' Heather gasps wetly. 'He was fine yesterday.'

'Of course I didn't. He's died. That's all.'

'I go away for a night, not even a night – did you put bleach in it?'

'Certainly not. What an awful thing to say.'

'You always hated those fish. You wait for me to leave, then you attack them. You want us all gone. It's no reason to take it out on George, he was helpless.'

'I thought the other goldfish was George Harrison?'

'The orange fish is Oliver Sacks,' Heather says shrilly, 'always has been.'

'Then I've been calling them the wrong names this entire time. But I didn't kill it. What's gotten into you?'

She sobs into her hand. 'You treat animals like things, and they aren't, they're real, with feelings. You torture them and destroy them and you can't help it because they're materials to you and you have no sympathy.'

'I'm taking a shower. I suggest you go back to bed.'

'I have college today. And work. I have commitments.'

'Do whatever you like, this is not my problem.'

Heather uses a slotted spoon from the utensils rack to lift out the dead fish, although there ought to be a little net for the purpose. On a piece of kitchen roll he looks tiny and drab.

As Cara goes upstairs she hears Heather saying, 'What a good goldfish you were, who ate your food and swam so gracefully. We won't forget. Poor Oliver has no one left to talk to in his own language. How you twinkled when you were alive. Somewhere your soul twinkles still. Our tank is half-empty without you.'

She thinks, Christ, you weren't this upset when your mother died.

At the end of the supervision he says, 'I'm struggling, Cara Mia.'

'I'm Dr Brenner in here, and—' She clears her throat, making it sound as if she's forgotten.

He takes up space. 'Hal is fine.'

Not as in Prince Hal, she thinks. 'What can I do for you?'

'My parents were over the moon when I was accepted,' says Henry. 'They brag about how well I'm doing to their friends.'

'Why shouldn't they? They must be very proud.'

'Perhaps they were also relieved. They have a specific idea of what success looks like, it wouldn't cross their minds . . . They made sacrifices for me, and I haven't questioned their choices. Living on my own schedule for the first time, I have a chance to think.' Henry juts his chin. 'I hate to admit it, but it's becoming harder to ignore the critical voices in my head and carry on. It's starting to show.'

'In your work?' It would explain a few things, she thinks.

He nods.

'And who have you discussed this with?'

'You.'

'Oh dear, you are in trouble.'

He smiles. 'You're quite funny.'

She crosses one knee over the other. 'I can't advise on how to tackle pushy parents. Mine were the opposite.'

He ruffles his hair. 'It's more a family tradition.'

'I'm sure it is. Either way, parents have expectations because they tend to see their children as extensions of themselves, not as individuals. I agree with you that this can be an issue.'

'I don't want to give less than my best, but sometimes the challenge is greater than my motivation is. I can't talk to them because I know what they'll say: knuckle down! I don't lie to them. They hear what they want, if you get me?'

'Let me guess, you have a brother.'

'I'm the youngest of three brothers. One did biotech; the other practises environmental law. They're both married to great girls. Sprogs.'

Cara fidgets. 'I'm glad you brought this to my attention – well done for that. Feeling some pressure at this stage is perfectly normal. Your lab work is solid, and you're a good communicator. Which parts are you struggling with precisely? I can support you by going back over topics, suggest additional reading . . .?'

He lowers his eyes to a notebook of boyish script. 'I don't know what's here for me.'

'Based on what you've said, I'm not too concerned. The world doesn't end because you're having a wobble. I wish I could reassure you.'

'How do I explain this? I meet people who are passionate for research – have a fire in them – like you do. But I don't. And I wonder how I can get it? Then I think, if I have to ask the question, it'll never come. Because I should know by now if I'm on the right path.'

'I thought you were going places. You made a point of it, remember? Head of research by the time you're thirty.'

Henry doesn't reply.

'Tell me what you want to achieve. What do you hope to gain from your experience here?'

'A purpose.'

'Excellent. I am delighted to hear it. Specialising – finding an angle – is like getting a stone in your shoe, as unappealing as that sounds. What you're looking for is a tiny detail that you've noticed, and that no one else is noticing, which irritates you. It might be very small indeed to begin with—'

'They tell me this is what I'm good at,' he says over her. 'But I'm not sure I believe that life is a competition. I had enough of that at school. I get sick when I think about it.'

'Demoralised?'

'Physically sick. A rash on my chest. Palpitations.' He gestures through the small window. 'Doesn't this strike you as false?'

The view outside is of busy traffic. Across the road is a company that teaches English as a foreign language, and which has nothing to do with the university, other than proximity. Presumably if the students can't understand English when they apply, this detail is lost on them. They might even return to their homelands claiming they 'went to Cambridge'. But Henry isn't referring to that.

'Don't you love your work?'

He shrugs. 'It's okay.'

Cara reddens then says, 'You have a lot going for you. Put the hours in and you'll be all right.'

'Which is what the family wants too. Only, what if these years produce nothing of significance?'

'Significant how?'

'That it doesn't do any good in the world? What if what's on offer is *all right*, when what I need is food for the soul? What if I get to thirty, and realise I've wasted my life? By then it will be too late to change anything.'

She stares out of the window to see what she's missed. 'I thought you were asking for help with your studies. But it sounds more like you're having an existential crisis.'

He rubs his chin in an affectation. 'Should I give up?'

'I wasn't suggesting that. For what it's worth, I have no doubt that if you apply yourself, industry beckons. You have a promising career ahead.'

'I was the cleverest in my class—'

Weren't we all? she thinks.

'—at home I wasn't as impressive. They're happy when I deliver.'

'Are you saying you're here by mistake?'

He breathes heavily. 'I said I didn't love what I'm doing. I suppose I can keep my head down and carry on. Figure out my next move.'

'Like staying with a woman you're not really into until someone hotter comes along? Like that? I'm afraid I can't help you, Henry. You're doing a degree for the wrong reasons, in a subject you're not especially interested in – in the world's palace of learning.' She rubs her eyes behind her glasses, fumbles them off. 'Isaac Newton. Paul Dirac. Darwin, for God's sake. Dorothy Hodgkin and more Nobel prizes than I can remember. Scientists are called to this place. Many great talents fought to be here. They were told they wouldn't make it, and against the odds, they did. If you want to contribute to human knowledge, there is nowhere better. And you talk as if muddling through is acceptable?'

'I don't want to cause hassle.' He flexes his large hands. 'Maybe I should reconsider my spot?'

'You will get criticised if you leave. You think your parents talk about you now? Throw this away and watch what happens: you'll be fed up of explaining yourself. And if you decide to stay, fine, but you'll get no special treatment from me.'

'I wouldn't deserve it.'

'You're searching for a purpose – it's a mystery to me how you've come this far without one. I am too busy to turn the average into above average, and I don't care how many emails they send trying to convince me otherwise. I'm sorry, but I have no opinion on your issue. My advice is to come back when you've made your choice. In the meantime, some of us have work to do.'

He mumbles an apology on his way out.

Heather

Heather has an Anglepoise lamp directed in her face. Her hair is pulled back, her shoulders are bare, and in her peripheral vision she has an impression of *orange* from her roots to her cleavage.

Betty tilts her by the chin. Looks at her intently, without looking at her. Her gaze stopping at the skin.

She dusts outlines on Heather's cheeks, then sticks silicone prosthetics around her eye sockets and on her cheekbones, exaggerating her features to monstrous proportion. Blends the edges with a gelatine mixture on cotton buds until they're seamless.

Betty wears gold cuffs in her hair and a denim dress with spatters that haven't come out in the wash. Her room is an ordinary teenage bedroom, apart from the chicken wire, bottles of stage blood, and a papier-mâché demon work-in-progress. She likes haberdashery. Horror. Nubian art. She collects images and turns them into mood boards: seabirds, reptiles, moths; Afrofuturism, carnival, Kabuki; tattoos, scars, anatomy.

Tests make-up on the back of her hand. Switches from sponge to brush. 'Don't move,' she whispers as she leans close.

For this character she's using a picture called *La Llamada* by Remedios Varo and what appears to be an enlargement of a red planet. The colour palette on the dressing table is mainly reds and oranges, with saffron, goldish-bronze and muddy grey. A few powders, Fuller's earth, plus plenty of gunk.

'Is it Mars?' Heather asks, trying not to move her mouth as she speaks.

'Blood moon. She's more of a lunar witch.' She leans back to compare both sides.

Most of the projects in Betty's portfolio were done on her half-sister, 'Never sits still for me, she's got ants in her pants,' and on herself. 'You control the pressure when it's your own face. Get in a zone. Part of the skill is communicating with a model, to get her to relax and feel involved. Otherwise the work suffers. Looks lifeless. They don't expect me to be good at white people as well, so I have no choice but to be outstanding. I need more practice on male models too, but they're only interested in fresh-kill zombies.'

They share a joint, passing it back and forth.

'I'm pretty relaxed,' Heather rasps. 'Shall I come with you?'

'No, dumbass.' She dips a brush in a tiny pot.

'Why not? We can get a flat together.'

'That isn't how it works. I'll be living in halls of residence. It's done.'

The brush tickles Heather's neck. 'You'll be with your arty mates?'

'Stop moving, why are you awkward?' They go silent while Betty paints some finer detail. Then she says, 'I swear episodes of *Friends* are what they show these days instead of telling kids bedtime stories. Did anyone ever live in a loft apartment in New York, working in fashion – or as an actor – or waitress? When there were only six of them it was okay. Now it's everybody you've ever met, plus thousands more you'll never meet, being sexy and funny all the time. Thin. Popular. Super-successful, yet somehow incredibly grounded. On a beach doing yoga. Who are these guys . . .? None of them live across the hall from me. They don't hang out with me every night. They don't choose me over their parents and their romantic partners. They definitely don't want to hear me play 'Smelly Cat'. Everyone I know is struggling, trying to make their money last till the end of the month. Those photos are nothing special either, not when they're easy to manipulate. If photography used to be a serious art form, it isn't any more. Billions of worthless pictures . . .'

Heather blushes through layers of red make-up. 'Yeah, they're crap.'

'I like what's tactile.' Betty sighs with concentration. 'Louise says it's not too late to switch, and train to be a legal secretary. Her dream for me is answering phones and filing. Taking minutes at meetings. Being perved at by my boss. I know why she says it – I know why – she's worried about student debt. And she doesn't want me to end up in the jam factory like she has. But if she's not going to be encouraging, she should keep her mouth shut.'

'Does she mind when I stay over?'

'No. My mum likes you. She thinks you're tragic.'

'Do you mind?'

'I'll make it clear when you're getting on my nerves, don't worry. My dream is . . .'

'What is your dream, Bets, or can't you say it out loud? Is it like a wish?'

'A poster – no – a movie trailer, with the lead actors in special effects make-up that I've created. A fantasy or a slasher film? Even a romcom with convincing ageing would do it for me. I don't mind a terrible script, as long as my artwork is believable. Central. That my art tells the story on screen.'

Heather tries not to frown. 'And studying in Grimsby will make that come true?'

'Can't hurt. Keep still.' She makes a correction with her fingertip. 'We'll still see each other.'

She can tell it's a lie, but it feels wrong to point it out. At least this way, Heather's face is going with her. 'I'm happy for you.'

'Are you?'

'It is possible to be happy for a person,' she says, 'and on an unrelated note, feel sorry for myself.' A sketchbook is open next to them, the pages wriggling with characters. 'Where'd you get it from?'

'Spirits are in us. I set them free so they can have a life.'

'It's weird in there.'

'Thanks.' She adjusts the lamp—

It causes spots in Heather's vision. They flash and fade, red, lurid green, fuzzy black.

'You remind me of Rachel?' Betty says.

'Yeah?' Heather is rather pleased with the comparison.

'Yeah, I think you'd marry money if you could. I don't relate to any of them, but I like Monica's strength and perfectionism.'

While Betty backcombs, Heather takes *Claribel of Tunis* from the fold of her sleeping bag. The pristine first edition from Ruth's room at the care home is now scuffed and tatty. Here, in Betty Willis's room, there is definitely a good chance of getting greasepaint on it. Heather doesn't mind.

Betty looks over her shoulder between hairsprays. 'Any good?'

'A bit subjective.'

'Does it – sorry if I sound funny – remind you of her?'

'Mum kept it, didn't she, which I think means something? He inscribed it to her. It's odd, whenever I read this, I feel like someone isn't being completely honest with me. That it's been done for effect. It feels made up.'

'Don't get excited, they call it fiction for a reason.'

Heather says, 'Do you ever listen to grown-up conversations and wonder how you'll get there? Do you ever doubt that you're going to manage it, be an adult, without feeling – strange? How do they know what to say, and when, and how to act right, and are we going to know too, eventually? Where do you learn from?'

'Maybe they're faking?'

'All of them?' Heather has an itch on the nose. Resists scratching because she senses Betty is nearly done. 'Mum was the same as you are. She knew what she wanted.'

'What was that?'

Me, she mimes.

'Lucky.'

'Yeah, but Cara definitely didn't want a stepchild, so it balances out?' The novel thwacks on the floor.

'Do this.' Betty opens her mouth as though in surprise and Heather mimics. She applies a finishing touch. Repositions the mirror.

Heather takes in the full effect of Betty's creature.

Every patch of skin on her face, ears and throat is covered in reds, brown and orange. She's cracked like dry earth, with sunken eyes, pointy features and bronze veins. Her hair is wild, more auburn than familiar ginger. Glitter on her lips.

'Whatever you do, don't lick.'

'Not everyone makes it, Bets. You will. You'll have your movie, loads of them; a studio is waiting for you. And the faces you're going to paint exist already, a person who isn't even a star yet is going to be your best work. They're out there, pulling you towards them. I am the Moon Witch, and I predict it shall be so.'

Betty lifts a brush to make an adjustment. Changes her mind. 'I like showing my best self. Louise says it's what we can do. I have to.'

Cara

Is there such a thing as grant application fatigue, Cara thinks, and is funding available for it? There should be.

She clicks through pages of criteria. Instructions. Boxes to write in. It is oh-so-familiar territory, although not similar enough that she can copy and paste with ease. The award amounts are reasonable; which means expectations are high, the process onerous, and her chances of winning are slim.

She emails the link to Dr Stewart. Gets on with a draft.

Cara needs to persuade the funders that her research priorities align with theirs, which requires – not lies, but spin.

There is flexibility under each of the headings: *Perception*, *Intention* and *Theory of Mind*. They're broad and vague from a neuroscientific point of view. The implication is, *We're not sure what we want, surprise us.*

She rejects a call, missing the days when you could take the battery out for emphasis. Given that improvement comes through repetition which strengthens synaptic connections, she should be the queen of grant application forms by now.

She's trying to come across as professional and detached, yet also passionate and completely immersed. She thought she was being clear a moment ago, then rereads and thinks, Um, no, without being able to put her finger on what's wrong. The saved version doesn't match the version she was aiming for.

The cash she needs for her research slips further away.

Suddenly, Cara realises she is alone in the lab, hungry and stiff. She's been down the funding rabbit hole for hours. A text from Dr Stewart invites her to the pub so they can work on a draft together.

What took you so long? she thinks, and replies, *OK*.

Cows and cyclists cross her path as she walks via Lammas Land and Coe Fen. The city centre is full of tourists and day trippers standing in the middle of the thoroughfare to admire the architecture, check maps, and pose.

She tries to avoid eye contact, to look as harassed as she feels. Her heart sinks at being approached.

'Excuse me, where is the university, please?'

A better question would be, 'How do you get to the university?' because she has a witty retort for that: excellence.

Hard work.

Sleepless nights mentally screaming at herself that nothing less will do.

She understands the mystique that brings them here in droves, to stare, to study, to forge a career. When Cara was younger, she was awed by sunlit glimpses of green lawns through college gates. Would have sold her soul to walk on them.

Today, she barely looks up at King's Parade. Instead of blackboards and chalk dust, it's PowerPoint and laser clickers. Instead of leisurely lab time and tranquil analysis, it's grant applications and feedback. Instead of debating the mysteries of the universe in a secret society over brandy, it's snotty emails and arguing in the comments.

Excuse me, where is the university of Cara's imagination? That's what she wants to know.

At the Eagle pub on a lunchtime in 1953, Crick and Watson announced to Cavendish Lab colleagues that they had discovered 'the secret of life', the DNA double helix. In addition to receiving a Nobel Prize for their achievement, there is a blue plaque on the wall, because they were braggarts.

Cara imagines what her career-defining moment might be like, a discovery of such significance that it changes everything which comes after it. Then she imagines dashing into the nearest café.

'Hey, guys, check out these results. I've found the secret of human consciousness. Lattes for everybody!'

It's never going to happen, and it's why nobody knows where Rosalind Franklin ate lunch. Women in STEM don't shout.

Dr Helen J. Stewart is tall and hearty, with a side-swept fringe and reading glasses on a beaded chain. She wears a smock dress with chunky boots and a floral anorak, as though she's going to a festival. She's drinking gin and tonic in the smaller room with the preserved graffiti ceiling, a traditional dark wood bar and cask ale handpumps.

She waves to Cara, who joins her gracelessly.

'Guilty conscience?' Helen says. Her expression falls as Cara opens the laptop. 'What, no chitchat? We're actually going to do work, are we?'

'Aren't we? It's what you put in your text.'

'True. You don't come for social visits any more.'

Now she doesn't know whether to show her or not.

Helen beckons, 'Pass it here,' and before long is tearing it to shreds.

Cara sips a G&T served in a goblet garnished with cucumber.

'Have you got to the part about philosophy research being eligible? We're competing with the humanities these days.'

'I like Spinoza,' Helen says, tweaking her hair.

'Philosophers want the best problems for themselves. They call us reductionist, as though it's an insult. Since when do you read Spinoza?'

'If he were alive today, he'd be a neurobiologist. Maybe we should get one for the lab, what do you think?'

'A philosopher?'

'Worth a few euro. Very interdisciplinary of us.'

'I'm the one who'll end up looking after it.'

Helen smiles briefly. 'You put in for a half?'

'Yes, I've made that up. I don't know what to ask for.'

'Personally, I think we should be aiming higher?'

Cara flattens her mouth, slightly relieved to hear the word 'we'. 'Can you remember the good old days, before neuroscience was churned into TED Talks and clickbait? When we were unfashionable and could get on with our research quietly?'

'Are you complaining that there is too much interest in the field?'

'The wrong type of interest. Verging on hysteria. Pots of money sloshing around. Forget slow, deliberate experiments. They want results they can put in a press release. Unreal expectations aren't conducive, not in my opinion.'

Helen types in changes. 'Trust you to complain there're too many opportunities to be had. There is nothing to be gained from purity, Dr Brenner. You're in business now, not academia. We need to make the most of it before we go the way of string theory.'

Cara swizzles. 'Hang on, before, did you say *guilty*?'

She looks over the tops of her glasses. 'Yes, it's not nice making little boys cry.'

'Has he complained?'

'Then you *do* know who I'm talking about. No, not officially. I think he was taken aback by your directness, as well as your, er, brilliance.'

'I offer the kind of supervision I wish I'd had at their age. What more can I possibly give?'

'No wonder they're rude about you in evaluations.'

'I don't believe in coddling them. And by the way, if I was a man speaking to a female undergrad using the exact same words and tone of voice – and she went off crying in the loos – nobody would remark on it.'

'Is that how you wish to be?' Helen asks heavily. 'You're better than that.'

Through the bulb of her glass, the ice and fizz, the pub windows are forced into ovals. Cara mutters, 'He's taking someone else's spot.'

'Okay, I'm not going to interfere with how you supervise. I'm sure you've done everything right. Would you also like me to tell you that you are more deserving than the rest? Give more than they do? Yes, I see you working exquisitely hard. You send emails in the middle of the night. You join committees nobody else wants to. You investigate with gusto. When you fart, you publish a paper on it. And I should think that you're Reviewer 2 on a few occasions . . .? Guess what, Dr Brenner, you have abilities. The microphone loves you, even if the camera doesn't. You're busy and it is great. Are you *special*? Needed? I would say that you have interesting layers, but you didn't come here to change the habits of centuries. Allow me to congratulate you on fitting in.'

She saves their progress.

Cara is waiting to be served when Silvia comes into the

pub. Keeps her back turned because she doesn't want to buy *her* a drink.

In the mirror on the back bar behind the spirits, Silvia taps Helen on the shoulder – squeaks – and gives her a hug. She sits down next to her and, alas, appears to settle in for a conversation.

'You look amazing,' Silvia says in a gooey voice, which she only started using after Helen transitioned. 'Did you have a glorious time in Egypt? Was Karnak amazing?'

'*Amazing*,' she replies.

But you can't stand her either, Cara thinks in Helen's direction. You used to complain about her more than I did.

Nonetheless, Helen is scrolling through holiday snaps on her phone; pauses at each temple and tomb so Silvia can ask asinine questions.

Cara speaks slowly to the barman while watching them out of the corner of her eye.

'We were part of a big group tour, which felt safer, and I tend to cover up in the sun anyway.' Helen beams. 'I needed the break. And our team is ever so good at letting people have time off when they ask for it.'

Cara sets down the gin and tonics. The amount of twigs and salad in them is absurd.

Silvia leaves after she's extracted a promise to go out, just the two of them, for a proper catch-up.

'She's a sweetie. You shouldn't be mean about her.'

'I didn't say a word.'

'Have you taken annual leave yet? You look like you could do with it. You can't keep carrying over.'

'I know. I look haggard.'

'I don't think you've missed a day in the lab since we met and considering what you – you were with him a long old time? You get less for robbery.'

For a moment Cara is confused. 'Paul? Well, wasn't that destined to fail? You might've warned me.'

'When Spinoza wrote, *the mind and body are one and the same thing, which is now conceived under the attribute of thought, now under the attribute of extension*, the paint was still wet on Rembrandt's canvas. It is painfully slow, Dr Brenner. Little by little towards less uncertainty is what we signed up for.'

'I didn't realise you like Rembrandt either. If we're at a conference, I go to the museums by myself.'

'And how is Heather doing?'

There is such a thing as oversharing, Cara thinks. She unlocks the screen and says, 'Let's win some money, shall we?'

Heather

On the bus.

Claribel had disappeared into the black darkness of the cave. I called her, my voice echoing through the cavernous spaces, but there was no answer. I considered the possibility that she had returned to the surface and left me there as a test to see whether I could find my way out. She was perfectly capable of such a trick. Then I wondered how long the torch I was carrying would burn for? As I looked at it, it appeared to grow smaller. The thought of abandonment filled me with dread, and I started walking in a random direction, I could not tell if it was up or down, and I kept calling her name. Still there was only silence.

However, I did not feel completely alone. It was as though there was some cave-dwelling creature watching and waiting for me to show my fear. Perhaps to attack me once I had wandered too far into the labyrinth and collapsed with exhaustion? At that moment, even Claribel's dragon of a sister would have been a welcome sight.

Eventually I discovered her deep in the belly of the cave in its oldest part.

'I thought I had lost you,' I said. 'I cannot see in the dark as well as you can, and your footsteps make no sounds.'

'I hear yours very well,' she said. 'They are like boulders falling down a mountainside.' She was insulting my size as well as my clumsiness.

Before I could answer, she took the torch and held it aloft, revealing dozens of hand stencils on the wall. In the firelight they appeared to push out from the rock, to reach across thousands of years and move like souls. I gasped with amazement.

'This is the moment we were awake,' she said in a faraway voice. 'When we first tried to bridge the gap between the seen and unseen. We then became ourselves.'

I was enchanted. Everywhere I looked I saw more decorations, not only hand shapes, but also hatches, rings and dashed lines. I longed to decipher their secrets, knowing that such a task would take a lifetime of study. 'Surely these were painted for some special purpose?' I said. 'Was it part of a ritual? Are they symbols? But what can they possibly mean?' I was thinking aloud.

'Protection,' she replied, placing her hand inside one of the ancient handprints, where it fitted perfectly. 'These were made by women.'

There was no way she could be certain of this, and I suspected her of trying to mislead me. 'What a pity we will never know the artists' names,' I said.

'Tanit,' she said, her hand still pressed on the rock as if communing with it.

She misses her stop.

Cara

This time it's a wireless printer. Last time it was getting rid of the futon by donating it to charity. The time before, a scheme to install solar panels which were supposed to generate income as well as electricity (they don't).

Glenda says, 'Amazing how it knows what to print without a cable telling it to.'

'You don't question how mobile phones work, Mother.'

'That's different, we had a cordless telephone in the hallway for years. This is creepier.'

The printer is by the writing bureau where she keeps bills, bank statements and postcards from Wales. The bureau is near the dinner table, with the Constable place mats and a tablecloth from Tenerife. Next to the settee is a magazine rack, with diet books, gossip magazines and the *Daily Mail*.

The software hasn't been updated since last time Cara looked. No wonder it's taking for ever.

Glenda brings in coffee. 'Mellow Birds,' she says, setting it down. 'I can't get on with the posh stuff you like, it creates ever such a mess and I find it bitter. I put more in yours to make it stronger, so you won't notice any difference.' Her hair colour is fresh. She is wearing a twinset, Uggs, and a squirt of Obsession.

'I'll let it cool a while.'

'Chocolate tea cakes too, real ones, not own brand. Would you like pink wafers to go with them? Have you heard from Paul lately?'

'If there's no news, it means there's no news. Please don't mention him again.'

'You can't tell when they're headed for a nervous breakdown, can you? They act normal, same as the rest of us. You couldn't've stopped him, it's no one's fault but his.' Glenda arranges the biscuits. 'With hindsight you should've got pregnant. I know you were trying to do right by waiting because of his poorly wife – but if you had got on with it, then you would've given him a reason to stay. If a man's having his entitlements, a woman should have hers. You could have started a proper family if you'd tried. You don't wait for permission. Like when I had you, you were a mistake, but in fairness to your father he sorted out his priorities quick smart.'

On the mantelpiece is a photograph of Bob Brenner wearing a paper crown at Christmas. There's Cara's first graduation photo (her ceremonies were 'much of a muchness' after that). The rest are of the Jones sisters on a glamour-shoot experience day.

'The word you're looking for is accident.'

'You like thinking that, don't you, thinking you know what I mean better than I do? I've been around a lot longer than you have, I know what's changed and what hasn't.'

'All done.' Cara shows her how to send a document and change the settings to save ink. 'You can print pages from anywhere in the house, for example if you're watching TV or in bed—'

'Oh no, using a computer in bed doesn't sound civilised, you'd be hunched over.'

'You read in bed.'

'Not if I can avoid it, it doesn't make sense paying for a wireless one when a normal printer does just as well. I mean, the computer's practically next to it. I'm having buyer's regret. Maybe we should return this and get a different model?'

'The laptop is faster now that I've taken off the malware,' she says as if she didn't hear.

'Was it slow? I thought it was supposed to be like that. Help me bring the washing in if you aren't drinking your coffee.'

They unpeg sheets from the line. Mirroring, they shake them out by the corners. Fold lengthways. Step together and fold in again.

'What's Heather up to?' Glenda asks.

'Why, do you want her?'

'Awfully vague when you try talking to her, isn't she? I think she must have a boyfriend tucked away somewhere, it's the only explanation I can think of.'

'You'd have to ask her.'

'I did when she stayed over, but she turned shy. Be a hell of a change for you when she eventually moves out.'

'Heather's plans are not my plans.' She puts the squares in the laundry basket.

'Crowded you used to be. Living in an empty house after all this time is going to come as a shock, I expect. I hate to remind you, but I won't be around for ever. Then you'd be a spinster, and an orphan. Unless you start making the effort to put yourself out there again, there's a very real possibility you'll end up alone. You'll develop strange habits ... Working hard, May?' she calls across the fence to the lady who lives next door. 'Nice day for it!'

The neighbour Cara has known for her whole life is humming while she weeds a border.

'Hey?' May squints from under a bucket hat. 'He looks lovely, doesn't he?' She means the chrysanthemums engulfing her. 'Is this your daughter? Hasn't she grown tall?'

'Yes, it's me, May. I'm the same height I was before. Can I interest you in a pet goldfish to look after? It comes with a top-of-the-range aquarium.'

'No thanks, I already got one,' and she carries on weeding and humming as if they weren't there.

They touch fingers with the penultimate fold of a duvet cover. Glenda resumes: 'I'll be honest with you, I had no idea if my marriage was going to survive after you left home. Empty nest syndrome they call it, I saw an article. I had to ask myself whether we had anything in common besides you? Not exactly Richard Gere, was he?'

'I know, Mother. All those times you've been mistaken for Julia Roberts.'

'You can laugh, but I've had offers along the way.'

'Flirting at the post office doesn't count as offers.'

'I lived my life for you and your father and I should be grate-ful – is that right? Because there couldn't possibly be anything better for me out there in the big wide world? This, here, is the nasty side of your character. As it happens, there was a gentle-man who was interested in me for myself.'

Cara sniggers. 'I'm sorry. I take it back.'

'He told me that he wanted to bring me cocktails on sandy beaches.'

'I'm sure it was very emotionally charged. Did I ever meet this mystery man?'

'You knew him quite well actually. It was Duncan.'

Her smile fades. 'Duncan, as in the pharmacist? Mr Westgate?'

'That's right. It was just friendly at first. Your father worked all week and played golf on the weekends. You either had your nose in a book or were grubbing about in the dirt like a tomboy. I used to go to aerobics with Duncan for something to do and then we'd have a ploughman's.'

'But he wore a wig.'

'It was a toupee, and I built his confidence enough that he didn't need it in the end. He was emigrating to Australia to retire, and he asked me to go with him. Cara Mia, I seriously considered it.'

'Hang on, are you saying this was a physical relationship?'

'None of your business how physical we were. That's private. What I will say is we had a special connection, and it was different to what I had with your father. When it was gone, I ached.'

Cara is folding a pillowcase until it can't go any smaller. 'And how long did this *relationship* last?'

'Not more than four years. You used to love seeing the back of his shop, with all the potions and prescription drugs and stuff, do you remember? Why do you think he kept giving you free cough sweets?'

Cara finds an old tissue in her pocket, balls it up and, in a gesture which doesn't feel quite natural, takes off her glasses and wipes them with her top. 'How could you do that to my dad?'

'Oh well, you're a fine one to talk. He never noticed, and if he did, he didn't let on. Whatevs. I had the chance to leave him and I didn't go through with it. I do wonder sometimes what might have been.'

Her mother knows 'whatevs' but can't get her head around wireless technology. 'He gave you everything you asked for.'

'Get off your high horse, this was yonks ago. I waited for the good parts of having a family to come along, and they never arrived. You made no secret of the fact that this house wasn't good enough for you. I thought you were an intelligent person.' Glenda shakes out a towel and they fold it together, although one folder could manage. 'Heather's a breath of fresh air, isn't she? A courageous girl with a really positive attitude. I think if I had my time over, I'd be like that.'

'What's stopping you from going to Australia right now?'

'I could go, couldn't I? I'm not exactly sure what it is I'm saving for. Old age, I suppose. Australia's further away than Wales, though; I'd miss my sisters dreadfully.' Glenda straightens the step-pyramid of linens. 'I offered to help her. She wasn't interested. Someone's put it in her head she has to prove herself.'

If Heather wants to make it on her own, then that's a win, and Cara will take the credit. 'How long did she stay for?'

'Couple of nights. She slept in your old room.'

Cara couldn't wait to get away from the narrowness of it; a mattress full of doubts, and woodchip walls. Doesn't mean she wants to share them with Heather.

Glenda says, 'She's a pleasure to be around. Lovely company. Only I forgot she's vegetarian, didn't I? I think teenagers do it to be trendy. Thank goodness you weren't a fussy eater, I could always rely on you to finish what was on your plate. I gave her a baked potato with beans in the end, and she covered it in brown sauce. She makes me laugh.'

Cara catches her reflection in the patio door. Her hair's still up from the shower and she's wearing a hoodie with black jeans. She looks like a before photo on daytime TV.

Heather

The spare key isn't under the mat by the back door. And it isn't under the plant pots of various sizes, nor poking out of their tops. And it's not in the shrubbery. It's the middle of the night and the only light source is the torch on her phone.

Heather isn't too drunk. Searching has a sobering effect, and she is doing a terrific job of making no noise whatsoever.

Fumbles with the green man ornament staring out from the ivy: he comes away from the wall and there's a gap behind with a key tucked in.

Congratulates herself on finding it without waking Cara. It can't have taken her more than ten minutes of rummaging? The next thing is getting it in the keyhole, which seems to have shrunk, or stuck, or changed somehow.

There are no lights on in the kitchen, other than the time display on the microwave. Her eyes adjust.

Cara is there, with the laptop closed in front of her, a bottle of wine on the go and paperwork fanned out. She can't see her expression, only her outline.

'Sorry, I forgot my—'

'Shh.'

'Why are you sitting in the dark?' Heather whispers. 'Were

you watching porn?' She senses she's being glared at. Takes off her leather jacket and sits opposite.

'Women my age do not look at porn.'

'Then you must be the last people who don't.' Sips from Cara's wineglass.

'Did you have a nice evening?'

'It was fine. My friend said he was playing a gig, but really it was one of those open mic things where you put your name down and have to wait your turn? His song was towards the end when people had had enough and were starting to leave. I wasn't keen on the music, to be honest; maybe if you're into that folky scene it was all right. I would've liked it more if Bets had been there because Hal had his group of friends, and I invited her, but she didn't come. And probably she was right not to, at times I felt ...' She scrunches her eyes trying to remember. 'I don't know what?'

'Is he your boyfriend?'

'Not really. He's not an especially good mate either. He tells me how much better he feels after we've spent time together, and that I'm good for him – what, like vitamin C? – and I think, Yeah, because you were talking about yourself all night long, and didn't ask me a single question. He can be nice, and he has a house in France, well, his parents do. They're giving him a rough time at the moment. He's a musician, he's sensitive. Is that quiche?'

She can make out a piece left on Cara's plate.

Heather starts eating it and says, 'Sorry, did you want to finish this?'

'No more for me, thanks, it's mainly butter and cheese.'

'You should eat what you like.'

'I would, if I didn't worry about my health and I believed in mindless pleasure.'

'Nope, your problem is at the other end of the scale, not enjoying yourself enough. You have frown lines, you know. I think, if I could make one wish for you, it'd be to have more fun.'

'I'd be rich,' Cara says, visible in shadow, 'if I could only change one thing. I can live with the rest.'

'You're pretty rich already.'

'Where do you get this idea from that I'm wealthy? I'm not. I save for holidays.'

Heather has another mouthful.

'I'm not,' she repeats. 'I could earn more somewhere else, four or five times the salary I'm on, and with a cheaper cost of living. Better labs as well, I expect.'

'Change jobs then.'

'I can't. Cambridge is special.'

'Glenda is nearby too, I suppose, sort of?'

'Families.' Her silhouette glances at her. 'I saw your poster on a tree. You shouldn't have done that.'

'Why not? Who cares?'

'It's useless to think a flier will bring him back, plus, you could get into trouble for hurting the tree.'

'You saw it, why wouldn't someone else? Maybe somebody has already? Maybe he has? Maybe it helped? We don't know. It's worse not having tried. Me, I mean, not you, you've done everything right, as per usual. I need to – reach out without him feeling chased.'

'I don't understand how you stay so calm. I was in pieces when my father died.'

'I remember.'

'Do you? I thought you weren't old enough to notice.'

'It was the same time you took me for swimming lessons. We went twice a week, on Sundays and Wednesdays, until I could swim a thousand metres, which felt like miles when I started and couldn't even manage a width.'

'Right, I forgot.' Cara refills the shared glass.

'Plenty of kids don't have a relationship with their parents; I'm winning really. Dad is what he is.' Heather clears her throat. 'Why *are* you sitting in the dark?'

'I was listening.'

'To me trying to break in?'

'To a blackbird.'

Then Heather hears it too. A low, abrupt whistle and trills, excited twitter, and raspy conclusion. 'Is that what that is? Why's he singing at night, does he always do that?'

'They sing because of light pollution. It must be exhausting for them. Shortening their little lives.'

They listen for a moment.

Cara sighs. 'About your idea of going abroad to find yourself ...'

'No, that doesn't sound like me.'

'Okay. You said perhaps that you'd like to take a gap year and go travelling, to decide what you want to do with the rest of your life – discover what you're good at – and until you did, you couldn't see the point of committing to a plan, education or career-wise ...' Cara passes her a Post-it note with a number written on it. 'I've done some checking. This is Paul's money. From your dad. When I asked him, he began setting it aside for you. You studied; therefore, you should have it.'

Heather shines her phone on the figure and her heart leaps. It's more money than she's ever had. A swan with three eggs. 'What's the catch?'

'There isn't one. It was Paul's, and now it's yours.'

'But what am I going to do at the end of my trip?'

'That's the beauty of it: whatever you like. The point is you go away, not knowing, and when it's over, you know. Take your time and come to a view. You are capable of this. Think of it as an assignment. This is your budget.'

Heather traces the digits in the dark; she can just make them out. Funny how it ends in zeros. Cara might have topped it up, and if she has, why doesn't she say so, so Heather can thank her? Why is she being serious? 'You couldn't live on this for a year?'

'Well, it's enough to send you on your way. Nobody goes on travels with all the funds they need. There is nothing wrong with bar work in a sunny resort, or picking fruit, being a chalet girl – earn some extra cash as you go along, meet new people and have a great time.'

'It sounds complicated.'

'It's a spontaneous way of living, which is fine while you're young and not tied down. You'll see the sights, learn about different cultures, gain skills. Not only for employment purposes, but as life experience. It's practice for the real world.'

'The real world, what's that?'

'Trust me, you'll figure it out. The brain isn't fixed. It's plastic. It adapts. We can cultivate the skills we want most – grow into a better version of ourself. Which means the present is always the right time to try something new or attempt what's difficult. Even when we're older, it is possible to improve. And you're a baby, you could do virtually anything you want to.' She scratches her shoulder. 'Not everything, of course. Not perfectly. We prioritise, don't we?'

Heather drops a pinch of fish food in the tank. There's a gleam as Oliver swims for it. 'Why have you been holding on to it if it's my money? Why didn't you give this to me sooner?'

'Are you saying it's not enough?'

'The amount is irrelevant. I'm confused because, was it mine

107

in the first place or wasn't it? Aren't you giving back to me what I paid in rent?'

'It's almost twice as much. Weren't you keeping track?'

'If I had Dad's money to begin with, I could have decided for myself who I pay rent to, and I wouldn't've needed to scrub toilets.'

'Why don't you take it up with him then?' Cara tuts. 'You're getting exactly what you asked for. You should be thrilled. It is a perfectly nice sum for a girl to go on travels with. If the situation were reversed, I'd be out of here in a flash and not look back. Shall I do a transfer into your account, will that help? D'you want me to throw in an air fare since you seem to think I'm made of money? I've been more than generous. I have been patient.'

They aren't whispering any more.

Heather wills her brain to go faster. 'What about my stuff?'

'What stuff? You haven't got any stuff. Stuff is furniture and the contents of a library and family heirlooms. Stuff is curated. It has a story behind it. You have knick-knacks from Tiger and some face cream.'

'You know what, Mum was right about you.'

'Oh, you only say those things to make yourself sound more interesting.'

They hear the blackbird again, louder, and look out the window as though an orange eye and beak will appear. Fronds emerge in the garden in grey light, and edges sharpen in the kitchen.

'Where would you go if you were me?'

'Venice is at the top of my list, to see the frescos and canals, and spandrels of St Mark's Basilica. I'd learn Italian. Go wine-tasting in the Veneto. Not Australia, that's for sure.'

'Sounds like you're the one who should travel.'

'I can't, it wouldn't look good to take a sabbatical.'

Heather doesn't completely understand what that means. Taps out a message. *Is it ok if I come stay with you please?*

Cara stretches noisily. 'Where will you go?'

'Betty's place then ...' She necks the last of the wine.

'Will there be blackbirds there?'

'I don't know. Maybe I'll get back to you?'

Heather was stupid to think she felt sober before. This is sober. The uneasy feeling that she should be doing something, without knowing precisely what.

She drops on her bed, leans down to reach her favourite Chucks from underneath. What Heather has saved for best is what she's going to live in from now on – that's the first decision made.

Her leather jacket was a present from Paul (with Cara's help because he wouldn't've known what size to buy), useful in different weathers and with zip pockets.

The hand charm necklace which was Ruth's, that Heather treated as precious, will be in active service.

She chooses a healing crystal from her shelf of positive energy. Yes, and a spare wallet for keeping separate bits in like an adult does, although hers has ladybugs on it.

The sunglasses got muddled in with the totes and ought to be returned. Heather tries them on.

They're too good to let go of.

The office is full of filing and science gubbins. She needs a flash drive, among other things. Rifles through a folder to find her passport, which is kept with Cara's rainy-day credit cards. There, another decision has been made.

What she stands in and can pull behind her is what Heather is taking.

You may stay for as long as you like, he replies.

Cara

She has a ritual like a pigeon in a Skinner box. Lays out her T-shirt, underwear and leggings the night before. Downloads an episode to listen to, alternating between *In Our Time* and *The Infinite Monkey Cage*. Gets nervous. She puts on her left sock and trainer before her right sock and trainer. Cringes, because she knows it shouldn't matter.

Not running. What she does can generously be called 'jogging'.

A woman Cara's size and Cara's age wearing Lycra. Is there shame in it? She reasons, when you're a blob, it hardly matters if you're a red, melty blob.

Once out there, people give her right of way. She even has an occasional nod from runners in the opposite direction. Any remarks and catcalls are from ugly men.

She knows, rationally, they shouldn't bother her. Nonetheless, she changes her behaviour. Buys sports sunglasses to replace her lost pair, feeling less conspicuous behind them.

She enjoys the data: distance, time and burned calories. Endorphins are pleasant, but she wouldn't call it a high. This is different from her memories of cross-country running at school: effort as opposed to torture.

I'll relent when I have pain, she thinks. Later, she assigns colours to pains of different intensity.

The solitude and the fresh air. How her body changes from cold and sluggish to hot and invigorated. The British weather isn't as bad as its reputation (put it down to climate change) and when it rains, it cools.

A run after work means taking advantage of the green spaces and towpaths. Her superstitious pigeon behaviour is modified. She wears a sports bra under her blouse; has a water bottle by her computer; keeps spare trainers under her desk. When the last colleague leaves for the day, Cara counts to twenty-six-point-two.

She runs down the avenue, across a paddock, through an archway and around the courts. She runs to Reality Checkpoint at Parker's Piece, and back again. She passes the perpendicular gothic of King's College Chapel. Takes a detour through the crescent to smell the kebabs at Gardies. Dodges market stalls, pedestrians with rucksacks and a professor in a gown.

Cara does a body scan. A green twinge in her left quadriceps. An amber stitch in her right side.

She slows to a walk in Petty Cury, busy with shoppers. Steals a lover's glance through the window of a chocolate retailer. Presses her fingers into her abdomen and gasps the stitch away.

A busker seems to be getting louder. Loud enough to compete with a spirited discussion on the paradoxes of infinity that she is trying to listen to.

He plays in front of a shop *To Let* and directs the song towards her, some ballad about a *cold, haily, windy night* and a soldier who begs a maid to let him in.

Cara gives Henry a withering look from behind her sunglasses. The first time in her life she's serenaded, and it's with sarcasm. He is more Cambridge Folk Festival than Cambridge University.

Has missed supervisions without sending his apologies. If there's no improvement soon—

Henry doesn't falter, misconstrues her attention as appreciation. He projects.

As soon as he finishes his song (and it seems to be taking a while) what she'll say plainly is that he needs to apply himself, or quit. No third option.

He is near enough to speak to and sings on and on. Surely he is inventing new verses to keep Cara at bay. And now it looks as if she's stopped to listen to him.

She thinks, I tried my best for you, and you complained.

She thinks, You're the type who's born with all the advantages and squanders them.

She thinks, Don't overthink, tell him off or he'll keep failing up.

The song is over and Henry waits as if she's going to applaud.

Several figures cross the space between them, and as she steps forwards, she sees herself reflected in the empty shop window. Plait unravelling. Muffin top. Underboob sweat.

There's laughter on her earphones. She *pauses*. Drops a fiver in his guitar case with a yellow leaflet stuck to the lid.

Chills and heat soak her body, and she's off again, hates how he isn't playing any more because it can only mean one thing as she shuffles away. Takes the corner at pace and pushes past her comfort zone – keeps pushing until she can no longer do the mental arithmetic to work out how many Ks are left, never mind infinity.

It'll be harder to motivate herself next time, which means more crazy pigeon rituals and, oh, the very thought of it. Please let no one find out. No one can ever know.

Heather

Passenger jets are parked like lorries and the runway is a horizon. Take-offs and landings are frequent and predictable, as though each one was not a miracle.

Heather watches through a window miles long, gripping the handle of her wheelie case until her knuckles turn white.

She looks for *Claribel* in the airport bookshop. Under *E* in fiction. Under *Classics*. In the paperbacks chart and on a table of special offers. She has seen reviews online; it was a big deal back in the day. Insofar as novels can be, because they're only novels after all. Would have been nice to see it here too. A good sign.

She checks the screen. Stares at the screen. Wills the gate to open. All Heather needs to do is get to her seat. Yawns. Betty gave her a send-off last night, and she's had maybe three hours' sleep.

Overhead, her pixelated ghost walks into a clothing store.

The sales lady says, 'How many?' and allocates a tag, shows her to a cubicle, puts the dress on a hook for her. Treats her as though she can afford to be there. 'Let me know if you need another size?'

Heather tries on a skimming dress that makes her seem older.

Not in a bad way. Sophisticated. The design is what Ruth used to call strappy, years ago, when she still took care of herself; when she managed to look both elegant and comfortable, stylish and natural, an impossible in-between.

The full-length mirrors are angled. As well as her reflection, Heather sees an image *not* reversed. Her profile looks back over her shoulder, without catching her eye. Opposite-opposite. She takes a fitting-room selfie and shares it.

Steps out for a better view.

The sales lady says, 'I had the exact same dress when I was your age. Nothing's new, everything comes round again.'

'Reminds me of what my mum wore.'

'Nice mum, is she?'

'The best.' Heather turns on the spot. 'She's a bit famous, actually. There's a character based on her in this cult novel which changes the lives of people who read it? It's sort of a self-help fairy tale, like, you read it for the story, but then you start thinking about how you can be a better person. It makes you feel lovely. The author said she was his inspiration. If it weren't for her, he might never have written it. And it's really good.' Her voice goes quite high.

The sales lady blinks. 'I never met the daughter of a fictional character before.'

'You've probably heard of it?' Heather crouches to her carry-on bag to show her. 'There was going to be a movie and everything. Sadly that fell through, but it could still happen. This is my second time reading it; it's different when you know how it ends.'

The lady excuses herself, saying that there are customers waiting.

Heather finds a spot on the concourse where she can watch the flight announcements, takes out the tattered hardback.

I laid my hands on her face in what I thought was a tender gesture, but she brushed them aside.

'Your gaze does the work of an artist,' Claribel said. 'Rubbing out flaws and exaggerating perfections. You want an impression of me, not my whole self, admiring a few scattered parts. You would turn me into a hollow bauble and fill me with your dreams. How pretty I should be then, reflecting back your favorite colors.'

Her voice was raised, and I looked over to the mat where her ancient sister was sleeping under a rough blanket, decrepit and withered as a pile of leaves, worried she might wake up and I would no longer be able to express my thoughts freely.

'I want to help you,' I said, as quietly as possible.

Claribel withdrew further. 'So you play the doctor next, and my pain is a trinket? What a skillful physician you must be if you can diagnose and cure my ailments with such ease? You wish to rid me of my suffering, not out of kindness, but because then I will be a simpler thing, closer to your ideal, and grateful. What you consider failings, I consider substance. I am better for the experiences I have lived through. I never once prayed for a savior.'

I watched the candle burn lower as if it represented her diminishing affections. Only then did it occur to me that her hag-sister was probably pretending to be asleep and listening to our every word.

'We might be happy together?' I said.

'No. Your desires are too ordinary. The perfection you crave does not exist in this life. You shall grow resentful.'

'My heart is breaking,' I said.

'Have I deceived you?'

I confessed she had not.

'I would rather be flawed and alone, than fake and dependent,' Claribel said. 'I will never be with a person who does not see me *and accept me as I am. It is the lowest standard of love I can tolerate.'*

Heather's phone hums, *You look like her.*

She sends another—

Cara

—chime.

Cara starts replying then deletes it. Deletes the whole damn thread. See how they came in and out of her life, like a flood she keeps cleaning up after. No matter what she does, the marks are still there.

Opens some wine.

Takes it upstairs with laptop and headphones. Draws the curtains, and the screen throws a bluish tinge on her bedroom wall.

Ostensibly she is researching a rail fare to Venice; then to the rest of Italy; then the nicer parts of Europe. A sabbatical isn't a bad idea, and Cara's turn is overdue. She hasn't pursued it before, partly because she is unwilling to relinquish control in the lab, and partly because she thought she would need maternity leave someday.

No. This isn't bold enough. It is time for a change.

She browses jobs and institutes to remind herself how marketable she is. Not change for change's sake; it needs to be *better*.

California. Hong Kong. Stockholm. The words have different flavours, she thinks, like lexical-gustatory synaesthesia.

She imagines waking up in a foreign land to a brand-new routine: a running route before the breakfast she will get in the habit of eating. Imagines going to work as the new girl, and meeting her colleagues for the first time in an unfamiliar lab, with innovative approaches and pioneering – even audacious – techniques. Immersed in a language she doesn't yet speak . . .

Entire cities lose their appeal when she considers them as places to live. Prestigious universities quickly lose their shine. Where on earth would she rather be than here? Unless she can figure that out, she should be grateful for what she has.

Blows her nose and drops the tissue to the floor.

There are some interesting projects once you start searching for them. She reads a few blog posts written in the first person. Anonymous, playful, instructive insofar as they claim to be true.

She clicks on a black-and-white video of a smartly dressed woman at a desk, reading aloud from a novel. A soft buzzing is picked up by the mic out of shot. The woman reads solemnly to camera at first, then slowly loses control and collapses into giggles.

Cara takes the thingy out of its box. Purple, ergonomic, silicone.

Another site is videos of facial expressions: breaths, rising, exclamation! And that's all. A few minutes in length, and each person makes it look easy.

Her body tenses because it's not. It's not bloody easy. She can't remember the last time. How she got there. How it felt.

Gifs. Inordinate gifs. Tiny looping frames of action.

[lower, look back over shoulder, lower, look back over shoulder, lower, look back over—]

[slide and contact, kiss; slide and contact, kiss; slide and contact, kiss—]

[curve, curve, curve, curve—] in perpetuity. There is something nice beyond the edges.

She tries reaching for it.

No to more than two people in a scene. No to canned music, strong lighting and stories taking a turn for the worse. No to violence, misogyny and hairlessness. For such a supposedly normal, healthy activity, it's turning out to be very complicated.

She searches for *ethical* and *female-friendly* next. Cara is meant to pay for content if she has these standards, apparently. When she can't find a credit card she is willing to risk it with, she closes the tabs to be on the safe side.

Doesn't want to hurt anybody. That would be awful.

Rests. Sips. Tries again. Teasing brings her closer. Less is what she finds, oh God, what's the word?

Sexy isn't in Cara's vocabulary. Not unless she describes a secret passage behind a bookcase as sexy. She thinks a shower with high water pressure is sexy. A freshly painted windowsill. Mozart tunes. The Enlightenment. Dissecting a specimen. A Sunday roast with crumble for pudding. And being awarded funding is pretty damn sexy.

It tapers. Has gone.

The vibrator was a mistake. It causes a bad sort of friction, even on its lowest setting. Switches on the bedside lamp and rereads the instructions down to the last page. Discovers it needs lubricant *sold separately*. Well, if that's what it needs, why doesn't it come with any?

I'm really bad at this, she tells herself, knocking back the rest of the wine.

Perhaps it wasn't Paul's fault after all. If she doesn't know what she's into, how on earth could he possibly divine it? Didn't she have to teach him everything, from what boiling water looks like to not clapping between the movements at the symphony?

Goes to fetch a snack; at least she can get this right.

119

She used to ask him what he was thinking – and his answer was nothing.

When she expressed enthusiasm for an idea – he said he didn't mind.

If there was a problem to solve – he left it alone until she solved it, or she nagged him and then felt guilty.

Cara was project manager, treasurer and caretaker; and she persevered because the good stuff was just around the corner. She assumed after Ruth, you know – died – their relationship was bound to improve. Paul's focus would be on her for a change.

They discussed the future together. Only now it dawns on her that she was discussing the future, and he was nodding along.

She waited for him to try without being asked, to show that he understood her. Her likes. He must've wanted to. Must have.

Because it is inconceivable that she has a PhD and spent that long in a one-sided relationship.

'Cara Mia,' says the goldfish, 'no one is on your side.'

Heather

'You're on the wrong side,' Paul says. 'The gate's on the other side of the terminal. Cara said they take your suitcase out of the hold if you aren't there.'

Heather's lost the power of speech the way Ruth did. Can only think the words, *Not her problem*.

'Cara knows more than us. She said you're too young. I'm sorry for you.'

But look at me go, Heather thinks, as she's running through a straight, gleaming tunnel. She's on a travellator which means by rights she should get there faster, except her feet aren't touching the ground. More like treading water. She uses her arms as well, tries swimming for it.

Paul takes Heather's suitcase out of the van.

The airline makes a final call for 'Passenger Wycliffe'.

She sits up. Rubs her eyes awake. Didn't hear the gate number and cannot see it listed.

It's true, Cara would never let this happen. Cara was in her element at airports, dictating weights of luggage and quantities of liquid in sealable plastic bags. She'd let you carry your passport and boarding pass, like an adult, and periodically ask you where they were, as though you were a child. She'd buy you a perfume from the duty-free; covered in testers, they'd say to each other, 'Ooh, lovely, is that you or me?'

Once seated, sweets and wet wipes on standby, Cara would order tomato juice and tell you about the place you were going, whether you wanted to hear it or not, and laugh at idiots who miss their flights.

3

T2Rs
Type 2 Taste Receptors

bitter

Heather

There are three shirt colours worn front of house in the Tree Frog Café.

Team captains like Debbi wear a black shirt and a four-star froggy pin. From the moment a team captain greets a party and shows them to their table, to wishing them a *happy, successful day, come again soon,* their job is ensuring customer satisfaction.

Teammates in beige shirts take the breakfast orders. They know how and when to offer sides and upgrades, and can advise on special dietary needs. Because they spend the most time with guests, it's easier to earn bonuses using their LEAF skills: *L*oyalty, *E*nergy, being *A*ttentive, and having *F*un. Crucially, they get the checks paid. Beige-shirt teammates include Pilar (two stars on her pin), Ashok (two stars) and Valentine (three stars).

Heather's shirt is green like the glossy indoor plants. Green like the tessellation print on the seating. Green like the laminated menus, with breakfast combos named for rainforest creatures. Her froggy pin has holes waiting for stars to be added. Green shirts pour and clean up.

Magnificent smile.

'Hey, can I get you a drink?' is the standard opener, as though she's buying.

Heather pours coffee from a never-ending coffee pot, taken with half and half. Pours ice water from a jug with a flick of the wrist to prevent it leaking. Pours tea which isn't hot enough – when Brits order it, she tries warning them via telepathy. She'd love to be shown how to make cocktails and artisan coffees, but is rebuffed each time she asks. So she has stopped asking.

She heaves away dirty dishes, brushes away crumbs and blots away spills. Sprays and wipes surfaces, lays mats and cutlery, folds napkins into fans, replenishes sachets, and finishes each table with a 'silk' orchid. Heather makes an area clean and tidy, so the guests can make a mess. Then she collects the empties and makes it clean and tidy again.

Debbi says, 'We create a flawless experience for our patrons. We each play our part to the best of our abilities. We don't bother teammates who're busy. That's everybody. You're in one of the most famous hotel chains in the world. Working at the Magnificent is a privilege, and a pleasure, and it's why we smile our Magnificent smiles as often as possible. A frown costs five bucks.'

Heather wipes sticky condiment bottles. Smiling contentedly.

Bartenders are all men and wear black ties, suspenders (braces) and rolled-up sleeves. The occasional bar towel slung over the shoulder. They express individuality through their facial hair, from designer stubble to old Dutch.

Cocktail waitresses have big hair, short skirts and glamour make-up even at six a.m. They glide across the floor and pose for photos, hand on hip, like contestants in a beauty pageant.

Housekeeping and maintenance have uniforms in khaki, with extra pockets, and lanyards with swipe access to industrial chemicals, hardware and a fleet of buggies.

The cigarette girl looks as though she's time-travelled to work.

Stands as though the tray on her neck strap isn't heavy, and everything she's selling is good for you.

Dealers wear maroon bowties, stiff white shirts and grey vests (waistcoats). They wash cards by mixing them face down. They shuffle a deck with terse precision. They stack the chips as if they're worthless plastic. *Clap* to show their hands are empty. Some use slow mornings as an opportunity for practice.

'Real or fake?' Heather asks, pointing at her collar in case she can't be heard over plunking, blarey slot machines.

The dealer flips his bow: it's pre-tied.

The clienteles' habits take longer to learn. Heather is still looking for patterns.

Vacationers who dress as though they're in their own back-yards tend to stay put once they've found a bar, buffet or game they like. They sit in a comfortable seat, sipping through a straw, and part with their money in a predictable trickle. Unless they can be persuaded they'll get extra value; then they willingly go over their limits.

Pleasure seekers (male and female) here for a weekend of parties may wear as little as they can get away with. Bare legs. Bare shoulders. Tops that come off sooner or later. Sportswear and summer dresses are popular. They're high on FOMO and YOLO, among other things. Getting their attention in a town dizzy with distractions can be the issue.

Cosmopolitans curate their spending. They've come for a city break, bringing with them a capsule wardrobe of stylish, interchangeable pieces. Their bucket lists are considered ironic, as opposed to lowbrow, not that it makes a dollar difference. Occasionally they go off-Strip in search of local culture. Like they're in New York; Paris; or Rome.

Not the New York-New York.

Paris Las Vegas.

Or Caesars Palace. Everything is big here, except punctuation.

Business-trippers have a dress code based on whether they're buying or selling. A suit is compulsory for sales. Investors, however, wear smart casual, and are thus harder to spot.

Debbi seats a group of twelve in her section, several with convention passes dangling from their necks.

'Are you having a lovely stay here at the Magnificent?' Heather says, remembering her Magnificent smile. 'What can I get you to drink?' The Lempriere Inc. pen tucked in her hair is for show, since she doesn't need to write it down.

Four coffees, two caps, spicy Bloody Mary, dirty chai, OJ, mimosa, tea (sorry in advance), one just-water and six waters-for-me-too.

'Perfect. Where're you guys from? Colorado? Cool.' She takes straws out of her apron, puts them on the table. 'No, I'm not Australian,' which is the go-to guess when they can't place you.

With that, she hands over to a beige teammate.

Debbi says bussing is a good job, and Heather can wait tables when it's her turn.

Debbi says this is a service town with a service industry, and there's a future here for anybody who works hard enough.

Debbi says if Las Vegas didn't exist, you'd have to invent it. As though Las Vegas weren't invented.

'Shall I clear this away for you?' Heather asks when they've finished their steak, eggs, Canadian bacon, hash and waffles. They've left the rinds, fruit and wheat toast. 'Shall I pack this in a box for you?' The American art of asking questions that have no more than two possible answers.

She heads back to the kitchen with the dirty plates.

Before she makes it to the swing door, there's a blur of hair extensions, gold and tan, as a young woman is knocked over—

Pinned to the floor by security guards.

Conversations break off. The gaming pauses. Music dies away. Seems to.

They hold her down by the arms – the stomach – hold her ankles to straighten her legs. The woman doesn't resist. Presses her face towards the carpet. One of the guards talks on the radio. Another turns her head up as if he's going to perform mouth-to-mouth. Is touching her cheeks and neck. She stares at him from under Amy Winehouse eyelashes.

Debbi says don't stop, no matter what, keep going and keep it smooth.

Heather thinks, I must get these to Camilo.

Noise fades-in.

She goes to the kitchen and crashes the stack down by the sink where Camilo is rinsing. She scrapes them off into the trash, then passes each item to him. He sprays and lines it up in a rack for dishwashing while she does the next. Synchronised.

Instead of high-fiving, which is actively encouraged, Heather asks how long he's been here for.

'The United States? This city? Here in the hotel? Too long and counting.'

She wipes the edge of the garbage can with a wet rag. A soupy smell of chewed meats, grease and hot water. 'I just saw something,' she says quietly.

'No, you didn't.'

By the time she's back out in the café, it's all over, and here's a new party in her section.

'Good morning, how are you?' Smiling. 'Can I get you something to drink? Handy, I brought the coffee with me. There you go. Where are you from? Florida? Cool, I always wanted to go there. I'm from London.'

She never says Cambridge and they never say Vegas.

There aren't any windows on this level of the resort. Temperature and light are constant. Comfortable. There is no sense of day or night, nor seasons, and twenty-four hours isn't hyperbole. Sometimes it feels as though they're controlling the conditions as part of an experiment. The eye in the sky watches to see what Heather will do next.

And something else is cycling through the air filters and blowing in the vents – top note of potpourri, base notes of smoking and dust.

Pilar, a lifer at the Magnificent, has medical bills and a knee that isn't right. She can point out everything the resort does which is *intentional, egregious* or *discriminatory.*

Ashok has family back home who rely on him to send money. They think he's an executive at the hotel and a personal friend of Cuthbert L. Holthouse based on the selfie he uses as a profile picture.

Valentine is a financier by trade who came to Vegas for a business venture which went bad in 2008. Now he's saving to buy the motorbike of his dreams so he can leave again.

These stories are just beneath the surface, waiting to be shared. In the land of free speech, there is a dearth of listeners.

Even Debbi. Her husband is a veteran; they have a daughter in school studying to be an accountant, and a grandchild who lives with them four nights a week.

Somehow the Magnificent absorbs them all. The casino hotel is a changeable, nervous thing.

You aren't supposed to take leftovers, but they throw away a staggering amount of food, and Heather isn't getting her fair share of tips. No, she's not being paranoid. She keeps track of the receipts and has done a calculation. She knows enough not to complain. During onboarding, she asked Debbi if there was a union.

Debbi says, 'The Magnificent is a unique brand. Don't confuse it with someplace else.'

Heather puts toast, waffles, omelette and berries in a polystyrene container. Changes her top. Puts on her sunglasses, which she'll need; and her jacket, which she won't, over her arm. Spins the combination on her locker.

She walks past tables for blackjack, baccarat, craps and roulette. Poker. Between rows of slots that ka-ching ka-ching ka-ching with exaggerated loudness. Past the pearly gates of the high-limit lounge, where bets start at five hundred dollars—

And Monstrosity Mansion where it's Halloween all year—

She passes restaurants (fifties nostalgia, Thai, and Mexican) and themed bars (art deco, Irish pub, and sportsbook).

Pauses by a window, Heather's first sight of the sky since she started her shift. Presses her palm to it, drinks in white daylight.

The Magnificent swimming pool is a bright blue lagoon, and the pool bar a line of beauty. The umbrellas are white canopies, and the bodies on the sunloungers beneath a spectrum of sizes and types. Oily. Bulging. Baked.

A bikini girl dives in.

Heather holds her breath in empathy as her shape slips along the bottom. To be submerged. Weightless. Quiet within and without. Employees aren't allowed to use the resort facilities: it's automatic dismissal. She doesn't wait for the swimmer to come up.

The lobby and desks and, finally, a glimpse of an exit.

A concierge (wearing a navy-blue pantsuit, red lipstick, and crossed keys insignia on her lapel) is talking to a lady (cinch belt over a dress, nude lipstick, Tiffany heart tag bracelet). The women lean in together, muttering short sentences. They exchange tips: information for cash.

Heather averts her gaze as she's learned to do. Steps into the Mojave heat.

The Boulevard shimmers, sunlight glares off every surface.

The famous hotels have ubiquitous outlines. The needle. The tower. The statue. Pediments. Pyramid. Swerve.

The Magnificent is one of this cluster of landmarks: a tapering prism of dark pink glass called a 'pinnacle'. Not the word that sprang to mind when Heather first saw it.

Out-of-towners can struggle with the difference between a prestigious mega-resort and a cheap one, but it's clearer on the inside. Like when Cara once explained to her that Trinity College is posh, and King's isn't.

She takes an escalator down to street level where luxury cars flash past, palm trees grow taller than lampposts, and flowerbeds are cultivated so you can't tell real from fake. Waits in the shade of an advert for *Meditation Classes, Dharma Discussion and Tea*, Buddha's hand extended in wish-granting.

The Strip imitates everywhere, and nowhere is like it. Even the sun doesn't behave as it should. By mid-afternoon strong colours have leached away, leaving pale cut-outs on a blue background.

The bus comes, and riding a short distance takes ages since it stops every few metres. At least it's cooler in here.

Heather settles in a corner, feet throbbing now she's off them, Clean Bandit on her earphones. You can tell who lives here because they'd rather sleep than stare at the attractions.

*

The Apostles Motel is on a highway that disappears to a vanishing point and the purple smudge of mountains. It has a mint exterior, is E shaped and two storeys tall with a railing wide enough for a child to fall through. A neon star pulses faintly in the sunlight, and underneath it says, *pool, TV, a/c, wifi*, in various fonts. The *vacancy* arrow could refer to the plots on either side: *Utopia Bail Bonds* is a space for rent; while the only sign left of *Peacocks Hotel and Bingo* is the sign itself. City Hall protects the street neon, which can stay lit for years after a business goes under.

When the Apostles was described to Heather as 'old', she thought it was a joke. 'The ivy on our wall is older than—' She stopped there. Stopped taking things literally.

She crosses the concrete parking lot to the office where Lars, the manager, keeps the American flag flying. Keeps a photo of himself in Marine Corps dress uniform. Keeps a gun on a magnet under the counter and conceals another on his person. He insists on ID and calls them all guests, no matter how long they've stayed there. Some have been at the Apostles for years.

Heather slides a hundred and fifty dollars cash through the gap for Lars to take in his clenched fist. When he doesn't acknowledge it, she says, 'You're welcome.'

Marble, by the payphone with a small square of knitting, laughs at this. They have a beard and a polka-dot apron. They say, 'Ignore me. I'm waiting for an important call.' They loop the yarn and click the needles.

'How long have you been waiting for?' Heather asks.

'The length of time waiting is a secondary consideration. The contact is essential. I can't afford to miss it.'

'What if you need the bathroom?'

They raise their chin. 'Lars will answer it for me, won't you, Lars?'

He waves vaguely from behind the Plexiglas. Slides the window shut.

Marble whispers, 'He's a war hero.'

'It's no excuse for being rude. But what if you're in the bathroom and he's out the office – what then? Is there voicemail on this thing?'

'Someone will hear it. They'll pick up and take a message. Don't you have faith in folks?'

Heather examines the payphone on the wall and a shelf that's bare except for a metal ashtray and a couple of dead flies. 'There's nothing to write on?'

'Doesn't matter. I'll be here. I have to, it's too important to miss.'

They both watch the payphone for a few seconds.

Watch a few seconds more.

When it doesn't ring, Heather brushes the surface clear of dirt. She takes the pen out of her hair and puts it next to the phone. 'There you go. Find some paper and you're all set?'

'Don't you need your pen for work?'

'They give them away for free. I'll get another tomorrow.'

She walks past the hole in the ground that constitutes the swimming pool. It's mottled blue and grey, tagged with graffiti, and has steps down to a bone-dry floor. Debris has collected in the bottom of what ought to be the deep end: leaves, grit and rusty lawn furniture. The pool edge warns, 8 *Ft*, with a picture of a diver struck through with a red line.

She taps on a door on the second floor (first floor) and lets herself in.

The twin beds have moss-green bedspreads, an oversized lamp on the nightstand between. The walls are cream coloured, with a mishmash pattern. A concertina door separates off a pink-tiled shower room.

She calls him *EE-lee*, like the Cambridgeshire city with a thousand-year-old cathedral. Americans call him *EE-lie*, like White Pine County, Nevada. It remains unclear what Reginald Ely calls himself.

A tall, thin man with stringy veins and a kaftan, he doesn't bear much resemblance to the chubby youth of his author photo. He hunches over his computer picking out keys with his right hand like a beginner on the piano, his left hand limp at his side.

She turns on the fan and wafts her top. 'The least Lars can do is put a safety barrier around that pit if he's not going to fill it with water. Before anyone gets hurt. It's listed as having a pool here, it's such a lie.' She unlaces her Chucks to rub her feet. Sees scuttling across the floor – throws the shoe at it.

Ely stops typing. 'Nunus?' he says in slurred speech.

'Cockroach, over there. Little bastard.' She raises her other shoe as a weapon and hunts for it in the closet.

'I thought you were a gentle vegetarian?'

'I don't eat animals. Doesn't mean I won't kill them in self-defence.'

He smiles his uneven smile, opens the takeout container Heather gives him. The smile subsides.

'Have you eaten today?' she asks.

'I might do if you brought me a chop.'

She shakes out her hair and checks her freckles using the selfie mode as a mirror. Helps herself to his lighter. Flops on her bed clutching a small glass pipe with colourful waves running through it. Starts to pinch green flowers into its tiny bowl.

'What do you like other than that?'

'Blue Diesel when I can get it. Mm, that wasn't what you meant. I like going on road trips?'

He huffs.

'I like camping at Bridalveil Creek?' she continues. 'Giant sequoias so big I couldn't believe they were true. I like swimming in snowmelt.' She keeps the flame cool, thumbs the carb. Gasps. 'So freezing my body still remembers it. I like it when people tell me stuff? The amount of effort they make, you can hear it in their voices sometimes, I haven't met anybody who is happy when they're planning for the future but – you never know.'

'Paradise in the next life is the oldest trick in the book. It worked so well the first time, they used it again in the secular world.'

'Is that what it is?' She switches her gaze between smoke and the ceiling. Mentally tracing spirals and ridges.

'The plan is there is no plan. Where have I heard that before?'

'What are you writing, is it another novel? As long as it's not about me, I don't mind, I will not be fictitious. What's the opposite, please?'

'Authentic.'

'Urgh, everyone is trying to be that.' She blows coils of smoke. Holds her phone to her chest where it slowly becomes warmer. 'And pictures,' she whispers.

'A focus helps us.'

'Helps us do what?'

He pauses his typing finger.

Heather leans on her elbow and articulates, 'Focus helps us do *what*, Reginald?'

'We choose a spot. And we resist the urge to look at the next thing. Stay with it. The world starts to reveal. As a tiny view.'

'That's nice. Why don't you write it down now you've thought of it before you forget?'

'It needs work.' He resumes his staggered typing.

'I like dapples.' She can see herself in the liquid dark. Distorted light. The walls are dissolving.

'Have you met Holt?' Tess asks, reapplying lipstick in the restroom. Electronic dance music pounds through the walls. 'I heard him give a speech on corporate leadership. Great leaders inspire their workforce. They "crush the enemy" – and the enemy can be a rival – or the voice of doubt inside us. Most of all, leaders understand the meaning of self-sacrifice. You see, it's not purely about Holt the businessman, or his brands, or how to make a profit, as fundamental as they are. It's about leaving a legacy. It's Holt, the father, creating a better world to pass on to the next generation.' Tess Kendrick wears a navy jersey, ankle-strap stilettos and a WWJD ring. Her hair is a thick ponytail. 'Powerful and poetic. Do you see him at all? Have you met him yet?'

'No.'

'He can come across aggressive on interviews, but on a podium I find him soothing. He says you should practise visualisation because whatever you're able to picture clearly in your mind is bound to happen; you simply cannot be a leader if you don't have vision and aren't drawing success towards you. Did you know that we only use ten per cent of our brains? Imagine what we'd be capable of if we tapped into the rest of our potential?'

Heather laughs the way Cara did when she repeated this from the internet. (Cara said, 'Then you wouldn't miss it if I gouged out the other ninety per cent . . .?)

Tess puts her lipstick away in a wallet she wears on a chain across her body. Adjusts her bra. 'Can you arrange for me to meet him?'

'I promise if I ever speak to Mr Holthouse,' Heather says slowly, 'I'll tell him about you.'

'You'd do that for me?'

'Yeah. I would.'

'You're sweet.' She rests her head on Heather's shoulder, smiles at her from the mirror. 'I checked online, I'm younger than Holt's wife.'

It's a Monday night and the dancefloor of Kite is filled with people. The cage dancer glows with ultraviolet body paint, and lasers slice through space in strobing green.

Tess says she loves to dance, that it sets her free and she can express herself. She steps side to side, nods to the beats as if uncertain what they're saying.

Heather isn't much of a dancer. It might be insensitive to send Tess to the bar when Tess doesn't drink, and anyway, it's too expensive in here.

She resorts to funny poses and shimmies to pass the time.

Tess says they should leave soon if they want to find a decent spot.

Crowds gather in the street, and implosion parties are in progress on balconies. Sound systems compete with one another and with the flash-bang of fireworks.

They lean on a street barrier to watch.

Tess says, 'I've seen castles on the BBC. You're good at protecting your history. We should learn from you how to value the past.'

'I'm not sure the Riv counts as history?'

'Dean Martin played here, Liberace too. It's a crying shame to let it go.'

Boom, great trailing spiders in the sky.

'Like Guy Fawkes night,' says Heather. Except instead of

being frozen and knee-deep in leaves, she's wearing flip-flops and a shirt dress at two a.m.

'I'm going to look awful at work tomorrow. I mean today, don't I? I need to catch up on my beauty sleep.'

'I think you always look beautiful.'

'Ahh, thank you.'

'How is Steve?'

'Tremendous.' Her grin widens. 'And yours?'

'He's not my – I don't have a – he's a friend of the family.'

'Right, you did explain. Are you seeing anyone special?'

Heather pouts. 'I'm not into dating.'

'You say that, but when you meet the right man you'll feel different. Someone who shows you how life can be, who is capable of bringing out this whole other side of your personality. Your strengths. Creativity. Working together as a team, to overcome obstacles in your path.'

'Is that why you came to Vegas?' she asks between bursts of falling stars. 'To elope?'

Tess shakes her head. 'Same reason we all do: for a fresh start.'

'And how is Connor?'

She laughs as if it's written in a post. 'Hehe getting big. He drew a picture of us living in a treehouse. It had a telescope on it, and a tank for suspended animation? I'm afraid he's turning into a nerd. We're going to visit my parents next week, Connor and me. Steve has to work. They have an orchard – which Connor loves, he could spend all day long playing in it. When you grow crops, it really does bring the whole family closer together. It's a supportive community where I grew up. We cherish each other. Not that there isn't a community here too . . .'

The fireworks spell something Heather can't make out.

'Was it the same when you were growing up? Is a piece of your heart always aching to go back home?'

'Um, we weren't a real family.'

'Oh, but they must've done right by you, you're a cutie.'

The Riviera is bathed in spotlights for the last show. The countdown isn't precise, and the extended pause is long enough for the audience to wonder if it's gone wrong.

The twenty-four-storey Monaco Tower pops with flares and a sound like gunfire coming from inside.

Then it's a collapsing sandcastle. The hotel keels at the top, losing its corners first. Walls shred inwards and the building is sucked down as though dropping into a sinkhole. *The Riviera* sign stays lit as it falls – how does it do that? – and is swallowed seconds later.

Heather sees the demolition before she hears it and feels the rumble through the bones of her feet. Covers her ears too late.

Dust.

Dust spreads up in clouds like colourful ghosts, then dissipates, until you can see through the space where the hotel was standing seconds ago.

Cheers from the spectators.

'That was incredible,' Heather says. 'Now what? Do they – what happens to it?'

'I expect they'll keep the neon at the Boneyard and build a new venue on the same spot.' Tess takes a last look at the vacancy and creeping haze. 'As *thou hast fallen thou mayest be redeemed.*'

Ely is slow typing when Heather gets in.

'Did you hear it?' she says. 'It was loud, the whole city is awake.' Her feet are covered in a layer of dry dirt. She goes to the shower to rinse them. 'I wish you'd come with us, it happened slow and fast at the same time? It was right there – then *gone*.'

'When you've seen one casino implosion, you've seen them all.'

'Wow, that is some kind of jaded. Tessie's right, it is a loss. Those stories?'

'A money-making venture for,' he hesitates, 'bad men who belong in prison.'

'Are you up late because you're working?' She looks over his shoulder. 'The amount of time you spend on emails which you could spend on proper writing, if you tried?'

'You think because this is meant for one person it is unimportant? I'm surprised at you.'

'No? Maybe yes?'

He takes a moment to reread, not quite silently. 'Stone crumbles. Language and ideas are harder to get rid of. You didn't think you were my only correspondent?'

'Reginald, you don't have to explain. Write whatever makes you feel good.'

He lingers over *send*. Saves instead. 'I'm glad there was a novel. I'm happy for readers who took something from it. When I look back, I see flaws I can't undo. It was an attempt. To show love. As a force.'

'I'm not big on love.'

'Of course you are. We all are. All beings that feel devote our lives to finding love. Its words and actions. True love is sacred.'

'Is it?' Heather hugs herself in a ball. She's only told two people in the world that she loved them. Two and a half. (It's half when the other person doesn't say it back.) Wonders if the gritty taste in her mouth is minuscule bits of hotel.

Cara

Cara kneels down on a folded Magaluf towel on her mother's kitchen floor. Places a washing-up bowl of hot water on the freezer shelf, making threads of steam. She has a tray to catch pieces of ice as they fall and a butter knife to help them along, carefully, so as not to damage the appliance. Without consulting Glenda, she throws away the ready meals and the sauces frozen solid. Half a chicken is stuck at the back, preserved like Ötzi.

'Don't you want my hairdryer?' Glenda asks, bending to look in. 'Make it go faster?'

'I don't think mixing electricals with water is a good idea, do you?'

'Is that your scientific opinion?'

'Yes. Unless you want to hold it for me.'

She straightens. 'You know I can't. My back. Crouching for a few minutes means a week on the settee, and I don't want that. Boring with only the television. Shall I get you the hairdryer and the extension lead then? Shall I? Be easier. How is work anyway?'

Cara dabs the iced-up compartment with a tea towel, willing it to thaw. 'Frankly we're in a state because I don't know if we're still getting our grant.'

'Certainly you are, you were in the paper. They have to give it to you.'

'They don't read the *Cambridge News* in Brussels, Mother.'

'You're fretting over nothing. We paid way more in than we ever got out.'

'Not for R&D we didn't. Europe was my sugar daddy.'

Her mother scoffs. 'Perhaps you haven't noticed, Cara Mia, but we made a decision as a country. I don't understand why you're moaning. There's going to be more jobs for people born here. More investment in the NHS. You can't argue with it.'

'Aren't you adorable?'

'Your attitude is outrageous, you know that? No one appreciates being patronised. You're my child, not the other way around.'

Against her better judgement, Cara chisels at the freezer with the knife. She dislodges some peas and a shard of ice large enough for a murder weapon.

Glenda prods the packed snow. 'This is infuriating. I'm getting you my hairdryer, it's the only way. Make yourself useful while I'm at it and have a read of that letter.'

Cara stands. Her runner's knee stabs with pain. No sooner did she get the hang of regular exercise then the physio is telling her to come off it for a month.

A letter from Glenda's financial adviser, dated *22 June 2016*, is on the bureau.

Markets are entering a phase of volatility and therefore we are revising our forecasts. If you consider the Band IV strategy you are currently invested in unsafe and wish to withdraw from world equity markets by switching your investments to cash which is very safe, you must notify us without delay. Should you decide to retain the Band IV strategy you are currently invested in may I remind you that profitable outcomes are not guaranteed. May

I also remind you that switching incurs a fee should you decide to do so . . .

Glitter on her fingers.

Cara fights the urge to wash off the microplastics, fearful that they'll end up in the guts of a poor unsuspecting fish.

Between the sunny postcards of Conwy Castle and Aberystwyth, an international stamp shines like a silver dollar.

Hiya Glenda!!!

I hope you are OK? America looks the same in real life as it does in the movies, but they let you find out yrself how hot it is. Folks here are friendly and ~~every~~ a lot of things stay open 24hr. Great if you like pizza at 3am which I do! And smoothies for when I am being healthy. I promise to give you a guided tour if you ever visit. It is amazing. & weird in a good way.

Love, H xxoxxoxxxo This is my view. In my dreams. LOL

Cara turns it over and more glued-on glitter comes away from the fluorescent skyline. Imagines Heather rubbing her fingers on her jeans as she wrote it.

'Here's the hairdryer, but blow me if I could find the extension. Can you manage without?'

She slips the postcard back and pretends to read the letter.

'It'll settle down pretty quick,' Glenda says, 'it has to, it's what the people want.'

'They voted for what's inside the mystery box. If they don't like what they get, who are they going to complain to?'

'It's perfectly obvious what's going on. Public services are under pressure. Space is limited. We're swamped.'

'Your ballot paper must've been different to mine.'

'I'm not saying I don't want to see new faces ever again. I'm saying that anybody who is here by choice, instead of by birth, should have to wait their turn. It's only polite. The government

144

should stop faffing and get on with it. Look at this mess.' She's referring to the jars, cartons and tubs that are yet to be sorted into edible and out-of-date. 'Chutney from last Christmas – it's the only time I buy it. For other people, mind you, they expect it when they pop round in December.'

'*Blut und boden.*'

Glenda flares her nostrils. 'I'm glad your father isn't alive to hear you talk like that. Nasty to stir up ill feeling purely because you're in the wrong. Will my eggs survive, do you reckon, or shall I get rid of them? Seems a terrible waste. I know, we'll put what we're keeping in the garage. It's cooler in there.'

Cara unwinds the hairdryer flex, which is shorter than her arm. 'Mother, how is this going to reach the freezer compartment?'

'You're the scientist, you figure it out.'

Heather

He texts last minute asking her to meet them downtown. Ely the novelist is treated as a guru by his small, ardent readership. He replies to each journalist, academic and fangirl out of a sense of obligation that confuses Heather. It's not as if they're paying him for his expertise. When a thoughtful email isn't enough, they might ask for a meeting.

That's where Heather comes in, like being fluent in a second language.

The venue for the interview is Atomic Liquors, where customers sat on the roof in the 1950s to watch mushroom clouds appearing over the Nevada test site, sixty miles away. Red light seeps from the vintage signs and there's street art of a face with a red stripe reminiscent of Ziggy Stardust.

'The writer who ghosts,' Ely is saying in his skewed speech, 'or a painter who accepts a commission for a portrait she otherwise has no interest in. A pop singer who cannot choose his songs, let alone write any.'

She joins them as he taps out a cigarette single-handed, his bad arm resting on the table.

Ned, a grad student, lights it for him.

'Work that is intended for consumption,' Ely continues,

'which aims to please. We look back after a time and find it shallow. Where there's no thought process, it isn't truly art. This is how I distinguish creative types from genuine artists with a point of view. The issue lies in compromises made for the sake of the patron. Creatives make work to appeal to an intended audience. Their projects have, uh, other virtues.' His impediment is cutting his words in half.

Ned glances at Heather who says, 'Creative people make stuff to *appeal* to their audiences; their projects have *virtues*.'

'I see. We were doing well for a while there, Reggie?' Ned inches his phone so Heather is picked up on the recording. Taps on a used *Claribel* paperback. 'But they're selling out. Is that your objection?'

'There is such a thing as entertainment, and attractive designs, what have you. I'm not detracting from the effort involved. Or skill. There're, er, happenings. Spectacles. Show business gives pleasure to many and is difficult to do well. But purchased content isn't – cannot be art. This is what I outlined in our letters.'

'What are you looking for in genuine works of art?' Ned asks.

'A sense of a person in a moment. Unconcerned with material consequences. An artist lets go. Page, canvas, choreography—'

'*Choreography*,' clarifies Heather.

'Medium is irrelevant. The work the artist has to make, whether she is paid to or not. When what we see is herself.'

'Ooh, intimate,' Heather says. Then, to the phone, 'Sorry, that was me.'

Ely smiles crookedly.

'It's risky?' says Ned.

'Very much so.'

'Colossal.' He clears his throat. 'And do you agree that the aim of art is to represent, not the outward appearance of things, but their inward significance?'

Ely seems to lose his focus, and for a second Heather thinks she'll need to intervene. 'Who wrote that?'

Ned checks his Hemingway-style notebook. 'I don't have the exact source with me. Aristotle?' It sounds like a guess. 'Should I look it up before we continue?'

'Unreferenced on the internet, where mistakes are repeated until they pass for true?' Ely shrugs a shoulder. 'Did Aristotle say this? Possibly, may've done. A sentiment is enough for readers of websites.'

The boy looks chastened.

'In *Poetics*, Aristotle says good metaphors are a mark of genius.' Ely rolls the burning tip of his cigarette to a point in the ashtray. 'And Leonardo da Vinci believed that a good painter has two chief objects to paint: man; and the intention of his soul. *Two* objects . . . Of these, it is harder to paint the intention of the soul because that is shown by the *attitudes and movements of the limbs*. Doesn't it sound quaint? It's not, though. It is a beautiful observation. By one of the best observers of nature who ever lived. I wonder what he'd make of me.'

Heather interprets as best she can.

'Showing the unseen. Is what we're up against. A contradiction since the beginning of us we are yet to resolve.'

Ned nods. 'Which brings me to my next question. What's in Las Vegas anyway? Why aren't you in a place more conducive to your art?'

'I visited for a weekend and I never left.'

'Do you gamble?'

Ely's turn to waver. 'Plenty of people come here to die.'

'To *retire*,' she says.

'Any chance you're writing another novel? You left the ending ambiguous . . .'

Ely studies the items on the table as if memorising them. Drinks, cigarettes, phones. The bookish contents of Ned's man bag. 'Is this another of your jokes?' he says to Heather as his arm slides off.

She helps keep him upright. 'What's wrong?' she whispers.

'*Claribel* is my favourite book since high school,' Ned is saying loudly. 'If I read it once, I read it fifty times. I keep finding these new ideas that I didn't notice before. Truths literally leaping off the page. When they hit you, it's right there – and huge – and I'm thinking, Wait, how did I miss this? It blows my mind.'

'Literally leaping truths?' Heather isn't supposed to be repeating him.

He smiles like a singer in a boyband. 'This book has more layers each time I read it. Some days I'm not completely sure what it's about. Like the connections the narrator makes with these other characters? Because we're all connected, aren't we, by sympathy, and the environment, and chains of events. Fate? The book feels fresh as the first time. It makes me want to quit school, quit my girlfriend and my job at the waterpark – pack a bag – go where the road takes me. Because we need that, don't we? To test our limits just once. The big *know thyself.*'

'Where are you from again?' Heather asks.

'Fresno. I drove here in my mom's car.'

'These insights come from the reader mainly,' Ely says. 'An author can only go part of the way.'

'But you are the unnamed narrator? He is you? How auto-biographical is it anyway? The woman is real too, right? Were you close?'

Heather bites her thumbnail.

'We were travelling companions for a while. It is a different way of being in the world with a person. You're never the same when you return.'

'Driving on the interstate yesterday, I saw these bright colours in the distance that got bigger and bigger, and I realised when I was close enough that they were these painted boulders, arranged in a circle, in the middle of nowhere. Forty feet tall. In these ravishing shades of neon – yellow, pink, green, silver – so I pulled over to take a look. It's an installation called *Seven Magic Mountains*. I love how it sounds. The idea of climbing magic mountains; I can't stop thinking about them. What goals are worth having? Which summits do we want to reach in life, simply because they're there? For rock climbers, sure, there is Everest. For the rest of us, it can be anything? Making it as a stand-up comic. Flying a plane. Marrying your childhood sweetheart. The published novel is one of the peaks we've all contemplated at some point. A work of literature that touches people because the writer is being themselves, as you put it, Reggie. No compromises. Sheer authenticity. And you made it all the way to the top. You are living the dream.'

Ely's expression stays fixed.

Ned blushes. 'I admire it. I admit, it is one of my dreams. I don't know if I've got it in me, but you inspire me to keep trying.'

'You are being kind,' he replies.

'I wish I could meet her. This woman. It'd be like meeting the real Alice in Wonderland.'

'Huh. She is the nearest we have to a character in the story.'

Ned stares at Heather with a gleam in his eye. 'You're Claribel?'

'No. She is Ruth's daughter.'

'Are you? That's wild. I'd love to be introduced. Is it possible? Even a video call if it's not too much trouble?'

When she realises Ely isn't going to speak, Heather says, 'She died.'

The spark dims. 'I'm sorry.'

'Ask her then,' Ely says abruptly. 'A few questions. She doesn't mind.'

Heather touches the Hand of Miriam necklace through her top.

Ned beams. 'Outstanding. I haven't prepared, but no problem, we'll go with the flow, be ourselves in the moment . . . What were your mom's thoughts when she read the novel for the first time? Was she aware this character was based on her?'

'I don't know. Mum never mentioned it.'

'But if you had to guess her reaction? You must have some idea what she thought of this portrayal of her . . .?'

'Remind me what this is for?'

'I'm a doctoral candidate, is the main reason I'm here. I'm fascinated by what you might call singular novels of the late twentieth century – books which cause a stir when they're first published, but are never followed up. Especially when the author appears to stop. Stop completely. *Why*? Is it a choice he made because he said everything he has to say? Was his plan to leave his readers hungry for more? Was success damaging to his gift somehow . . .? I think first novels are like first loves – they're hot. They have fire in them. And once you've been burned by that fire, maybe you never get over it. I don't know, it's what I set myself to find out.'

She says, 'They give PhDs for that?'

'I hope so. I expected Reginald Ely to be out of reach. I didn't think when I started that I'd end up talking with you in person. Both of you. Maybe there're ley lines which led me here?'

Heather closes her eyes, listens to her skin. 'You could be right, there is something running through this valley? Feels prickly.'

'Or is my destiny to bring Reggie's book to a new generation? Yeah, I think I need to write this up for the student paper as well.' Ned makes a note to himself. 'You've read it,' he says to Heather. 'Most of us don't get to see our parents as young people; and here your mother was, walking and talking on the page. Do you recognise her? Were you ecstatic?'

'A little. I think maybe she'd be flattered by the way people are still reading it years later. How this storybook version of her is forever young, and beautiful, and helping complete strangers with whatever they're going through? She comforts them. So I'm okay with it. But Mum was more complicated than that.'

Ely frowns lopsidedly.

'Claribel is kind of ideal,' Heather says, warming to her theme, 'because she has her own thoughts, but also is always available to tell the man what he wants to hear and meet his needs, and that's fine, I guess. A made-up story is not supposed to be real, is it? It's supposed to be sort of easier. Basically, you can tell what's going to happen because it goes along and – say if there's a boy and girl who fall in love in a novel, then they're bound to end up together, aren't they? Or die. It's fiction. They have to. And it's nice and everything, but real people are puzzling because they don't do quite what we expect? Mum did the unexpected; she was free and natural. Sometimes she got angry about things that weren't in her control and she could be selfish, like the rest of us. Let you down. But Claribel is fictional, and behaves like she is. Claribel isn't real.'

'Let me tell you about real people,' Ely says, pointing over his shoulder. 'Drive in that direction for an hour and you come to an air force base. Do you know what they do in there all day? Pick off civilians, *children*, on the other side of the world, like a videogame, using,' he groans, 'tiny weeny flying machines. I'd rather see the limbs fly apart and smell the burning flesh if I

152

was a killer.' He looks across at customers drinking beer at other tables. 'Is that them?'

'Time for a break, I reckon,' Heather says. Pauses the recording.

While Ned goes inside to buy another round, she reaches for the paperback curling with annotations. His marginalia includes *Unreliable narrator* and *Is he hallucinating/lies/dreaming? REAL???*

Her eyes cross. The words go blurry, her focus somewhere on the other side.

Incongruous. Relevant!

Ely leans on his elbow. 'Is this yours?'

The lighter. A pencil. Devices. And a scrunchie she had on her wrist which is what he's referring to apparently.

This is the first time Heather sees the casino magnate in real life.

Cuthbert L. Holthouse is a spry octogenarian, with tar-black hair, a gold curb chain and Armani hanging off him like a bathrobe. Holding hands with his wife/daughter, he strides through the Magnificent flanked by bodyguards. Several young executives hurry to keep up, burdened with tech, briefcases and clip-clopping shoes. They are headed towards a private elevator that goes up sixty floors to a lavish boardroom.

They're coming this way.

The Glacier MxCool800 the breakfast café relies on is dispensing warm water only. So Debbi sends Heather to fetch ice water from Bebop Bill's, the nearest neighbour on their level with whom Tree Frog are on friendly terms.

After a quick experiment, Heather decides that balancing pitchers of water on a tray on her palm is best, leaving one hand free to adjust the distribution of weight.

Two jugs is inefficient.

Four jugs is impossible.

Three is manageable, she concludes.

It's not as if she's carrying it anywhere other than across a room, albeit a large room, and she can see the faux-greenery from here. Yet Heather is only a quarter of the way when her bony wrist and soft arm start protesting.

Heavy, slick with condensation, and spillable.

She is almost halfway, though. She can tolerate the discomfort, and truthfully, this is probably good for her. To turn back would be to fail. But if she does her task with a Magnificent smile, she is bound to get a bonus.

Heavy, full to the brim, and slippery.

The only resting places between the nineteen fifties and the tropical rainforest are gaming tables, busy with patrons this morning. There is no choice. She simply has to get there.

Heavy, heavy, and heavier.

She stops in the middle of the thoroughfare. Tries swapping the tray to her other palm. Spilling a bit deliberately is better than dropping the whole lot by accident.

Her arm is shaking and her muscles ache. Her wrist is hurting in new ways.

And this is when she feels a difference. Like air currents blowing across a warm sea, stirring moisture and heat.

It is a dense, humid realism the Tree Frog Café has never attempted before. Sticky. Static.

She imagines herself as a speck stranded in the middle of the Atlantic. Both shores far out of reach. Can visualise rings of isobars getting nearer as an eye of low pressure creates a funnel and churns through the resort.

The shake and heat get worse.

154

Instinctively, she pulls the tray closer to her body. The jugs of ice water clink in an ungainly fashion. She braces.

Teammates go about their business with grander gestures and louder voices – she isn't imagining that – to draw attention to their professionalism. Security guards stand to attention and salute. Admiring looks from guests who have seen him on TV shows, tabloids and the jackets of his books.

This is how he thinks the world is, she thinks, because it is like this wherever he goes. Employees buzz with purpose. Interiors warm and wet, as though the air con has died. Doors opening. Paths clearing. He makes a wish – and it's done.

Heather is going to meet Holt.

If she causes an incident, she'll lose her job or worse. It's too late to change her mind, she has committed to staying put.

Without changing speed, Mr and the fourth Mrs Holthouse (country singer and brand ambassador) let go of each other. They pass on either side as if Heather is a hazard cone. Likewise the gaggle of executives and bodyguards split down the middle, and for several seconds she is inside the inner circle.

Close enough to see his taut eyes, plumped cheeks and chin implant. Close enough to hear the grunt in his throat as he breathes. Close enough to smell the Lempriere cologne—

A memory of Ruth burning incense sticks; and then, years later, Cara explaining that the sense of smell is the first to deteriorate in old age.

—the entourage regroups and carries on, leaving Heather in its wake.

The storm passes. The turbulence subsides. She finds her momentum.

Heather crash-lands at the host's station, the pitchers intact if somewhat splashy. Moans and rubs her wrist.

Debbi says, 'I hope Holt runs for governor someday.'

The bartender who has a problem with Debbi takes pity on Heather and loans them ice buckets until the machine can be fixed (maybe this was Debbi's plan all along).

Debbi says, 'Nothing less than perfection, today could be the day Holt stops by for waffles.'

There are tables to be cleared. Heather pounces on them. Scrapes dishes while counting down the hours and minutes left on her shift. Prefers dirty work with Camilo to being on display front of house. 'Why did you come here?' she mutters.

'This country? This city? Same as everybody: it's my dream.' He lifts a crate of steaming clean dishes out the washer.

She sanitises the lid of the garbage can. 'I didn't realise dreams were still a thing?'

When work is over, Heather discovers that the staff lockers have been ransacked. Bags are turned out. Valuables stolen. What's left is sprayed with foam.

Her cash is gone and she finds her phone among the carnage with a cracked screen.

Slumps against the window of the bus, making room for a passenger who sits next to her with a carrier bag on her lap.

The woman dozes off instantly, leaning towards Heather's shoulder. 'Sorry,' she says, rousing again. 'Did I fall asleep on you?'

'I don't mind. Tell me your stop and I'll wake you when we get there?'

'No thanks. I'm fine.'

'Have you just finished work?'

'No. I'm homeless.'

She nods. She doesn't know how to say she looks too nice to be living on the streets.

'People think it's drugs, but it's not, it's sleep deprivation. They

156

rob you if you fall asleep. You have to keep moving.' The woman looks at the back of her hand.

Heather looks too and can see, briefly, the jewellery that used to be there. Twists of gold. Sapphires and diamonds in floral shapes. 'I'm sorry to hear that.'

'Yes, it is a terrible thing to lose a home.'

'I'm Heather.'

'Erica. Almost the same.' Erica stands. 'This is me. Pray for me, Heather.'

'I will.' She gazes out at a hotel portico, with sculptures, fountains and topiary. Wonders how many vacancies they had last night.

Cara

She rereads a clumsy paragraph and frowns even more. 'You must stick to your thought process. I need to see you draw these threads together, show how they connect.' Turns to a section heading. 'This tangent is worthless, I don't understand why you left it in. And there aren't nearly enough citations. Call it laziness, shall we, instead of plagiarism.' Cara adds a comment in the margin. Adds another. Hesitates to add a third since they'll become meaningless.

Naomi takes out a packet of mints with a couple left in the roll, foil and paper coming away in slivers. Sucks one. She has a plaster on her knuckles.

'You were – are – ahead of where I was when I was your age. If we were peers, I'd have been jealous of you. Now I barely recognise this as your work.'

'Can I get an extension?'

'I'm not going to support a deferral unless you tell me what's gone wrong, and how you're going to fix it?'

She grinds the mint against her teeth. 'Bum.'

'Don't you have an excuse? I've heard them all, by the way. "My granny is in hospital." "I have anxiety." "I was dumped." I made myself available to you, you promised to deliver, how on earth did we get here?'

'I'm not in the mood for a bollocking.'

'It's your prerogative to mess up, even if it makes us both look bad. I'd lose my temper if I was that way inclined.' Cara closes the document. 'You're not pregnant, are you?'

'No.'

'You don't sound particularly sure?'

Naomi picks at the plaster. 'I can't be. My parents think I'm saving myself.'

Before the girl elaborates any further, an unwelcome image of *doilies* pops into Cara's mind. Suddenly she recognises this evasiveness and knows what Naomi is about to tell her – or rather, what Naomi will avoid telling her if she can manage it.

Doilies. Complimentary bathrobes. Victorian four-poster. Never in her young life had Cara experienced such grandeur. Then a story as old as men and women having different expectations.

'Dr Brenner, I just need to gather my thoughts like you said. Keep it together.'

She does her best to listen to Naomi's version, which is difficult to do when memories of her own keep intruding. Shame has buried some details so deeply, she couldn't excavate them if she wanted to (and she doesn't want to). Others resurface. At breakfast the next day, still in a placating fog, Cara broke her egg yolk for the sake of appearances and offered to split the bill equally. This backfired: he made a fuss because he had paid for everything in advance; her job was to eat the breakfast with enjoyment. So she ended up apologising to him.

'Then he . . .'

It was Cara's first Shakespeare play; her first B&B; her first serious boyfriend. At least it wasn't her first time.

'And then I . . .'

Cara stayed with him for a month longer after it happened, which suggests on some level she was okay with it?

'Processing begins with the basics. Do you hear me, Naomi? Like remembering to eat and sleep. I am giving you permission to rest this weekend; you'll be in a better frame of mind to decide what's for the best.' Is this Cara talking? Can she hear herself? What her student has just disclosed is an outrage, where is the *calm voice* coming from? 'I've plenty of free time on Monday to pick up with you again. My diary is wide open. And my phone is always on. You've invested too many hours not to salvage this.'

Naomi is too smart to reveal all the relevant information. She has confided only up to a point, not enough that it becomes actionable. Stops short on purpose.

Give me his name. It's on the tip of Cara's tongue. Is he a student here? I will have him jettisoned by the end of the day. Is he staff? A fellow? God help him, losing his dining rights will be the very least of it. Give me his name, Cara thinks, and his future will be smashed, not yours.

She pushes down her private pain, which is an old wound after all, not a fresh one.

Naomi has been clear about the support she wants. Cara's role is to be the trustworthy adult in the room. An adult who listens kindly, without judgement, who only gives advice that is specifically asked for, and can be counted on to respect the young woman's boundaries. It's more than she had.

Cara offers her hand. Naomi's handshake is small and dry, and the plaster sticky where it's begun to peel. She grips back.

When Cara is alone, she checks her phone. Goes onto the social media she's all but abandoned and her most neglected inboxes. To make sure.

160

Heather's status seems pretty upbeat.

Women should shake hands with each other more often, she thinks.

Heather

Cars streak past the Apostles like meteors. Nightlights bleed into the sky for miles around, an electric sprawl visible from space.

The neon rose of the twenty-four-hour Miranda wedding chapel hangs in the dark, blooming and shrinking in perpetuity. Heather watches it from a beat-up sunlounger in the shallow end of the dry pool. Matches her smoky breath to it.

Offered. Wilting. Offered anew.

What does she want, anyway, other than to be here in the company of dark and lit windows? Some open. Some with curtains drawn. Snatches of movement.

That's Wade Jr, watching television. He used to be in a touring band years ago, before the lead singer was shot. The gunman was never caught, and Wade doesn't like talking about it. What Wade wants is the chance to play the blues again for a sympathetic audience.

In another room is Ramon with the love of his life, Sukie, a purebred Pekingese. He carries her in his arms, so her paws don't touch the dirty ground: he wants both of them to stay clean, as it were. There he goes, taking her out for late-night walkies. Heather hopes that's all.

Their nearest neighbour, Maria, is a dancer who did time for

162

roundhouse kicking a man in the head. Sequins and cuffs, she has worn both. Maria wants to put the past behind her, start her own dance studio and mentor the next generation of talent. She's at home. Her laundry is hanging out to dry.

The window with a glimpse of bare chest is where Mel and Claude live. Whenever Heather sees them, they're dressed the same: today they were construction workers. They just want to start a family.

This room is Prabjot's, the human computer who devoted her life to finding a perfect system. She lost a fortune when it landed on 30, and she became hysterical. Caused such a scene that she was banned from several casinos. Prabjot's window is dark and closed tight. Wants to figure out what went wrong. Wants to win it back.

And Mr Seahorse, who wants to make memories.

Electric pink, burning orange and reddish fog rolling over and over. Heather looks through it for her heart's desire. Something's in there, but it won't hold still. How it scampers, pounces, tussles, then slinks away. How it changes shape and it wants to play. And Heather wants to indulge it. A hard world makes people hard-hearted, and she doesn't want to be that.

'I keep waiting for a sign? You haven't left a trail for me to follow, or words of wisdom. It's yours I need, not someone else's. It's odd. I like living most of the time. I don't mind long shifts and the work other people think of as beneath them. I'm not a fan of recognition. But I am confused. Is it supposed to be this much struggle? When I'm tired and achy, I can't think straight and I worry that I'm doing it wrong. Further away from what I'm meant to be. Because it's not going especially well?'

Ruth doesn't reply.

'That was a mean trick you played on Dad. Are you still around? What are you?'

Pure spirit.

'Where are you?' Ely calls to her.

She shivers, zips her jacket to the top. What they told her in school is true: the desert can get chilly at night. She answers, 'I'm in the pool.'

'By the pool?'

'In it.'

She hears his shuffle, and sees his unsteady outline.

'Careful, you'll crack a bone if you fall.'

Ely pants that he can manage and is now negotiating the steps – *scrape* and *clunk* as he fumbles a rusty chair from the pile to upright. Sighs with satisfaction as he sits down.

'I was telling Ned about our trip to Bridalveil Creek,' he says. 'I've decided to take him there. He loves natural beauty.'

'You're seeing him again?'

'Certainly. Ned is my biographer.' The tip of Ely's cigarette glows.

Heather hasn't got anything left to smoke until next time she gets paid. 'He thinks you're stuck because of illness and gambling debts. He basically called you a one-hit wonder to your face.'

'Just for that, you aren't invited.'

(As if she was ever invited.) 'You don't have to pretend for me,' Heather says. 'I don't care, not as much as I thought I did.'

'I told myself it was a practice and my real novel was going to . . .' He draws an arc of light in the air. 'The best story. In the best way. Oh well.'

'Try again? Why not? If you had something new to work on, as well as living here, the parts you enjoy and need most, I think

164

you'd feel happier overall? Unless you really do love cards more, which I wonder sometimes. Pick an idea you like; write out a plan of how it goes; then add bits in to make it longer. How hard can it be?'

'You hear this music?' he asks.

She listens. Blues harp is playing thinly from one of the rooms.

'I get lonely for other artists. I like sharing my thoughts with someone who can appreciate them.'

It's a good thing he can't see the face she's pulling.

'A writer is always talking to another person, in a quiet voice. Without a true point of view it is, what you might call,' he hesitates, 'a clever copy of a painting?'

'Counterfeit?'

'Close enough. I don't want him seeing my manuscript. If something happens to me, can I trust you to destroy it?'

'Don't be melodramatic. Write a different book if it bothers you. Do it properly this time. Put in everything you've been saying and giving away for free. Stop being distracted by nonsense.'

He gives a cough. 'The second is supposed to kill you.'

'Cut it out.' She bumps his shoulder with her fist to bring him to his senses. 'What if you're wrong to keep hiding it? Maybe if you show it to Ned, it might do you some good, bring you closer together, if that's what you want? Or someone *better* than him.'

'Rotten thing,' Ely whispers, brushing his weak arm as though it might come away like a scab. 'Did you do this?' And before she can ask what, he falls off his chair.

She giggles. Then helps him back into it. 'Be careful. Does it hurt? You don't try with your exercises, let me help?'

'Fuck off, hectoring harpy.'

'Reginald, you're doing it again.'

165

'What am I?' He goes quiet. Turns aside to light another cigarette single-handed.

She watches the wedding chapel rose for a moment, a stuttering bud. And flower. Droop. Bud. And flower. 'I bet you never spoke to Mum that way?'

'I promise you we said far worse to each other. The fights we had. Amazing one of us wasn't killed. Sorry. Condolences, etc.'

Droop. Bud. 'Did she wait tables like I will when I get promoted?'

'Ru drifted in and out of jobs. Perhaps yes.'

'D'you think it's strange that she never mentioned you, not a hint? I hope you aren't offended.'

'I would describe it as consistent. She never answered when I wrote to her either. Not even a card. We lived in different parts of the world and lost touch. You can't remember what that was like. We partition ourselves. We can do that. Separate parts that don't belong.'

'What, that doesn't make any sense? In daily life, possibly, but not with a person who matters to us? Otherwise we're just sides? What's the point of living if nobody can ever know us whole? You couldn't know anyone else either, not even yourself.' She shakes her head because she gets muddled when she tries to discuss these subjects. 'Why did you two break up?'

'How could we break up?'

'You know what I mean.'

'We were kids. Kids fall out.'

'Wasn't it friendly, though?'

He hums. 'Have you seen siblings fighting over a toy they both desperately want? Have you heard the appalling things they scream at each other, and how quickly it descends into threats and tears …? She was used to getting her way, and for once I wouldn't give in. Tell me about the man she married in the end?'

166

'Oh, he's a great dad. Out there doing his thing like I'm doing mine. He asks me when we're going to see each other again.'

'And what do you say?'

'I tell him I'm busy and doing really well, thanks. He does, um, security systems. Encryption for big companies. Technical stuff. And loves the ocean. He has a boat.'

'He's a sailor?'

'Yep. A sailing boat. He's always tinkering with it, fixing it up, tying the knots. We used to go out together when I was small, but then we had to stop because I got seasick. He's just finished a huge contract and is on a voyage around the Greek islands and having an amazing time. It's why he hasn't been in touch recently, the signal isn't good out at sea.'

'You must miss him terribly. What is his boat called?'

'*Little Joan*. She weathers the storms.'

'Aren't you lucky having two remarkable parents? It explains a lot. You must've grown up believing you could be anything.'

'I was wanted, and I'm grateful.'

'Did he fall in love again after her?'

She closes her eyes. Remembers finding a bridal magazine hidden in Cara's sock drawer as though it were shameful. She'd marked the bridesmaid's dresses as well: emerald green was her first choice. 'What about you?'

He demurs. 'I had books. We don't choose our parents; they don't even choose us. One can cultivate, however: Seneca wrote that *we can choose whose children we would like to be*. I think it applies to any writing we crave. Take up a thread and we become theirs ... Remind me to explain this to Ned. He'll want to know.'

'That's a great idea,' she says enthusiastically, 'a children's story, they're pretty short.'

'I have no desire to make an enemy of your adventurer father by keeping you from him. It wouldn't be proper.'

'Oh, he doesn't mind . . .'

'Ruth expected too much,' Ely says firmly. 'She was dependent on me for too long, it was her least attractive quality. It didn't enter her head that my needs were different to hers. I take my share of responsibility too. Perhaps if I'd told her sooner that it was time for us to move on, we might have salvaged our friendship.'

Heather still has his message saying that she could stay for as long as she liked. Even if he meant it back then, he's changed his mind like a politician.

He says, 'We parted on bad terms. A grief I hope not to repeat.'

She unscrews a bottle of pills and pops one dry. 'Understood. I'll be late if I don't go now, it takes for ever.'

Ely is looking at his phone as if she's left already.

Heather gets off at the bus stop as it's turning light, details enhancing slowly like a photograph in developer fluid.

Her reflection in a store window – the contents shady – with reflections of lone passers-by and occasional traffic. Of an Australian steakhouse, of a giant candy mascot, of billboards for strip clubs and legendary shows. The whole Boulevard is in this window in panes of black glass, splitting the world apart. In there, in there, and in there.

Multiverse Heathers meet her gaze.

Is this Heather doing better? Has this Heather got anything right yet? Does this Heather know secrets Heather doesn't? Is she content? Reckless?

On the other side of here, is a Heather living at home with Ruth and Paul – and is she rebelling because of how dull and reliable they are? Is it Norwich, Lowestoft and Great Yarmouth in there? Is it teas with Aunt Kathy and Uncle Trev? Is it being spoiled and then ghosted by Hal, or has she married him for his money? Is it sharing a purple apartment with Betty, and coffee on the best sofa with their funny, attractive friends? Is there a scientist on the news talking about her research who is nothing more than background noise?

She takes a photo on her phone. The pills rattle in her pocket. To work.

She plays with how many dirty dishes she can carry in a single sweep, and how full she can keep the cups and glasses – flowing to the brim. She dowses a highchair with detergent, cleans into its very joints, so not a speck of beans or toddler spit remains. Zero tolerance of stains on her patch today. When a dude knocks over his beer, she's here for him with a cloth before he can even ask. (Beer for breakfast, why not?) Then Heather's on her knees, scrubbing gum from the underside of tables.

Debbi says, 'Are you trying for a world record?'

'Hey, you made a joke, it must be a holiday.'

She carries armfuls of plates and cutlery to Camilo, and scrapes them like she's ringing bells. Arranges them into a sky-scraper that could withstand an earthquake.

'May I take these?' he says.

'So what other clichés do you believe in?'

'Excuse me?'

'Like, "Fake it till you make it"? "What doesn't kill you, makes you stronger"? "Shake it off" ...? Catchy, right?'

He concentrates on rinsing.

'Out of interest, exactly how far are you willing to go for this dream of yours? In a nice way, I'm not being funny, I'm gen-uinely asking out of genuine interest. I kind of need to know for me too.'

'Whatever it takes.'

Heather smirks. 'Why? Like us – is this better than what we had before, someplace else, and if it's not and we stick to it, why are we doing that? Because of what you said, *the dream*, which I guess makes sense to a lot of people? Then again, if it was because of a dream *you had*, well, it probably might be weirder? Something good is coming, any day now – isn't it? – allegedly – and we keep making these promises to ourselves – we try our best – and that is definitely how the system should work. Does it, though? Does anybody check? And if it doesn't . . . ? It's not as if we could return it and get a refund. Can we? So we have no choice but to carry on believing whatever they sell us – sell us? tell us – tell us? – mainly because,' she exhales, 'it sounds convincing when they've got a private jet.'

'Take it easy.'

'I don't think they're lying as such. Deep down they're explaining it to themselves.' She rubs her temples.

Camilo lifts a crateful of dishware into the washer. 'You're a realist now?'

'It can't all be true, can it, not all the time? Is this how it would be if it were?'

'You think hard work doesn't count? Self-belief is not worthwhile?'

'I'm only—'

'Here's a reality check: you cannot go back. What you leave behind, you change. It doesn't exist any more. You have got what's in front of you, what's to come. This is why you hold on, no matter what. You chose a path. Don't complain you got what you asked for.'

Debbi comes in through the one-way swing door.

Heather dashes out the other side and says, 'Good morning,'

to a father and son in matching green caps in her area. Gives a kids' menu to the son, and a Magnificent smile for the father till her face hurts. 'What can I get y'all to drink?'

The dad (AC/DC T-shirt and hairy toes) orders coffee and a lemonade.

'Perfect. Is this your first trip? Have you seen a cirque show yet? Did you come far to be with us *here* at the Magnificent?'

'All the way from North Dakota,' he says.

'Wow, I always wanted to go there!'

He stares.

In a flash of inspiration, she adds, 'You have spectacular scenery.'

'We do. Theodore Roosevelt National Park is simply wonderful. You must be the first person we met who heard about it.'

'Although it's warmer here in Vegas. We're having another sunny day again, er, I hope you like sweltering?'

'Do you live here in the casino?'

She grits her teeth. 'No, sir.'

Heather brings crayons and an activity sheet for the boy. And as she's pouring coffee, the man pushes his hand up between her thighs.

'What the living fuck?'

Coffee trickles off the edge, onto the carpet. The child looks at them both with interest.

He withdraws to reach for the half-and-half, saying, 'Please don't curse in front of my son.'

The touched skin is still shrieking when Heather is clearing out her locker. There's a drub in her chest like twenty shots of espresso. Hives pop out on her neck. When it becomes obvious that Ely isn't going to answer her, she calls Tess next.

'I just got fired.'

Tess makes cooing noises on the end of the line. Offers to meet her within the hour for fried chicken.

'Were you stealing?' she asks gently. 'You're lucky not to be in jail if you were.'

'They don't eat the fruit, I don't see what's wrong with it when they throw food away? There was this disgusting man and his repulsive child, and if I knew management weren't going to back me up, I'd have poured coffee right on his ...'

Tess nods regally. 'I wish I could go to London. I like the sound of Piccadilly Circus. You know Piccadilly Circus? It reminds me of Mary Poppins. I love her. She's smart and sophisticated, she doesn't sweat the small stuff. No one messes with Mary.'

'I liked it best when the Poppinses flew down from the sky and slayed the demons.'

'Huh, I don't remember that part? It was in the book, I guess. I could be a nanny for a rich English family, I'd be good at that. Lord knows I have enough experience.' Tess drops skin in her mouth. 'Can I come stay with you?'

'Where?'

'London, baby.' She points. 'You've got a rash all across your neck.'

Heather covers her throat and mumbles that she's freckly.

'You look as though you didn't get any sleep last night. There's stuff you can do to help with that, called sleep hygiene? I've read about it. I'll send you the link. What's Piccadilly Circus like? Is it posh?'

Heather says, 'There are shops, and restaurants, and theatres, and giant illuminated signs, and nightclubs, a famous fountain, and I've been with my—' She drops her head on the greasy table.

'Right, you take it for granted. I'm the same, I need peace and quiet. I avoid the Strip entirely.'

'But we're on the Strip, aren't we?' Heather glances over her shoulder.

'Other than for work, or a party or something.'

You all say that, she thinks.

'Your boyfriend must feel sad now that you have to leave? What did he say when you told him?'

'He isn't my – I haven't had a chance to – this has just happened to me, Tessie. Can't you listen for once like a decent human being? I am stuck.' She daren't nibble her fries for fear of the oil they were cooked in. 'I asked them for housekeeping, I'd have been fine as a maid. It was management who put me on breakfast in the first place.'

Tess's smile fades. 'I'm sorry for your troubles.'

Heather can see hundreds of Magnificent bathrooms with corner baths and gold faucets. Towels and bedsheets to be laundered by the sackload. Meeting rooms, staging areas, a dozen commercial kitchens. Miles of carpets for vacuuming. Acres of floor to mop. It is constantly in use, it'll never be clean, it's time to start again before you're finished.

Yet somebody's job is to quantify it. To work out the square footage. Supply the pillow chocolates, toilet paper and tiny, pungent Lempriere soaps. An army of invisible maids who never get any credit, and no one asks them how they are.

Heather says, 'They make profits out of problems here, not dreams.'

'The devil knows they can be one and the same thing. Can't you go home?'

'I took her bloody money, didn't I? She ended it. I could tell.'

'How are you going to live?'

Heather leans on clasped hands, still and wide-eyed. An unintended thought, but also unsurprising. Of blending into her surroundings, moving through them with ease. Like Tess does.

'Hehe no, I've seen this before. Not when you've been lying the whole time.'

'When have I lied?'

Tess snorts. 'Since the day we met. I'm serious. You think it's okay just turning up in another country, undocumented, and do whatever you please? No skills. No resources to invest. Take what you want for as long as it suits you? Ignore the rules the rest of us have to follow? It's not fair. I don't agree with it. And I don't see why I should help. What's in it for me?'

'I haven't asked you for anything.'

'Yeah, you did.'

Thousands upon thousands of Magnificent surfaces to shine. She could devote her life to them. Until a girl can see herself from every conceivable angle.

Tess is saying something. 'Service is a performance. Pace yourself. Red flags are red for a reason. Avoid timewasters at all costs. Prayer helps you to conquer the day.'

'Prayers don't work,' she whispers, 'they're wishes into thin air.'

'Be careful how you speak, young lady. This is not the solution you think it is, it's adding on a bunch more complications that I don't think you're ready for. And are you even listening to what I'm telling you right now . . .?' Tess looks her up and down. 'You're arrogant. Frantic. There is no intention as far as I can see. I have absolutely no idea what you hope to get out of this? Do you even know?'

Heather sees herself polishing a great mirror until it disappears. Sees herself falling through it into a space where her skin is cool, and her limbs and spine and face relax. The words come out as bubbles. 'To swim every day.'

Cara

'Someone who is blind in one eye is likely to turn their head to compensate, like this.' Cara demonstrates. 'Patients with hemi-spatial neglect, however, don't. This motion – I should say, lack of motion – is a clue to what's going on.'

The slides are projected hugely, the rest of the room is dimly lit. Two-thirds of the seats are unoccupied, and no student is taking notes. She is never sure whether it's a sign they're listening intently or that they've zoned out.

'They don't try making up for their disability,' she says, 'because they don't notice they have it. As far as they're concerned the world stops at what we regard as the middle. Over here, there's nothing to see. Half stays hidden.'

This isn't as bad as back when lectures were a big deal and she over-prepared for them. The material no longer requires a full read-through the night before. She can afford to riff. Clicks to some line drawings next. It's a spotty slide transition, which she meant to change to a subtle fade.

'When you give a patient who has hemispatial neglect the task of copying a clock face, what they might draw, for example, is a shape with numbers one to seven on it. But they do not perceive, and therefore won't copy, eight-nine-ten-eleven. They're

175

also likely to draw a daisy with petals on the right-hand side but none on the left. And if you ask them to draw a clock of their own choosing, they might put the numbers one to twelve, but squash them in, like a waxing moon.'

The audience are kids with knobbly elbows and over-styled hair. There's also a colleague in a hooded sweater, leaning forwards on his chair; or he might be a student from one of the mature colleges, Hughes or Wolfson.

Cara is wearing the same top she wore yesterday. Her nail varnish is chipped. Her underwear is grey downstairs and peach upstairs. There are some nice clothes in her wardrobe that she's saving for – what?

'Hemispatial neglect is in the memory too,' she explains.

—Venice, which never comes.

'Ask the patient to describe a town square they remember as if they're facing north; where is the bridge? Where is the restaurant? Where are the frescos . . .? What comes to mind is what's east. West is blank. And I'm using the example of vision on the right, and blank on the left, because this accounts for the majority of cases. Hemispatial neglect is commonly caused by damage to the right hemisphere, a lesion on the right parietal lobe, although there are exceptions. Be mindful of that.'

She's having an out-of-body moment when she speaks automatically. When she watches her thoughts unfold. Is this what happens to a musician playing a familiar piece, the same notes in the same order, knowing it has more to give? Tension in the gaps and changes in emphasis. With ease.

'I reiterate, this is not blindness as we tend to think of it. Both eyes are *functional* and have sight, as it were. The patient is ignoring a side. Does not attend to it. An intriguing aspect of this condition, therefore, is to ask ourselves how many people

176

are in fact living with this, um, condition without realising it. Walking among us, undiagnosed. Because the other side has to be constantly pointed out to them – it really needs pointing out. Repeatedly. They aren't aware there is a problem and wouldn't be, if left to their own devices. They need *strategies* to be able to see more then they do. Indeed, it is miraculous once you turn an object around and show them, for instance, that half their plate is full of food they haven't eaten yet. Or some fabric has a beautiful pattern that they didn't notice. They're amazed.'

She puts her glasses on and the blurred faces slot into place: her prisoners in the cave.

'Shall I use my point of view as a further illustration? There are perhaps forty-five chairs in here, but only a dozen or so are occupied. You're mostly bunched on this side for some reason, I don't know why, maybe you're friends . . .? To me, the chairs in this room would appear empty and I would think I was alone; therefore, I wouldn't begin speaking unless somebody pointed you out to me and said, "What about these students over here, don't they matter?" Then I'd think, Where did you lot come from? I'd feel relief and maybe suspect I was being teased. Another example is the man who shaves half his face, but leaves his beard on the other cheek.'

Cara recognises everybody now, including the man, who strokes his stubble.

'Hair which resists being cut,' she says, 'or a plate that refills like a porridge pot in a fairy tale. Except the beard was there all along, as was the dinner made by a loving partner. Life must be full of surprises.'

Asbjørn Scandi-something, she thinks. He is a running bore, as indeed she is.

'Let's be careful, however, not to romanticise a disability. If you have this, it means your world is narrower and filled with halves of people. When you look in the mirror, you see half yourself. Yet this feels natural. Half is normal. Half-finished is complete. And I wonder what it must be like, how different their experience is to mine. I wish I knew. Then I wonder if I know already, and I catch myself checking.'

Scandi-something? What's the matter with her today?

'I apologise. I seem to have lapsed into a stream of consciousness.' She clicks to another slide.

Asbjørn chats afterwards.

While she's packing away, Cara says, 'I didn't know you were part of the university. I hadn't put two and two together before.' (She pats herself on the back for remembering the running connection without needing to be reminded.)

'I'm not. I wanted to hear the lectures.'

'Aren't you? What do you mean, did you gatecrash?' She says it as a joke.

'Technically, no. I'm on an email list. It's moderated.' He shrugs. 'I don't pretend to be something I'm not. I suppose you could say I was curious when I read about your talk. I'm not usually interested in science. It caught my eye.'

Her expression falls. 'Seriously, you are stealing lectures from us?'

He gestures towards the vacant seats. 'How was my being here depriving anybody? I've done you a favour really.'

'But they earned their place. They – I can't believe I'm making this argument – paid fees. There was a process. You're trespassing.'

'It's more riding on your wifi than stealing, when you think about it. You were excellent, by the way; you make it very engaging. You helped me to think deeply how it is for people who're disadvantaged in this hemibrained way, and perceive less. What they miss out on. I was enlightened.'

'Don't try getting round me, I should report you.'

'Please don't, don't be cross. I'm sorry.'

Cara files her notes, pulls out her USB, shuts down. 'You put me in a difficult position.'

'Yes, and we should talk it through. We hardly speak because you're too far ahead of me. I'm not as fast as you are. Do you enjoy wine?'

'It's eleven o'clock in the morning.'

'A cup of coffee with apple cake then, for elevenses? I call it apple cake, but my friends tell me it resembles an English trifle.' He pats his belly.

'I'm busy.'

Asbjørn huffs. 'What if I promise not to attend lectures again that I'm not supposed to? I don't want to cause trouble. Unless you invite me to yours? If I'm your guest, then I can't be doing anything wrong; only when you invite me, though, okay? A text saying, *Asbjørn, I'm giving a talk tomorrow and my students prefer staying at home to watch reality shows, please be in the audience so it isn't as lonely.* And I'll say, *Fine, I'll be there, stop pestering . . .*'

She laughs somewhat.

'More people should have heard you today. You told it well.'

She's laughing at herself because she did her make-up in a hurry this morning. Her hair is greasy. And, of course, she is still wearing old knickers that don't match her bra.

They talk about training. Training as an individual versus in a community. Training plans for a marathon which neither Cara nor Asbjørn are ready for. They discuss PBs, routes and carb-loading. She mentions her black toenail because this is the

179

only context in which it's permissible; he replies that his insoles smell like dead rats, but they reduce pain so he's not parting with them.

The occasions they've met before, and Asbjørn seems to think it's more than twice, it was with a group at the park, which is slightly embarrassing for her. When you run with the guys, you're one of the guys. Nobody wants you when you're sweaty, farting or free-bleeding out of necessity.

Nobody wants you, Cara.

Certainly not a hairy Dane in a flat above a bike repair shop. Who buys the *Big Issue*, plays percussion and does hygge.

She glances along his bookshelf: he reads Russian literature and biographies of jazz musicians; there is a photo of him volunteering at a loggerhead turtle sanctuary.

Cara can't speak another language, let alone 'four or five'. She had an app on her phone to learn Italian, but kept missing her daily targets and got discouraged.

They skip ahead to travel and interests. She hasn't asked him what he does for a living yet, and now is afraid to, in case he says tree surgeon. Or art restorer. Or working with troubled youth to reduce knife crime.

As soon as he finds out what she's really like, he'll go off her. She has a realistic view about that.

Cara has never been camping, and has no desire to. When Radio 3 is too pompous, she switches to Classic FM like a philistine. Instead of being constructive in online discourses, she trolls chaotic politicians who are clearly out of their depth. She struggles to make friends, and obviously doesn't deserve Helen's loyalty. Cara thinks that poems should rhyme. She looks horrible in hats. She doesn't give enough to charity. And if Asbjørn knew how bad she is in bed, well, he wouldn't want to touch her.

180

What Cara *can* do is spend an entire evening shopping online for a lampshade without buying one. She can consume a whole bottle of wine and a fish pie that is supposed to be two servings by herself. She can give a speech – and have a conference eating out of her hand – only to burst into tears the next day, because Glenda took a taxi to lay flowers on Bob's grave because Cara wasn't around to drive her.

And while we're on the subject, it's a miracle her goldfish hasn't died, the tank is that filthy. What does it tell you that she neglects the single beating heart that relies on her?

Cara thinks babies are ugly. Cara can't get the hang of contact lenses. Cara doesn't know how tennis matches are scored. Or how to play bridge. She calls religion 'folklore' and allows herself to be drawn into arguments with people who disagree; perhaps that's why she is never invited to dinner parties. She can't sing in tune and has appalling handwriting. Her jokes never work.

She is not a whole person.

Asbjørn says, 'I want to shower.'

Oh no, she thinks, I can't let you see my mascara running, or me with wet hair, or my saggy bum, fat thighs and weird labia, I hate them, and oh God peach bra and grey pants, what was I thinking? She'll never forgive herself for this.

'You're tense. Is there someone else?'

'No,' she says quietly. 'It's just me.'

This stuff is for the glow of candlelight and inebriation, not office hours. Cara isn't allowed.

She isn't allowed to imagine what it might be like if this man were hers. To imagine how it would feel if, on a Saturday morning after a brisk 5K, they went back to his flat, stripped off their running gear and left it in a damp, muddy heap. And what if, with John Coltrane on the speaker and coffee percolating in the coffeemaker, they shampoo each other while comparing times and injuries. Then, clean and dimpling, they ate æblekage and screwed till lunchtime on the bed he built himself.

Imagine if this was Cara's life. She didn't know she wanted it until she just thought of it.

Heather

'—it lies next to him,' Ely mutters, 'on a pillow like mine. He can't close a drawer because of fingers sticking out of it. Then an arm barely concealed behind the shower curtain. He's minding his own business and it reaches for him. At first, he thinks it's a prank. Then discovers his nightmare is real.'

Heather rubs her eyes. 'Did you have a nice evening with Ned? What time is it?'

'Late. I have an idea. I know what I'm going to write about.'

'Great. Well done. I'm happy for you.'

'A Poe-style short story. Neon and Gothic. A hand that follows a man everywhere he goes. To the store. When he's tying up his laces. While he's out on a date ... It can be the first of a collection? Ned helped.'

'Yep, I hoped he might.' She snuggles back down.

'He reminded me of a rule that writers must follow if they are to make lasting work.'

She moans. 'Please tell me in the morning?'

'Over-writing is bad writing. It drags. It has to be lean and swift.' He puts a clunking duffel bag in the shower room. Turns on more lights, making her squint. 'Concise.'

'What are you doing, Reginald?'

'Cutting the dead weight in order to reveal the truth. Have you heard, *less is more?*'

'That's what you woke me up for?'

'Simple. And resolves a lot.' He stands with his hand on his hip. 'I'm seeing him again tomorrow. I want you gone.'

'Fine, I'll go out. I have to anyway—'

'Totally gone. You're in the way.'

'Are you having an episode?'

'Certainly not, this is clear thinking. Look, no cigarette.' He waves. 'I might quit as of today? Yes, I think I will.'

She puts on her lamp. 'You know what? Fine. I'll be gone first thing in the morning. But seriously, I'd love to know what good it'll do when I've been trying to help you with this for ages – and then pretty boy comes along . . .'

'There's more to it than that. He believes in me.' Ely is rummaging in the bag on the bathroom floor.

'You love how you look to him – not *him*. It's pathetic. Also, it's mean of you. Luckily for Ned, he's too thick to understand.'

He comes over quickly and pulls back her sheet.

'Hey, I might've been naked down there?'

'Leave. Before I call the authorities to report you. And I won't stop talking until I can't undo it.'

'Saying what?'

'Everything I know. More, if necessary. You shouldn't be here.'

'You're a crap bluffer. It must be why you keep losing.'

'I don't play poker, poker is a thug's game, I play baccarat.' He picks up her shoes, opens the door, and throws them over the balcony.

'What the—'

'You've outstayed your welcome. I should have done this long ago.' He throws out a hairbrush next; some shorts; a book Tess insisted on lending her. At the same time he has his cell phone under his chin and is trying to dial – limps from the room to outside. Drops more of her stuff over the rail.

Her best bra. Condoms. Froggy pin. The healing crystal he throws as far as an ordinary stone. A bottle of sunblock *splat* on the asphalt.

'Stop, freak.' And she grabs what's within reach. 'I can't handle this any more. It's time to ask for help from a doctor – an expert – I know someone we can ask for free. You need a new prescription. Why are you doing this?'

'Jealousy. You never let me have relationships that're just mine, Ruth – Claribel – Clare.'

'Heather?'

'I would've got there eventually.' He holds up his cigarettes to show her. 'See? I won't be needing these.' He tosses them out after. 'Hello?'

She lowers her voice. 'Reginald, doesn't this strike you as a little bit subjective?'

The dispatcher asks for his emergency.

'All right,' she says, 'I'm going. Please stop. Lars will go ballistic.'

It would be possible to knock him off-balance. To take away his phone and scream for help.

Instead, Heather walks calmly past her scattered possessions.

Hi please call as I haven't got credit. Thank you
Heather uses the twenty-four-hour pizza wifi to message Tess on smashy phone.
I need a place to stay for a night.
Can I stay at yours 1 night please? 2 max long story! xoxo
*[sofa] ok

No reply. Tess always replies. She is addicted to replying.

Can you ring me asap you get this? I really appreciate it and I will owe you one!! [blows a kiss] thanks, sweets.

Nothing is happening on her socials either.

[purple heart] [wrapped present] xxo

The battery is 52% and Heather has left her charger behind.

I'm not in trouble with the law lol

Arse. She shouldn't've sent that.

She takes a stroll over the footbridges. Passes a girl who could be her sister.

[see-no-evil monkey]

Heather was almost on to the interesting thing. Had started to feel feelings other than mellow that were worth having. Begun to – what is the word? – like discriminate, but not. When you recognise what's proper, without especially trying.

It is right in front of her. Further away than ever.

?? [wilted flower]

There are two chances remaining: that Tess is feeling more Christian than usual; or the contents of her ladybugs wallet.

Heather runs her fingers over the raised numbers and letters like Braille. This must be how you felt when your experiments didn't work, she thinks.

Cara

What's left when Cara's desire goes flat is self-conscious breathing and repetitive relief. Her phone plinks and brightens on the bedside table, and it is as much as she can do not to reach across him and look.

Rather, she watches his outline in low-key light. Reminds herself how often she went without in the past, and if she pleases this man, perhaps he'll return the favour on another night. No? That won't be necessary. His patience is astonishing. The body has a mind of its own. It smothers her.

Of course in the morning, she wishes she had checked. Because it turns out some so-and-so stole her identity.

The text was an alert for unusual activity on her credit card, and she could have stopped it sooner had she not agreed to cuddling and fallen asleep. Dopamine. Oxytocin. Annoying.

Now she's on a helpline with a fraud investigator in Northampton who keeps calling her 'Miss Brenner'. He says, 'I'll cancel your card straight away, Miss Brenner.'

'Is it very bad?'

'Would you mind holding the line please?' Without putting her on hold, he starts humming an Oasis song and typing in the background.

Asbjørn is slicing a kiwi fruit. She mimes *coffee* because he ought to know by now that is her first priority in the mornings.

'Can I check you're calling from the UK, Miss Brenner? Have you been abroad recently? I'm seeing transactions for a Clover Inn, Target, an airline, Salieri's?'

'No, I'm at home, none of those are mine. Is this going to affect my credit score?'

'Uh-oh.'

'Why? What are you uh-oh-ing at?'

He chuckles. 'Nothing to worry about. I'm reading the addresses, that's all. Whoever it is is having more fun than we are.'

'I should think that's a given.'

Asbjørn brings her coffee and a fruit salad. She shoos him away because there is noise at the other end. Is her fraud investigator doing an Elvis impersonation?

'Don't worry, Miss Brenner, I've taken care of everything. Do you have any idea how your card details were stolen in the first place? There are steps you can take to help protect yourself against fraudsters in the future. Would you like me to run through them with you now ...?'

She sips her coffee. The effect is instantaneous and not remotely scientific. 'Which airline?'

Heather

And when she bought the ticket, part of her thought it wouldn't work. Has a grocery tote for baggage. A *fabulous* sweatshirt it's too hot for. And complimentary hand lotion for her sunburn. Drinks water from a Coke bottle.

She is being filmed: CCTV records her every step.

Heather is playing the part of a normal passenger without drawing attention to herself. Like an extra. Walks slow circuits of McCarran. Pauses to look at her phone even though she can't go online – looks like she's looking – because that is what adults do while they wait for check-in to open. A tangle with a uniform is the last thing she needs.

Pretends to take a call within the sight-line of a guard.

What normals don't do, however, is use their single digits of battery life to take phantom selfies. In the restrooms. The sheen of escalators. The polished floor. Not to would be a lie; this is the conclusion.

Turns at the wall for another lap of the concourse. A glance at the screens that haven't changed and the clock which has barely moved along a few minutes.

Passes Ely, who sits as though he's also tired of waiting for the desks to open.

It suits her fine that he hasn't noticed her, since she's made up her mind never to speak to him again. She'll contact him from a safe distance. Another continent will do.

'If this is supposed to be a stakeout, you're rubbish, I went up and down four times?'

He's grey and clammy. Raises an eye like a fish.

'Are you going on vacation?' she asks cheerfully. 'I always thought they live on vacation here, I never knew what there was to get away from?'

He chews his lip. 'I brought you something.'

'How did you find me? Have you been here since yesterday? Today? Whoa, spooky. You should find a table before your luck runs out.'

He tries reaching into a pocket, unsuccessfully. 'Did we part on bad terms?'

'Well, they weren't good, Reginald.'

'I expect you forgive me.'

'Yes, I do forgive you. Please fuck off.'

'Is there a drink . . .?'

Heather sits on his good side, on the bench that appears to be holding him upright. Unscrews the water bottle and lifts it to his sloping mouth. Blots it with a tissue.

'You aren't like her.'

'Neither are you.'

His jacket covers one shoulder, and he has a filthy hammam towel rolled up inside it. Mumbles, 'I feel bad.'

'I should hope so.' The sight of him is making her light-headed, and gives her a ringing in the ears. He smells sharp, like cooked sugar, and is drained of colour. 'You couldn't just let me go? Would've been kinder. I didn't cry. I didn't cause any trouble. I haven't messed with your life, have I?'

190

'You treat me as a whole person. I'll miss that.'

'But you won't have to if you treat yourself like it more? A touch of self-care goes a long way.'

He doesn't reply.

'Get help from a professional.'

He doesn't reply.

'This isn't my problem.'

He doesn't reply.

She thumbs her phone in the silence. 'Nothing from you. Or Tess, for that matter. Do you know who has been calling non-stop? Lars. And I bet I know why. I did try telling you?'

He doesn't reply.

'Then again, you tried telling me that I should've moved out by now. Maybe he'll let you pay for the damage in instalments?'

He doesn't reply.

'You have these brilliant ideas, it is a shame you don't make something of them, something substantial. I think you could, if you were willing to devote a tiny amount of attention to, um, the current areas of neglect. Look, I honestly don't care who you spend time with or what you do with your money, it's your choice . . . I like weird stuff too. I'm not having a go; I'm putting this into practice for myself. I've thought about it and decided that I'm ready for a change. I had the best of, er, this experience. So you haven't scared me away. I like you. I would've let you know I was all right?'

He doesn't reply.

'Why are you bundled up? What's with the layers? My skin is burning. I'm using hotel hand lotion,' she takes out the min-iature to show him, 'as aftersun. Do you think that's okay? Do you? My poor skin takes for ever to go down. I'm not angry with you, I promise I'm not. This is me being grown up. Only, there are no blackbirds here. I checked.'

191

The screens switch over. Passengers gather their luggage and cross the hall to join the line.

He holds out her sunglasses. 'Take these.'

Heather imagines herself in Britain wearing them. Shivering in her *fabulous* sweatshirt not warm enough for there. 'I forgot to order a veggie meal, oh no, do you think they'll have spares? I was looking forward to it. I definitely need to go, I can't hang around. Airports make me peculiar. Thanks for letting me stay and what we shared; I think Mum would be glad we met. It was fun while it was fun.' She stands to hug him goodbye.

Ely is in no rush to reciprocate. He keels to one side.

She leans in and pulls his jacket open. Then sees what he sees: a piece of meat gone bad.

She sees that he hasn't felt attached to his other hand for a long time, and has simply tried to resolve a contradiction which became intolerable. A clean, bloodless cut is all it would take to free himself. If it felt separate already, what harm could it do?

The rolled towel is a brown-stained sleeve, partly rigid and partly moist.

Cara

M11. M25. M23. The car in front sends up spray and the windscreen wipers beat like bats' wings. What should take an hour and a half takes two and a half hours (although conditions stay fine for the avatar in her satnav).

Cara jogs to arrivals.

She chooses a spot by the barrier. Is torn between watching the exit and the announcements.

The plane must be taxiing. Or perhaps it's parked and having that awkward moment where the seatbelt sign is still on, but passengers ignore it and begin freeing themselves.

She breathes unsteadily. Bolsters herself as if she's about to give a lecture. Indeed, she is about to.

Cara will be stern, factual, humorous. Make it clear it is not the money she objects to – it's the secrecy. It was never her intention – she'll emphasise this – that they should lose contact completely; that is not the same as, as it were, not being, um . . .

Loses her train of thought.

Her attention flits back to the sliding doors. To wasp-coloured signage and family reunions. To the smells of magazines and fast food and vulcanised rubber and circulated air and boiled sweets and floor wax and unwashed bodies. The din.

193

What Cara will say is this: I'm glad you're okay. I'm glad you felt able to turn to me in a crisis – which this had better be – because you always can – within reason.

Heather must have anticipated that she would look at her email. Her *boring* email that she's had since her teens, the account Cara insisted she set up for job applications and online purchases, and that ever afterwards was nagging her to change her password for. She said she did, although clearly she didn't, as it's the same password Cara chose on her behalf, *TemplVil567.*

I can't understand why you weren't straight with me, she'll say. Why the subterfuge? (She can hear Helen laughing when she retells this as a funny anecdote. 'Subterfuge.') How did you end up stealing my credit card instead of asking for my help? Were you ashamed? And if you had to go off gallivanting like a wild child, there are many more attractive cities to choose from. Didn't my taste rub off on you at all?

Cara will say this is partly her fault, this gap. She'll be big about it. Oh, she is looking forward to that! And she'll ask calmly, without prying, Heather, what were you doing?

What have you been doing for this whole time?

I mean, what have you done?

I mean, Heather, what are you doing now, as in next?

What on earth did you think you were doing?

Maybe Cara should buy a blueberry muffin. Then she can eat the muffin and breathe into the paper bag.

Actually, she knows what's going to happen.

Heather will step off the plane looking fresh and faintly surprised. And she'll say hi, and tell her she's making a fuss over nothing. She'll be polite and vague, and offer some kind of explanation she's had eleven hours to work on. Then she'll

194

ask if there's any Paul news? And finally, disappear again. And that will be that for several months, or years, and Cara will kick herself because she missed work for this and keeps letting the Wycliffes disrupt her life and why did she ever want to be one of them?

Bags delivered.

Heather is in baggage reclaim. They are specks in the same Gursky.

Travellers exit through the automatic doors. Cara thinks, not quite literally, that unless they're show girls, brides reeking of tequila, and Barry Manilow, how can she be sure they were on the same flight?

She fancies that a couple in double-denim are the right demographic. A worse-for-wear stag party. The retirees. Therefore, Heather is coming along soon.

She sets her face to passive.

Details scroll as more information is inserted into rows above.

Geneva . . .

Belfast . . .

Alicante . . .

Heather's flight falls down the ranks, tumbling like sterling after a referendum. Why does the last-chance duty-free lane look empty?

She cranes to make sure she doesn't miss her. Stays put.

Cara isn't sure how long for, but after a while, she asks a woman with a silk scarf tied jauntily around her neck. The lie comes easily because it is sort-of true:

'I'm waiting for my stepdaughter. Can you tell me if she has arrived, pleased?'

Hesitation. This is the barrier of confidentiality she warned Heather about. She wasn't making it up. It is a real thing.

Cara shows her phone with the hacked email. 'Here is her itinerary? I don't want to give her a hard time for making me wait. These are my payment details, by the way.'

It is enough. The woman is typing on the system. 'Yes, steps are important.'

'I'm sorry?'

'When they treat you like real parents,' says the passenger service agent, called Anoushka, 'that is when they become yours. The day my stepson broke his leg ... Here we are. No, Miss Wycliffe didn't board the flight.'

'It can't be. Are you looking on the right page?'

Anoushka says, 'Did you try calling her?'

Her face reddens. 'You know what, she said her plans might change last minute, I remember now. God, it's been one problem after another since I switched providers. I expect if I checked my – settings.' Cara walks purposefully in the wrong direction.

Her heart pounds as though she's done parkrun in under twenty-eight minutes. Passengers cross her path. Trolleys cut her up. Arrows send her in circles.

Cara has another long drive ahead. Arguably this is an occasion when it would be okay to fill her face with carbohydrates.

She walks past boxy outlets. Costa. Burger King. A pirate selling Cornish pasties. Her insides claw. If she doesn't pick one soon, she risks being treated as a security threat.

What she finds is the multi-faith prayer room.

What did she think was going to happen? Heather is an adult who does whatever she likes. She has no hold on her – no claim on her – who is she going to complain to?

The tiny room is like one of those American ministries which steals people's money. It is low-ceilinged, artificially lit, with carpet tiles, and a place to wash your feet. Symbols are pasted onto squares. The blue-sky wall bears a resemblance to a screensaver.

Cara leans on the chair in front with her head in her arms. To anyone passing by, it looks as though she is praying. She won't, though, never. It would be a betrayal.

4

Autobiographical Memory

*complex and diverse brain
activation patterns*

Cara

The rye bread he calls rugbrød, dense and dark brown and filled with seeds, which Cara assumed he ordered from some online bakery, he is making from scratch in his upright cooker. It is perfect running fuel, and she scoffed the thin squares topped with smoked fish and avocado as soon as they were placed in front of her, forgetting that when you're in a new relationship the girl has to pretend she eats daintily.

He has a jar of runny dough made in advance, and she thinks, Quick, bake it, then we can eat it hot. But this is just the first step: he adds the cracked rye and wheat, flax and sunflower seeds, and an unappetising dark liquid.

'Pizza bases,' Cara says, 'shop-bought. I didn't make them. They were terrible, and she put these dubious toppings on them. Pineapple went on there, definitely, with some olives, and paste from a jar. Cheddar, no mozzarella; and, I think, some broccoli? I must've eaten dozens of better pizzas, yet that is the one I can remember.'

He says it needs to rest for eight hours but, like a television chef, has prepared a batch earlier. There are more ingredients to add, and mixing.

'I wanted to give her a sense of how far women have come,'

she says. 'That our opportunities mustn't be taken for granted. We have to push harder – she has to. I took her to view Cecilia Glaisher's schematic drawings and early photoprints of snow-flakes. Meticulous in their geometry, and requiring exquisite observation of the natural world. She made them to illustrate her husband's published papers – uncredited. He was a celebrated meteorologist, whereas she was, out of necessity, an amateur. The Victorians wouldn't have known what snow looks like up-close, were it not for Cecilia Glaisher. I mean, can you think of Victorian Christmases *without* snowflake decorations? A lot of interesting work arises when a person follows her curiosity. But it is a provocation when one doesn't know what will come of it, when one's contribution might, conceivably, never be acknowledged. Glaisher was a mother too, of course.' The old pang, biology digging at her with a sharp instrument. 'I reasoned that if I didn't get my ducks in a row it didn't matter, because Heather was bound to get pregnant one day. Eventually there'd be a newborn around the house, and I'd have a bit of the experi-ence without it damaging my career. Be a step-grandparent who helps. That scenario wasn't too terrible to me.'

Asbjørn's alarm tells them it's time to spoon the dough into bread tins, like fruitcake mixture.

'I suppose I was able to pick and choose the girly parts with her. She had sparkly hair slides that she liked putting in my hair. Sometimes I kept them in all day.'

Cara realises the oven isn't on yet, which means they're going to have to wait for it to heat up. Then is dismayed to discover that this wasn't a mistake on his part: the dough needs to stand for two more hours. Her shame for the speed with which she ate the first batch deepens.

'I could always see what potential she had. She is capable,

202

animated and personable. I might even go as far as saying that she has an aesthetic ... But she won't apply herself. Wouldn't even try, despite my efforts, and who else was going to notice her talents and encourage her? Long term doesn't exist as far as she's concerned. I wanted to show Heather how important it is for girls to have work that belongs to us. To value what she calls her own. It's not pretty. It has to be earned, not mystically channelled. It bothered me when the lessons didn't come through the way I intended them ... She turned what happened to her into permission to do whatever she feels like doing. Not remotely grounded. She is determined to be an outsider – for how much longer?'

Heather

Marble corrects her: it's not a ball, it's a skein. And this is a hank.

Heather raises her helping hands, holding up the orange yarn in a thick, loose loop, while Marble winds it in a ball on their thumb, carefully, like applying a bandage.

'She promised me pizza for tea if I tidied my room,' Heather says, 'which I did, I was really motivated, only our usual place wasn't open because maybe it was a bank holiday or something? I wasn't going to let her break her promise though, so she bought pizza bases from the minimarket saying I could put whatever I liked on them. I got carried away in the veg drawer, there was baby corn on there and all sorts, it was the most fun we had cooking a meal together. She said we could do it again, but she didn't mean it, and we didn't.'

Perhaps the payphone will ring while Heather waits for them to get to the end.

'The snowflake lady,' she says. 'She made these enlarged pictures of individual snow crystals which no one had looked at properly before? Very precise drawings, and she used, um, multimedia I suppose, to turn them into early photos by pressing them against the sensitive paper? It was science, but design as well, almost. Loads, with coloured inks, and they looked like cut gemstones. Same, but different. And her husband took all the credit because it was historical times. Her name, which I've forgotten, didn't appear anywhere. Glacier? I liked how she was experimenting to get the images she wanted. I liked comparing them.' Her heart nuzzles inside her. 'Snow annoys Cara, mainly because she makes the effort to go into work, and everyone else calls in saying they can't ... She's not huggy; well, once she hugged me. I don't know why, and I was afraid to ask because she'd been crying and was trying to stop before Dad got home? There was something going on there. She was moving, slowly, in her comfy pjs. Maybe it was a heavy period?'

It's the end of the orange yarn, finally, in a neat ball that won't get in a tangle when Marble knits from it. However, there is a yellow skein to go.

'She taught me how to do a French plait, which she learned to keep her hair out of her eyes when she was working in the lab. She was kind without spoiling me, and she wouldn't do surprise presents ever, it was always what I chose or what we chose together? I don't mean matching – never matching! We do not have the same taste. Although if I felt cold, I'd borrow a cardigan without needing to ask.'

Another colour of wool: Heather rotates her wrists in order to keep helping.

'She tries too hard. She has this never-ending to-do list she keeps adding to, constantly, and she doesn't think to put on it, *be okay with this feel pleased with the last thing before moving onto the next.* She waits – she needs the validation – for somebody else to tell her how well she's doing. No one does, other than me, and my opinion doesn't count because I'm not academic ... She dominates, in a good way; she takes charge, even in terrible situations with Mum, when Dad went to pieces. Seemed fearless?

I was a handful at times, and I did shout, and she'd yell back. Hmm, I know it's funny, but I didn't mind the occasional argument because it meant overall we were all right? Anger doesn't last if you get to share it with someone you trust. When she's rationalising – that's when alarm bells started ringing. You have to be vulnerable and stupid together, don't you, if you can? It's where the best stuff is. She gets bogged down in details; whereas I like not knowing what's happening next, because there's space for possibilities. She'd be heartbroken when she wrote something that got rejected, or her research didn't go according to plan ... She's into the whole prestige side, er, even though it's only cosplay and fancy dinners – and she's clever enough without them – and they can't see what she has to offer. She is a brittle person who saves the worst criticisms for herself. She doesn't like being alone with her thoughts.'

Cara

It's Cara's turn to make rugbrød. She is learning the recipe so in future she doesn't have to wait for him to.

'I no longer keep track of her status updates,' she says. 'They're excruciating. I accept – as I'm sure she has – we don't have anything in common any more. In what way is it my job to worry?'

Heather

Heather holds a purple hank in both hands. The colours Marble needs aren't available in pre-wound balls, and Lars won't help in case it compromises his masculinity.

'Her name pings up in searches and she is always busy,' she says. 'That is her passion, being busy, then moaning she can't get anything done. Officially, I wasn't part of the plan, and I'm over it. Unofficially, she is not unlovable.'

5

Cone Cells

colour

Cara

Let's say new goals are a part of her process, and this book deal will pay for the terrace she wants to build. Some landscaping. New garden furniture. Pots of herbs. Not that she needs additional commitments.

Cara is redrafting chapter five, which is about psychoactive drugs, including the most widely used and unregulated in the world, her beloved caffeine. Ideas leapfrog in her mind. She sets them down as bullet points: *performance enhancement, anxiety, panic attacks.* Nothing tainted with personal experience though.

Without being asked to, she cuts the hooded figure that carried a head in a basket and stood at the end of her bed in childhood. Self-indulgent. Chapter six, *sleep disorders,* is under control.

Chapter seven is about fallibility and includes, among other sections, *magical thinking, confirmation bias, optimism bias, placebos, pareidolia, the misinformation effect, confabulation* and *cognitive dissonance.*

Chapters eight, nine and ten are reheated lecture notes. She has had this material for years, there's only tidying left to do.

Her editor wants her to sex up the AI and cyborgs of chapter eleven. A few references to pop culture seems to be what he's after. Isn't writing books supposed to be difficult?

Hits *ctrl S* from habit.

Twelve is a beast. It's obvious that she has squeezed in too much, and it needs separating to make better sense. She reads the editor's note, and smirks.

Lovely. Except you haven't explained what consciousness is? Do tell!

He is being facetious. At least, she hopes he is.

Perhaps it's a nudge towards a more conversational style. Or maybe, just maybe, he hasn't fully understood the issue and genuinely believes that she has a theory of consciousness tucked up her sleeve.

This is part of the problem with the hard problem. Certain neuroscientists have, to all intents and purposes, been promising a breakthrough any day now. And so, not unreasonably, the public expects one. Even though that isn't going to happen. And in the meantime, an industry has evolved to fill the void, based entirely on neurobunk.

Her editor isn't too bothered by this, nor by the discussions scientists have among themselves. He wants content and doesn't seem to realise that if Cara actually *knew* what consciousness was, she'd be a rock star by now. Dr Cara Brenner would be able to do whatever research she wanted, anywhere she wanted; they'd be falling over themselves to throw money at her. Cited for ever. Awarded a Nobel. Interviewed by Oprah, thus inspiring a generation of girls to go into STEM. Olivia Williams would play her in the movie of her life.

If she knew what consciousness was, there is simply no way Cara would be writing a popular science book for this piddly-arse publisher.

She leans away from the computer screen.

Throughout her career, consciousness has lived in her

imagination as an object waiting to be discovered. What it is. How it looks. Where to find it. How elegant if there were a vivid and unique pattern of activity to test for. A distinct wave, spike or network that lit up in conscious brains.

In her dreams.

They make do with patiently pursuing the neural correlates of consciousness. Her research is respected precisely because it is thorough, meticulous and dull. It's not the stuff movies are made of, and there hasn't been a biopic of Rita Levi-Montalcini yet, who is arguably the better candidate.

Cara zooms out of chapter twelve, hating its sprawl and lack of spirit. There's nothing in here to show how profoundly bizarre the human brain is; for example, its incredible adaptability is reduced to a sidebar. She hasn't conveyed that consciousness is not only subjective, which is deeply problematic, but ephemeral, making it trickier to pin down.

Everything she's written describes an isolated object, out of context. Separate from other brains, like a jellyfish washed up on the beach. Dead or almost dead, only fit for poking.

She has skimmed over the aspects that are most unsettling for her. That consciousness can emerge out of myriad versatile processes. That non-human animals, including all mammals, birds and octopuses, have the neurological substrates of consciousness. (Along with a group of colleagues, she signed the Cambridge Declaration that this was unequivocally so, although it hasn't stopped her eating calamari.) The potential for sentience in organoids – dots of brain tissue – supposedly an ethical alternative to 'human' experimentation: some react to light stimuli in vitro; some vascularise in a host mouse cortex; some produce networks of activity disturbingly similar to premature neonates.

That the role of consciousness is reconciling the mess that's out there with the mess that's in here, through a pinhole. And if it weren't obvious to every waking person, it might be considered a miracle. She has managed to write about the greatest human mystery and make it boring.

And nowhere does Cara admit that when she looks back at her own research, even when it has stood up to malicious peer review, and the results are reproducible, it seems clunky.

You see, this is why she needs a patio. To have a space to think and stop making these stupid mistakes.

Then again, if she's doing it for a patio, why doesn't she just give the publisher what he's asked for and be done with it?

To break the chain of thoughts, she clicks on her inbox and stares at the top line, as if anticipating it'll appear. Milliseconds later, it does.

Then Cara hoots with laughter. Even though it's wildly inappropriate. Because she didn't know Norfolk had any cliffs.

Her attention is drawn to a display of ambiguous images on the wall of the psych lab. A [rabbit-duck]. A [vase] made from [two faces in silhouette]. A cartoon gestalt-switching between a pretty [wife] and a crone [mother-in-law] (she has never seen a husband/father-in-law equivalent). The [Necker cube]: a 2D wire cube with its nearest plane popping out in space – and which retreats as soon as she thinks it the other way.

Helen turns on the amp so they can hear what's going on through the two-way mirror. Cara pretends to be absorbed in a file of self-report surveys and ERPs from previous participants.

In the next room, a volunteer is wearing an EEG cap, like a vintage swimming hat dotted with electrodes. He keeps still while Iqra adjusts them.

'We monitor your electrical brain activity as lots of wavy lines,' Iqra explains. Her lips move over there, and her voice is thrown in here.

'Brainwaves?'

'Precisely. The experiment is better if you can relax, please, and not move too much.' She's working on a screen with red dots and green dots which resemble a theatre seating chart, and turns them all green by adding gel to the contacts on his scalp and wiggling the electrodes.

The volunteer sits in a digital glow. Wires trail from his head like tentacles.

'I'm a fan of negative results,' Helen is saying to Cara on the dark side of the glass. 'They save duplicated effort. They help us check what we think we know. A scientist who reports garbage is honourable in my opinion.'

'Agreed. But I still won't be pressurised into finding virtues in a failed experiment.'

'Yours always work, do they?'

They can see the volunteer obeying the instructions to keep still and watch the screen. They see the electroencephalograph measure and record his neural oscillations as visual traces. Pulsing sine waves.

They wait.

It is a chequerboard at first. Black and white squares alternate in a hypnotic rhythm.

[black-white, white-black, black-white, white-black, black-white]

Gradually the program filters out background noise and the EEG trace becomes a consistent waveform. Then video clips start.

They are snippets cut together as quick montages. Of debates. Of statements. Of off-the-cuff remarks. Of rallies, of interviews

215

and handshakes. The glare of the studio. The formality of the chamber. The thud of the street.

Convention.

Hustings.

Town hall.

A doorstep. A platform. And a podium. Microphones poised like daggers.

.

.

[Etonian] ... *[Grey scowl]* ... *[Leopard-print heels]* ...

.

...

.

.

[Londoner] ... *[Clown]* ... *[Having a pint]* ...

...

.

.....

..

The segments are shorter than soundbites, but in this lab they might as well be feature films. Any event-related potentials – the discernible shapes in response to a stimulus that are most valuable – are lost in interference. The graph is a meaningless scribble.

.

.

[Shades of pink] ... *[QC]* ... *[Nondescript]* ...

..

.

.

'She isn't making it easy on herself,' Cara whispers.

'Can't you admit when someone else has had an interesting idea?' Helen whispers back.

.

.

Cliff edge ... Seven-and-a-half out of ten ... £350 million a week ...

. . .

. . . . .

.

. . .

'When was the last time one of the plebs made you show your university card?' says Helen, shaking her head. 'Rude remarks. Freezing out. I asked her if she was having any problems? She looked me straight in the eye and said no. It's *Lord of the Flies* out there; I expected you of all people to understand.'

'I meant it as a compliment.'

. .

.

Take back control ... You deserve the truth ... Fist fight ...

. . . . .

. .

.

. . .

The volunteer twiddles his thumbs, then appears to remember not to.

Iqra's attention switches between him and the data pouring in.

.

. .

[Black] ... [Orange] ... [Pantsuit] ... [Surrogate] ... [Tall] ...

.

. . . . . .

. . . .

.

. . . .

. . . .

Cara looks at her phone. 'Shall we go to lunch after this?'

'Why, what's wrong with you? Are you dying? You haven't invited me to lunch since the old days.'

'It's only lunch.'

.

. . . . .

Nasty woman . . . Glass ceiling . . . Pay for the wall . . . What is Aleppo? . . . Deplorables . . .

. . . .

. . . .

. .

.

.

. . . . .

Snatches and frames loop with intervals of blank. The ERP waves like liquid.

.

. . .

Grab 'em by the . . . We go high . . . LOCK HER UP . . . NASTY WOMAN . . . Alternative facts . . .

. . . . . .

. . . . .

. . . .

.

. . .

. . .

The volunteer has slumped like a man in an armchair.

. .

. . .

Sovereignty ... Will of the people ... Dark days of the 1930s ...
Vi coactus ... Had enough of experts ...

. . . . .

. . . . . .

. .

.

. . . .

. . .

Fluctuations.

'Hmm.' It's the noise Cara makes when she's looking at
her own data.

.

. . . . . .

There is no plan ... Russia, if you're listening? ...
Do – dooo – do – do ...

. . .

. .

. . .

. . . .

Helen clicks the top of a pen to make a note.

. .

. . . .

More in common ... Without a single bullet ... A citizen of
nowhere ...

. . . . .

. . . .

. . .

. .

. . . .
. . . . .

The light comes back on, and the volunteer blinks at Cara.

She is taken aback by how hard he is staring at her, then remembers he can't see through the mirror and must be looking at his own reflection in the silly hat.

Iqra carefully lifts the cephalopod off his head.

He is thanked for his time and shown out.

'How's the book coming along?' Helen asks. Although not really because she's spinning through data, comparing frames to ERPs, waves expand and contract at her touch.

'Oh, it – should be okay.' She watches her colleague's profile. With a Necker cube drawing, Cara is able to force her perception back and forth, swapping the emphasis of squares at will: with Dr Stewart, however, she concentrates harder to see both views. Yes, there is definitely a fixed plane with Helen Stewart in the foreground, and a separate plane with Murray Stewart who recedes.

They first met as postgraduates. Cara was giving a presentation at journal club on a study of auditory nerve action potentials. She invited any questions from the floor . . . ? A boy with *Four Weddings* hair and wire-rimmed glasses raised his hand, and called her incoherent. Honestly, she mistook it for flirting.

Helen pauses on a violent blast of activity. 'I ask you, what kind of brain does that to other brains?'

Cara says, 'I need you to cover my teaching and supervisions for a few days. Do you mind?'

'All of them . . . ?'

She shows the email on her phone rather than trying to explain.

Helen reads through her spectacles on a beaded chain. Gives

it back. 'When the time comes to execute traitors, it won't be the media warlords or brat princes of Silicon Valley who are led to the scaffold. It won't be the peddlers of salvation or Wall Street Ponzis and offshore billionaires. It'll be us, dear. You and me. The geeks and the pedants.'

Cara nods slowly.

'Call her.'

'Well yes,' Cara replies, thinking she'll forward the email and attachments, which amounts to the same thing.

'Call her,' Helen says again. 'And book a hair appointment before you go. You've had it this way since New Labour was credible.'

She touches what was supposed to be a messy bun.

Later, when Cara is alone, and after some procrastinating and squeezing the phone in both hands as hard as possible, she scrolls to *H* in her contacts. 'Hello, you.'

A sigh on the other end. 'It's the middle of the night here.'

'Sorry. I didn't think of that. I'm coming for a visit, I had to tell you. You're still in *Las Vegas*, aren't you?' She says it as if it weren't a real place. 'I'm taking back toil, and turning it into a thing. I thought you'd like to know, and maybe meet for a drink?'

Muffled movement. 'Don't. You'll hate it here.'

'What are you talking about? The Rat Pack? The Hoover Dam? High-stakes gambling? Those are up my street. Tom Jones. David Copperfield. Nicholas Nickelback . . .' Cara wants to kill herself.

'Don't come.'

She laughs, barely. 'But I've got my heart set on it – it's not up to you. Wouldn't you like to see me while I'm in town?'

A pause. Perhaps she's with someone.

'Are you still there?'

'Yes. Are you?'

Cara is, she's right here. 'Is this a bad time? Have you been on er, substances?'

'I'm sober. I was asleep.'

'Then I'm sorry I woke you. I'm excited, that's all. I'll send you my itinerary and we'll make a plan? Dr Stewart – Helen – has offered to cover for me, so that's not a reason not to.'

She sniffs. 'Is the fish all right?'

'Yes. Yes, fine thank you. Mooching around in his tank. I'll send a picture, shall I? Go back to sleep.' She hangs up before it gets weird.

The sign is a red star on a white diamond, with red uppercase letters and a blue flourish.

Welcome to Fabulous Las Vegas.

At night it appears suspended and has chasing gold spangles.

If you're madly in love, you can have a spur-of-the-moment wedding. Then a honeymoon. Then you double down. Eat meals in restaurants with Picassos, or flying wine angels. Experience Gold Spike like a local, Green Door, and the alien heat of the Mojave. Treat your hotel like it's a hotel, thanks to the army of hospitality workers.

From performers in Pleaser heels, to high rollers betting thousands on a hand: make it here, and no one can deny you've made it.

But none of that is going to happen to you, Dr Brenner. Don't panic, your Vegas life will be short.

Heather is dressed in black as though about to give a presentation. She has stayed pale except for a few darker freckles, and her ginger hair is dyed Jessica Rabbit red. Red, white and black, something of the playing card about her. She wears a hamsa-charm necklace and has an enormous handbag in the

222

crook of her arm which Cara covets at first sight. She could be Heather's evil twin.

They peck on the cheek and sit across from each other in a booth. Cara orders a mojito and Heather asks for sparkling water.

'Aren't you drinking with me?'

'Alcohol is for civilians.' Heather scans the bar for a minute. 'Actually, I changed my mind, I could do with one now that I've seen you. No offence.'

'Have mine when it comes. We'll order another.'

The waiter returns. Heather says she doesn't want a cocktail after all, but Cara says she, Heather, might change her mind again, and if she doesn't she, Cara, will drink it for her. They order the same, then fall silent.

Jazz piano in the background filling the gap.

'Dad's dead,' Heather says. 'I can't think why else you're here? Was it suicide in the end? Trouble is, when I imagine him trying, I worry that he'd get it wrong.'

'He's not dead.'

She raises her inked eyebrows. 'You don't sound convinced.'

Cara gets out her tablet, opens the email and attachments.

A security-camera shot of a thinner, bearded Paul alone on a veranda. His hands are in the pockets of a padded jacket, which is unzipped and has an X underneath. Saggy sweatpants. Trainers with white socks.

Fifty minutes later, according to the timestamp, he is walking across a deserted golf course – where the greens and shrubs drop away to an abrupt horizon.

The last attachment is a map with two markers.

'Is it from the same Lauren we saw when he went?' Heather asks. 'She became a police officer then.'

'I talked to her, it was pretty blah.'

'When she says *found the van*, what does she mean? Was it abandoned, was his stuff inside?'

'He parked near a coastal path. There wasn't much in the way of possessions, but he slept in there at least sometimes. Left it locked, as if he intended to go back. They need to hold on to it for a while.'

Heather swipes through pictures. Expands his blank, bristly face. 'These are from . . .?'

'The clubhouse CCTV. It's possible he was lost as – it was dusk by then. The lights are motion sensitive, usually it's owls and foxes and things when they look at the tapes. This is three kilometres from where the van was.'

'By some cliffs?'

'They aren't especially high.'

'Wow, a golf course on the Norfolk coast; I cannot think of a more boring way to go. I bet you can't stand the fact he's wearing his *X-files* T-shirt.' She drinks from Cara's side of the table. 'Is there going to be a funeral?'

Thank God when a second drink arrives.

'No,' she replies uncertainly. 'We mustn't assume what his intentions were. No note, you see.'

'He doesn't leave notes. He didn't before. He's no good at sharing.'

'Your father is still a missing person as far as I'm concerned. He chose a kind of life . . . I'll be honest, I didn't think he had it in him. Maybe he was meeting a friend in the village? We don't know unless there's—'

'A body? You can say it, I don't mind. A piece of him washed up more likely, am I right? Maybe a bloaty torso?' She gazes at her. 'I thought you had something important to tell me, Cara.

This is stupid. We would both be better off if you'd forwarded it and left me alone.'

'That wouldn't be right.'

'Let the record show Dr Cara Brenner did the right thing, because that's what counts?'

'If you want to, uh, see for yourself . . .' She sips because she's forgotten what she was going to say. 'This is a firm lead. People have dog-walking routines in the evenings. Knocking on doors and asking residents if they've seen him – posters in the local pub – it might just work? A page in the parish newsletter? It won't take us very long.'

'Nope. Can't.'

'I realise this is a lot to process, but we need to do it while it's fresh in people's minds. I'll help.'

'No, I truly can't, if I leave the country, they'll never let me back in. I've overstayed. That's it.'

Cara runs her fingers through her new pixie cut. The nape of her neck still feels bare. 'You said how important it was to try, not for his sake, but for yours; that you were giving him space to reach out when he was ready, without feeling hounded. Words to that effect. It was wise for a young person.'

She smiles. 'And how many years exactly should I spend searching for a father who lost interest in me? And where will I stay – at yours? You'll be sick of me in five minutes.'

'We can figure out the details, of course we will. Make a plan.'

'Based on what, some CCTV of a golf course? I'm not going anywhere.'

'Being able to return afterwards, if that is really what's keeping you here, we can find you a lawyer. It's not an issue.'

'You've got answers for everything. I said no.'

'But you aren't being rational.' It occurs to Cara she should

225

reach forwards, although she isn't sure. 'Soon it will sink in. You can't ignore this, you'll regret it later.'

'No, *you'll* regret it, because if I stay, how else will you stop feeling so freaking guilty?' Heather's smile stretches. 'This is about you, the way you want me to react, never mind what I want or how it disrupts my life. We both know he had, like, a nervous breakdown right in front of you. He was a perfectly nice, normal man, and you're meant to be good at this stuff. And showing up in person – telling me that I should drop everything and fly back to effing Cambridge because *you* suddenly decide it's urgent – is not going to undo the fact that you let Dad down. You let him down, Cara. If anyone should have noticed what was happening, and helped him, it was you. Instead, you made it worse, like you're making this worse, for me, because I like it here. It's a laugh.'

Cara uses a napkin in case there's mint on her lip.

Heather exhales. 'Please stop pretending.'

She takes back her device. Gets on the wifi to forward the message – which swoops out of her items and pings into the Louis Vuitton. 'There, you've got the same information I do.' Clicks it off.

The pianist is playing standards from the American songbook. A guest takes his photo and dollars are added to a glass vase.

'Aren't you scared someone's going to report you?' says Cara.

'What sort of person would do a thing like that?' Heather lays her phone in front of her and stares into it. For a moment Cara thinks she's being snubbed. Then Heather throws her head back to look at a mirror design on the ceiling and takes a picture.

Cara looks up too, briefly. 'Not exactly safe here.'

'Neither is England. They love immigrants really, without us, the economy would collapse. Don't believe fake news.'

'I might understand it if you were seeking enlightenment in an ashram in India . . .'

'I don't know what an ashram is, but I'm pretty sure there is one nearby. And if there isn't it's only a matter of time. This is a magical valley. Lots of energies meet.'

Cara laughs drily. 'It can't have been very magical when you bought yourself a flight on my credit card?'

She rolls her eyes. 'I knew you were going to bring that up.'

'Did you think I wouldn't notice? Clearly you at least considered—'

'Here, have it back, I don't need it, I can repay you with interest if you like? Trust me, it isn't a problem.' She starts rummaging in the designer bag.

Shit, Cara thinks, even the lining looks good, it must be genuine.

Heather puts the card on the table, the one Cara bought granite worktops with.

She sips. 'Keep it.'

'Even if I was desperate, I wouldn't use it again.' She slides out of the seat, smooths her outfit.

'Where are you going?'

'To work. Thanks for my drink. Leave a decent tip – they're arseholes to the staff here.'

She watches Heather wend between tables. A waiter half bows, and she barely acknowledges him. And Cara can remember teaching her how to order from the children's menu at Pizza Express.

In the lobby of the hotel she chose because it had the best last-minute deal, and the least ridiculous-sounding name, the top of a giant aquarium disappears into the ceiling.

Cara gazes in.

A bright blue room with glass walls, no doorways and too many fish for its volume.

Great fish like silver platters. Rays fluttering like black capes. Blobs of colour hang like Christmas tree decorations.

They circle. They form groups. Break up and reform. They slink away to hide in rock formations. They're peaceful and private, until they panic and scatter.

There is a person in there.

Guests gather round the tank to watch her and to wave, their faces blue in aquatic light.

She has princess hair; a bikini top; and a fishtail. She waves back, blowing them kisses. Moves her arms in a slow-motion dance and works her hidden legs to stay upright. She is diving without scuba gear.

Cara holds her breath in response.

A mother picks up her daughter and says, 'It's Ariel,' in a sickly-sweet voice.

Ariel like a water-nymph, Cara thinks. Another work of fiction. Yet the discomfort must be real enough. Aren't her lungs aching to expel air and inhale? Cara wants to, wants to breathe normally again.

Oxygen in the blood, please.

The underwater girl has treats which the fish are eating from her hands. Nibbly contact, no sudden movements.

The aquarium is deep.

They won't reach her when she starts to drown. They'll never make it in time.

Her chest tightens. Any second now. Can't breathe until the swimmer does, otherwise it's cheating. How is she doing it? Is she freediving? What other explanation could there be?

Heather

Dear Valued Guest,

We are pleased to announce that THE APOSTLES MOTEL has been acquired as the newest member of the Lempriere Inc. family.

Daily operations of THE APOSTLES MOTEL will continue under your existing management team. Therefore, Guests will still enjoy a full range of services and facilities – without experiencing a reduction in access or quality!

Your comfort is our mission. In order to maintain the high standards of excellence that we know you have come to expect of THE APOSTLES MOTEL, Lempriere Inc. is eagerly awaiting your feedback. Should Guests have any questions, comments or suggestions, please do not hesitate to contact your customer service agent at the reception desk.

Have a nice stay!

Sincerely,

Margery Starre, Vice President

Lempriere Developments

It's displayed in the Plexiglas window. The window is closed and the office behind is empty.

'Have you seen this?' Heather asks.

Marble clicks their knitting needles. The rainbow knitting snakes around their shoulders, gathers in their lap, and trails down to the floor. 'We've all seen it.'

'Look what I brought?' She shows them some complimentary notepaper with an embossed logo.

'Ah, that is exactly what we need. We can take as many messages as we like from now on.' They rest their hands on the woolly bundle. 'As it happens, I'm waiting for an important call. It is essential I'm here, or that a person is able to take down details on my behalf, if I am not.'

Heather picks at a roll of tape to make a sticky loop on the end of her finger. 'You think somebody is going to then?'

'Call? Or take a message?'

'Both?'

'Yes. And yes. They will. One of the helpers, who come in different sizes and shapes. As do phone calls. There are various kinds of phone calls. Important calls. Urgent calls. Non-urgent calls. Greetings. Directions.'

'Pranks?'

'Hopefully those in moderation. Humour is ...'

'Subjective?'

'Indeed.' Marble counts stitches along the needle. Spaces them evenly. 'Mr Ely seems better?'

'Yeah, Reginald is okay.' She has taped a knot by mistake.

'He is lucky to have you as a friend. The packaging we come in is not of our choosing. We weren't born with *fragile* printed on our butts.'

She sticks loops to the back of the notepad. Presses it on the shelf where a pen is tied to a bracket with a piece of orange yarn. Gives the payphone a quick wipe clean. 'Perfect. There's plenty more where that came from, in case it rings a lot?'

They both watch the payphone for a moment.

The pause runs on and on.

She says, 'I like how your scarf has turned out.'

Marble gives it a pet, and resumes knitting.

Ely is in his room, trying to get his foot in his shoe.

'Were you going to mention the letter?' she asks, leaning with her arms folded.

'Not a letter. Edict.'

'Where will you go?'

He massages the arm through the support sling. Stands with the aid of a Nordic walking pole. 'I haven't decided.'

'Are you sure you're well enough for this?'

'You wanted me to walk.'

'I was thinking more around the block, and maybe build up from there?'

'Just imagine the satisfaction you'll feel when I get into difficulties. You can say, *I told you so.*'

She can't stretch out on what used to be her bed as it's covered with stacked papers and publications. In the middle of his filing system is a paper parcel, with a shredder next to it. The fan rustles loose pages. 'Is that what I think it is?'

'It's nothing,' he replies.

'Can I have it?'

'Certainly not.'

'Why, what are you going to do with it? It doesn't matter if you aren't keeping it any more.'

'Lower your voice, please. There shall be no more arguments in this house.'

'I do not approve of you having a shredder in here.'

'Objection noted.'

She licks her lips. 'Ned would wet himself if he saw.'

'Nevertheless, some things are best not shared. His is not the right sensibility.'

'And what about whoever comes after him?'

He skews his expression at her. 'That is cruel, Heather Wycliffe. I am surprised at you. Are you all right today?'

She nods emphatically. Straightens papers disturbed by the fan. 'Give this to me and I'll shred it for you?'

'You won't – you'll do no such thing.'

'I don't like the idea of you alone with a shredder in here – sorry, not yelling – I can show you the pieces if you don't trust me.'

'Respect my choice to keep my thought process private. I beg you.'

She turns her back and pouts into her phone. 'I'm looking up this place because I'm not entirely sure how you get there. Isn't there anywhere nearer and less volcano-y you'd rather go?'

'Volcanic.'

'Less volcanicky, then?'

'Did you bring plenty of water? Hat? Hiking boots?'

She points to her battered sneakers and holds up a red umbrella for shade. She says, 'Poor Lars. Shouldn't someone take his guns away?'

They drive twenty-something miles (or a million miles, depending on your point of view), where real estate creeps into the wilderness lot by lot. They lose their way on unfinished roads until they mute the GPS and Ely navigates from memory.

The pinkish pale waves of Sloan Canyon sharpen into ridges.

Once there, it's as though you're standing on another planet. Its stony slopes. Its rocky soil. Its igneous bands. Packed columns. Jagged layers. Sheer faces.

They climb extinct volcanos, grey and sandy underfoot, with maroon and black mica. The ground scurries with lizards like tiny dragons.

Plants grow here, despite the hostile conditions. Ely, panting and slipping on the loose path, names them.

'Creosote,' he says of the yellow and green bushes. 'It smells medicinal. It's used to treat ailments such as cramps, tuberculosis and snakebites.'

'Snakebites?' Heather says, checking down by her feet.

'Beavertail prickly-pear,' he says of a cactus with flat, speckled stems and magenta flowers. 'A valuable food source.'

'How do you eat them if it's got prickles on?' She lifts a finger towards it.

'I wouldn't, if I were you ... Mojave yucca: its fibre is for rope, weaving, and to make sandals with.'

'We had a yucca in the office I used to clean.'

They lost sight of the visitor contact station more than an hour ago, and they've followed a trail ever since.

She kicks at the dust and spins the umbrella on her shoulder. 'We're in trouble if you have an episode out here, I couldn't carry you back. Would they airlift you if they had to? Are there patrols?'

'Is there anything I can do for you? Tell me what's on your mind.'

'Mainly I'm concerned that we're going to end up on the news.' She marches ahead of him, each step scrunching like Aldeburgh beach. Finds a strip of shade to stand in.

He catches up to her. Wipes the sweat from his brow. 'We've come too far to turn back.'

'Did I say I want to? I can march all day long, but these had better be some damn pretty rocks.'

They carry on, eventually making their way through a natural entrance.

What she sees next is like a chalk drawing on coloured paper. Except the picture is scraped through the burnt crust of the rock surface: a bighorn sheep.

Then she sees a coiling shape which could be water, or a reptile come to think of it. And crescents. Hoops. Grids on another plane.

More petroglyphs emerge, the more she looks for them. Of humans. Of critters. Loops, darts and polygons. A hawk with open wings. A skeletal plant – or is it a centipede – or a map?

Visions grazed into stone.

As they go further on, Heather realises there must be more, higher up on walls she can't make out, hidden on undersides and wrapped around panels. They might be abstract. They could be calligraphy.

The canyon is a picture gallery.

She takes her phone out of her back pocket.

'Before Rumi had written a couplet,' Ely says, resting against a ledge. 'Before Hildegard of Bingen sang a note of praise. Before King Canute tried and failed to repel the tide. Or the first entry was made in the Domesday Book. Southern Paiute people – and others, perhaps – were telling stories here, making music and passing on their traditions. Each strike cost effort. Every mark is a spirit.'

She touches her palm to a purple boulder hot like an animal (careful not to disturb the art). Takes a sidestep and her umbrellaed shadow overlaps it.

'You're turning into a Vivian Maier.'

'I haven't heard of him.'

'I know.' He gestures into air. '*I think good thoughts whilst other write good words.*'

'I can help,' Heather says again. 'Only what you need me for, not what you can manage by yourself?'

'It is a kind offer. I decline.' He spikes the pole in the soft ground. 'Living never stops feeling uncomfortable, that is the price we pay for our turn in the world.'

'Do you want an Ativan and what's left of the water even though it's a bit warm?'

He accepts the bottle. 'I forget, occasionally, that you are hers. It doesn't fully hold together. You are observant and generous. Tough. Courageous in your way. You must get these qualities from your father, because you did not inherit them from Ruth.'

Nature or nurture? she thinks, then stops the thought in its tracks because she doesn't want to resemble anybody. She wants to be like what she is. Herself.

He lowers his slurred speech. 'The evening we spent in Atomic Liquors discussing aesthetics, when I was supposed to be the one providing answers: you were nearly right when you said intimate. You were almost exactly right.'

A nude city without her make-up on.

The Strip is bare and broad. Bleached with morning light. In the absence of crowds, the streets are being washed clean. The signs softly lit.

It must be around six a.m. And is as temperate as an English summer. Birdsong is louder than traffic – the birds who make their homes in cosmetic trees and in the cracks of towers for hillsides. When the fountain isn't dancing, they treat it like any pond.

Heather walks with cash in her purse.

Over there is a jogger in fluorescent pink and black, wrapa-round sunglasses and headphones, making the most of the basin breeze. Nobody runs here unless you're being chased by cops.

Weirdo, she thinks. Ah, what?

The runner runs straight and strong, crosses between parked cars and picks up speed. She isn't looking. (Why isn't she?) Running as if she is keen to meet her fate.

Heather goes after her shouting, 'Cara, Cara, Cara Mia?'

Cara never drops pace, never alters her rhythm.

They pass an advert thing, a shiny thing, a twirly thing.

Heather's hair is wild, her shoes click like a metronome. She lags behind and she'd laugh if she could because Cara's really fit, and she really isn't. How can they both be here, in adult Disneyland, instead of home, in adult Hogwarts?

She has a stab in her side. Shouts again, drawing the attention of street sweepers and a woman walking an Alsatian.

Cara slows (and Heather thinks, Thank goddess) briefly, for a delivery truck unloading barrels in her path. No, she's not stopping for it, she weaves past the dray, then—

Oh no, she wouldn't, she really is the stupidest professor you ever heard of.

—looks over the wrong shoulder.

Dr Cara Brenner, the brilliant Cambridge scientist who dedicated her life to unlocking secrets of the human brain with clever experiments, was knocked over and killed in a road traffic accident today, because she didn't know left from right. Witnesses say she was jogging on the Las Vegas Strip at the time ...

You couldn't make it up.

She lunges and grabs her by the elbow. Pulls as though she's weightless.

A car brakes on the corner. They lose their footing – it screeches short – and the driver blares the horn.

They fall down. Heather on her side with her purse still attached to her body, Cara on hands and knees, her sunglasses knocked off, headphone wires trailing along the ground.

Activity paused.

Heather shakes with giggles. 'That was unbelievable.'

'What the hell were you—'

The driver's swearing can be lip-read through the windscreen. He scowls and accelerates away.

A drayman says, 'Are you ladies okay?'

'We're fine,' Heather replies. 'Thanks. Sorry, our fault.'

Cara gets up, rubbing her knee. Helps her to her feet.

They brush down.

'For your information, I looked before I crossed.'

'They come from that direction, not *that* direction. Some of the turnings aren't clear, and the drivers think they're more important than pedestrians, and they can get pretty mad too, and they should, because jaywalkers are constantly being hit on this stretch of road – or you can get a thousand-dollar fine if the police saw you, easily, or sent to jail – I'm not exaggerating – which is why you have to be extra careful not to go running out in front of moving cars here and check the other blimming side?'

'I was looking both ways.'

'You *weren't*. You'd be dead if I wasn't here. I am basically a superhero to you. Hey, I saved your life; I can treat you however I like from now on?'

'Please explain how that is different from before.' Cara checks her wearable and mutters under her breath.

'Is it broken?'

'No. My time. It was supposed to be fast and flat.'

Heather giggles again. 'You were a geek and now you're sporty. Who saw that coming?'

In Cara's hotel room, she stays for a while in the en suite. When she steps out again in a towel, her wet hair combed like a boy, Heather says, 'Don't you like the food here? Is it your period?'

She swigs green water from a sports bottle. 'Running cramps, nothing to worry about. I drink the electrolytes and take an Imodium. I have my routine.'

'It's disgusting. Don't let real people hear.'

'You think that's bad?' Cara puts her foot on the edge of the bed: her toenail is black and purple, with a yellow callous and a fresh white blister.

Heather grimaces. 'Eww, put it away!'

Despite the amount of nakedness she sees these days, she averts her eyes when Cara takes underwear from a drawer and drops her towel—

Cara

—nice undies, not the ugly knickers Glenda made her wear till the elastic perished. Back when Heather was a tween who couldn't swim further than a width, and being naked together in the changing rooms at Abbey pool was normal—

Heather

—no embarrassment with Ruth's body, not when it was well and clean, not when it was sick and soiled either. Cara getting dressed shouldn't be a big deal. Her legs are brown to the thighs, then light at the top as if she's wearing stockings.

Heather says, 'Nice tan lines.'

'I run in shorts. They're a badge of honour.'

'You've lost weight too. Not in a gross way, the same as what you had, but cinched in? You look strong. And I like your hair this way, it's very Tamsin Greig.'

'Maybe she should play me in the movie of my life.'

'Ooh, are they making a movie about you?'

'No, not at this rate.' Cara brushes on face powder, glances at Heather from the mirror. 'I still can't believe we bumped into each other. You appeared from nowhere.'

'I told you. Energies in the Valley. Weird stuff happens.'

'No, that isn't the reason. It's unlikely, the probability is low, it is not . . . inconceivable.'

'Seriously, you get used to it. There's squillions of people, but also you see folks you know all the time, or you meet somebody new, then you get chatting with them and realise you know someone who they know, or you're both regulars at the same

240

deli. And there's lots of gossip about . . . I want to say local politics, like town-and-gown? Like that, except Vegassy.'

Cara stops adjusting her bra.

'This can feel like a small town,' Heather continues, 'but you didn't hear that from me, okay? You chose a good hotel, with nice pools. They get funny about non-guests using the facilities, but if we say I'm staying with you, it'll be all right?'

'I spent the day by the pool yesterday. It was loud, and I didn't get a lot done.'

'You were *working*? You're supposed to be having fun. What else are you planning to do while you're here?'

She runs an eyeliner along her eyelid. 'I don't know, I thought maybe . . . I haven't really thought about it. Is there a gallery?'

'Haven't you seen where you are?'

'I just stuck this in my eye . . .' Cara grabs tissues to rescue the mess she's made. To avoid another catastrophe, they don't talk while she applies her mascara.

Heather says, 'It's a plastic city.'

'You can say that again.'

'I mean it's plastic like you said a brain is. Not rigid. You make it what you want it to be? Please don't work today? I'm not. I'll spend the day with you.'

Cara pulls on a pretty top, and Heather hooks a tiny button at the back of her neck. She opens her mouth as if she's going to ask a question. Instead, puts on lipstick.

Heather looks out the window at the Boulevard below thrumming like a vein. 'The first thing to do is book you a mani-pedi.'

'That really won't be necessary.'

'It is – it's done.'

'I'm fine without, thank you.'

'You don't understand. It's done. Booked, see?' She shows her the confirmation.

Cara

The chair in the salon is larger and more comfortable than any chair she ever sat in. The soft leather supports her every bulge and there's room for her to spread. It is hideous, a sensible shoe in chair form. Cara could die happy in it.

Her scarf-coloured gels don't elicit the same gasps of approval as Heather's choice of black with a gold pattern. Cara wants her fingernails round, whereas Heather asks for claws.

The bottles are lined up, ready.

'I'm not used to having my feet touched.' This is the polite version. What she means is she can't stand being touched in intimate places by strangers, and this ordeal is happening against her wishes.

The pedicurist is perched on a stool with castors. She is Southeast Asian and wears a surgical mask. She checks from time to time that Cara is okay. Is ma'am okay with massage? Is ma'am okay with lotion? How is the pressure? The phrases are basic, but the rubbing is intelligent: she finds the spots of tension and dissolves them.

Of course reflexology is drivel without any proven health benefits, and beauty treatments a vacuous waste of time and money. Nonetheless, Cara is starting to see why wealthy housewives make a habit of this. She closes her eyes. The smell of acetone is overpowering, and the strokes and dabs feel magnified.

When she opens her eyes again, she cries out, because Heather is about to pay. Thus the efforts to relax her are undone.

Heather takes her to a café where the staff swerve behind the counter to avoid one another, and they have to shout their order over loud music.

Heather struts, balancing a tray one-handed and collects cutlery with the other, as though marks were awarded for style as well as execution. She is wearing a kimono-style top and denim shorts with the pockets showing. It is studied casual, with heels and unsubtle jewellery, like celebrities wear at airports knowing the paparazzi will be there.

Cara tries to introduce the subject of Paul again.

Heather makes a show of biting into a sub and having her mouth full. 'Why have you given up social media like a cavewoman?' she asks, which is annoying, because if she'd checked she'd know that the combination of bad news, bots and troll farms was getting Cara down.

'Time suck,' she replies for the sake of simplicity.

'Helen and me follow each other, so if I ever want to know what particular neuron you're researching ...' Suddenly, she's on the subject of Dr Stewart, and how marvellous and resilient she is, an inspiration to all of us to be more like ourselves. She is demolishing her sandwich and fries while she talks as if it's her last meal, and when she's finished, picks Cara's plate clean of whatever hasn't been contaminated by bacon. Cara hasn't seen her eat like this since she had a growth spurt.

They pass a thick police officer outside, with a buzzcut and white lines from ears to eyes where his aviators have been.

Cara does a double take. It's one thing to see armed police

guarding government buildings in Whitehall; it's another when they're chewing a burger in a car park and have relish on their chin.

Heather makes brazen eye contact with him and beams. She grabs Cara's arm, taking her by surprise, and slips hers through, opening their hands to compare manicures.

Cara finds herself striding in the same arrogant way just to keep up.

Heather

Heather can hear a remark forming in Cara's mind.

She purses her lips as they move through the show garden – at golden eggs, at LED stars, and doll-children with floral waistcoats. Scarlet and orange carnations create blocks of colour, to enhance the everlasting cherry blossoms, the acid-house daisies, the roses the size of triffids. Scale is irrelevant here in this frivolous menagerie. A single fluffy chick could terrorise the occupants of the model Shanghai hotel, like a monster in a B movie. Among the plants, red and gold figurines and babbling stream is the centrepiece: an animatronic rooster. It shakes its tail feathers, flaps its wings and cock-a-doodle-doos at pre-programmed intervals.

'Very elaborate,' she says, which wasn't the first draft.

Heather describes a few highlights on their way to a shopping mall (careful to say 'mall' as in 'malware', not like what a tiger would do). Tells her there'll be a test later. Then says, don't panic, she's only joking, there isn't going to be a test. Concentrate on having fun.

It is full of choices. Customers drift from one flamboyant retailer to the next. High-end units compete with worse-for-wear, and flimsy walls are all that separate a hot trend from economic decline.

Cara perks up when she sees a brand she likes. Holds clothes against herself to compare smart and casual, plain and busy colourways. Converts the price tags to sterling.

'These'll look good to show off your lovely legs?' says Heather. 'Wear them with a neutral top and I swear they'll really work? I can buy this for you as a present if you like. You should try them on.'

The cubicle door in the fitting room has a frosted panel down the middle, and there's movement and a hint of cheek within.

From the waiting area, Heather tells her that before Vegas became a city it was traditionally a water stop for travellers – which is ironic really because now the water is running out.

'Pardon?'

'I said, there's always a drought on. When you visit Lake Mead, you can see how far the water level has dropped. They call it the bathtub ring. No one takes it seriously, though. I haven't worked out why? Maybe if you hustle to get through each day, it's harder to think ahead.' She glances at the translucent pane. 'Are you trying on the white one? I can give you an opinion if you aren't sure? I promise I won't let you make any fashion mistakes.'

The sound of annoyed unzipping, a scrape of hangers. Cara's voice is muffled by material. The end of the reply is, '. . . the water does run out.'

Heather must have misheard. Cara wouldn't be that insensitive about a creeping catastrophe. 'This is like a TV makeover show,' she says lightly, 'and I'm your stylist, only it takes way longer in real life, you don't have a transformation in the next, er, scene.' She taps her foot. 'What did you say?'

'I said, it will be a blessing if the water does run out.'

No, no good.

247

Heather shoulders her purse. Won't say goodbye because there's no point. Cara doesn't listen to what she means. Takes a sidestep toward the exit.

Wonders if she'll emerge in the same moment, and would she try to stop her if she did?

Doesn't matter. Forget her.

Cara

'You were right about the print—'

Heather has left the changing room and gone to browse something else. True, Cara was taking ages, mainly because the sizing makes no sense.

The complimentary carrier bag makes Cara's heart beat faster. It's proper too, stiff, with cord handles and smart typography.

She looks for Heather in the store. Then outside the store. Then in the store next door.

Checks for texts.

Does a circuit, remembering a time when she got lost in the supermarket, and Glenda asked a supervisor to put a call out on the Tannoy. 'Can a Miss Cara Mia Brenner please make yourself known to a member of staff? We have found your mummy and would like to return her to you.' She was embarrassed to hear her name announced in public that way.

Heather reappears (or was there all along). Patters her phone with one thumb, the other tucked in her shorts pocket.

'Oh, there you are. Have you seen anything you want?'

Shakes her head, mm-mm. 'Sorry, I was catching up with socials. They get funny if you make them wait.'

'No such thing as a day off, is there? Work and leisure are

merged for ever. This has been nice ... Listen, I was thinking, if you need to take off ...'

Heather is absorbed in the bewildering assortment of apps she has on her phone.

'We probably had the best of it this morning,' Cara continues. 'And I didn't give you much notice. I don't mind.'

The girl flits her eyes. 'Am I that unbearable?'

'No. No, I want to spend the day together. I do.' She unlocks her phone too. Notifications are piling up. It takes all her self-control not to dive in and sort them out. 'You smell citrusy.'

'Yeah, I got sprayed by the fragrances?' Heather slides her phone into her back pocket. Peeks at the garment Cara has mixed feelings about. 'I was going to pay for that?'

'Pay for the next thing if you want.'

Heather

They're meatier than Heather imagined, like turkeys and hams in human form. Peeled, chopped, portioned. The bodies have flaws that wax models don't have – including pimples, flaky patches, follicles, scars, swelling, asymmetries, wrinkles, lashes, broken nails, fillings, moles and tumours.

They're pink and taut. They're red and draped. They're grey and knotted and slashed and splayed and separated into constituent parts. The skin, the flab, the muscles, the tendons, the cartilage and ligaments. And bones, from what's minuscule in the ear to chunky femurs. Hearts and lungs and livers and gums and gullets and guts and bladders and tongues and lymph nodes and nipples. Cortex.

Dismantled.

Posed like mannequins. Lit like treasure.

Cara leans on a glass case. She murmurs, 'I remember the first time I held a brain. Such a privilege. Touching a whole record of a person's thoughts and all the emotions they ever felt. Their humour, their memories and impressions. Pain. A personality resting in my hands. Most of the time it's tissue, it has to be. But the first time, it isn't. I couldn't stop thinking normal things like, This brain liked sandwiches, and, This brain played chess.

I didn't know who it was, obviously, it's only what was occurring to me in the moment. This brain got married, and had anniversaries, and babies, and then it had grandchildren. I couldn't stop. The normalness was overwhelming.'

'How do you know it was a *normal* brain? What's normal, anyway? Like what society says is normal *is* normal? Being married, and straight, and white, with two children and one and a half incomes is normal, but anything which deviates from that isn't? No matter how miserable you are? Funny shade of normal.'

'You know that isn't what I said.'

Heather walks around a standing exhibit. His limbs are fixed mid-action, his eyeballs peeled like onions. 'When his face goes into shadow, you can see how he looked when he was alive. Like meeting him in a club or something.'

'Maybe he deserves his anonymity.'

'But is it what you want for yourself too? To be *normal* and disappear into the crowd?'

'Well, no, that's not what I – no.'

'Because I've got news for you if you think it is. It's too late for that.'

She frowns. 'Exactly how old do you think I am?'

His ribs are spread like claws. His penis is shrunken. His belly eviscerated with the surrounding layers scraped back like wallpaper, leaving a selection of organs. His veins and nerves are colourful fibres. His pulmonary arteries and bronchi are coral.

Heather takes a big inhale and says, 'It's not that you're too old for it, nowhere near; I'm saying it's too late for you, personally, to take the easy path. Precisely because of what you said. The rest of us, the vast majority, don't find blobby, crinkly gunk worth looking at, even if we knew how. When you held a brain for the first time and fell all in love with it – that was

252

the point of no return. Boom. It was over. You'd hate yourself if you did anything else. You can paint your walls beige if you like, have a tasteful wedding with perfectly balanced centre-pieces, and no stepchildren attached, and – hang on – you're seeing someone?'

She blushes. 'On what do you base your assumption?'

'You are! It explains a few things.'

Photography of the specimens is forbidden. The slanting spotlights, however, with the black backgrounds and glass containers: Heather can't help but reach.

Cara waits for her by a case of skulls.

'Stop working. Switch it off.'

She winces as she does so. 'It's so empty in here. Where is everybody?'

'Feeding the slots. Gambling. D'you want to learn how? I'm not into it, but I can teach you blackjack or craps. Baccarat as well, unfortunately.'

'I can honestly say it doesn't interest me.'

'I bet your boyfriend is nice? I can tell by how you're looking after yourself. There's less stress here compared with last time.' Heather mimes an eye mask. 'Still some, though. What's his name?'

Her tone is cooler. 'I don't have a boyfriend.'

'Fine, don't tell me. But I have contacts, I can find out whenever I like. I won't think you're being unfaithful if that's what you're worried about?'

They're next to a glass coffin with a female cadaver in slices.

Cara says, 'And what's going on in your life, romantically speaking, and professionally?'

'If you're not telling, I don't see why I should.'

'Okay, that's fair.'

'Maybe you should move your research over here? They'd go mad for you.'

'What a horrendous idea.'

'I'm serious. Within six months, you and Hels will learn more about people here than you ever did in *Cambridge*.'

'I'm not interested in people. I'm interested in brains.'

Heather laughs. 'Well, I think generally that people are under-rated. I like how they come and go, and what they tell you. And I like when they're ever so sure of themselves, but then they clearly aren't? It's sweet. Not always, there are plenty of arsehats too. I think it has something to do with behaving differently when they're on vacation. You see another side to them. Everything is new, and there aren't the same consequences here as there are at home and . . . Desire is constant. Doesn't matter what they've got, or how much of it. I watch them every day. Desire is so basic it's untrue.'

Cara makes a funny noise. 'Not Spinoza again.'

'What's Spinozart?'

'Some reading I did to keep up with – nobody. I'm sorry, please continue.'

'Only that enough is never enough. And it's crazy-making. Like when they're winning, for example, they get addicted to the thrill, because good luck comes in a big rush and they're swept along with it? When it goes badly, however, they chase their losses. Even though they *know* it's designed to be unfair, deep down – deeper than rational – they believe that they're going to win a fortune. That exceptional definitely applies to them. And they keep going until their money drains away. Then they get disillusioned, and then they *do* go home, don't they, and have to carry on. Unless they don't, which is worse. Have you ever seen a million dollars in cash? There's this place you can go

254

and have your picture taken with it. A pile of money right there in front of you – in a secure box, they don't let you touch it. I'll show you if you like.'

Cara smirks. 'But is a million dollars still worth a million dollars? Because if not, doesn't that defeat the object?'

Cara

'No horror, I'll be laughing the whole time. No nudity either, unless – no, nothing with nudity. No magicians.'

'What's wrong with magicians?'

'Everything. And no shows based on a hologram of a performer who has died. That's just a glorified PowerPoint.'

'You aren't leaving many options?'

'In fact, you can avoid the whole tribute act area completely.'

Heather goes over to a desk. Greets the staff as though they're friends of hers.

Cara hangs back, not only because she was asked to, but because Asbjørn is trying to call her.

'How is it?' His furry face fills the screen. 'Are you having too much fun already? Where are you?'

She looks around at a decadent lobby. 'Some casino or other. They merge into one.'

'Have you lost track so soon? What has she done to you?'

'No, you don't understand: they literally merge into one. They are joined up. You walk along thinking you're in one of these resorts, and before you realise it, it turns into another. They're interconnected.'

'Ahh. Like the colleges.'

'Not like colleges. You're as bad as she is. I've been tracking my steps, I've done ten thousand since we've been out. She's at the desk, trying to get us tickets for a show. I don't know if she's having much success.'

'May I see?'

Cara points the phone towards Heather, in conversation with a staff member in a navy suit. 'She might be too far away.'

He squints. 'Have you tried talking again?'

Cara shakes her head.

'You should.'

'It's not that straightforward.'

'But why not? You went there to be with her. She seems a pleasant, reasonable young woman who respects you. You are having a relaxed and friendly time. No work. No men, um, none I care to know about. Try. For your peace of mind. Then you can let it go and move on with your life.'

She says, 'How are you today?'

Asbjørn turns his phone to some cauliflower on a chopping board. 'I am making soup for dinner. These are the ingredients. This is the recipe. And this is the sweater I found for two pounds.' He holds it against himself. 'I was so happy, I paid three. Nothing else to report other than it is boring here without you. Did you talk about me?'

'Your name hasn't come up, I'm afraid.'

'Very well. Will you place a bet for me, please?'

'I won't. I'm not into gambling, and being here makes me like it even less.'

'Don't waste your chance. Especially if this trip is the only time. Enjoy the experience. Afterwards, I'll meet you at the airport.'

'That won't be necessary.'

'I will meet you there, it will be better for you; and if I think you're going to like this recipe, I'll make it again. I bought too many cauliflowers. I went on a spending spree.'

Cara decides against showing her purchases. She can't compete with cauliflower soup and a charity-shop jumper. 'I should go. Bye, Asbjørn.'

They click off.

'Perfect,' Heather says, coming back with a glossy leaflet. 'This is the best hypnotism show in town. Usually it's sold out. The reviews are stunning.'

'I said no magicians.'

'He's not a magician – he's a hypnotist. He had an original series, and he's an influencer. He has these celebrity clients who he helps to get over drugs – and their abandonment issues – stuff like that? He even helps them remember who they were in past lives. He's incredible. This is in your ballpark, I swear.'

Heather

Paradise sinks and the ground drops away. Walls obscure the view, then part gradually, like the lid of a slowly opening jewellery box.

Colossal casinos shrink to the size of stacking-boxes. Tower blocks and spires become building blocks and needles. Flashy landmarks, floodlit billboards and brutal multi-storey parking slide into a mosaic.

Up they go. In a bubble.

Seen from above, the city has texture.

Cara stays seated in the middle with her ankles crossed.

Heather stands on tiptoe, palm pressed against the glass. 'Did you feel sick at the start?'

'Your body detects motion which your eyes don't perceive. In nature, the only reason your senses receive contradictory inputs like that is due to toxicity: hence, motion sickness. Sapiens haven't evolved to ride on Ferris wheels.'

'I didn't say I felt sick. I asked you if you did. You can see your hotel from here. Your room is, hang on, two, four, six ... Roughly there.' She points as though on a wall chart.

Cara gathers her bags by her feet. Shields her face.

'I can't believe I haven't done this before? This is my first time too. Whoop, we're growing taller.' She turns three hundred and sixty degrees. Stares around at the blood-orange mountains and purpling valley as broad as the sky. 'Isn't it big?'

Tourists are having a party in the cabin next to theirs, complete with a bar and a kissing couple who are ignoring the view.

Cara ignores it too. She seems more interested in the wheel itself, as though calculating its dimensions or worrying about the tensile strength of its spokes. (Is tensile strength a thing?)

'You aren't afraid of heights?' Heather asks.

'I am not particularly fond of them.'

'I'm sorry. I didn't realise. It's perfectly safe, I'm fairly sure it is, and if you want to get rid of any vertigo, what better therapy is there than this – landscape? It's not scary, how can it be, it's sensational.'

'Vertigo isn't a fear of . . .' She mouths something. Takes her glasses off and examines them for smudges.

Heather remembers she's wearing Cara's sunglasses. Goes to the opposite end of the pod to take them off. Shoves them in her purse.

Liquid reds deepen. Cloud forms trail after a sinking doubloon.

'We should come up again when it's proper night-time, and in the middle of the day when you can see really, really far, and maybe – yes, at dawn, because it would be different too then, wouldn't it? The sun would be over there – or over here. There, I think. I've forgotten, is west on the left?'

Highways stretch for miles like gold chains lying in dirt. The swimming pools are semi-precious blue.

'My new place has a pool,' she says quietly.

'A pool? Gosh, that sounds great.'

'Don't be too impressed. It's shared. It's almost harder to rent an apartment without one here.'

'Even so, a pool. Will you show it to me?'

'Can't. Not ready. At the moment I'm still in digs.'

'Would you like me to check your lease agreement for you?'

'No thanks. I'm fine.' Heather leans into the sunset, her face burning. Pouts to keep from saying more.

'I have a little confession to make,' Cara says to the girders outside. 'I thought you'd find it too difficult living in uncertain circumstances. I had this idea before I saw you – completely irrational – that if you were desperate to stay, you might be tempted to do something stupid. A quick fix. I got myself worked up because I wouldn't be around to talk you out of it, and then you'd be truly stuck.'

'Like what? What did you think was so awful?'

'What I thought is, you might get married. As a strategy. I had this scenario playing out in my mind where you were introducing me to some ghoul as your husband, and I was acting like I wasn't shocked, and being polite to him. And you were living in his mother's basement, or a trailer, someplace grim, and I had to pretend to be okay with it. I feel ashamed. For some reason I really thought it was a possibility.'

'I wouldn't get married and not tell you. I won't. But even if I did, haven't you noticed I'm an adult?'

'It's because you are an adult that I was wondering.'

She thinks Cara could do with some mattifying powder, only Heather can't offer hers because it's a couple of shades too light. Says, 'I like Vegas in the in-between times when you glimpse her slightly unready. Most people don't notice. Suddenly it's evening, and she's in business mode and off to work again, all service, and showbiz, tits and teeth. They say such mean things about her, and she takes every insult with a smile. I never felt this way back home.'

261

'I see.'

'Do you? Don't you think there's something wrong with it?'

'Well, of course your city is different to mine. How could they possibly be alike?'

'Let's make a pact,' Heather says. 'Whatever else is going on, no matter what happens, even if we have a massive bust-up, if one of us is going to get married, we promise to invite the other to the wedding. Deal? And texting is allowed.'

'Ha.'

'Poor Cara, you look miserable over there? You should've said, I wouldn't have suggested it if I'd realised.'

'I'm okay with heights, usually. I just don't like being able to see under my feet. I need solid floor and for it not to be moving.'

Heather sits next to her and offers a bottle of water; Cara hesitates, then sips; Heather sips and offers it again; Cara shakes her head.

Heather says, 'Are you making a pact with me or not?'

'All right, I'm in.'

'Be careful, because you're way more likely to tie the knot before I do. You are, seriously, you're the one who wants to, and is in a relationship.'

'I'm not.'

'You're such a liar! Fine, I'll go along with it. But I cannot imagine getting married, not for any reason, not unless I go for one of those solo weddings and marry myself. Have you heard of them? They're amazing. You still have a party and a dress and a bouquet, the works, only the bride celebrates her independence and commits to being her own best friend and champion for ever.'

'How vain. I'll RSVP no to that.'

'I don't mind as long as you send a present.'

The mountain range is burnished. The horizon blazes amber. The desert recedes into dark. A zillion electric lights.

'Cara Mia, you're missing it. Please come and look with me?' She steers her towards the edge. Squeezes her clammy hand.

The party cabin with the kissing couple is above them.

They are descending.

'Over halfway. We shan't be long, a few minutes left. Take steady breaths and the queasiness will soon pass?'

'From a distance it seems, uh, prettier.'

Ochre, faded red and mercury. One or two stars starting to show like sequins—

Cara

—faintly on steel blue. The streets sprawl like crystals under a microscope in polarized light.

'What do you do?'

'I'm a virtual concierge. I freelance for a company that has contracts in several of the smaller hotels, and a few corporates who use us when they're in town for conventions. It's more like being a PA than a traditional concierge. Organising. Some local knowledge when online searches won't cut it. The money's okay, but it can get hectic, although it's seasonal of course. When demand dries up, that's frustrating; January is deader than dead. Client requests can vary dramatically. What shows are suitable for families? Where's the best sushi? Where can they print extra delegate packs? Discounts and recommendations, nothing fancy. It is twenty-four hour. Ice cream for thirty people isn't difficult, unless it's five o'clock in the morning, then you need to think on your feet. I meet loads of new people, which is interesting, and when I do well, they tip well. I welcome the client, provide a personalised service, and basically they go home feeling great.'

'Be ye followers of God, as dear children. Walk in love.' An evangelist with a loudhailer matches the dance music piped out of entrances. 'Fornication and all uncleanness, or covetous-ness, let it not once be named among you, as becometh saints. Neither foolish jesting – no dirty jokes, no locker-room talk – but give thanks.' He turns up the volume. 'For this ye know: no whoremonger, no unclean man, no covetous man hath any inheritance in the kingdom of Christ and of God. More bitter than death is the woman who traps you, whose heart is snares and nets. Her hands are chains. She will make you her slave. Walk as children of light, for it is shame even to speak of those things which are done in secret.'

Cara is sweating in unladylike places. Swaps her shopping to the other side. 'You can choose a poem or a song you like for the service?' she is saying to the back of Heather's head. 'You can write a letter and I'll read it out on your behalf?'

'Wait a minute, you said there wasn't going to be a funeral, but now you're saying there is?'

'A vigil – not a funeral – and it wasn't my idea.'

Heather halts, forcing other pedestrians to divide around them. 'OMG, Aunt Kathy? I bet she loves the drama.'

'I wasn't keen either, initially. Then I thought about how we could make it work for us.'

'On what planet . . . ?'

'It's publicity. A way to raise awareness about his case. We have the CCTV pictures and a location, more than we had to go on the day he left – and that's what we should be focusing on. I'll help you make it nice with music and tributes, it'll be exactly how you want it to be.'

'I want Aunt Kathy and Uncle Trev to stay out of my life.'

'I agree none of this is ideal, but there is an opportunity here, and I doubt there'll be a better one for – for – for finding answers. You might thank me later.'

'Thank you?'

Cara almost says, *You're welcome*, except Heather doesn't look the least bit grateful.

'You expected me to be a crying mess and beg you to take me back, you'd prefer it that way because it would confirm your, um ...' She sags on her hip. 'You're worse than they are for getting in the middle of things that're none of your business. I wish you'd stop this charade,' which she rhymes with *parade*. 'I'm fed up with clever people, and how selfish you are, and manipulative. I am not your project.'

'Why are you being spiteful?' Cara waves aside a handbiller slapping cards advertising hot girls delivered to your door.

'Dad's gone; you can't seriously think he isn't? There's *sceptical* and there's *denial*, even I know that.'

'Please reconsider? You would if it were Ruth.'

'I forbid you to say my mother's name.'

Finally, Cara understands. This is what she wanted to do in the piano bar, isn't it. Cause a scene. Well, Cara didn't allow it then, and she is not going to allow it now. 'Are you okay, H? Is there anything you want to tell me?'

'What are you asking me for? I should be asking you. I'm fine. Don't I seem fine to you? Isn't there some important science thing you're missing out on while you're bugging me with questions I have already answered?' Heather's voice is verging on shrill.

'Suppose you're right,' she replies, calmly scraping away a card stuck to the sole of her shoe. The ground is covered in erotic card litter. 'Then this becomes more of an acknowledgement, to give him his dignity, and I can help with that.'

'Yeah, aren't you lovely when somebody's died? Give Aunt Kathy whatever she wants, I don't care.'

'Right, I'll come up with . . . I'll make your wishes clear.'

Heather tilts her head. 'Did you enjoy the exhibition?'

'It was super.' She tries smiling. 'What a good suggestion of yours.'

'You know they might've been executed in prison camps?'

'What? Is that true?'

'Could be? It is conceivable perhaps that there were some human rights abuses along the way, is all I'm saying.'

'What are you telling me now for, when I can't do a thing about it? Why did you bring me if you knew?'

'Well, they might've donated their remains willingly, we can't be totally sure. What difference does it make? Killing and dissecting is part of your job.'

'The two couldn't be further apart. We have mechanisms in place, ethics, they give their consent first—'

'You don't ask the dogs and mice and monkeys for their consents. Do you? Have you ever?'

'I swear you misunderstand me on purpose.'

'Seriously, why are you here? Why are you still involved in this?'

'To keep my promise.'

'What promise, Cara?'

'You know perfectly well *what promise*. You waited for me to come back to the house so you could ambush me. You acted like you were about to have some kind of meltdown and, to be clear, you made me promise that if I heard news first, I had to tell you myself. I'm here because you insisted.'

'Great. Big of you. I'm utterly impressed.'

'I can't do anything right for the Wycliffes, can I? You made me promise. Don't you remember how you made me?'

'I also told you not to come here because you'd hate it, and I was right, because you do.'

'Forget it. I won't bother you again.' She turns on her heel and starts walking back in the direction they came from. Looks over her shoulder and says, 'It's too bloody bright. I can't remember my way back to the hotel.'

Heather points. 'That way. Keep walking in a straight line. Don't stop.'

While Cara is walking along the Strip, louder and lighter than day, she reassures herself that she has honoured her commitment. She kept her word to Heather, and can take her at hers without feeling too guilty about it. If there was a grey area for a while, it is no longer the case. Cara has tried her best. Has done what she set out to do. Hurrah. It's over.

Now there is nothing left to stop her eating a big plate of pasta, getting rotten drunk by herself and dropping twenty dollars on a bet so Asbjørn won't think she's square. Then she can go home with a clear conscience.

At last her life will be back on track.

More work. Better work.

Running further. Romance, as in more sex. The travelling she actually wants to do, once she's paid off this hoopla.

Maybe – yes, why not? – she *should* relocate, hang the consequences. Glenda is in robust health. Asbjørn didn't have plans to settle in the UK even before the hostile environment, it's something they could do together – or not – either/or. If Heather can muddle through in another country, then Cara certainly can.

Heather, bumbling along in the gig economy. Without status. Or purpose. Getting by on attitude. She isn't Cara's problem.

A message is forming in her mind to close the matter in writing, to the effect of I *wish you well*, short and sweet. Nothing that can be construed as *stay in touch*.

She slows down – she is practically powerwalking through the twitching beams of a lightshow. She passes a pirate ship. And the Lord of Misrule.

Is there an opposite to Stendhal syndrome where, having been exposed to such unrelenting tackiness, one becomes immune to it? Is that why, when a gondola appears to float a few feet above the ground, Dr Cara Mia Brenner is unmoved?

In fact, it floats in clear, shallow water. The visible hull and the shadow cast underneath create the impression of floating on air. Quickly dispelled.

Cara stands on a walkway with a white balustrade. She is looking up at a *sort-of bridge* and down to a *sort-of water's edge*. Touches her chin, as though they are worthy of analysis.

The enclosed bridge joins two wings of a casino and crosses a canal. Yet, not a canal. The 'canal' ends suddenly at a wall in front of her.

Pasted on the wall, under this arch, is a blown-up stock photo which shows what you might expect to see in the original setting.

[*Venetian waterway flowing past baroque residences*]

The colours are problematic. She is standing over chlorinated water, whereas the real waters must be murky green-brown. The image has been Photoshopped, and she can see where the air-brushing stopped – leaving grime on the palaces, eroded bricks, weathered cladding, and a layer of green slime along a brilliant turquoise waterline. Hints of authenticity left in by mistake.

Her brain crawls.

And there were reflections when the photograph was taken. Upside-down blurs, with eddies and ripples. These are reflected back, here, in real life, at incongruent angles in the sterile pool beneath her feet.

She steps back to better see the enclosed bridge, bolted on to the resort.

Movement within: there are people in there.

Which means it is a fake bridge. Being used as a bridge. And it resembles the bridge it is supposed to be. It is *being* the bridge.

She sighs.

She can't decide whether the angelic faces staring down at her are stone or Styrofoam? Neptunes recline in corners. It has crests of oligarchs, neoclassical pilasters, and two square windows. Above is Lady Justice with her sword and scale.

As Cara studies it, her thought process is interrupted by the tingle of being studied herself.

'What are you looking at?' Heather asks.

She shrugs. She has no idea. 'Are you hungry? Is there somewhere round here we could eat?'

'Oh, I never come to the Strip.'

'I thought we were on the Strip. Isn't that what it's called?'

Heather skips on the spot. 'Yes, but *I never come*. Except for work, and socialising, and wanting to, apart from those times . . . I've been waiting ages to say that to someone, it's what the locals say. They make me die.'

They arrive in Italy through a colonnade decorated with frescos and marble, smothered with gold leaf. It turns out the bel paese is a room-temperature village, with a flat cobble floor and scudding clouds painted on a vast ceiling. Venetian toy land.

The Doge's Palace, Ca' d'Oro and Torre dell'Orologio have been reproduced in miniature. Ornate arches are bunched together, your view strictly limited to their icing-sugar fronts. The Grand Canal is a water feature, with candy-cane mooring poles and gondolas squeezing through narrow lanes.

She can't fault the level of detail, except for the details they've left out.

There are no signs of decay, nor scaffolding to show restoration in progress. No cautiously preserved artworks in their original settings, no graffiti or irreverent street art.

Instead of a medieval labyrinth of bridges and passages, their way is clearly marked, lit by disproportionately large streetlamps.

Heather takes Cara to a restaurant in tiny Piazza San Marco where there are no pigeons and thus no pigeon poop, no resonant ring of bells, no pilgrims, no 'skip the line' line. No guided tours of historical landmarks. No louche students drinking Aperol spritz. No sparrows pecking crumbs under the tables. No Vespas buzzing by.

No breeze. No waves plashing on the promenade. No puddles to negotiate.

There's no aroma of salt, or drains, or sun-baked Istrian stone. No underlying dread that this City of Water will sink due to the climate crisis, centuries of culture washed away.

It's a back-up.

After Heather's margherita and Cara's seafood linguine, they agree they can't manage a whole dessert each and order a tiramisu with two spoons. Take turns eating from opposite sides of the plate.

'I stayed up to watch the debate.'

'Fun, we were watching at the same time. I wish I'd known, we could've texted. It took over the whole city, it was like a boxing match. Not what I'd call a debate, though. You know they don't like her?'

'Why not, too professional for them? Too experienced? Insufficiently orange?'

Heather scrunches up her face. 'His side told the best story. Doesn't matter in the end whether or not it's true.' She does a sarcastic wave.

Cara realises that she was staring into the distance. 'When it's this farfetched, where do we start? How can we undo it?'

'Have you learned any Italian then?'

'No, I'm too old. I couldn't become fluent.'

'That wasn't what you said before, and I believed you. You aren't too old for learning basic phrases.'

'I don't have time. I'm writing a book.'

'Yeah, you all say that.'

'But I really am. I do take your point, though.' Cara wipes her mouth with her napkin, and Heather copies her. 'It's popular science. The publisher is following a trend – it's not that they think what I do is important. I happen to know their first choice dropped out. The brief is rather vague, and my editor isn't much older than you are.'

Heather pushes a strand of red hair behind her ear so it won't fall in their dessert. 'Don't you worry it gets in the way of research?'

'It is worthwhile if one does it well. He – my publisher is a boy – auditioned me. They call it training, but ... he wants me to appear at festivals, be on podcasts to promote it, do interviews. I don't know, it sounds tiresome.'

'You're good at that stuff, aren't you? Isn't it more of what you do already?'

'Yes and no. Depends on what I'm supposed to be talking about. You see, there are two books, potentially, as I see it – sorry, I don't know why we're discussing this.'

'Like a sequel? I like sequels. I don't understand why people are snarky about them, and reboots, and alternative universes, if those are different? Betty posts which are the best ones so ...'

'I mean that there are two possible *approaches* I can take. One is the book they've asked me to write, a text for lay readers, and it's fairly straightforward, with chapters pretty much like public lectures. Which I can do. And it's a safe, sensible project, although there's a lot out there like it already. I'm not sure what I could add. Then there's another kind of book, which has a lot of the same content and yet is more . . .'

Heather looks as if she's going to say a word, then licks a spot of tiramisu from her lip.

'More of a book I'd want *you* to read. To show what I see, rather than explain what I know. You finish that.'

She scoops the last morsel. 'It's your book. Can't you write whatever you like?'

'Doing what I'm supposed to is the path of least resistance. I'm torn, though. He's not the brightest. He's given me a lot of leeway without meaning to, and it's not strictly within my – this is not the same as what I usually – it is a huge risk.' She blinks, as though to clear the colours from her sight. 'Also, why should I bother? Why should I share thoughts that I otherwise keep private? Why put myself through all the crap that comes with it?'

'Say what you want to say, the way you want to say it. And have fun.'

'That is,' it takes a moment to spot the flaw in Heather's argument, 'an oversimplification.'

'Okay then, take the cash. Who could blame you? Write a boring book, and then go back to the lab, which is where you feel most comfortable. But don't complain afterwards that you've missed your chance to do something different. There're plenty of writers out there who are desperate to tell what they know – and how it makes them feel. Be taken seriously, because the world hasn't been kind enough to listen to them. They ache to.' Heather empties her glass, turns it by the stem. 'Somebody should? The rest of us need it too, by the way. To be let in.'

'Since when do you know all this?'

'I just know things.'

Conversations subside the closer a gondolier gets to the high note of 'Nessun Dorma'. He almost reaches it.

Heather says, 'People tell me things anyway, feel like they can.'

'You're approachable. It's a great skill to have, especially in your line of work.'

'It must be lovely to be clever,' she murmurs, 'be treated like an equal by other clever people ...'

Cara tries not to scoff.

'Solving problems I don't even have the brainpower to understand what they are? I'm too stupid. Don't argue. I am. My body is more intelligent than me.'

How can Cara explain that her calendar is full of admin tasks, and urgent projects not of her choosing? That she's at the mercy of deadlines, and budgets, and a never-ending mass of emails. That one setback could effectively end her career. That the students she's supposed to set on a path to greatness are a constant source of worry to her. And yes, she does a lot, but at the same time has done so little it frightens her.

'Maybe I'm jealous? I didn't think it was in my nature. I am jealous of you, Cara.'

'What can you possibly be jealous of me for?'

'You and Helen have a purpose together. You share an energy.'

'Not necessarily. Just because we align now doesn't mean we will in the future. Heaven knows, we didn't in the past. She'd drop me if it suited her career; that is how it works, I'm afraid. Here, I've been hogging this.' Cara shares what's left of the bottle, giving Heather the most. '*In vino veritas.*'

'Wouldn't you be upset? Especially if she had grown tired of you – suddenly, you weren't interesting enough?'

274

'What choice would I have? You can't force people to stay. Or go before they're ready. They make up their own minds, you taught me that.'

She gapes. 'But you have an understanding – there's a part of you you can only share with each other, not with your families, not me, not some man ... Why do friendships have a way of hurting us?'

'They do sometimes, I'm afraid.' Cara swipes and taps [crescent moon]. 'They have a temperature. It doesn't make them less than they are: it makes them real. Your friends can let you down, make decisions you disagree with, exclude you on purpose. And you can't help comparing yourself to them, for better or worse. It's rough. The alternative is not having them in our lives.'

Heather narrows her eyes. 'I really didn't want you to come. I tried telling you – I *did* tell you. And I want you to know I'm annoyed that you didn't let me get on with it in my own way. But since you are here, and I wasn't able to get rid of you, I admit this is not totally horrible.'

'I appreciate your feedback. While we are on the subject, it is ludicrous to think you saved my life today. Please stop behaving as if you did.'

'You're welcome. You'd do the same for me.' Heather empties her glass. 'I'm a lightweight these days. I'll read your book too, or maybe the first chapter, to get the gist. I'll order a copy and you can sign it for me.'

'Save your money, I'll send you a copy. I'm going to get trolled, aren't I?'

'For being clever, and a woman, and putting your voice in the world all at the same time? For sure. They can't help themselves, they're very emotional. Mustn't it be wretched being a man?' She checks the time on an eighties-style digital watch.

Cara checks her activity tracker. 'No wonder I'm flagging. I won't keep you any longer. Thank you for being my guide today, I can see you're a capable concierge.'

'Hey, you can't go to bed yet, we haven't done the best bit?' She mimes for the check. 'The hypnotist show, remember?'

Cara thinks, Isn't there a way we can give him a miss?

Heather

On the fourth attempt, the room keycard bleeps, and Cara staggers across the threshold. 'I retract my previous statement,' she says. 'You were right, and I was wrong. I'm in love with gambling.'

'How much were you ahead in the end?'

'Two hundred and seventy of your Earth dollars. I'm finished with science and turning pro.'

Heather locks the door after them. Should she remind her that it costs more to spend a single night here?

'Not only blackjack. I reckon I'm going to be great at other card games as well, as soon as I learn how to play them.' She drops her winnings on the nightstand, fumbles with the combination of light switches.

'Leave them off. I waited all evening to do this.' Heather opens the automatic drape as wide as it'll go. The window turns into a triptych of black glass.

Neon night.

Illuminated hoardings. Megastructures, including the tip of the wheel. Moving beads of traffic. Hotel windows repeat like tiles.

Cara looks at the view too. 'Urgh, it's a giant vanitas.'

'Don't listen to her,' Heather whispers, and blows the city a kiss.

'You're welcome to stay if you like.'

'Thanks, I think I will. I like hotel rooms. I'd sleep in a different one every night if I could. I bet there are more hotel rooms on the Strip than nights I have left to live.'

'How cheery. You can leave the curtains open as you seem to have a thing about it.'

'I bought you a present.'

'You didn't have to.'

'Don't get excited, it's only silly.' She rustles tissue paper.

Cara opens her hand to receive it, and sighs. 'A Las Vegas snow globe.'

'Yep. See, it has the Stratosphere, and the Statue of Liberty, the hot air balloon, Egypt, Camelot, the Magnificent – they're all in there – and out there. And look, there's playing cards along the base to remind you of the night you broke the bank. Put it somewhere you can see it every day.'

'How droll. It doesn't even snow here.'

'Occasionally,' Heather says. 'Maybe once a year there's snow on the ground.'

'What are you talking about? It's the desert. How can it possibly?'

'They have snow. I don't know how it's made, it just does?'

'You mean fake snow like at a ski resort? They do it at Christmastime for tourists?'

'No, actual snow falls out of the sky and settles on the palm trees. When there's enough for a snowman, they show it on local news. You're not doing it right.' Heather takes it out of her hand, gives it a shake, then gives it back.

Cara looks into the globe like a fortune teller. A blizzard

of glitter obscures the tiny city, then disappears, but for a few sparkly flakes. 'Post-post-truth. What a beautiful thought.'

Heather giggles. 'It's a piece of trash, even I can see that. Don't keep it if you don't want to. I'll put it in my new apartment.'

'No. I like it. I'm wrapping it up to protect it. Where's the box it came in, I'll carry it in my hand luggage. *Tak.*' She doesn't manage to repack it neatly.

Heather stays by the window curled in a chair. Unhooks her earrings.

Cara discards her clothes and crawls into bed, plumping a pillow. 'You look like an Edward Hopper over there.'

'Who's he?'

'He was an American painter. You'd recognise his work if you saw it. He shows – what's the word? – separateness, I think. Do you want to borrow a T-shirt to sleep in?'

She hums no. 'I feel separate sometimes, as if I'm not totally myself? When you work in hospitality, you need to keep the real you out of it. You pretend to be a thing for someone else for a while. Creating this image.'

'Please, we all do that. Inevitably, we take on a role. It is the fundamental difference between work and private life.'

'I thought you loved your work?'

'I do. I'm also aware that some element of theatre is involved.' She adds quietly, 'I walked on the grass once when no one was looking.'

'Rebel.' Heather watches the restless illuminations: compares them with the lurid glow they make behind her eyelids. 'I have these different sides to me, and I never show my sides all at once? Makes me feel like I'm deceitful. Whoever I'm with, I hold so much of myself back. Being real is more of a – dare?'

Cara yawns. 'Assuming you exist, and the self is not an illusion.'

'Whoa, how much did you drink?'

'Same as you.'

'I switched to sparkling water hours ago.'

'I didn't notice. The weird feeling, frankly, it never goes away, not even when you get to my age. Would you like to borrow my toothbrush?'

'I brought mine.'

'You came prepared. What else have you got in that gorgeous bag of yours? A house plant?'

Heather checks that it's zipped closed.

Cara groans. 'Dr Stewart is such a smarty-pants. I'm not a purist – not in the bad sense. I just like doing things right. Haven't women made important discoveries before me? Aren't my opportunities better than theirs? Because that's what it says on the tin ... I had a boyfriend when I was an undergrad, my first serious boyfriend, he had big teeth and a private education. A chemist. He had this bearing and, I don't know, a way of getting by that I couldn't put my finger on. I'd be doing extra hours in the lab and the library, and I had a part-time job of course, so I wasn't always available when he wanted to see me. Then he'd call me a workhorse – and I'd cave. I wanted it to look effortless.'

'Sounds exhausting. What was your job?'

'I worked in a greasy spoon. It wasn't too bad. They'd give me free meals.' Cara's eyes are wide open. She is watching the city too. 'Did you know I wanted to be a surgeon when I was little? I used to perform operations on my dolls with kitchen utensils. The tongs were for taking out an appendix. The tin opener was for a lobotomy.'

'Why weren't you?'

'Bob was fine with the idea; he'd circle *Casualty* in the TV guide for me. Glenda found it hilarious. I stopped talking about it.'

'She was probably right,' Heather says. 'Your sewing is atrocious.'

'They teach you to sew at medical school.'

'Not you. When you sewed on my swimming badges, I told people Dad did it.'

Cara yawns louder. '*It's nice to be important, but it's more important to be nice,* no Cambridge man has ever been told in his life. *Stop showing off* was the other thing she used to say, like when I scored full marks in a test. I hope I never said it to you.'

'Since I never scored full marks in anything, no, that would be amazing.'

'I promised myself whatever you ended up doing, however strange it sounded or wrong it went, that I was going to support you. At least, I'd make supportive noises at first, and figure it out later.' She laughs softly.

Heather scrolls through her photos from today and yesterday. 'Is that why you were asking about my passion every five minutes?'

'Us girls shouldn't miss out.'

'I still don't know. I might never know. Why can't I just live a nice life, hang out, and feel good about myself more often than I don't – and want for the planet not to be burning up and the seas not to be choked with plastics? Isn't that enough?' Her thumb is itchy. 'A passion is just another expectation. Telling a person she's a failure because she doesn't have it figured out is as bad as telling her she's fat. You have no idea what's going on with her, and criticising makes it worse.'

Cara doesn't reply.

Heather says, 'I hope you broke up with that guy before he broke up with you. He sounds typical.'

'I did.'

'What was his name?'

'Dominic.' She pauses. 'He's still around. He's a tenured professor, not at Cambridge, thankfully. I feel an email coming on.'

'Don't, Cara. It's never a good idea.'

'Not *him*. I was thinking we could try some simulated blackjack in a scanner. Then I could see their mesolimbic pathway active with their mental calculation subregions . . . Dr Stewart will know what I mean.' She pokes her phone in the dimness. 'Must you work tomorrow? I've got time for breakfast before I go.' She flumps back on the pillow. 'The ceiling is spinning.'

'I remember people used to think Mum was drunk, and she let them. She preferred to be thought of as a party girl rather than admit that her illness was catching up with her. Would you want to know if you were me?'

Cara breathes heavily. 'It is terrible knowledge.' Eventually she says, 'Yes, if there was a chance of my getting pregnant. I wouldn't risk passing it on.'

'You think Mum was selfish for having me?'

'I didn't say that.'

'But wasn't there meant to be a cure by now?' Heather waits for her to answer, and when Cara doesn't, she tuts. 'How would you know? You're not a real doctor, are you?'

'I read medical journals. And there might be some good news in the pipeline about alleviating symptoms which will improve quality of life for – for people, hopefully.' She raises her head. 'I thought you talked this through with Paul?'

'Of course I did, I just want you to remind me, that's all – and I can change my mind if I like, is that okay with you?'

'It's your body.'

Heather deletes a photo. 'You should've been the one who discussed it with me. You knew he was no good at that stuff. She wasn't a mutant.'

Cara snores quietly.

Heather puts a glass of water next to her, hangs up their clothes. Lies by her side, saying, 'I'm going to sleep in the same bed as you instead of the couch. Please tell me if it isn't all right?'

She rouses. 'I'm the partner Paul ran away from, what a dreadful woman I must be. Poor you, are you going to throw up?'

Heather tries saying she'll be fine, and is busy tomorrow, let's stick to the plan. Feels herself sink past the edge of sleep.

To the true place where you sweep clutter away.

Except Cara's voice is pulling her out, she won't shut up—

[*Threads and flashes turn into umbrellas floating down from the sky*]

'—she slayed the storybook villains and banished the nightmares. I loved that part. I don't cry at TV very often, but they took me by surprise. I was tearful.'

'We both were,' Heather replies automatically. 'Wait, what are we talking about? I lost track? I could see them for a moment. The figures in the sky? And Voldemort, Cruella and the Child Catcher. She beat them all, no drama.' She touches her cheek to Cara's shoulder. 'Did we drink real champagne? You said it was a special occasion and I was allowed.'

'Yes, we got tipsy that evening. Can you remember the lines they used at the start of the ceremony, *Be not afeared; the isle is full of noises . . .?*'

'*That give delight and hurt not.* Sorry, I don't know the rest.'

'Our country was the magical island for a while. Brunel was

283

the sorcerer because he made everything appear.' Cara exhales. 'At his urging, all was spectacular.'

'Hmm, I remember the sheep, and the metal workers, James Bond and the Queen. Suffragettes. The "Heroes" song playing. I remember talking about it days later with total strangers. We were tricked, though. The words belong to a slave who has dreams like us. How do they go again?'

She feels Cara reaching for her phone.

Heather is too sleepy to listen.

Cara

What she sees in half-light is Heather, half-dressed, taking a photo. From the way she is standing, it must be a selfie.

'None of this is in Las Vegas,' she is saying. Gestures to the Strip like a magician's assistant. 'Neither are we. We're outside city limits.'

I'm dreaming, Cara thinks.

'What happens in Vegas happens everywhere else eventually.'

That isn't how the saying goes.

She wakes: sunshine blaring in.

Rubs her head and berates herself for the morning-after cliché. Remembers she is supposed to be going to the airport and panics that she has overslept.

Dear Dr Brenner,

I am delighted that you are enjoying a winning streak and I admire your ability to count to 21 like a gangster. Unfortunately this email baffles me. I take it you intended to copy in the entire department?

Kind regards,

Dr Helen J. Stewart

Cara rereads the message which she sent with oodles of confidence last night – and which makes her cringe this morning.

Damn.

Will she follow it with an *oops-silly-me* apology? Or is that drawing attention to her mistake? There are no other replies. Even her drunk emails aren't worthy of comment.

And why did Heather leave without saying goodbye?

Cara stabs out a text.

She replies at once. *wtf I said bye and you said bye to me to [confused face]* Before Cara can query this, she replies again. *Wait [green face]?*

[laughing face] [laughing face] [wink]

She drinks handfuls of tap water, spits in the sink.

Right on all counts. Coffee will set me straight! I will let you know when I get home. Yesterday was fab. Let's do it again soon? Hugs. C Xxx

She looks like one of the bodies from the exhibit, plastinated and not entirely dead. Turns her washbag upside down for the paracetamol—

Its contents clatter with unspeakable loudness.

Heather doesn't reply.

And she doesn't reply.

And doesn't reply.

Cara swells the glitter in the globe. Underneath it says *Made in China*.

6

ipRGCs
Intrinsically Photosensitive
Retinal Ganglion Cells

*sleep/wake cycle and
pupillary light reflex*

Heather

A fleck in a jar. Her body is alive with cold. Submerged, she scissor-kicks down, eyes open in a blue haze, the taste of chlorine on her tongue, menthol pinpricks on her arms. Sounds are muffled, as though pillows are pressed against her ears, yet she can hear glugging like a bottle of water poured in the next room. Loose. Strokes along the bottom touching the tiles. She is making rings and stars.

Her lungs squeeze with the urge to expel breath. Swims harder, blowing bubbles in a string. Swims as if she's chasing a record, the first length underwater, the fastest and the best.

Slaps the side and surfaces, white sun blinding her. The pool is a Jackson Pollock of splashes and splinters of light. She turns, sinks under to pull back her hair, then kicks off before she catches her breath.

Heather swims on till her face is hot and she's dreamy with exhaustion. Then rests at the edge as if washed up by the tide. Her hair dries unevenly as she listens to the burr of cicadas. Her fingers are wrinkled, and the water-resistant sunblock has all but washed off.

The shared pool is an oblong with grey benches and shabby dwarf palms. It was probably an afterthought, to get extra value out of the square footage, and is underused, which is fine by her.

Starts the timer on her digital watch. Pushes off.

Once you're in the water, it doesn't matter how scruffy the pool looks above, or how clumsy you are. Even with eyes open, it's runny and blurred. Her concentration is on her strokes, on banging the heel of her hand on the ledge and turning to do another length. On counting harder. Face down she follows the tile line along the bottom, dot dot dot . . .

A hotel corridor with ellipses of rooms repeating on either side and a vanishing point further ahead than she can see. She keeps going straight, sticking to the middle of the swirly carpet pattern, tracking the numbers on doors like an odometer. Heart rate increased. Scanning for security. Takes corners with conviction. Memorises the route she came in by and her choice of exits.

Checks her digital watch. Pushes on.

Clare Pembroke is punctual. Wears a smart jacket and heels. Uses Britishisms. Is white – whether she approves or not, it makes a difference here when you're trying to move around unchallenged. Several currencies are accepted.

Clare drinks fizzy water. A spritzer in a pinch, saying it has the least calories.

Acts natural.

This is work: being groomed, smiley and organised. This is work: making a strict screening process seem easy at the other end, and fixing a price before she gives anything away. Showing up looking gorgeous and bland. Unflappable AF. This is work.

Her bicep bulges carrying her handbag in the crook of her arm as though it weren't a toolbox. The contents include, oh wow, tons: phones, condoms, lingerie, wipes, biodegradable body glitter, black ribbon that only she is allowed to tie, a dinky toothbrush, a frisbee (how did that get in there?), massage oil, lube, pepper spray in a legal quantity allowed by state law, and a banana. Everything she needs, she has on her person. And this book she just started—

Clare began reading between appointments when she realised how much waiting around was involved. Guests in the resorts don't bring many books with them, not unless you count the ones about gambling systems, and she does not. There is no Heffers, of course, but Amber Unicorn is pretty cool and so is The Writer's Block. She never tires of self-help. (Loves *Grit*. Loves *Quiet*. Loves *Bounce*.) Is interested also in economics, American history and the occult. Plus, it's on brand.

Clare is discreet about peccadillos and tragedies alike. Clare charges by the hour with a two-hour minimum. Clare's mental map of the Valley grows more detailed with each passing week. This is Clare Pembroke: a work in progress.

A man. Give him a face, an age, an accent. Give him height, weight and skin colour. Give him her Ts & Cs, and then hope he sticks to them.

Mike.

This is Michael-Is-My-Father-Just-Mike from Massachusetts. Side-parting, preppy pants, polo shirt.

'Our generation hasn't bought an album in our entire lives,' he says, 'and streaming has failure baked in. Musicians with an iota of talent have but a single goal these days: video games. Video game music is rich. It's lustrous. Gamers are connoisseurs. They don't tolerate inferior product. They've got a multitude of platforms to tell you what they hate, and why, and what should be better. They demand high quality, and I respect them for that. Big production in the ears is what they're accustomed to, an immersive experience, and the industry has evolved to deliver. Game music way surpasses film scores as the standard modern composers should strive for. And you can forget about the classics, nobody is listening. Let me tell you this: Beethoven is dead.'

They've agreed a fee, and still he tries for a discount.

She smacks his hand away, showing him she's prepared to walk out.

He laughs it off. Mike is an honourable man and wants Clare to enjoy herself. Can he offer her anything to help her relax?

'Thanks, but no thanks, I'm on a detox.'

Soon it becomes obvious that Mike hasn't had much experience with real women. He's fast and verbal. His refrain is, 'You like that,' which he repeats until it's noise.

She does her best not to disabuse him. Keeps an eye on the clock, which he'll try to run over. Although they are a similar age, the Mikes of this world make Clare feel old. He's acting out what he's watched online, and when he gets to the end of his checklist, gives himself a whoop.

Clare spares a thought for the girl who is going to marry him someday. Saving herself for this.

Afterwards, Mike checks his phone before putting his pants back on.

Joseph.

They meet in a bar of his choosing. Joe from Wyoming welcomes Clare with carnations and a pink greetings card, with a gift inside.

'How thoughtful,' she says, throwing her arms around his thick neck.

He holds her as if it's a reunion, not a first encounter.

In addition to a significant height and weight advantage, Joe has a ponytail, wristbands and plaid. He offers her beer, rethinks, then offers champagne.

Clare says she'll take fizzy water, thanks.

'I've been researching tells,' he says, 'from the animal king-dom. Ever heard of thanatosis?'

'Sounds interesting, but I don't know what it is.'

'You do: it's playing dead. It happens all the time at the table. Instinctively, we know the way to avoid drawing attention to ourselves is to be passive, right? Our bodies have the knowledge deep in our respiratory system, in the instincts given to us by Mother Nature. Being inconspicuous is how we survive; ergo, when a player has a weak hand, he freezes like a possum.' Joe does an impression and Clare giggles. 'I'm kidding – not really. Not collapsed unconscious in his chair. It's subtle. If a player goes deathly silent, if he fakes ease, if he is nonchalant to the point he stops breathing, *then he's bluffing.'*

'Can the opposite be true, though? Could playing dead suggest a strong hand to draw you in? Do predators do it too? Does it work?'

Joe drinks. 'Darling, I lost a lot of chips tonight.'

'As long as you enjoyed yourself, that's the main thing.'

'Right again. That's exactly what Beverly says. She says it's only money, and you can't take it with you. Spend it while you can, and hang the kids' inheritance.'

'Is Beverly on vacation with you?'

'No, back home. She can't leave the house much.'

'I'm sorry to hear that. I hope she feels better soon. Have you got a picture of her? I'd love to see . . .? Gosh, she's pretty.'

'She knows I'm a poker player, knows all about that. As long as I stick to my limit, which I mostly do.'

Clare squeezes his knee. 'Your luck will change.'

'You're an angel. You could be on television. You should take an acting class and find yourself an agent who'll turn you into a star. How did you end up doing this?'

Her mind flits to the dollar bills in the unbirthday card. 'It just kind of happened as a side thing. It suits my lifestyle, while I decide what to do next with my career, and I love spending an evening in elegant surroundings, with good company. I love being spoiled and having fun. I'm enjoying myself before I have to settle down and be a proper grown-up.' She sticks out her bottom lip comically.

'You remind me of what Beverly used to be like before she got sick.' He finishes his beer and says, you'll never guess what, he was bumped up to a honeymoon suite for free, and it has a giant heart-shaped headboard.

Afterwards, Joe talks about his daughter who lives in Portugal and the grandbaby he Skypes with but hasn't met in real life.

Leyland.

Leyland, originally from Iowa, starts by apologising in his first message. *I'm not much to look at. I have an ostomy pouch. Other ladies have turned me down.*

Clare's reply is standard. *If you have good manners, stick to our agreed times and have freshly showered, then I really do believe we'll have an awesome date!*

Leyland has a shaved head, a cold handshake, and his breath is minty and sour when he pecks her cheek.

'Excuse the mess,' he says of the studio apartment, 'it's only temporary.'

'Why did you move this far?'

'To escape the humidity. I took early retirement.'

Bottles of meds are lined up, and she asks permission for a closer look. 'What was your job?'

'I ran a boarding kennel and doggy day care. Dogs all over the place, different breeds and sizes. A nursery for them to play in, a big meadow for chases, and luxury dens for VIDs – very important dogs – which they all were because each pet has a unique character. Dogs deserve love and respect. They let you know how they feel. Every day at work was fun.'

'I like fish. You can't tell what they're thinking.'

Leyland's expression falls. 'I'm not fond of fish. They don't live for very long.'

She warms his muscles, encourages his blood to flow, asks if there's anything he likes?

He whispers, 'Surprise me.'

Balls, she thinks. It probably means there is something he's after and can't bring himself to say out loud. She says she'd prefer it if he could be specific, please. What did he imagine before she came over? She won't be shocked, and any difficulties they'll work though.

He clams up. And if Clare isn't confident enough for them both, he'll start apportioning blame.

Afterwards, Leyland has cramp and needs help getting to the bathroom.

Although he's local, she doubts Leyland is going to book her again, which is a shame because Clare could do with some regulars for the quiet season.

She turns to Scarlett Days for advice.

Scarlett tells her she's a fool for offering GFE in the first place. Wasted energy. Too messy. The tip never reflects the amount of work you put in. Scarlett has a menu for precisely this reason: because she isn't a mind reader. And hasn't she said a bajillion times that managing expectations is part of the skillset? 'But don't kick yourself too hard for losing out on steady money,' she says. 'What a shame you can't go back to vanilla work, it's clearly what you're suited for. Is this how everybody does it in England?'

Clare huffs because she is kicking herself a bit.

Okay, fine, what does Clare want to learn? How to tickle him with feathers? How to drip candle wax safely? What to do if he barks like a dog? You know, that's probably what the whole kennels speech was about, only she didn't pick up on it.

Clare baulks. 'Is that what that was?'

Scarlett shrugs, now they'll never know. 'Remember, full service is still a performance: build your fourth wall high.'

Clare Pembroke has a sense of humour. She laughs at his jokes, but stops short of coming up with her own.

She is intellectual enough to appreciate his intelligence, but not to an extent that would challenge him.

She is a great listener. Anything he's got to share deserves her close attention. She lets him talk at his own speed about family, careers, sports, land, collecting, start-ups, politics, investments, health, betrayal, lawsuits, the good old days and what might've been. She listens for the sting.

Yep, there it is. She gets it.

'You weren't to know, how could you possibly have known?' or, 'But you weren't really lying, you were trying to stay positive,' or, 'You spoke truth to power, most people haven't got the guts for that,' or, 'No one will ever understand how much you've done to protect your family,' or, 'Credit where credit's due, it isn't about the money,' or, 'Have you got a picture of your cabin/wife/band? I'd love to see.'

Clare Pembroke's diary was empty until their date began. She has been looking forward to this all day and is delighted by the choice of venue. Says she would have chosen the same herself, it is definitely worth travelling a bit further for. (It's not as if it's a three-day weekend and she squeezed in extra bookings and had to dash across town to get here on time.)

Clare Pembroke doesn't have bills or rent. She has *expenses*. And these are mainly fashion, candy and perfume.

Clare Pembroke is always sober. She doesn't get silly. Interestingly, she doesn't get periods, either.

Clare Pembroke is a natural blonde, she'll swear to that.

Clare Pembroke exists in the present. No baggage. Isn't complicated. She won't ask him to drive her to the clinic or help her unblock a sink – not so much as open a jar.

The vigilance every woman feels alone with a man she doesn't trust, Clare feels.

She provides a service *with boundaries*. If he follows the rules, she will feign enthusiasm. And when a transaction is complete, she thanks the client and walks away. Never to bother him again.

Limited access to the outside is what he's paying for. Access to her real name and inner life isn't.

Clare steps onto a travellator – changes from heels to flats, switches her phones back on, eats a banana – before stepping off the end.

Mike, Joseph, Leyland, dot dot dot . . .

She slams her palm to mark the last length and stops the timer. Rests at the side, limbs prickly, sunlight peeling off the moving water.

She hears a shrill *woot-a-lee* from nearby, then an embarrassed *tak*, and a more abrasive *woot-a-lee*.

Woot-a-lee. Tak. Woot-a-leee.

It's a black bird on a branch. Vermillion shoulder pads fluffing up on black wings.

She lifts herself out. Towel dries in the shade and eats a banana. Her body thanks her.

It takes Heather a few seconds to remember that this is a walk-in closet which now has an air mattress in it, and is the second bedroom in a ground-floor one-bed apartment.

She gets up precariously, wondering if she'll puncture it by standing. Extracts her orange bathing suit from the shelf and a sunhat for the walk.

She still has the LV, and honestly intended to return it sooner. Sits cross-legged while transferring the contents to a satchel from Target. Gives the empty purse a pat of thanks.

'Come out with your hands up. Or I'm coming in. And you'll be sorry. Bughole.'

She raises her hands. Peeks out at the miniature cop with a plastic badge on his pyjamas and a police hat that doesn't contain his black curls.

He shoots her. *Pop.* 'Heh, you're dead.'

'You aren't supposed to do that when I'm surrendering?'

Connor shoots again.

She puts her hands on her hips. 'I have a no-guns rule in this house, including toy ones. You can't play with that in here.'

'Oh, but he's cute,' Tess says. She's in sweatpants and a kitty-cat robe, scrunches him close. 'D'you want some breakfast? It's Cheerios?'

Connor takes his cereal to a bankers box for a kids' table, along with a handheld game making electronic blasts.

'Did you sleep okay?' Heather asks Tess.

'If only. *Her candle goeth not out by night.* I'm working on it, it's one of my areas of improvement if I am to maximise my potential. I was thinking it over, though, and I decided we're the ones who should be on the airbed. I didn't mean to kick you out.'

'Please, you two stay in the bedroom, I want you to.'

'That's nice of you.'

Yesterday the living area was almost bare except for a goddess wall-hanging and a thrift-store rug, the Billy bookcase that leans, and breakfast bar stools from a used casino furniture sale, which probably saw action as regular bar stools.

Today, Tess's cases, her storage bags, her tech, her shoe collection and Connor's cartoony toy boxes are piled up by the wall, across the floor and spilling out onto a tiny strip of patio.

'I'll get more organised when he's at school and I can do it right. I can't stand chaos either, I'm really, really neat. We won't stay long, I promise you. The moment I've found a place, we'll be right out of your hair. A week or two. And if you want us gone any sooner, no matter the reason, just say the word and don't worry about hurting my feelings. You shouldn't have gone to so much trouble making room for us. By all means put your TV back where it belongs.'

'I haven't got a TV.'

'Oh dear, were you robbed?' Tess unwraps and rinses crystal goblets. Takes Heather's hodgepodge tumblers out the cupboard and replaces them. 'I'm putting these away because they're fragile. Whenever he eats sugar, he is as excitable as a Labrador.'

The music gets doomier as Connor tries to level up.

Heather says quietly, 'Doesn't it worry you when he plays like that?'

'He's a kid – kids play video games. I agree with you, though, it's too loud for this early in the morning. Connor, please? We are trying to have a grown-up conversation.' She points to her ears.

Without hesitating, he pauses the game, plugs headphones in and carries on.

Heather frowns.

'Wait a minute, you meant earlier, when he was shooting at you? You have a guns phobia. I totally respect your point of view, and we're your guests. I'll talk to him and make the rules clear. He shouldn't have disturbed you when your door was closed; I swear I taught him better than that. I have several things to go in storage, and he won't miss a few toys for a while. It can be his contribution to make our shared space more homely.' She nods and nods.

'Tessie, a cop costume? I'd be . . . I don't know.'

'You think a brown kid can't be a law enforcement officer? That's pretty vile of you.' She pulls her laptop open. Types swiftly. Clicks a test site. 'Let me see what kind of bandwidth you've got . . .? Oh well. Yet another issue that could turn into a problem if we allow it to, but we won't, right? Like not fighting on our first day. Anyway, when I cut his hair he passes for white.'

Heather steps away. She returns Tess's Louis Vuitton handbag, mumbling her thanks for the loan.

'You're welcome. Hehe.'

'What?' She looks down.

'Are you really going for a swim in that freezing pee pool? I couldn't. You are insane.'

Heather slings a towel over her shoulder, regretting she wasn't out there sooner.

Tess hasn't moved an inch when she gets back, still typing away. Connor is on the patio, rolling backwards and forwards on a kick scooter.

'Hey, how was the water? Refreshing? You're glowing from your workout.'

'I can't remember whether I told you this.' Heather says, combing back her wet hair. 'I'm a concierge?'

'You did. And FYI, I work at an old folks' home, Scarlett is a sweet old lady I nurse for and take to play slots. She is extremely good at it! Not that he'd even know what a bordello was.'

'All right then.'

'Great. See, we can make this work. We just need to feel out

300

the kinks. Be sensitive to the other person's needs. Have some coffee to go with your banana?'

She accepts a giant cup of a better brand than she'd normally buy. Rests on the towel to avoid getting the seat damp.

'Thank you for looking after it,' Tess says of the purse, which is still next to her. 'Not a single mark. I hope it did the trick? You should get one for yourself, they're handy. Was it for a date, may I ask? A civilian date? I can set you up if you're interested. Nice guys – not ex-clients, I wouldn't do that. Come to think of it, I could be a full-time matchmaker if I wanted to? I've done it for friends and had a lot of success. I even considered setting up my own agency. This could be a perfect time? People are tired of letting algorithms decide who they should fall in love with. And I'm good at it. When I meet someone new, I'm able to see past their flaws to their inner beauty. I always ask myself, how can I be of service to this person? How can I enlarge her happiness?'

'I'm not interested in men.'

'Sometimes I can't tell when you're joking. You're odd.'

'Why am I?'

'Because you have no centre. You make me feel as if you're not really here. What else do you do in your spare time, other than swim in the cold and take photos on your phone? And get high, which I hope you already know I cannot permit you to do in front of my son. You're an intelligent, vibrant young woman. What kind of life is that? I'm not judging. Merely making an observation that you have more to give. You need to believe in yourself.'

'I do.'

'Do you really? Don't you want to build a home, start a family, put down roots? Do well? Give back to your community?'

'I have you guys,' Heather says with her mouth full.

'Yeah, you're part of our story now, mine and Connor's. Do you believe in God and the kingdom of heaven?'

'Nope.'

'How can you be sure? Don't you believe in an afterlife at all – that your soul lives on?'

She touches her necklace. 'If there is an afterlife, Mum went ahead to it and didn't look back. I think she would've found a way if it were possible. So that's what I believe.'

Tess lowers her long eyelashes. 'You know they say that a parent's worst nightmare is something happening to her child? Well, isn't a child's worst nightmare something happening to his parents, even more so than separation and divorce is? A child cannot imagine anything worse than one of his parents dying in a car crash, or a fire, or terrorism, can he – leaving him to face the world all alone. Not knowing if anybody is going to step in to take care of him. And no loving mother wants her child's biggest fear to come true. Arguably, from his point of view, it's worse. I think about that when I meet other working moms who don't have the same security as I do. I'm sorry you had that pain.'

'Thanks.'

'What if, instead of you being the one who helps us, we've been sent here to help you? What if we're supposed to change your life somehow? Like, on some level you were expressing a need when you invited us in. Your heart was talking. I definitely sensed something in the moment, but I pushed it to the back of my mind because I was so caught up with my own situation. Only I'm starting to think maybe Connor and I have a special purpose with you. That this wasn't a coincidence.'

'Hmm.'

'Look at how basic your life is – and it doesn't bother you. I'm paying you a compliment. I'm saying it is phenomenal how well

302

you cope. We are very different women, you and me. Neither of us has completely failed, because we each accentuate the different qualities of womanhood. There's a lesson there. We shouldn't feel anxious when we could be feeling ultra-positive.'

'Is it not just some things . . .?'

'Positivity attracts merit. That's what we've got to remember.' Tess grins. 'We don't have to understand it – we just have to understand that it works. *In God have I put my trust: I will not be afraid what man can do unto me.* How is custody even a thing, when a child obviously belongs with his mother, period? Words on a piece of paper written by greedy lawyers. Not real. It's not love. It's not grace, like the grace you've shown us. I have my sister with me, and she has sheltered me and my baby. Therefore, I'm going to do right by her.'

'You honestly don't have to do anything.'

'With change, there is bound to be pain. After it, comes renewal. Good news is on the way, Heather, I know it. Success is transformative, but first we must transform ourselves to *be* successful . . . I can mentor you if you like? I can help you figure out what your goals are and how to attain them? We can look at your photographs together, and I could give you constructive feedback? It's one of my areas of expertise.'

'No.'

'No? Of course not. Maybe later. I'm glad you stuck around. And grateful. Humbled by your spirit. And I'm here for you too, more than you can imagine. Anything you want, name it, and if it's within my power, you shall have it.'

'Awesome. Can I borrow your car, please, for errands and – for errands?'

Tess smiles unevenly. 'Okay. You can use my car.' She slides the designer handbag towards her. 'Why don't you hold on to this for longer? It suits you, and I have others. We're roommates, it's fine to borrow each other's stuff. We're like a sorority.'

Clare wears her hair in a donut bun, and a reliable cocktail dress zhuzhed up with a scarf that she tied in a fancy shape following an online video. Rarely does girlfriend experience mean, literally, a companion to go out in public with.

She says, 'Are we going to a retirement party, or an awards gala, or is this for investors? Do I need to remember any names? How long have we been seeing each other? And, um, remind me what you do again?'

A velvet rope is unhooked, then hooked behind them.

Her date's hand is shaken vigorously by one executive, and fist bumped by another. His business partners and their romantic partners show a polite interest in Clare when she is introduced.

She explains they met at a hardware store by the adhesives (isn't that adorable); they've been dating for four months, although he's been busy with the Juno project lately so they keep missing each other; they have a shared love of Ron Howard movies; and she's a concierge. (Detailed enough to satisfy. Dull enough not to encourage questions.)

Guests keep arriving, and the serving staff circulate with trays of drinks and hors d'oeuvres.

Clare takes sparkling water.

'Are you pregnant?' one of the wives asks casually.

'I'm on a seven-day detox.'

'I could do with that. I find ridding the body of toxins from time to time to be beneficial for wellness. I always say that when you feel good physically, it sharpens the mental faculties. I've done them for years – detox diets, juice cleanses – done them all. Great for energy levels. We're all chasing our tails, aren't we?

But I love having irons in the fire, love it! It's also vital, I think, to set time aside for personal development. There's this raw foods place I'm desperate to try. We should go together for brunch?'

'Yes please, we should definitely do that, I'll give you my number and we can arrange it.' Clare's date needs her, but she promises she'll be right back . . .

An area of the ballroom is dedicated to a display of the Juno concept. There are floor plans and swatches to admire, alongside testimonials from exhilarated entrepreneurs. In another zone, they've set up a full-scale JunoPod so guests can experience for themselves the stylish comfort and dynamic solutions it has to offer: to imagine *this* as their daily workspace, set in a vibrant community of inspirational, ethical and empowering influencers.

The centrepiece is a 3D model of the entire JunoLV complex to interact with. Rendered in sophisticated detail, it animates at the touch.

Clare swipes to explore.

JunoLV. Transformational JunoPod desk provision, plus multilevel meeting places, and state-of-the-art conference facilities.

Tiny figures jolt into life in a futuristic office. One is talking exuberantly on the phone, leaning back as though stunned by excellent news. Nearby, a meeting is in progress in a glass cube, which looks important, but there is also time for sharing fruit from a giant fruit basket.

Iris Atrium. A multisensory playground for creative synergies, plus continental café and picnic area. A girl with purple hair skateboards down a winding path. A skinny guy is sitting on a swing to work on his laptop, swinging at regular intervals. A woman reads a novel between business deals. After a few beats, the skateboarder skates along the path again in the same direction.

Ferdinand. The elite destination bar and nightclub, for intimate gatherings AND *transcendent parties. (Dress to impress.)* A man and a woman stare into each other's eyes and sip their cocktails wordlessly. They sip them. They sip them. They sip them. They keep sipping them.

Honeydrops. Modern dining and microbrewery.

Pine Fitness – open 24/7. Heavy-duty gym equipment, airy studios and mindfulness sanctuary. Starting in anjali mudra, a yogi is saluting the sun, while over at the weights, a bodybuilder is doing barbell squats. The yogi comes back to prayer position, namaste, and performs another salutation; the bodybuilder continues doing reps like he's lost count.

Wherever Clare points, they repeat the same actions. Start on the same mark. Go in the same loop. The man on the office phone is as elated as the first time he heard the news. The fruit basket in the meeting is a cornucopia.

'You designed this?' she asks.

'A few of my ideas were included, yeah. These're mine.' Her date points to the 3D flaming sconces. 'We haven't broken ground yet, but any day now. Provided we keep on visualising the project as finished in our mind's eye, this will happen.'

'And become stinking rich?'

'That is the virtuous circle of wealth. We've had terrific interest already, there's a real buzz. Ultimately, the forces of success flow towards the worthy.'

Yep, there it is. She gets it. 'You've worked incredibly hard in very challenging circumstances, and given it your best – who can do more than that? Everyone here is proud of you, and you ought to be proud of yourself. Enjoy the party. What will be will be.'

'It is intense sometimes. I love being part of the JunoLV

community and I was honoured to be headhunted for the project. I do wish ...'

She does her listening face.

'I've lost relationships in the past because I had to put work first. My career trajectory is important to me, I don't want to change who I am. I think about being with the right woman, who understands. I imagine what she looks like, what our house will be like. Staying up late to watch movie marathons in our home theatre, surrounded by children. Imagine all of that. Maybe we'll get married in a Hollywood-themed wedding?' He attempts a public display of affection. His colleagues and their spouses are mingling nearby.

Clare pouts. 'The day JunoLV turns a profit, the company goes public, and you become a billionaire? I'll marry you in whatever wedding you want.' She pinches his face, hard.

The din of voices increases. Heaves of laughter. Jostling for prominent positions and sightlines. The air is muggy with pheromones: the men puff out their chests, and the women hold in their tummies. The thermostat has gone berserk.

Clare knows what's happening without turning round.

Somebody tings a champagne glass, calling the guests to order.

And Cuthbert L. Holthouse steps forward, opening his arms in a ta-dah motion as if the Magnificent ballroom and its contents have this very second appeared. Then he brings his hand to his heart, to acknowledge the applause and cheers of support. Black hair, white teeth, yellow jewellery. Tight skin and a saggy suit.

Phones turn to Holt like cyclops' eyes.

'Tough times are the greatest times. Adversity is a friend who helps us discover what we're made of. Lord, I love a disaster. I love seeing folk react because that's energy I can use. I love to fill an empty space. We see ourselves in our creations, whether it's in fine institutions that we help shape with our generosity, or in our offspring who love us back, or in ventures of supreme perfection such as this is: *JunoLV*. What a beauty. What vitality. To call this a business complex doesn't do it justice. It is organic, vibrant. It's alive. Don't listen to the naysayers ... My wife tells me they're called haters nowadays ... Call them what you will, but pay them no heed. Because they're scared. Of you and your abilities. They have never seen business done like this before, it is beyond their comprehension. We are here to leave an indelible mark on this noble land we were born to, and on the whole world. We take pride in the struggles of the past that our forefathers overcame. We pause to count our blessings in the present and cherish what we have. Mostly we look ahead into an uncertain future, and an exciting one, a radiant horizon. We clench our fists and paw at the ground, because we want to get there first. I have been in business since the age of thirteen, when I went door-to-door selling pear preserves to the neighbours out of a wheelbarrow. It was hard work, but no hardship. I couldn't wait to earn my first dollar. Because I fully intended to turn that dollar into two dollars – and I did. Then I turned my two dollars into eight dollars. Eight became sixty. By the time I had a thousand dollars, I knew it was possible to make a fortune, and so I carried on until I earned myself a million dollars by the age of twenty-six, back when that was a lot of money. I'm still going strong. Success like mine comes at a cost. It's been back breaking, and it was a dirty fight sometimes. I loved every minute. I want to see you succeed too. To have everything you want, and everything your families deserve, and I want you to have fun doing it. Our competitors are nervous at what we came here to accomplish.

We're resolute. We're originators. We have hot blood running in our veins. I won't say thank you, or congratulations. Those words are too small for the greatness inside you. Instead, I'll say keep it up. Keep going. Go further. Be the first to reach the luminous horizon. There's magnificent talent in this room, and magnificent rewards sooner than you know.'

Covered by more applause and closing remarks, Clare says to her date, 'Why don't we leave?'

'We can't. I can't be the only one who didn't get to meet him. You have to come too.'

'What for?'

Holt poses for photos with his admirers, is shaking hands like a candidate running for office. 'You're doing excellent work,' he intones. 'Go for it. You're in at the ground floor – it can get rough down here. Dig deep. I believe in you.'

Her date says, 'Take a photo of me.'

She shakes her head. 'The smart thing is to do nothing.'

'What sort of advice is that? We should lean in.' He joins the huddle following Holt. Risks being swept aside by partygoers and big-yourself-up suits.

Clare whispers, 'I wasn't talking to you.'

She stands in a space in the path of Holt's entourage. Takes a copy of *Business Powers* and a sharpie from her purse: holds them in front of her. Magnificent smile.

Holt veers towards her, like a dog sensing a treat. 'You brought this along for me to sign?'

'To Tess? T-E-S-S. She's my roommate,' she adds in a carrying voice. 'She is a superfan of yours, attends your courses, buys your products, follows your strategies to the letter. She must be one of the hardest working, most determined people I know. And my best friend here.'

Holt signs his jagged autograph. 'Glad you could make it. Is this your boyfriend?'

Clare's date is at her side, his arm hugs her waist.

'I've read it too,' she says, tilting her head. '*Business Powers* is a great title, and I read a lot of self-improvement books. Tess raved about it, so, made sense. I wish she could've been here to hear you tell the pear preserves story, because she grew up on an apple farm. But isn't it true that your father was the largest manufacturer of preserved fruit products in the state? A supplier to the US army, if I remember.'

'You have read my book, Miss . . .?'

'Clare Pembroke. He made you sell jars door-to-door for a day, didn't he, you and your siblings, to see who could sell the most?'

'Correct. I should've been playing football.'

'He often came up with ways to get you competing against each other, didn't he? He hoped it would prevent you from turning out spoiled because you had so much more than other families in your area. He also sent you to elite colleges, I think. Wasn't your brother, Jules, his favourite, who died of a bee sting?'

'My brother died of anaphylactic shock.'

'Anaphylactic, yes, that's the word. Your father said he wished the bee had stung you instead? That is what you put in your autobiography. Which makes me wonder what you didn't put in . . . Books have a way of doing that, even if they're ghosted by some loser. They have traces of truth in them.'

'Precisely what is your involvement in this project, Miss Pembroke?'

'None. I'm just the photographer.' She steers her date into position next to Holt. Takes a few snaps on her phone.

Cara

Asbjørn's T-shirt hangs off her as she brushes her teeth. Automatically, she places a hand across her chest to lean over and spit – chokes – spraying toothpaste in the basin, on the mirror, and down her chin.

White spots.

Cara asks Asbjørn to stay on his side of the bed tonight. Yes, she was up for it before, but the moment has passed, and she has an early start. Is too hot for cuddles either. He doesn't question it and falls asleep first.

Leaving her idling in the dark.

Cara has never been one of the worried well. Thanks to Glenda, who had no qualms about sending her to school with a runny nose, headache or temperature. There weren't any sick days in childhood for Cara, not unless a teacher sent her home. As an adult, she's found you can get a surprising amount done with over-the-counter drugs and Shiraz.

She curves around Asbjørn's back, rising and falling like a hibernating bear. Walks her fingertips to her armpit. This isn't worry. No. There is nothing to worry about.

Although she has to feign worry to be referred along the

pathway. Forces herself to make it sound worse than it is, or she risks being brushed off.

Perfect: Cara wants to be brushed off. It will be more convenient. Please *do* send her away with the snide implication that she has wasted NHS resources by taking an appointment she doesn't need. Then she can get worked up about that instead.

It feels big (it's tiny). It feels hard (sometimes she can't even find it). It feels wrong (there's one on the other side for all she knows). She is doing neurotic woman *now*, so she can do righteous indignation *later*. It doesn't even hurt.

Cara is examined by a GP; a registrar; a radiologist; and a consultant; and each uses some version of the same words. A *ninety per cent chance it's nothing.*

The next step is making sure. To make her safe. All she has to do is go along to the scanning, and the mammograms, and let strangers touch her boobs.

Inconclusive means inconclusive.

By now, quite possibly, they are the ones who are exaggerating.

We're all too busy and important for this, she thinks. I'm needed elsewhere.

The hospital is part of the university.

Cara walks past medical students chugging coffee and dragging on cigarettes between lectures. She's wearing her ID, so if anyone notices they'll think she's on her way to the brain bank.

Dr Cara M. Brenner has a Baconian belief that knowledge is power. Nothing less than close observation of phenomena and rigorous investigation of their underlying causes will do. Shadows on screens, lesions, tissue samples – she loves them. There is no such thing as too much information.

Nevertheless, she is turning away from the core biopsy needle the consultant uses, a cross between a piercing gun and a skewer.

312

He aims at a black blob on the ultrasound (yes, the same as you'd find on a maternity ward).

The local anaesthetic works. *Clack* without any pain. This would be fascinating if it were happening to someone else.

The nurse holding Cara's hand calls her a good girl for having it checked. Reaches across for tissues.

'Sorry, I'm bleeding a lot.'

The consultant shows her a pot of clear fluid between his thumb and forefinger, with tiny squiggles inside it like tequila worms. They set a date to give her the results.

A Friday afternoon. Excellent. She's got nothing in the diary.

Cara is going to act surprised when they tell her. Trouble is, with being able to think through all the permutations in advance, it takes away some spontaneity from the moment of truth. Like a reality show where they prerecord different endings to keep the winner's name secret. Ideally she'll be shocked in a calm, detached way.

The original reaction she had in the bathroom about a month ago – the convulsion and the minty spewing – was crap.

A month? Huh, it's like old times. If Asbjørn is wondering why they've stopped having sex, he hasn't asked.

Therefore, to conclude: (1) premonitions are bogus; and (B) it's a nonsense lump of nothing. See footnotes.

Heather

The rain is like gravel being dropped on the car, and Strip lights run like paints. Traffic backs up. A scrawl of lightning in the sky.

She looks at her messages in case the client is being impatient.

Hey Roomie, are you in the Monsoonie??? [umbrella] [rain-cloud] [tidal wave] Hype!!!! Don't forget to check in [mwah] oooxxx

It keeps falling overnight. By morning, the basement parking of the hotel is a dirty river with rapids and urban flotsam, the roofs of the cars just visible. It gushes out, joining a weir under a footbridge. Along comes a suitcase in the deluge. Along comes some polystyrene. Along comes a shopping cart, which gets stuck.

Walkie-talkies buzz with damage reports.

Tourists watch, holding up their phones as if it's another attraction.

She had the sense to park on level two, but there's no driving out of there for a while. It's flooded down the street, too deep to walk through. Her breakfast appointment won't be put off. She has to find another way.

'Neddie. Ned-head. The Walking Ned?'

'Are you drunk?'

'Only a bit knackered.' Heather opens a menu. 'I'm going to

order American-style pancakes – or as you call them, pancakes – see it works both ways? What do you need, Ned?'

'I'm not annoyed,' he says, adding sugar to his coffee. Stirs it for an overlong time. 'I make a point of respecting other people's personal space. Easy come, easy go is how I feel, because if it's meant to be, it'll stick, right? Have you heard from him?'

'Who?' She goes blank.

Ned scowls. 'I was afraid you were going to do this.'

The TVs on the walls are tuned to local coverage of unpassable roads and submerged tunnels. The emergency services keep advising motorists to turn back from flash floods: doesn't matter how often they show drivers being rescued from their cars, some still try. Spewing manhole covers. Downed power lines. Tilted trees. A man and his dog are in a canoe, paddling serenely down a street.

'I'm familiar with his moods. He's given me the silent treatment before, but not for this long. He won't answer my calls. His social media is frozen. He's vanished.'

'Hmm.'

'Did he talk to you?' he says, not quite to her face. 'Has he mentioned me?'

The syrup is thick and warm on the pancakes. Heather's coffee is refilled. She looks into her cup, muddy brown with a sheen; scraps and sediment pass before her eyes. She drinks deeply. 'If I'd known how good this was, I would've swum here.'

'Look, we're on the same side. I'm not a threat to you. Can you reach him? Do you know where he went?'

'I don't know where the going-away people go. For some reason, everyone asks me as if I should.' She eats. 'When things go bad, isn't a natural human reaction to try and get away from what's hurting us? To have distance. Start a new chapter ...

Turn over a new leaf ... Simply living can be such a flipping pain. Yet we never say, Hey, this person hung in there for years even though they were uncomfortable and felt tired, aren't they brave? They get on with it, and if we can ignore them, we do.'

Ned's staring at the screen behind her.

'Sometimes they show up again,' she says.

'He invited me on a trip. I brushed him off, mainly because my girlfriend was nagging me to spend more time with her.'

Straight men are the worst, she thinks.

Ned checks his smartphone.

'Are you recording this? Is that your thing, going around recording conversations? Are you saving them up for a documentary?'

'It's a tool. So I don't miss any details.'

She leans towards it and enunciates, 'You are supposed to ask my permission first.'

'Before he went AWOL,' he says, 'did Reggie leave a package with you to give to me?'

'He did not.'

'Are you sure?'

'Positive.'

'You're not withholding something which maybe you wished was yours, but isn't? Think carefully before you answer.'

Heather frowns. 'I have literally no idea what we're talking about.'

'This matters.' He taps her half of the table like it's a debate. 'A man's reputation is at stake. A chance to gain a unique perspective into how a work of art was made – evidence of his process. Do you know how often a chance like this comes along in an academic career? Once, maybe twice ...'

'Poor baby.'

'I can see what you're doing. Where's the manuscript – the original, where is it?'

Above them is a copper-coloured lampshade reflecting the diner in a convex bowl, and the TV screens as quivering spots. Heather reaches for her bag. 'You might be surprised to hear this, but I said to him once he ought to show you the pages that were left. Not for research or anything rubbish like that, but because I thought it would help you both. He didn't take any notice.'

Ned rubs his third eye.

'If he talked about it, it was to keep you interested, I guess. He enjoyed being seen a certain way by you?'

'Yes, indeed. I could see him.'

'His writing didn't come easily. It took him drafts and drafts to get it right. It's not sexy. Not how it's meant to be for someone who had a talent – has. The struggle was real.'

'We had an understanding,' he says wistfully. 'I put it down to shyness. I let myself get strung along, for what?'

She says, 'Don't spoil it.'

'Have you read—'

'Nope, wouldn't let me anywhere near it. It was his – and Mum's. Theirs. It was private.'

'That was their world,' Ned muses. He holds his phone like he's on speakerphone. 'Ours is this world, rougher and less enchanting. Reginald Ely wants, however, to keep a small part of it ideal. A finished work. With no corrections or redundant passages, no signs of the effort and preparations that went into his creation. His artistic and physical *struggles* remain invisible, but they were absolutely there; the labours of his creativity were *real*.'

(She thinks, Didn't I just say that?)

'And he didn't explain this to me. Like a truly great teacher, he wanted me to figure it out for myself.' Ned stops recording. Looks into the distance.

Heather licks stickiness from her lips. Rereads the menu for what to order next.

'They keep showing those tunnels ...' he says, pointing to the local news.

'Yeah, they're flood tunnels. There are miles of them criss-crossing the city, right under our feet.'

'I never knew.'

'We're in a valley here, and when there's a storm, the water comes down the mountains in a rush. It's supposed to get channelled by the washes and drain away. When the rain is heavy, they overflow, like they're doing now. Thing is, street people live down there, and sometimes the water level rises too fast for them to get out.'

'Shocking.' He counts cash out of his wallet. 'I wonder how bad life has to get before you end up living in a drain.'

She pats her mouth with a serviette. 'Probably too bad to tell anybody.'

The scrolling headline updates. BREAKING: *Body Found After 'Severe' Storm Hits Las Vegas Area.*

'When he contacts you, please pass on a message from me: I miss our chats. I'm sorry I can't stay. My mom needs her car.'

Cara

'Don't rush me, Cara, this is an investment.' Glenda is reading a list of features on an ironing board in the laundry aisle. 'What's *ergonomic?*'

'It means it was designed to feel comfortable,' she says.

'It's the same shape as the rest of them, isn't it?'

'I'm sure they're comfortable as well.'

'No, I don't like the daisies, they remind me of hay fever.' Glenda moves along the row, squinting at prices. 'Somehow sixty pounds seems an awful lot to pay for an ironing board, because after all it's only an ironing board. And yet eleven pounds seems suspiciously cheap. You have to wonder what they're hiding.'

'Can I ask a favour?'

'Ask away. It wasn't this complicated the last time I bought one, although to be fair I've had my old one for . . . I don't know how long, I can't even remember where I got it. This is ridiculous. I'm starting to wonder if I can live with what I've got, and I should buy a new cover for it instead.' She picks a packet off the rack. '*As seen on TV.* Have you seen this on TV?'

Cara shakes her head.

'Not kittens either, I wouldn't like ironing their faces. Woolworths.'

'Pardon?'

'That's where my last ironing board came from. Are you feeling okay? You look peaky.'

'I feel fine.' She zips her hoodie. 'I have some news: I'm having an operation. I've got a dodgy lump – my body does – to get rid of. It's a day procedure, if everything goes according to plan.'

'Well, if they're sending you home on the same day, then there's nothing to worry about. We all get lumps and bumps as we get older.' Glenda lowers her voice. 'I can understand your embarrassment, though. I had a carbuncle right on my – you-know-what. Absolutely massive it was. There was oozing. Seemed medieval to me, I thought I was dying.'

'I recall.'

'The doctor prescribed some antibiotics and it cleared right up. Even so, I'm glad you're having it seen to. Better safe than sorry.'

'I'll be under general anaesthetic,' she says loudly. 'I shan't be able to drive myself. I need your help bringing me home in a taxi, next Wednesday afternoon. Is that okay with you?'

'No bother, Cara bach.'

'Really?'

'I can help you get in and out of a taxi and carry a bag for you. I can even stay over if you like and bring you breakfast in bed? Pot of tea, hot toast, marmalade, and healthy cereal with bits in it, how does that sound?'

She smiles somewhat. 'Wonderful.' The tension in her jaw loosens. She touches her forehead to Glenda's shoulder. 'Thank you, Mother.'

'But I assume by next Wednesday, you mean the *nineteenth*, not the twenty-sixth? I'm afraid I can't do the twenty-sixth because I'll be on holiday by then.'

'*This* Wednesday is the nineteenth,' Cara explains. 'My surgery is *next* Wednesday, on the twenty-sixth.'

'That's no good for me, I'm away from the Monday. Your aunties and I are renting a cottage for a week. Mumbles. It's a surprise birthday party for Dilys. I say a surprise – she's the one who suggested it. They're bringing the husbands as well, and grandchildren. We haven't been together, the six sisters, since forever.'

'Can't you go on Thursday morning? You'll be there for the rest of the week.'

'I already forked the money over, you see. As I'm the only single, I have to pay more than my fair share as it is.'

'You're not a single. You're a widow.'

'Can't you change your date? The NHS treats you as a customer now – if what they give you isn't convenient, you put in for another. They won't mind. Then I can help you out, no problem.'

'I have my date and a surgeon I like.'

'Your choice, the offer's there.' Glenda studies a silver model which promises efficient heat distribution, a stable work surface and professional-looking results. 'I might ask if I can take this out the packaging, so I can have a go and get a feel for it. I don't want it if it's going to snap my fingers off.'

Cara roots around for a plan B. The last time she was incapacitated, it was laryngitis, and Heather was the one bringing her hot Ribena. It was Heather who figured out that Cara's new office chair was giving her back pain. When her ear was blocked with earwax and the whole side of her head was aching, Heather used a pipette to administer drops of olive oil; she had no choice but to lay her head on Heather's lap, and she pulled her hair back in an unassuming way.

Cara gave free maths tuition to the child of her depressed cleaning lady: is that worth a lift from the hospital? 'I can cover the cost of your holiday?'

'How very like you, throwing money at a problem.'

Yes, Glenda's right. She could do that too.

Heather

Connor is making a pinhole camera for his science project. As Heather is babysitting and it sounds as though it will fill a few hours, she goes along with it. She sets up a work area in the yard and asks him to wear his smock while he paints a shoebox.

'Are you painting the inside or the outside?' she asks.

'Inside *and* outside,' he says authoritatively. 'Because you don't want any light getting in. Not even a tiny bit. And you don't want it reflecting off any printing on the inside either. It's going to spoil your photographic paper. And ruin your picture. You don't want that.'

'Right, good plan.' She covers her mouth. 'Er, did your mum give you this shoebox to use, specifically?'

The box Connor has chosen is for a pair of red seven-inch heels with evocative ankle straps.

'She doesn't mind. She has plenty.'

'Come to think of it, I've got one you can have . . .'

He's already begun – by painting a large splat of black paint across the lid.

'Okay,' Heather says, 'make sure you paint it all over, really, really well. In fact, you might need two coats to be on the safe side? I'm going to check the instructions on my phone.'

He nods emphatically. He's on it.

'You know, if you like making experiments, you could become a scientist for a job and be paid to do them.' Then she thinks, What am I doing?

Before she started adult work, Heather had no idea how much – she wants to call it adulting – was involved, which doesn't translate into cash.

She prioritises references, knowing other girls might lose money or more, if she delays. *[thumbs up] this gent is fine and does what he is told. $$. Immature humor, just laff I did? Yes I would date again.*

Weeds out timewasters from her DMs. *I am a well bred elite male who can heal you. I am a White knight and will treat you like a queen. I will sweep you off yr feet.* He's trying for free nudes.

She replies, *hey shame I'll never know irl. my loss [skull] [Block]*

Blocks unsolicited pics because it's worse than work looking at them if they aren't going to pay. *[Block]*

BadDate. Caucasian, brown hair, 7ft basketball player tall 'Pipsqueak' 40s but says early 30s, broker/financial. #Boulder #BoulderCity #Vegas. Socials of UFO conspiracies. Vanity plate. Screengrabs are attached.

Heather adds the details to her growing list of dates to avoid. *[flying money]* so the alerts can keep coming. She hasn't got around to managing Clare's diary yet.

Refresh. A lead.

She finds smiling as she writes helps her to get into character. *My rates are for my time and my rules are non-negotiable to ensure we both get the best out of our date!* Clare insists he follows her process to the letter.

However, he has a special request.

Heather grits her teeth. *Happy to accommodate safe requests. Let's hear it?*

The pause is unusually long for someone who seemed okay to her at first. The beep. He wants them to pray together afterwards.

Love to! Absolutely! Offering prayers is what I do anyway. She makes a note to dress conservatively, perhaps borrow a cross from Tess.

Connor shows her his camera obscura.

'This is coming along nicely,' Heather says, checking all around the edges. 'When it's dry, shall we work on sealing these? What do you think?'

'Okay, and I need a soda. In a can. It has to be *a can*.'

'Yes, you do. You aren't allowed to pierce it, though. You have to let me do that for you, understand?'

'I can do it by myself,' he answers, 'I'm not a baby.'

'No-o. Only grown-ups can use sharp tools to cut metal with. If you don't let me cut it for you, the whole project is off – *finito* – that's the deal. Take it or leave it.'

He makes a show of giving this his consideration.

'And, I promise I'll let you be in charge of the funky chemicals when we come to the developing part.'

While Connor is watching paint dry, she sends a question to a web developer because she wants to come higher up in searches.

Then spends time on her eBay – Heather's eBay – because she can't risk clients seeing Clare sell the 'presents' they gave her. She's currently listing a Victoria's Secret teddy which doesn't fit at all, a thesaurus and powdered beets (she thought he meant *Beats*). Whatever it is, Clare is always thrilled. Saves the packaging carefully. Then Heather can list it as brand new. What she'd appreciate more is the cash equivalent, or a gift card at the bare minimum. They wouldn't dare try paying their dentist with sneakers.

Swipes back to Clare's social media, which she needs to stay on top of.

. *Petal, you damage *all* women thru your actions and retraumatise yourself. Help to exit is the only way. I'll leave this here x [hotline and website] for a non-profit in cahoots with ICE.*

. *No one ~chooses sex work~ it is PAID RAPE. Whores are co-conspirators of TRAFFICKERS AND PIMPS. You're PATRIARCHY dog food.*

. *Filthy girrrl gonna cut you fm mouth to ass.*

[Report]

[Block]

[Repeat]

Not that this stops it. It is a constant mopping up of blood.

Connor might have lost interest in his attempt to make a working camera. He's singing, 'Just Keep Swimming,' and decorating the shoebox with Nemo stickers.

Which reminds her, she was going to recycle some of Clare's selfies and videos with effects, as there isn't much privacy for making new ones at the moment.

Filters. Cropping. Captions will breathe new life into them. Go brighter, and frillier, and cute – no, that's not Clare. Mellow, and chic, and romantic realness.

She is distracted by a photo she sent to the bin several days ago. A baseball cap pulled down on scraggly hair, knotted tank top and big underpants. Limbs lanky as a gecko. Mouth partially open and her grumpy face fogged out as she exhales. Clare wouldn't be seen dead like this.

Starts cooking dinner.

And Heather is sitting outside again when she hears, '—disrespectful of private property.'

She breathes out, hides the vape pen in her shorts.

'Clean it up, Connor, we're guests here.'

Because guests don't pay rent, Heather thinks.

'Excuse my yelling,' says Tess, joining her, setting down the vanity case, and starts to remove her make-up with cleanser. 'I earned half what I usually make, thank you for not asking. Mostly I used my room for crying in.' Bronze smears on cotton pads.

'Did Connor tell you he's made a pinhole camera?'

'Yeah, it's babyish. He should aim higher at his age. I cannot remember feeling this exhausted and having nothing to show for it. I've got to ...' Tess goes quiet as she pulls off her false eyelashes.

'Burnout happens. Can you take some time off?'

'Not really. I know my body best and what I'm capable of, I've got more in me. You wouldn't understand.'

'I do,' Heather says. 'I've been there.'

'Hehe, we are not in the same boat. Our situations are not comparable.'

Heather goes to her inbox. 'There's this meeting I'm thinking of going to? Well, it's more of a family picnic, you can bring kids along, then everybody chats. Talk about how we're doing. It might be lovely.'

'Let me make this easier for you. I am not into that whole scene. I spend days on end with a bunch of other girls who do nothing but talk about their personal problems. I'm really not interested in this "meeting". I appreciate the suggestion, though.'

'Won't Connor enjoy making new friends?'

'Obviously, he loves meeting people. He'd have a ball. Learning new words. Mixing with the drug users and the god-less communists. So that takes care of that.' Tess grins. 'You, on the other hand – you should go. Get out this bubble of yours.'

327

'What does that mean?'

She laughs. 'I'm being supportive. Go ahead, meet the hardest working women in the state. Gain a little perspective? Sign a petition, if it helps. I'm pleased for you, honestly I am.' She drops a used cotton pad. Extracts a new one.

'What's wrong, Tessie?'

'Nothing is *wrong*. I'm just thinking out loud. You see, those of us who have responsibilities, we are on a journey. We are constantly trying to make our lives better, and the wider world better. We're striving. Whereas people who kind of float along without a purpose are the ones I feel sorry for. It must be extremely lonely. Not understanding how it feels to be needed – not knowing what it takes to create something out of bare nothing. A child. A career. Marriage. These are things made of actual stuff. And they need to be taken care of. They're tangible. But because you don't love anything other than yourself, you don't have the fear in your heart that what you love *most* could be snatched away. You've never made anything real, Heather; this is all pretend as far as you're concerned, a lovely dream. No obligations, nothing at stake, and ... You don't know what it's like for the rest of us who do care. Playing with selfies like you're still a teenager doesn't count.'

Heather locks her phone.

'How nice it must be to work independently,' Tess hums. 'Swanning from suite to suite, eating in fancy restaurants. Finishing in the early hours with a purse full of cash (not even your purse because you keep borrowing mine) then able to sleep all day ...? Meanwhile, I stay on the right side of the law – work cards, fees, testing – clean, like I'm supposed to. I was born in this country. I pay taxes. Take shit from my managers. It is not fair you're doing well and I'm not. Yet somehow *my* fricking

328

name is on a database? Hehe, you shouldn't be here.' She sloshes more cleanser, rubs at her eye make-up, black smudges on tan. 'I have done everything right.'

'Oh?' Heather looks over the top of her sunglasses. 'Remind me, where do the legal sex workers come from?'

'We are *not* the same, why aren't you listening?'

'Why should I, when you sound crazy?'

'I sound emotional because I have emotions. You act like you don't need relationships, as though sentiment, or faith, or wife, are dirty words. It doesn't make you superior. You're as cold as a corpse.'

'Your son swam two widths today,' Heather says. 'I sat with him while he FaceTimed your parents. I made dinner. And if this is your way of asking for a loan, you forgot to say please.'

'Did you hear me asking for money? Stop, you're too much.' Tess throws her things in the case and disappears inside, leaving the mucky pads behind. 'I said clean this up, Connor. If I have to say it once more, I swear I will get those clippers out right now.'

To stay afloat. Is Heather's answer.

Whereas they're more likely to be paying a mortgage. Paying for a trip. For tuition. A portfolio. Or car trouble. Civvy work doesn't cut it. This is a cushion.

Because they have children. Because they have parents who need medicines which aren't covered. Because they have a disability and this is the most flexible work they could think of. Because of debts/a habit/a record that follows them everywhere. It's a safety net.

For the future and a better quality of life.

What Heather sees in the future, on the rare occasions she thinks about it, is climate meltdown and possibly zombies.

Difficult to know how to prepare for that without getting drawn into dark areas of the internet.

When pushed by one of the organisers, Heather says she's saving up for a plane ticket – or a consultation with an immigration lawyer. She hasn't decided yet.

Where you come from, and how you got here. Whether you're trapped and desperate to leave – or strutted in of your own free will – and all in-betweens. The mistakes you made, and the company you keep. What you look like and what's on paper, or isn't. On street, online – in a club, in a room. Someone will be here for you.

You won't be judged or reported to the authorities.

Heather nods, uncertain how she can help. Asks for a job to do since she hasn't contributed any food today.

'Why don't you ask everyone what they'd like to drink? Do you need a piece of paper to write it down?'

'No thanks, I can memorise it.'

They paint signs. Gossip and fundraise. Go through a box of tissues, because it's allergy season.

Clare is doing okay, thanks. Despite the odd no-show. Despite this guy who changed his mind about the physical side and it turned into a therapy session (the self-help books she's read came in useful). Despite a weird feeling she had in her gut within the first five minutes of an appointment, which led her to make her excuses and leave – she offered to give the money back, and he said no problem keep it, and didn't get in her way. Now she's second-guessing herself and wondering what she should've done differently.

The swimming pool has moving gridlines turning into spaghetti like a Hockney. Eyes open, she opens her mouth and bubbles come out, O, O, o.

Recovery isn't the same as rest. The body needs movement. Tempo. Push on. They're more forgettable underwater, whoever they were.

She climbs out, dripping, covers her shoulders with a pink jacket. Slips on her sandals.

From the poolside she looks back in, and what's down there is like herself from a moment ago. Coming towards her. A ghostly swimmer.

Cara

'I never had you down for a fish person?' Helen says, watching it blob in the tank. She moves ready-meal containers on the granite worktop to make space for a largish box.

'It was . . . an accident.'

'This place is a dump,' Helen says, donning Marigolds.

'Sonja is coming tomorrow.'

'Who is?'

'My cleaning lady. Don't!'

Helen hesitates. Stops tidying. Takes them off with a snap. 'I only hope you're paying her extra. I brought some work to keep you occupied while you're having this time off. Meta-analysis.' She holds up a USB flash drive, then drops it in the box.

Cara has no intention of doing any work.

'Some reading so you don't fall behind, and other bits and bobs.'

On the contrary. Dr Brenner wants her hours back.

Not her basic hours: she was paid for those. Not her lab hours: those are what she came for. Her *additional* hours. Every *extra* one. Every committee Dr Brenner sat on as a favour. The writing and assessing foisted on her that weren't her responsibility. The emotional labour that fell on her shoulders, regardless of how busy she was, or ill suited to the task. Every hour that she didn't need to spend responding to feedback from all sides. The casual consultations. The late-night emails. The papers and engagements the faculty urged her to do, then took credit for. The time she devoted to a project that was hers, until it was taken away. The skin-crawling maleness she sucked up without complaint; the oiling she was unaware of until after it had happened. Suddenly it matters.

The sheer amount of effort that Dr Brenner has expended on trying to position herself so she could, in theory, be treated the same as a privately educated man makes her howl.

Well, it's payback time. And if they don't give her exactly what she wants, she'll ... she'll ... she'll ...

'Here's your card,' says Helen, popping an envelope in front of her. 'There weren't many of us around to sign as it's the long vac. A couple of colleagues were surprised, as well as concerned. You haven't done a very good job of letting people know what's going on.'

'How shitty of me.'

So instead of flowers, she's got a cardboard box full of work. A big box. Perish the thought she actually uses this time to convalesce.

Dr Stewart is standing in her kitchen, hand on hip, moaning about the precuneus and self-referential processing research ...

While Cara has to concentrate to take her tablets in the right combination. Anything more difficult than telling the time and knowing what day it is is beyond her.

'Do you want me to say we're fine without you? That everything is under control, and you've nothing to worry about? Or would you rather hear that we aren't coping, and are desperate for you to return? Which do you prefer?'

Whatever happened to boundaries ...? Please, explain this to Cara, she'll wait. To respecting personal space. *Discretion*. When Dr Murray Stewart took his medical leave, Cara didn't pester him. She didn't make him feel guilty for being away from the lab – or complain that she wasn't being kept in the loop – or bring him homework. No. She managed his workload within the team and left him alone, until he was ready.

'Murray is my dead name.'

'Sorry?'

'You called me Murray.'

She shakes her fuggy head. 'I have breast cancer. I can say anything I like. I haven't got bandwidth for your names and pronouns.'

Dr Stewart looks away. Adjusts the butterfly bracelet she isn't seen without these days. 'That isn't how cancer works, and you know it. You're better than that.'

No, Cara doesn't think she is. In fact, she thinks she is precisely that bad. And this must be why she has it. It. Cancer. It is a plague upon women like her. A plague, for pushing too hard in her career. A plague, for being a bad daughter, an unfeminine partner and a reluctant step-parent. A plague, for not having had babies in a timely fashion. For sitting down too much, for eating and drinking too much when she felt tired, i.e. frequently. A plague, for being insensitive to social issues which her analogue upbringing did not prepare her for. Plus, the offences she didn't know she was guilty of, until they were shouted at her IN BLOCK CAPITALS FROM ANONYMOUS CORNERS OF THE INTERNET. A plague, for envying colleagues who do better than she does without trying as hard because they were born into more favourable circumstances, or because they're more talented than she is. Or because they dissemble and bluff

334

and never get their comeuppance. Whereas she is honest about her failings. *She works on them.*

And for overthinking.

And stress (far too much stress, it was her vice) because there were too many demands on her (she welcomed them, she believed in the trickledown effect), and which she turned into passive-aggressive behaviour towards other women who some-what resembled her, but not enough to be relatable. She rolled it all up into a tight ball. And this is what's caused it.

Cara has never been a smoker, but if she had known she was going to have this cancer, this soon, she might as well have been. She could have cultivated a Parisienne look.

Helen is asking her something. Cara asks her to repeat it. 'How is your treatment going?' says Helen more clearly.

The truth is a long list of indignities, she wouldn't know where to start. It unscrolls in Cara's brain. Fuck's sake, the bilateral mastectomy was only the first step, and she still hasn't recovered from it.

There are two lines of scabbed purple glue where breasts should be. Her 'flat' chest is a new subterrain of bobbles and snagging and twinges and stabs and bones and tenderness, sur-rounded by bruises that, weeks after surgery, still haven't gone down. She has numb flesh down the sides of her torso: poke her in one place, and she feels it sparking in another. Nipples airbrushed from history.

Cannot straighten her arms. Cannot roll her shoulders. Cannot reach things on a shelf.

This was before chemo, which has its own time.

The ebb and flow of sickness, as though she's on a ship lost at sea. Her legs bitten by invisible insects. The deadweight constipation, and forcing down old-lady bran to try to move it. The gentle walks she's supposed to do, but is afraid of collapsing in the street, so she walks from room to room like Miss Havisham.

Not eating the food she loves. No poached eggs, no brie, no bagged salads, no medium-rare steaks, no takeaways. No alcohol, just when she could most do with a drink. What she tastes all the time is the salt solution she uses as a mouthwash.

She's in a chemo haze.

She can't focus long enough to read a chapter of a book; it has to be a page or two. Her eyes hurt too much to look at screens for more than a few minutes. There's ringing in her ears as though she's been to a nightclub. And earworms. An experimental remix of 'You Should Be Dancing' by the Bee Gees, with extra brass, bongos and cowbell.

Her thoughts run on different tracks. She talks herself out of talking to anyone.

And all this punctuated with a bashing heart in her tissue-thin chest. Like the dongs of Big Ben. To frighten her, in case a few minutes go by where she might, conceivably, relax.

'I said: and what is that like for you?'

'Worse than the worst hangover I ever had, going on and on.'

'You don't recognise yourself?' Helen says. 'Living a day at a time is a necessity?'

Cara's fear response is in overdrive. Her amygdala is squealing.

'Where's your boyfriend? Why isn't he helping?'

'I murdered him,' she replies, instead of saying Asbjørn left her because this was more than he could handle.

'I'm sure he had it coming.'

Some patients with the same outcomes as hers refuse the offer of chemotherapy, the oncologist said. They weigh the risks and benefits, then decide against it; or they say yes at first, then bolt.

Cara wishes she didn't know that. The knowledge clatters like a key in a tin that she could be one of the ones who says no.

My hair is falling out.

'Pardon?' Helen comes closer. 'What did you say?'

'My hair is falling out,' she says, audibly. 'I brush it to get rid of loose hairs, and it keeps on coming away. I'm pulling it, I have to force myself to stop, before I pull it all. Makes a mess in the plughole, so Sonja – Sonja is my cleaner – is going to ...' She mimes scissors, although what she means is an electric razor. 'Next time you see me ... I don't want you to be shocked. It usually grows back.'

Her choices made sense in the consultation room. She was sure she was right. Meanwhile, back in the real world, she was going to expand her collection of dresses. Softness by stealth was the plan for Professor Cara Brenner, as soon as she materialised.

Not a boy chest. Not bald.

'I can't picture it any more!'

'You don't have to. I can. I can see you returning to work very clearly, and then you'll have to put up with the same nonsense as the rest of us. I know this doesn't feel like the best outcome, but trust me it is.' Her words fade into noise.

It's all very well Helen saying this: she's got cleavage under her *Save the Bees* T-shirt. The unruly fringe of old has grown out into a sleek bob. What else has Cara given up without realising it?

Helen prods her phone into life. 'Have you seen this yet?'

The video is shoved in Cara's face – of a sunny girl looking over her shoulder, the burble of amateur recording, and a corner of perfect blue sky.

This jacket makes me look like I'm in the Pink Ladies, Heather says, *so I had to stop by. A group of flamingos is called a flamboyance.* The camera turns: there are some flamingos standing in a pond.

6, 5, 4 . . .

Collective noun, Cara thinks.

0.

'Is that it?'

'They only last a few seconds. They aren't really messages, more of a short-form performance art.'

Groggy. Cara has to lie down. She finds the sofa mainly by touch. Splays out, because her chest wall might crumple if she attempts to lie on her side.

She's never known fatigue like it – a clingy pulling under. Has never experienced sleep this poor. Nor the strobing grids, columns of numbers and liquid pouring into graduated cylinders behind her eyes, along with a reproachful voice asking different versions of the same question: *What were you expecting? You weren't expecting this? What did you expect?*

'I'll leave you to yourself,' Helen murmurs.

Good. It's what she wants.

The pounding in her flimsy chest jolts her awake. She can't tell how long she has been asleep for because she feels roughly the same.

The kitchen fairies have been. Helen must have shown herself out.

Cara looks in the box.

It doesn't contain much in the way of reading materials. The space is mostly taken up by a smaller, prettier box with *Winona* written on the lid. Inside it is a wig.

She's too tired to cry.

Heather

Heather asks, are we using real names? Of course, Tess replies, as she's setting out soft drinks and tearing off raffle tickets. All right, real names and fake occupations it is.

'I want to express my gratitude to our amazing hostess,' Tess says brightly to the six women who show up, plus children. 'She is the reason we're here together today. Many thanks, I couldn't have done this without you.'

Heather remembers that's her. Acknowledges the polite clapping.

'How well did you sleep last night?' Tess asks. Lets it sink in. 'Were you up late last night, later than you'd like? Did you struggle to get out of bed this morning? Maybe the habit of staying in touch has a detrimental effect on your general sleep patterns; and when you do eventually go to bed, you end up surfing on your phone – and more than an hour goes by? Maybe you're worried for some reason, and that is what keeps you awake. Like, how am I going to pay my bills this month? Can I afford to give my kids the standard of living they deserve? Am I wrong . . .?'

She shakes her head, as do several others.

'Did you wake up this morning, refreshed and alert, after a minimum of seven and a half restful hours? Or are you reaching for the caffeinated drinks to get through the day? Are you wearing concealer on the circles under your eyes? Are you tired right now?'

'I almost didn't come over because I was exhausted,' says one woman.

'Right. Which is why I'm especially appreciative that you made the effort. When you're sleep deprived, to the extent you cannot face a simple social gathering, that is when you most need to come to a Somnate party. For showing up when you thought you couldn't, here, have a raffle ticket.' Tess gives it to the woman.

(Heather didn't get a raffle ticket for hosting.)

'Let me reassure you that if you have suffered from a bad night's sleep recently, you are not alone. Half of adults aren't getting their recommended seven to nine hours per night. Lack of sleep costs the economy up to five hundred billion dollars per year; and one and a half million workdays. Unfortunately, it's not only the cost to our pockets ... Health risks associated with sleep loss include obesity, heart disease, diabetes, loss of memory, depression, to name but a few. Shift work is shown to increase certain cancers, including breast cancer. Think what a catastrophe it would be if you couldn't fulfil your obligations due to sickness, when all along it was in your power to prevent it? *It is vain for you to rise up early, to sit up late, to eat the bread of sorrows: for so he giveth his beloved sleep.*'

Heather stifles a yawn.

'I slept great last night,' Tess says, holding a bottle of purple drops in the palm of her hand, 'and so can you. Starting tonight. I want to give you the sleep you deserve. The deep, quality sleep that keeps your immune system strong so you can be productive and powerful from the moment you wake up.'

Somnate – Holistic Sleep System.

She passes around several fruity-looking bottles, each with a logo of a woman asleep on a cloud.

'This is one of my favourites from the range: a blend of lavender for reduced anxiety and blueberries, which are a source of antioxidants. You mix them like any water flavouring.' She adds a violet glob to a glass of water, stirs until it dissolves. Sips. 'Each unit contains twelve servings. If you're unlucky enough to have insomnia, my heart breaks for you. I've been there. What helped me was these extra-strength supplements which have a unique added ingredient, developed by scientists, to relieve the pressures of chronic sleeplessness by restoring your circadian rhythm.' She shows them the sachets.

Somnate Serenity-XTRA: contains Integritine™

'Somnate is approved for vegetarians, with zero added sugar. All products are completely natural, in order to promote a natural, nutritious sleep.'

'How come I haven't heard of it?' asks a dancer hugging a baby to her tattooed body.

'Excellent question. Here, have a raffle ticket. Somnate isn't available to buy in stores or online, but is purchased exclusively from registered Somnate representatives. Like me. I'm a Sleep Helper.' Tess points to a pale blue *zZz* badge on her blouse. 'I can design a four-week Sleep Cleanse for you, including customised sleep hygiene advice and product selections to get you excited about sleeping well. It costs ninety-five dollars – or only thirty-five dollars, if you agree to host a Somnate party of your own? That's over sixty per cent off. Remember, to live our dreams, we first need to get a good night's sleep!' She fans out brochures, samples, and Somnate-branded sleep masks. 'Okay, it's raffle time, so grab your tickets. Anyone who wants to know more – including if you're interested in becoming a Sleep Helper yourself – I'll hang around to answer your questions.'

Over the next hour Tess sells a hundred dollars' worth of product and diarises a video call with a friend to discuss registering her as a Somnate rep. When the party's over, she texts her upline to report back on how it went.

Heather runs a knife along the burnt edges of the mashed potato in a hot oven dish. 'Shepherdess pie.'

Tess mouths a *wh?* shape.

'Sorry. Hasn't turned out how it looked on the recipe.'

'I should make funeral potatoes one evening. Cream of mushroom works nearly as well as chicken.'

Funeral? She must have misheard.

'I've got a present for you.' Tess pushes a hefty gift bag towards her.

Heather reaches into it warily. The packaging says *Nikon D800*, but without breaking it open, she isn't sure what that means.

'Mint in box,' says Tess. 'Thirty-six megapixels, full-frame DSLR. You could shoot a billboard with that thing. The AF in lowlight is outstanding (not so much for the video, though, I wouldn't bother). It's solid, practically professional.'

'A camera?' Heather says, frowning. It has multiple buttons with letters and symbols, two displays in addition to a viewfinder, and is as heavy as hell. 'I don't know how to use this.'

'Hun, you should learn.'

She presses some buttons and the display blinks into life.

'Aren't you frustrated by how limiting your phone is? Don't you want to see more? Show more? Hasn't anyone ever encouraged you to push yourself?'

Yeah, she thinks, because she was trying to compensate

for herself. The camera still has explicit photos on it: perhaps Heather can wipe the data and sell it on.

Tess flips through a Somnate brochure. 'If I climb to cloud five, I can become a Sleep Consultant, which includes a course on dream interpretation. Doesn't that sound interesting? There's a discount for introducing a friend . . .?'

Heather scrapes the crusted sides of the dish. Decides if it doesn't come away, it probably isn't edible.

'They like us when we earn, Heather. If I'm an independent businesswoman working from home – spending as much of the day as possible with my little boy – able to buy his uniforms and take him to practice – by selling health products to inspirational ladies – what family court can deny it for a fact? Are you sure you don't want to be my downline?'

She shakes her head. Again, no.

'This is a nice apartment. The type I have in mind for Connor and me. Except ours is going to be bigger.' Tess wrinkles her forehead. 'What's wrong?'

'Nothing. Only, I don't know, doesn't it sound kind of pyramiddy?'

'Hang on, Heather, I'm afraid I have to stop you there. Somnate is network marketing. It is *not* a pyramid. Pyramid schemes are illegal, and I for one would never go near them.'

Cara

Mentally, it's like meeting herself again. The predictable window of four to six days in the run-up to her next treatment, when Cara is lucid.

Physically, she is in disguise. Her head and body are inflated by steroids. She has covered the tree rings on her fingernails with vampish nail polish.

Flat, flat, flat. Cara spent her life avoiding horizontal stripes. Now she lives in some version of a Breton – with long sleeves to hide the puncture marks and damaged veins in her arm.

Putting mascara on a single eyelash is a nonsense, and her eyeliner game isn't up to much. Dumps a lot of smoky eyeshadow on there. Wears her thickest frames and oversized earrings to give herself features. After another minute of head scratching, she decides this is going to be a bald interview. Returns Winona to her box, like a pet.

'In your introduction, can you please avoid saying ... I'm not asking you to ... Only not to mention we're *not* in the lab, if you see what I mean?'

The podcaster, Sally Hicks, assures her she won't.

'I don't want to, you know, I'll be back there soon, and don't want to give the wrong um ...' Cara had a point to make about perceived weakness and women in STEM, something along those lines, but her mind has gone blank.

Sally tests for levels. 'I appreciate you doing this, especially at such a wretched time, health-wise. You must be getting tons of requests?'

'Actually, you're my first. Maybe when ...' Holy crap, the chemo has burnt her synapses.

'*Neurobubbles* is published, yes?' Sally takes out an advance copy with the spine creased and Post-it notes in marked pages. 'This is going to be light touch. I'll start with an easy question. How did you come up with the title?'

'I didn't.' Come on, brain, Cara thinks. 'A list went round. I wanted to call it A *Thoughtful Reader's Introduction to Neurobiology and Cognition*, because that's what it is. My editor's suggestions were more along the lines of *The Neuroscience Secret* or *The Consciousness Code*, and I said, no, those are silly titles for what I wrote, and terribly misleading.'

'Shame. *The Consciousness Code* sounds fantastic.'

There is an opening here, although Cara isn't sure what to do with it. Her eyes are heavy.

'I'll come back another day if you need to rest?'

'No, please don't go. I'm fine.'

'Don't worry about pauses or rambling. I'll edit it so it flows and makes more sense. Anything you want to do again is okay. What about explaining – commenting on – why scientists are on a journey to try and find out what consciousness is?'

'Curiosity.' Cara strokes her bald head. 'Altruism. Validation. Why do we do anything? There is something peculiar in this case, though, because we are constantly in it. It is part of who we are, right here; and if *this* phenomenon feels immediate and present to each of us, we really ought to have a better handle on understanding it. That's part of the appeal, I think. If I could tell you what . . .' The words stick in her throat.

Sally says slowly, 'It would be a world exclusive for *STEM and Us*?'

'Yes, it would be fun. Nonetheless, an inordinate amount is happening to model the brain and increase our understanding of memory and cognition. From time to time we get these tantalising glimpses. A hint. A shining detail which gives us – something. I'm extremely proud of my colleagues. I love their audacity. I love watching them work.'

The podcaster leaves a gap to make sure she has finished. 'Can the reality-based community still afford to research consciousness, or is it a luxury we'll have to let go of? Isn't this a time for pragmatism – more achievable goals – given the context of uncertainty we are entering into?'

'Uncertainty, you call it? If they were actively trying to sabotage experts, they couldn't have done a better job.' She presses her tragus to dull the ringing in her ears. 'Sorry,' she whispers, 'I landed on that a bit early. Perhaps we can swing back towards the end.'

Sally opens the book to a highlighted passage. 'You made some remarks in this chapter, and I'd like you to expand on them. What, if anything, can we say about consciousness with a degree of confidence?'

'Mm. We are swathed in qualia, that is, sensations of colour, and brightness, motion, sounds, temperature, pain and caresses, of ownership of one's body . . . Normally this is accompanied by an overall impression of seamless continuity. Of being whole. However, a slight disturbance is enough to break the illusion of cohesiveness. A lesion on the cortex; a change in chemistry; trauma. Some basic unit of perception that we fundamentally

346

rely on can be lost. For instance: being able to recognise faces and who they belong to? It is disconcerting – and gives research-ers plenty to work on. Minds are fragile, they shouldn't be taken for granted.'

'Isn't that perception, not consciousness? Should perception and consciousness be talked about together, or separately?'

'Good point. And a conscious person who cannot rec-ognise faces any more is still a conscious person, of course. Consciousness arises from perception, from perceiving and processing objects, and noticing patterns. It does a job of selec-tivity, of framing. It's not very big; in fact, it's pretty narrow. It lets us into a fragment of the world, but also misconstrues it! Francis Bacon, the forefather of the scientific method, observed how prone we are to receiving different kinds of data, and then interpreting them badly. What he called the "idols of the tribe". Experiences which seem immediate and meaningful to us are like distortions in a mirror. To get closer to truth, one must proceed with caution.'

'And from these kinds of discussions, your publisher came up with the title?'

Hasn't Cara got around to answering that yet? She thought she had. 'It's not an interesting story,' she says. Just a chain of emails until they wore her down. '*Thought Bubbles* was another suggestion they came up with, which I resisted. My name is on the book. I'm the one who has to live with it.'

'*Neurobubbles* is . . .?'

'A compromise.'

Heather

Boxes of Somnate are stacked up to the front door, which doesn't open fully when Heather gets home. Bangs into them. 'Tess, you promised.'

'Not here,' comes the reply.

She drops her keys. Rolls her neck, which crackles at the back.

Connor is staring at his Spiderman action figure, moving its limbs stiffly. His hair is short.

'Where's your mum?'

He shrugs with exaggeration.

'Did she say when she'll be back?'

He carries on manipulating Spiderman more roughly. Spiderman says no.

There are specks of hair on a plastic chair and on his towel.

Heather says, 'What's going on?'

He hangs the toy upside down. 'What will happen if I put Spiderman in a blender and press go?'

'He'd be chopped up into tiny pieces, and you won't be able to play with him again.'

Connor appears to consider this. 'How long will it take? A minute? A second? Twenty seconds?'

348

'Why are you being horrible to Spiderman? What did he do to you?'

He turns it over. 'What if I burn him, will he melt?'

She takes the figure out of his hand, stands it up. Poses it towards him. 'Why do you want to do these mean things to Spiderman?'

'Because he's a stupid bughole.'

'I see. And why is he a stupid bughole?'

'Because he is.'

'All right, well, what if maybe he isn't?'

'Maybe *he is*?'

'Maybe *he isn't*. And he doesn't deserve to be blended, or set on fire, or thrown into the bin, because nobody deserves that.'

'He's mine. He belongs to me. I can do whatever I like.' Connor scratches his scalp. 'I'm not crying!'

'I didn't say you were.' Heather looks from one to the other. 'Should I step outside and give you two some privacy?'

'You're like her. Bossing me around, telling me what to do, who I can see, what I'm not allowed to play with. I'm not allowed to do *this* – I can't go *there* – when I'm older then I'll be able to do *this*. But when it's my toys, you can't stop me.' He knocks it against the wall stacked with Somnate inventory. 'No more grown-ups. None of you listen, ever. Living here sucks. This isn't a real house. There are no cats. I'll go live with my dad, he has two cats, and he doesn't have blond Jesus because that doesn't make any sense. He likes me. But grown-ups go on and on, and they keep on making up rules, don't they? When it's perfectly obvious none of you knows anything. It's not fair.'

'I think, Connor, your parents are only trying to—'

'I'm telling you shhh . . .'

She mimes zipping her mouth closed.

He lies on the floor with his head on his arms, swinging his heels back and forth. 'I'm done with all of you.'

Heather retrieves the fallen action figure. Stands it on the skyscraper of Somnate. Glances around the shoebox apartment. 'Would you like to do an experiment with me?'

He turns his back to her. 'Not really.'

She lies on the floor next to him, leaving space for him to wiggle further away if he chooses to, or come closer. Closes her eyes.

They stay this way for a while, sighing, not crying. Until he says, 'What kind of an experiment?'

Patches of paint are flaking off the Apostles Motel. Brittle weeds push through cracks. The shooting star and *vacancy* signs are pale bones, and underneath some lettering has dropped off.

'It's old,' says Connor.

'It's not old,' Heather replies, lifting a step stool out the car, followed by a roll of black sheeting. 'The Tower of London is old. Conwy Castle is old. Stone-flipping-henge is.'

'It is old. Look at it.'

'One day I will take you to an authentically old historic castle – built hundreds of years ago – where kings and queens lived, with towers, and dungeons, and everything. I promise.'

He frowns. 'Why?'

She shoulders her rucksack rattling with a torch, staple gun and utility knife. 'Let's get a move on, shall we, as technically we aren't supposed to be here?' She hangs rolls of duct tape on his arm like bangles. Gives him some cardboard to carry.

Utopia Bail Bonds is not on one side, while *Peacocks Hotel and Bingo* isn't on the other. When the Apostles is torn down, the three unoccupied spaces will merge and become one.

They cross the neglected concrete.

'It's a ghost town,' he says, following her.

'Didn't used to be. See that office? Lars worked in there. Friendly chap. He flew the American flag everyday, and never said a bad word about the government, even when they treated him badly.'

'People really stayed here?'

'Oh yeah. Stayed. Lived.'

The swimming pool hole has been filled with gravel.

JunoLV. Transformational JunoPod desk provision, plus multilevel meeting places, and state-of-the-art conference facilities.

'This was Wade Jr's place. He played harmonica late into the night with the windows open, and it lulled you to sleep. Over there is where Ramon lived with his little dog, Sukie, who he pushed in a stroller because the ground was too hot for her paws. Be careful not to fall through the railing, walk this side of me, please ... This was Maria's room, a showgirl who could roundhouse kick a bottle off a man's head. In that room over there were Claude and Mel: the last time I saw them, they were dressed as brides. And this room was Prabjot's – the human computer who found the perfect system to beat the odds. She won a fortune when it landed on 30 and got herself blacklisted by all the casinos in the state. And Mr Seahorse.'

'You're making them up.'

'I'm not. It's true, every word.'

Iris Atrium. A multisensory playground for creative synergies, plus continental café and picnic area.

The door yields. 'And here was the room of a real writer, who would rather cut off his own hand than make bad art.'

They set to work.

The furniture has been reclaimed or destroyed, and the bathroom ripped out, leaving gaps in the tiles. Heather closes the concertina door so they can't see it.

The cream-coloured walls still have their textured pattern, but they have brought a sheet with them to use as a screen. She stands on the step to hang it. Staples it loudly in place.

They cover the windows with plastic, starting at the side panes and working inwards. The view outside – of motel rooms, palm trees, signage, parking lot, the Miranda chapel, a line of barbed wire, and relentless blue sky – is gradually obscured. They plaster the frames with duct tape. Block every chink of light.

'Did you bring a dime?'

Connor pulls it out of his pocket. 'Is this the right size?'

She doesn't know. 'Don't get your hopes up, okay, in case it doesn't work?'

'Don't worry. It will.' He draws around the coin on a piece of card. Cuts a hole with the knife she lets him use. 'What is this called again?'

'Aperture.'

'A-purr-ture. Can we do a selfie?'

Ferdinand. The elite destination bar and nightclub, for intimate gatherings AND transcendent parties. (Dress to impress.)

Heather frets over sticking the hole to the middle of the glass, layering on extra tape to make a dark centre panel with a dot of light.

'Stop,' he says, 'you've done enough.'

Finally, they seal the door closed, plugging the bottom with a towel.

They can't see.

Wait for their eyes to catch up.

Honeydrops. Modern dining and microbrewery.

The view outside is let in. Faintly. Watery. Inverted. It splays into the room, on the walls, cornice and ceiling, and on every bumpy detail. Projecting clearest on the sheet on the back wall.

The sky is at the bottom, and the balcony is across the top. It has colours: sandy; bright grey; mint green. Upside-down palm tree. Illegible white and yellow signs. Parked car. Chapel roof. It is what you can see from here.

Connor moves towards the picture, the sky and land rippling on him. His shadow like Peter Pan. 'This is cool.'

Heather's outline too. Weird and familiar. She says, 'You're right, Connor. Grown-ups are the worst for doing stupid things; way, way worse than anything wrong a little kid could do.'

Pine Fitness – open 24/7. Heavy-duty gym equipment, airy studios and mindfulness sanctuary.

'Phone ringing!' he yells.

She automatically checks her cell. 'No, it isn't.'

But he's right.

7

Tactile Corpuscles

gentle touch

~~I~~ₐ(She) was busy dyeing cloth and ~~my~~ₐ(her ancient) arms were stained blue to the elbows. The pigment was made by fermenting leaves and, when fixed, the fabric would be used for a skirt. I realised this was the first time that I had been left alone with the ~~Visitor~~ₐ(elder sister) and ~~he was watching me work in~~ₐ(I watched her work, determined not to break the) silence. ¶

'We appear strange to you,' ~~I~~ₐ(she) said. 'You forget that you are the stranger here.'

'I shall do everything in my power to continue earning your family's trust,' ~~he~~ₐ(I) said ~~proudly~~ₐ(, unwilling to be cowed by an old woman).

'Do you not care about the consequences of your attachment?' ~~I~~ₐ(she) asked ~~him~~.

~~The Visitor~~ₐ(I) replied: 'I understand your need to protect your little sister, however, my only wish is to fulfil her heart's desire.'

As ~~I~~ₐ(she) wrung out the textile, ~~I~~ₐ(she) gazed at ~~the poor boy who, despite all his refinements, was incapable of understanding his own heart, let alone someone else's~~ₐ(me with an expression akin to pity). 'Claribel does not need protecting,' ~~I~~ₐ(she) said at last. 'Your fate is less certain.'

357

~~He~~ ^(I) gathered up ~~his~~ ^(my) writing materials, ^(politely) doffed ~~his~~ ^(my) hat ~~in a forced way~~ and excused ~~himself~~ ^(myself).

~~I left my work to dry in the sun, thinking that the extra care I had taken had been worthwhile. It would make a splendid addition to our rituals. Suddenly, I was grabbed from behind and I jumped with fright. My silly sister had wrapped me in a great, hard hug. She knew I was still angry with her, but she was trying to pretend otherwise. I sternly pushed her away.~~

~~Claribel took no notice. 'We used to have fun together,' she said. 'But then you turned into a dull old drudge, toiling and fussing over menial tasks. I have to make my own fun these days.'~~

~~'Fun?' I said, disbelieving. 'Is that what you call it? I call it spite.'~~

~~'You would never have the courage to tell him your true feelings,' she said with a wicked gleam in her eye. 'If you did, he would recoil from you in horror. The best you can hope for is friendship. It is obvious that I stand a much better chance.'~~

~~'Is that how you justify toying with his affections?' I asked. 'It will end badly if you keep carrying on like this. Please do not act in a selfish way that you will come to regret later? I say this out of genuine concern. He is biddable and you are hasty. More than one heart could end up being broken.'~~

~~Claribel protruded her bottom lip, which was her habit from childhood whenever she encountered a truth she was incapable of arguing against.~~

~~I took advantage of my sister's silence and said: 'I fear no good can come from an irresponsible flirtation. Instead of pursuing him and forcing him to choose you over his family now, why not let him return to his homeland for a while? A temporary separation will give you both a chance to discover whether your fondness for one another is real or not. If it is merely infatuation, then you will have spared yourselves many griefs. And if it is meant to be then~~

without doubt you shall soon be reunited, knowing the sacrifices you have made are for true love.'

'You cannot build a dam in the torrents of emotions,' she said fiercely. 'They burst forth with greater violence.'

'Consider it a period of grace,' I said.

She answered with these words: 'It is a shame that you will never have children, for you are a wise and loving soul, and you have much to teach the next generation. One day when I am far from here, I shall have a beautiful daughter, and I will send her to stay with you for a time so that she can learn the mysteries from you. Even if my marriage is fated to be unhappy, and you are cursed forever with loneliness, there shall be a girl born of our village who will have everything she needs to be gentle, keep hopeful and stay free.'

Mon 2 Oct 2017

last seen yesterday at 17:45

Are you OK? C x
Hi H, it's Cara.
It is all over the news. I just need to
hear from you? Let me know.
xx
Post something please? Anywhere. I'll keep looking.
Were you or anybody you know involved?
Is there anything I can do for you?
Reply pls and I'll stop mssging. Cara x

Yes safe. I wasn't there.
Tak.

OK.

Tue 3 Oct 2017

Hey Cara, yes Im ok and not hurt and not involved. I was locked-down in a hotel a mile away, they kept us in there and it was like sheltering from an airraid. Noise outside. No one allowed to move to go out to help or go home. Fake reports of other shooters confused things. A lot of people dead and many injuries, the totals keep rising and the hospitals are overwhelmed, they are asking you to stay away if you're not fatal. My roommate was here already by the time I made it home is worried for a cousin of hers and we both have friends who work on the Strip like everyone does. We've been trying to hear from them we haven't heard from yet. Im frazzled and unwinding in our yard. Then I will go to bed for maybe ever.

Dear Heather,

Thankyou for replying. It was good to hear from you and I really mean it. The thought of you being that close to such a horrific attack is bewildering. They are saying it's the worst shooting the US ever had (?). I cannot comprehend how it's possible. And what is this reluctance to label it as terrorism, where does equivocation enter into it? I do not understand the mentality.

361

Do cities recover from these tragedies? How will it affect you? I'm thinking about whether the authorities will clamp down harder after this, or if you are in the least bit concerned for your safety.

How is it with you? (Aside from the world gone mad.)

Here at home the fish and I are fairly quiet. The house needs a few jobs tending to, but I haven't the energy for them. A picture fell off the wall (it was a breeze when a series of doors were open) it was the one of the Automat, so it needs to go back up. I have a noisy boiler in need of servicing and a mouldy patch in the bathroom I can't get rid of. Your old room is a dumping ground, I'm ashamed to say. None of these jobs are urgent; individually I can live with them. But they add up. I allowed my house to get uncomfortable.

Glenda is coming over tomorrow, she is all for making me chilli con carne in bulk. Sometimes it's bolognese. (Basically they are the same recipe, except one has spices.)

I did a stupid thing: I applied for a professorship. I couldn't have picked a worse time! I didn't get it, of course, and now I think I never will. God I sound petty. Sorry.

Are you seeing anyone? By that I mean do you have a person in your life who is on your side? I'm really asking how I'm going to know if something serious were to happen. I don't wish to meddle, but I regret not being better at staying in touch.

I hunker down of an evening with a blanket and an ice-lolly, and I listen to Nina Simone. Miles Davis. Oscar Peterson. Shirley Horn. The Jazz Messengers. Etc. Where has this music been my whole life?

Cara

Xxxx

Sat 7 Oct 2017

How will the city recover??
They built and dedicated a healing garden already
trees for victims were in the ground faster than the bodies were
[seedling]
Vegas is as busy as a woman.

Mon 16 Oct 2017

Dear Heather,

I had to share with you this incredible red sun like a laser dot, caused by Ophelia and dust from the Sahara. The whole sky is a yellow bruise. I wish you could see it. I'm sending you a photo which doesn't do it justice.

How are you? I am fine.

I am still quite upset about not getting the promotion. I thought it should have been my turn. I went back to HR for more feedback which was adding salt to the wound I know. It amounts to the fact that I have been too long in one place . . . Can you believe it? I have too much staying power. I'm too dedicated. They refer to this as 'academic incest', the idea being that one is better for having moved around, gaining experience in different research labs. While there may be some validity to this, it's not as if we don't attract a diverse range of talents to draw from; also, I don't think the work I have been doing these years is too shabby.

But mainly it galls me that if I were a man with the same career history, I suspect it would be regarded as longevity.

I had a good cry.

Stay safe and I am wishing you well. Feel free to contact me when you like.

Cara

xxx

Hi again. Stupidly I sent without attaching. Here it is. No filter ha ha! C xx

Sun 17 Dec 2017

Ho Ho Ho Heather, Merry Christmas!

For the first time in my life I am not doing cards. I think millennials are a hundred per cent correct on this matter. This way I get to say Seasons Greetings, be greener and to ask how you are. Are you well? Are you busy? How is it going with your roommate? How do things currently stand with your status, and have you any plans to come back to the UK next year just for a visit? If you are, I hope I don't need to spell out that I will be very hurt indeed if you were here without telling me. I'd want to see you for a drink and a pizza. It will be on me! Are you doing well?

I was thinking about staying power being used as a criticism. Clearly you have it. I recently have come to value the ability to hang in there, to stick it out in the face of the world sending you a great many signals to give up and move on. It is a female predicament, being the one who stays put and it not being considered an achievement.

A few Christmases have gone by without me bothering to put up a tree. This year I am in favour. And I think I will make more of celebrating small occasions next year. I want to go outside more too. When I have the time, I am thinking of taking up a post as a volunteer, perhaps in a heritage setting. Something other than the sciences. I want to see what's nearby that I have possibly overlooked when the weather gets warmer. I'm keen to be in the garden again and be adventurous with what I grow. I want to see more colours and attract wildlife as opposed to trying to drive it out. More invertebrates, not less. I used to get frustrated that my garden never looked how gardens in pictures do; that there was never a tea rose that didn't get black spot or an elegant peony which lasted. I underappreciated it. But now I think it's sweet it's an untidy organic thing, which is closer to how I used to think when I was a child. I quite like the idea of honeysuckle, rosemary and herb pots to attract bees.

These were the ideas that came to me while decorating my tree. Are you doing anything special to celebrate?

Love,

Cara

Xxx

Mon 25 Dec 2017

Merry Christmas Heather.
Wishing you a healthy, Happy New Year
filled with success of your own choosing. Take care.
Lots of love, Cara x

last seen today at 22:08

Wed 11 Apr 2018

Hi Cara. Im terrified for my friends and confused by how people can carry on oblivious af. The DMs are disgusting. I don't want to believe this is what they did on purpose but right now I can't think of anything else. it is harder to know what to do. fwiw I'm sorry you didn't get your promotion it is their loss. All this time I thought you were a prof anyway, how can you not be? that was strange. being on display is where stamina comes into it and that must be the same for you when you teach, you concentrate the whole time with all eyes on you knowing they are ready to tear in if you waver for 1 second. recharging takes longer idk its being on alert and checking my responses with everything on top [raised hand] [nazar amulet]

Mon 16 Apr 2018

Dear Heather,

Thank you for your message. We all have bad days and any-thing you want to unload is fine with me! What is going on in your neck of the woods? My phone is always on (as well you know).

I have a confession to make: I redecorated your room. In a way I can't believe I didn't get to it sooner. I thought about turning it into a posh guestroom, but I rarely have guests over so that seemed pretty pointless. Then I considered turning it into digs, but I'm sure that would be an ordeal for everyone concerned. I had to make a few tough decisions with regards to what was still in there. What I mainly got rid of was clothes you won't ever wear again and some old candles, soaps, etc. I kept anything you made at school and your certificates, etc., are in files. For your books, ornaments, pictures (including a few that were your mum's I should imagine) I bought some rather nice storage solutions but do tell me if it's all right to do another purge and I'll donate/recycle them. The cd player works in a manner of speaking.

I painted it oxblood and I bought a great new sofabed which nearly didn't fit up the stairs! My books are in there beautifully organised. So: it is an alternative place to read and enjoy a craft if I ever find one I do not regard as too difficult or an infantile waste of time. As you delighted in pointing out, I am hopeless with a needle. I also have a mat in there for stretches. The windowsill has globes and cacti in your honour. Am I making it sound dreadful?

Also it occurs to me, perhaps, that if Paul/you/whoever were to show up on my doorstep unexpectedly (which I know is unlikely, but if he or anyone else did for some reason) here is a space that can quickly and easily revert to a bedroom for a while. (To reiterate: I am aware that this is very unlikely indeed and isn't really going to happen. I am just saying that it could if it had to!)

I mostly stay off social media: it's the snake that eats its tail. But I look for your updates, and your hair is very pretty.

I'm signing off as I have to get ready for work tomorrow. Ciao x
*I put Duolingo back on my phone.

Tue 8 May 2018

Cara Mia I don't think of it as my room and neither should you. I don't hold onto much in case I feel like packing up and going to explore somewhere new eg I read a book once then pass it on. I just finished The Four Agreements by Don Miguel Ruiz and I can think of at least 2 people who might like it and get something from it. I reckon books have their time with us. But my roommate loves her stuff lol. I tell her she's going to be a hoarding lady. She counters by saying she's going to have a bigger house to put it in. She called me lazy but I'm not convinced the opp of lazy ~ obsessed ~ is a good way to be.

I don't think I am. I do have bad habits, but I don't like drunks and I'm sober for work always. Neither am I selfish but interested in other people's concerns and history? Sometimes I go to meets where there's a mix and I'm a fan of doing right by our community and our planet.

How is your garden? Send pictures of big smelly flowers and plump fruits and vegs. Better yet post them where I can see them like a real human? Get rid of whatever you want to including my possessions from childhood. I won't need them again.

One thing it will be worth my while getting good at is cooking. Both my roommates – my friend & her son – say I'm a bad cook. It means I must be terrible because she is and they live on takeout. Did I tell you she has a very raised voice?

I am ok thanks. If I'm relying on something to carry me through then I know that is a bad sign. When I can take it or leave it it doesn't have a hold on me and then I'm not stuck. I think I might give anything never to feel stuck again. good of you to stay in touch it makes a difference. my phone is on when it doesn't die of battery [blows a kiss]

Fri 8 Jun 2018

Dear Heather,

I saw a former supervisee of mine who is going to Toronto to research the mechanisms and management of chronic pain (which means long-term pain). I cannot think of a finer purpose for her to turn her abilities to. Most of our students go on to bigger and better things, that is what is supposed to happen. My impact on this particular trajectory was negligible. She is one of those who was always going to do well. Seeing her again, however, gave me mixed feelings. I shook her by the hand.

((Annoying Gap))

I wrote the above over a week ago and left it in my drafts folder to finish and send you the next day. You gave your email such thought and I wanted my answer to be considered also. But then what happened, in the lab, is that a visiting colleague kept snif-fling and touching our work areas (not only mine) and though I sanitised the surfaces and slopped on hand gel I came down with a stinking cold which knocked me out. Sorry.

I run myself ragged and am still behind. The prospect of a balance and/or recognition is further away than ever. I seem to

374

be getting neither right. Is it unreasonable that I want to benefit from what I put in? I wouldn't mind making sacrifices, provided I had made enough progress to show for it. I can't say this to other women in STEM because what they need from me is to 'represent'. I'm not up for it as much as I was when I was young and hungry.

Neither do I have a partner to console me. Cumulatively, I have spent over half my life with the wrong men. Forgive me if I shouldn't say this to you, because it means by implication that Paul was the wrong man, and he isn't here to defend himself. I mean me. I made poor choices. I think you tried telling me once, although I don't remember your exact words.

Single life is a valid choice and has many advantages. I admire those who do so joyfully. However, I'm interested to know who I might be with someone who knows me well. What it takes. How the right person could bring out my better qualities. Because I struggle to know what these are unless they are pointed out to me.

But no one is coming. There is no rescuer.

I have learned that tiredness and sadness are closely related in me. One feels very much like the other. I can wear myself out with sadness; and the tiredness makes me dwell on my failures and take criticisms to heart.

I try to defer to your example somewhat by embracing the lively parts of the day. I try sometimes to put my wellbeing first, even though it appears counterintuitive. Who knows, perhaps not doing so was my error all along.

Love

Cara

xx

Thu 6 Sep 2018

Hi, how are you? I am sending this link to everybody: a trailer for a new drama called Seven Vials which you must watch ideally in one go and then share it and talk it up to everyone you know! It's about two different families in a small town trying to survive a series of manmade apocalyptic events. My best friend from school, Betty Willis, is one of the make-up artists! I won't do any spoilers, but if it's bleeding/bursting/infectious, Betty probably worked on it. She is going to be a super-famous FX MUA, it is happening in the very near future. Please watch #SevenVials and support her [movie camera] [green vomit face] [syringe] [water not suitable for drinking] [mosquito] [skull] [kitchen knife] #apocalypse #postapocalypse #drama #7Vials #bloodandguts

Cara, are you having fun yet? Don't overthink. Please feel more.

I swam today. As usual. I love saying that! I don't know how to explain except my body likes it. In case you need to hear this today: Cara Mia Brenner shows up and does her best. That is your thing [black heart] [cherry blossom] xoxoxo

376

Fri 7 Sep 2018

> And I can count on you to see the good in people.
> I was drunk emailing last time.
> I'm fine!
> C xx
> I should bury my devices when I get like that

[cocktail] [glass of red] perfect time to tell it like it is
That thing you say.
I googled your book is on sale. Why didn't you tell me?
You haven't got many reviews [speak-no-evil monkey]
I can write one for you
The cover is [star-struck]

> I concede the reviews are coming in thin and slow,
> but I beg you not to write a fake one. If
> you finish Neurobubbles & like it,
> then maybe leave me a review. Please don't
> review what you haven't read.
> I allude to this very subject, the instinct to react

377

without deeper thinking.
What was once a survival mechanism has
become a constant hum of anxiety.
Even if well-intentioned.
I think
there was not the level of interest my publisher expected
[bandaged head]
I signed some stock for Heffers but it was a non-event.
There is a good podcast I did called STEM and Us
You might like that better?
than the book
Episode 40.

I don't pod.

Sun 9 Sep 2018

Hi H
I started Seven Vials. Gory, yes, and tense. I like it.
I had to put the lights on! Guess who likes it more . . .
Mother!
She reads rather gruesome memoirs, I shouldn't be surprised.
I put a comment on Betty's wall saying well done.
Cara xx

Tue 11 Sep 2018

A development;
I was headhunted by a university in Amsterdam which does
a lot of neuroscience research in collaboration.
They have invited me for an informal visit. I won't take it up tho,
I don't think it's fair to pretend I'm considering it when I'm not.
Cara xx
Nice to be asked [party face]

GO to Amsterdam! [facepalm]
See how you like it there and what's on offer before you turn it down
Don't take my word for it. ask literally anyone who will tell
you the same.
I bet you'd want Helen to go see if she was offered it. I know
you would.
Amsterdam is [peach] if I break up with LV I might see you there?

It's complicated.
Shall we switch to a video message,
or ye olde fashioned phone calle?

380

Doesn't work for me
No lets stay like this more convenient for timezones and work.
I think you should go for an in person at Amsterdam U is all
Stupid not to.

STEM AND US
EP 040 – THE CONSCIOUSNESS CODE

Cambridge Neuroscientist Dr Cara Brenner talks about the pleasure-seeking orbitofrontal cortex; the precuneus and the self; and neurobiology's ongoing quest to solve the riddle of consciousness. We also discuss public perceptions and STEM, plus her new book, Neurobubbles.

[play] 1 hr 1 min

[Intro, royalty-free ukulele]

PODCASTER: *Hi, it's Sally. Today, on* STEM and Us: The Consciousness Code. *What is consciousness? Are mind and body separate objects, or one and the same? Will scientists ever solve the hard prob—* [skip]

CARA: *—the OFC mediating fear and reward. When you hear an actor saying 'What is my motivation?' it has to do with their character moving towards a goal in anticipation of a reward; or, alternatively, avoiding punishment as a consequence of—* [skip]

PODCASTER: —*what attracted you to STEM in the first place?*

CARA: *Fairness, at first. Also because being a scientist helps me have fewer doubts about the world we live in. It is furnished with irresistible facts. Observing them; asking questions about them; devising experiments; and offering robust explanations for what's going on around us – there is no greater privilege than that. Getting closer to this world and becoming better acquainted with it, as it is. It wasn't what first attracted me, but that is the reason I stayed.*

PODCASTER: *Like a love affair?*

CARA: *Could be.*

PODCASTER: *As a successful female researcher, you must have ideas on how to attract more girls and women into STEM subjects?*

CARA: *Well, I confess I have been guilty of treating science communication as an optional extra in the past. It's only by attempting to write a popular science book myself—*

PODCASTER: Neurobubbles, *available from the usual booksellers . . .?*

CARA: *Ah, yes . . . Only by going through a process of trying to put across what fascinates me about the brain in a quasi-narrative form, did I give this subject the consideration it deserves. And I have my, er, Heather Wycliffe, to thank for that. Science writing is usually passive when it's written for other scientists. The passive voice is the very voice of objectivity. It is dispassionate, scholarly and remote; the human beings who worked in a lab are, linguistically, expunged. 'Mice were anaesthetised' is what ends up in the materials and methods section, instead of 'we anaesthetised mice'—* [skip]

PODCASTER: —*municate to a wider audience?*

383

CARA: *Too often we frame 'public engagement with science' as the problem to be solved – and yet how scientists engage with the public is what we have more control over. This is about putting evidence in a relatable context for laypeople, explaining why a study offers hope or causes concern (or neither of those things) and possible implications. What story do these results tell? And before we dismiss clear, humane communication as not-part-of-the-job-description, we should remind ourselves that we need more women in STEM; and that being a polymath was once something to be admired.*

PODCASTER: *Does the same go for political engagement? This is a post-truth era where the political classes can afford to ignore the opinions of experts, no matter how well presented ... Can't they?*

CARA: *If scientists have a weakness, it is that we can be naïve when it comes to rude social systems. We want to believe that if we show the evidence to the right committee or branch of government, then positive change automatically follows; that all policymaking is evidence-led. It hurts me to admit it, but we should stop being surprised this isn't so. Politicians deal in confidence, imagery, rhetoric, tribalism, um, emoting. To name but a few qualities that are contrary to a scientific point of view. It is tempting to get lost in the perplexities of post-truth, to be indignant and keep on taking swipes at it until we wear ourselves out. Another conundrum is this: should we, unelected folk, speak truth to power – even though power speaking truth to us is optional? Phrases like 'the will of the people' sound woolly to our ears. But a politician is only doing what he is supposed to: what is expedient. He could just as easily perform scientific piety if it suited his purposes.*

384

PODCASTER: *Surely being an expert means staying out of the mess of public affairs? You cannot say more than what has been observed, and what the science supports. Wouldn't it be compromising if you did?*

CARA: *Scientists are certainly more averse to muddy ambiguity than most people. But it depends on what you think science is for, whether you believe it has a purpose beyond the lab? We can't have it both ways. Either we're floating above it all in our own bubble, indifferent to the machinations of various governments, to potentially harmful decisions and insidious behaviours. Or we join in, because we can't afford not to? In addition to being scientists and academics and clinicians, we are also citizens of somewhere. We occupy a space together and, in theory, can contribute to a common good. We have ageing parents, or children in school, and colleagues of many nationalities; we all exercise in the park and breathe the same air. Our careers might be taken away from us, but we never stop being members of a wider community. I tend to think of it more as persuasion, rather than the fuzziness of changed perceptions. The natural world – our world – I find incredibly compelling. The more I learn about it, the more respect I have, and I feel responsible as well.*

PODCASTER: *Are you referring to the climate emergency?*

CARA: *The predicament of climate scientists is a teachable moment for us— [pause]*

[Mark as played] Completed

Fri 4 Jan 2019

not a vlog. don't @ me [classic camera] [shortened link]

[INT. Heather in a white shirt sitting cross-legged on a king-size bed with gold-trim pillows and an upholstered headboard.]

[play] Everyone takes photos, the world doesn't need more. Pointing and clicking isn't as difficult as what a painter or a special effects artist does, it is the easiest thing to do.

My photos were garbage when I was young. Taking a picture filled some seconds when otherwise I would have to think of something that was constructive or the opposite of that, or keep quiet and be bored? Easy as chewing gum. I find it hard looking at them now, especially the selfies, which is when I was most likely to be worried about my eyebrows being hairy or thinking I can't post this because I'm wearing the wrong jeans and what a disaster that would be? Kid stuff. By the time I had gone through my process of second-guessing how I should look, I totally missed my chance to see what it could have been a photo of. What I could've made. The moment has passed by.

Most of daily life is not much worth looking at when taken at face value, although I am keen on surfaces. I like the green of a glass bottle? The hood of mountains. I like repetition in the massive carpets you get in casinos. Behind the scenery, where it's textured and cracked and is functional. Faded colours by day. Colourful after dark. Which is not how it usually goes. I like the reverse; the other sides; the underneath; inside.

I'm not a person with characters writhing inside my head waiting to be set free, like an artist working on a comic book or a film or a novel. Creative types with strong ideas in them – they need to be expressed to get them out and give them a life of their own. That I'm not driven or intelligent is what I have been told by people who are. And I tried finding my thing, honest I did. And I felt sad for a while because I will always belong to a class who never makes anything with my hands or my brain.

I'm pretty blank.

Then I realised, the prize on offer when you have nothing in particular to say and can bear looking at a specific thing for longer than feels comfortable is sometimes a better image than I dared to hope for. I look at my photos and then I am sure I exist in the world. Yes, photos are stupid, no one cares about them and there are far too many, of course – I'm aware.

I could get carried away with edits. That is a real danger. You can filter and crop and distort it to death. I also think captions and hashtags are problematic; the second you try adding an explanation – and I have tried – it changes them again. And I'll tell you why: because commenting is not the same as looking. Even so, the urge to make a shot better – be clearer, emphasise – can be overpowering.

[Heather picks up a camera, looks through it, and focuses it towards a source of natural light. Her finger hovers over the shutter button. She lays the camera down.]

A photo leaves out more than it shows. It took me ages to figure out why I kept taking photos of the same objects and places over and over. I have these categories like: Roads. Corridors. Tiles. Bright red. Where I've stayed. Self-portraits – those especially because I reject my traditional selfies. They cluster, it just happens. Before I noticed I was doing it. By retracing my steps I am, um ... The rules are not written down, but they're there. They are the captions. #NoTitle. #NoHashtag.

A group of photos on the same theme has gaps in-between them: and then when you see them together it's like they're communicating. They come up with ideas of their own.

The temptation to make it fleek. Wow. It's like tampering with the evidence. Sometimes I cannot resist, though. Why should I feel bad? They're mine. Tak. [pause]

Wed 1 May 2019

vlog 2 overdue. i had time off finally and it feels good to chat with no one else around [drop of water] [shortened link]

[EXT. Heather wrapped in a towel over a nautical-theme swim-suit, her hair is wet.]

[play] I am fed up of being told that I should hate my body. Yes, I'm a ginger and my hair frizzes out. Yes, my skin is pale white and gets rashes. I've got freckles and spots, and marks from mosquito bites stay visible for ages. Yes, I have small breasts and a squidgy bum, and weakling arms. Yes, I have a cunt, it is a very nice one thank you. And knobbly knees. It's the body I've got. And I can be sure it belongs to me, in a way nothing else does. Money; possessions; document status; relationship status – they come and go, nothing lasts. But this body is what I had to start out with and is staying with me to the end. Hating is not really convenient.

It tells me when I'm hot or cold. Scared or safe. Delicious and bitter. It becomes achy, tired, tense and then some time later, as if by magic, it feels better again. Feels nice. And it swooshes

389

through water and I can't tell you how much that means to me. To be floaty, cooler. I love eating pizza too, I get excited about that.

My body has her own set of priorities: the first is staying strong and well. She isn't afraid of hard work, and she has an appetite. I feed her, exercise her and play with her. If she is wounded or ill, I do everything in my power for her to get healthy again – as I would for anybody I was in love with.

This body gets dirty. But is not dirt. It isn't filth or dust. It is not ground to be conquered, or scorched, or dug into. Not grabbed or walked on. This is my patch.

People make judgements at first sight of her, and often they misread me as a result. I didn't choose to be born like this. None of us do. And I will not apologise for how much space I'm taking up, what shape I am now or will be in the future. I will not apologise for choosing what to do with what is – always has been – wholly mine. I would fight for it if I had to.

My pulse, and clever cells with my DNA written all the way through them, and my breath. These are my physical property. You'd think the capitalists would have a better grip on that?

This body doesn't stay still and doesn't stay the same. If I have one complaint, it's that it always needs something like hungry now, sleepy now, need to go back into the shade. Need to pee. I am going to sneeze . . . Then you give it what it asks for and it doesn't take a minute for it to be complaining again it's after something else. Yet also it provides me the means to meet those needs, and is my first, best chance of survival. It has luscious moments of calm and pleasure. Until it needs something different again, probably for me to stop doing whatever it was that I was enjoying at first, then got carried away with?

My body tells me loud and clear there are others on this island with me. Others who might hurt me. Others going through pain, as I do, even though I don't understand their pain – of course not, I barely understand my own. Others I could try to help. I'm not alone. My body exclaims this.

It is a coward, however. That's an issue when I want to do the right thing to support my siblings: to insert myself in a fight for the sake of someone else who, maybe, might not return the favour, it has to be said. I don't know. I can overrule what my body instructs me to do, as in not do, out of self-preservation with supreme difficulty. And I do because . . .

[Heather rubs her hair with the towel and pulls it back from her face. Roughly folds the towel and sets it aside.]

The case to be selfish is strong. I'm as bad as the next girl is for taking what I can get. I like myself less when I think about that.

Many of us want to see improvements and that is my connection with other people. Not our features, or our backgrounds, or working arrangements. We have a gathering. Show up for a rally. Donate. Make reasonable arguments without sounding too angry, although we are. Collect the evidence that has been asked for, knowing we may never see the benefits! The good we do doesn't amount to much when they don't listen to you. On the contrary. Too often for it to be getting worse.

The body's answer is numbness.

Numb is how it copes with trying to reach a goal, but never being able to. Being thwarted. And the way it has been rigged makes it off-putting to show up for next time? Harder to know what the right thing to do is, if you're not able to get a feel for it.

My body is keeping a record. Of everything that's happened to me and that I do. What other people say about me, directly and indirectly. It gives me fears which are hard to ignore. When my body senses it's threatened, I notice it acting in strange ways. Trauma can leak out. We might think we feel okay, but maybe

391

we just feel mainstream for a while. Bodies, therefore, have a lot to answer for. Mine reacts. Unless I train it to recognise what's what – good, bad or neither.

Numbness is the body shutting down, persuading me out of action. Physical danger is the last thing my body wants and it will try to find shortcuts for avoiding that.

My body is my closest, most persistent and demanding friend. Who speaks in riddles. My body has memories stretching far, far back, to long before I was born. She uses pain to manipulate me – anyone else who did that I'd drop them in an instant. She is the roommate who will never leave.

I can't see inside my own body, not really, and not only the moist, fleshy insides that are roughly eyelevel. There's this whole other layer I do not have access to? A dark area where it keeps knowledge, preferences and bugaboos. I'd love to get in there and reorganise but that is practically impossible. I have tried reaching in; it lets me very rarely; and no I cannot grab on to much. But I notice movements happening in there when I'm extremely relaxed, or in my swimming zone. I glimpse them out the corners of my awareness. The flutter when I break a seal of a freshly cleaned hotel room. When I see a city view from way up high, never the same as on hundreds of previous occasions. The uptick of recognising a good photo from a bad one. When I'm asleep is when my body lets me in. It's busy at work. And sends messages through its mysterious method. Processing what I'm unable to. Nudging and prompting.

The body has a strong sense of privacy. Which is a shame because if I want to be a better person I could really do with it just being open and honest with me. [pause]

Thu 30 May 2019

posted this even tho i watched it back & saw how shiny i was [sunglasses on] i considered a do over but [rolling with laughter] no one saw the last one. what's the opposite of influencer??? [magnifying glass] nonentity [mist] [skull] [shortened link]

[EXT. Heather on a patio without make-up on. She is wearing a black T-shirt and occasionally vapes from a pen.]

[play] You start by doing different things in different contexts. Behaving differently as you do so. And you even look different and talk different. The work side. Friendships. Spiritual or not. Chores. In streetwear. What you did in the past. How you want to be in the future? What appears on flickery socials. Definitely your nationality on your document, if you have one. Age; race; sex; thighs; underarms; heart (the one pumping blood); and heart (the one with desires in it). On and on into these separate thingies, each a smaller piece. The more I think about them, the more fragments I notice, because they are divisible, and further divisible again, down and down to smithereens – and then atoms.

And that is not a nice story because it's like I was only made of these tiny bits . . .

I try showing it in my pictures sometimes, the frayed-apart human I feel. Seen as a shimmery outline. With varying success – usually no success.

Except then I'm walking around and people assume I'm a full girl, without the multitude? They haven't a clue that I'm floating along, and the fragments may disperse. With that, perhaps I am looking for something solid?

Dreams have a hold on us. People talk about their dreams and follow them, although they are vapour trails. Including at the expense of others and of the planet, like they did in the late 1900s. Or their dreams are put tight away where they are ignored and never shown to anyone, storing up trouble. Following their dream for even a little bit is not an optional extra: it is a simple human need. See, that worries me. Getting a dream from imagination into dimensions? The execution? Most of the real world isn't set up for that, even though this same world insists it is what you should be doing.

Dreams are a time and a place that is not here and now: and require the dreamer to go towards it. As if the dreams can only flow away from us – outward. Either forwards to the future or backwards into the past. That is because of us projecting them. That's fine, but I can't help thinking that in my present I am also being looked at – from ahead – and from behind. Like, I am in memories? I'm also in plans? I can almost feel the tickles of them.

Photographs are like this. They are both images to aspire to and quickly dating artefacts. Publicity and . . . Historical.

Boomers are harsh about selfies because they think it's narcissism. I think not. It is because if you believe you might never afford your own home, or have a stable income, or have access to the healthcare you'll need some day – and you know your electeds are dysfunctional – and you know the climate is already gone to poop – and terrorism is a fact of life and coming soon to a neighbourhood near you, ahem, 'legal' gun owners ... Well, surely it is only natural to focus on what you have some control over? And what we can control is what we decide to show online. Your best self. We want to make the world better, which includes it appearing better, and selfies are a stab at perfection.

Quickly it evaporates down the feed. I admit a selfie isn't a true self, which is why I stopped taking them. Only for work, and with mates, and whatever.

A photo is static. Taking photos is energetic: you are there. Physically. Which can be trouble.

I know my complaints sound stupid compared to other people's. My privilege gives me wiggle room which is not available to every-one equally. It is difficult to know what to do with that. Just as I don't want to be divided into a million pieces, I don't want to be isolated either. Sometimes, yes, I am going to need support, like we all do. I need support that fits me like a good bra. Choosing a bra for somebody else is pretty impossible to get right?

Grown-ups let us down. Children are right about that. I remember when I was small, I stayed at my aunt's, which I hated so much. I rang my mum and asked her to pick me up. I counted on her to listen to me, but she didn't come because that didn't fit with her plans for that particular day. She deserved to have her way, she felt. My way could wait till Sunday afternoon, instead of Saturday morning. I had to say thank you for having me, urgh ... I didn't get to meet her as an adult, and we didn't know each other very well ... Then there are the grown-ups who come and collect you, even though they have work which is really important to them. They just appear for you. They're there. You don't even have to try and talk them into it. That bugs me.

I still look for the grown-ups, which can be confusing because sometimes I'm the grown-up. I don't know how that happened. On the positive side, though, I get to be the grown-up in my life.

There is subtle kindness and agreement out there, among the mess. I've seen it.

If I'm small bits, I am easier to trample on. A whole rounded woman gets more in the way. Connected to the ground under my feet. Not only following a desire path, but adding to it with my weight and footfall.

[She sips from a red cup.]

The great and wise Phoebe Buffay was only allowed to do cups and ice at the party: so she did the most illustrious cups and ice, and made it her own. She could, because she had done the work to become the person who could do that. Her actions were an extension of her personality. Like her flowery hairclips and the rings she has on. She created the part of the world she was living in. It was intentional. She did that consciously. With true feeling. What was in her past didn't stop her, and neither did a domineering co-host. Phoebe turned them into cups and ice.

What people do with their privilege is interesting because it shows a process. Or lack of one. A chance to take better photos is the privilege I want most. The human gaze is an act of intimacy. It's why we feel violated when photos are taken without our permission. And it's what we hate about not being able to take them down from the internet.

We muddle through on rough, uneven ground. I might not be successful in the conventional sense. I might never change anything further than what's within arm's reach. Today I wondered if I could be in a relationship with a person who sees this problem the way I do, who agrees with me? I might not say no to that. I want to be with someone who tries, and I am with myself all the time, so. [pause]

8

Proprioceptors

position and movement

Heather

Arms by his sides as though he is an actor. But he's not. He hangs *do not disturb* on the doorknob and locks it after them before saying hi.

Average build. Average age. Average. Average. Average. Average. There are no toiletries by the sink. No luggage. The welcome pack and pamphlets are untouched. His ID said *Security Guard*, which is a go-to second job for a—

Clare pushes her sunglasses back on. 'What will it cost me to leave?'

'This is another party to you,' he says.

She doesn't reply.

'It's going to be fine. In fact, I'm easier than your usual clientele because there's no pretending between us.'

'I get to leave after, right?'

'Absolutely. I'm not going to interfere in your business.' He offers her complimentary water from by the phone.

She won't risk it, even if it appears intact. Takes a swig from some water she brought with her. Her mind flashes to the pepper spray in the bottom of her bag. Maybe there is no point if he has a gun in the room.

'I can tell you're a professional. You're smart, and I bet you had excellent reasons for choosing this lifestyle. You're a single mom, am I right? Boy or girl? I'm not prying, just trying to get to know you.'

She points with a playful, *yeah, you got me*, gesture.

'This comes with the gig. It's part of the deal you made at the crossroads: sooner or later it's your turn. Any apprehension you feel, I urge you to take responsibility for. You look like a waitress.'

She checks her bland executive attire, unsure how it can be construed as a server's uniform.

'Your hair is down in your pictures.' He reaches in for the bobby pins, pulling hairs out of the bun she styled less than an hour ago. 'I got this,' he says when she tries doing it. 'There, more natural. You can start by telling me your name? I know it isn't Clare.'

'If you aren't arresting me, what difference does it make?'

'For authenticity. I like keeping things as real as possible, to have a genuine connection with the women I make love to. Nothing should get in the way. No barriers.'

She wags her finger again. 'That isn't what we agreed.'

'Take your sunglasses off. They're great. I'd hate if they were damaged.'

She adjusts them.

'Everyone has aspects of his job he doesn't like. In my line of work, it's lowlife. I see mankind at its worst, doing evil deeds to one another, ruining lives, knowing I'm the guy who has to intervene – I'm it. The white knight who saves the day.'

'Am I being arrested?'

'Certainly not. I'm a gentleman. Quid pro pro.' Then he laughs. 'God, you're always emotional.'

'I'm sorry? We have not met before.'

'It's okay. I understand. Obviously you want to stay, America is the greatest country in the world.'

What other countries have you been to? She covers her mouth. Clare mustn't, she isn't that funny.

'We're indoors. You can lose the glasses.'

This isn't the time to kick herself. Clare needs self-belief, not negative self-talk. Imagines walking away from the hotel unaided: she promises it to herself.

'Miss,' he says with a hint of impatience, 'you'll start over again tomorrow.'

She puts them away, possum-calm. Magnificent smile.

[record]

'Your wife has no idea. Does she? I bet every effort she makes is to protect the life you've built together. Your home and place in the community. So this is insane to her. No way would she understand the thrill you get from jeopardising literally everything you have in the whole world. Your wife is gonna cry, and then scream for a divorce. Poor her. No. You need to pay attention to me now. It is all about to change. My mother is famous.

'Are your kids old enough to understand, um, this? They soon will, and they are going to need counselling. This is the story they'll definitely tell when they mess up their own lives someday. What their father did. You'll lose your job, your house, your reputation, and be broke. And alone, did I mention alone? Your friends won't want to know you, you can try, but they won't return your calls.

'Original is what my mum is. With a vicious temper. OMG, she'll chew you up. She made herself into a professor at Cambridge, she wasn't born to it. She lectures all over Europe, in Amsterdam, Italy, and everywhere. They listen to her because she is an actual genius. Harvard wants her but she won't budge, all the best ones do. She is on TV and wrote a bestselling book. I used to think that all parents went on the news to announce big scientific discoveries. Ha, even our prime minister knows her for her confidential government research. She has a Wikipedia page and a blue tick. She is the real thing. You aren't. I know because I searched!

'Don't worry, we'll make sure you're plastered all over the internet from now on, for eternity. Your name will never be separated from what you did.

'I'm sorry you wasted your chance to be heroic. You must've known if you kept on treating people this way, someone would make you pay for it? It's your turn, you see.

'Without the culinary workers, and laundry workers, and guestroom attendants, and utility porters, and bus girls and boys, and women with unbelievable stamina ... How many millions of guests with money to burn simply won't come here again? When I try thinking about it ... The amount we put in, so many of us, this city especially, you should be thanking us and shower us with dollars and benefits on a daily basis? And you should feel frightened of what we could do. I work alone; however, I am not alone.

'Other girls, we'll help them come forward. I have a mum who has devoted her life to telling the truth, she's so fucking reliable. And rich enough to end you. I don't mind waiting while you google her; drink some water? I'm a professional and I explained the rules. All you had to do was be appropriate.'

[stop]

Send or delete?

Schedule. [timer] [dynamite]

Implode it like the Riviera.

Cara

I had to think. I don't wish to hear from you again.

This must seem confusing when I reached out to you. I saw your other social media by mistake and then a website. I don't know what to say. There is no doubt it is you, don't deny it. I am stunned completely. Is it drugs? Don't reply, I won't read. Clearly I haven't done a thing right by you.

I wish I hadn't wasted my time. I am deleting you now.

Yours sincerely, because 'love' is more than Cara can manage. Send or delete?

Send. Absolutely, send it forth. They weren't a family in the first place; what difference does it make? Stop messing around in the drafts folder and get it over with.

Although *I have deleted you* is more impactful than *I am deleting you now.* A fait accompli.

Cara reads it back: it's like a cross between a Dear John letter and a suspension from the headmistress. *I don't wish to hear from you again . . . You have let yourself down, and you've let down the entire school.* Hopefully she doesn't sound like this in real life.

Is it drugs? which is non-specific because she doesn't know what the drugs are any more, presumably not ecstasy and heroin, that was the nineties.

Dear Miss Wycliffe? Was that the salutation she meant to put? *Yours sincerely, Dr Cara Brenner,* as though they were strangers? But they are, that's the point.

Don't reply, I won't read is clipped. Why not put DONT REPLY STOP WONT READ STOP and be done with it.

Notwithstanding, Cara wants to send it as it is. Should've sent it when it was fresh with anger. Heather is in the wrong. She, Cara, is the one who should be upset.

I am deleting you. Right now.

No sooner than she tries blocking Heather across various platforms does she discover that the handles stay in her blocked lists. How do you clear them? And a bunch of tags and comments are stuck to her posts, annoying snippets like *I see you fancy scientist lady in Downing Street did you meet Larry the cat? [happy tears cat]* and *dammit unicorn grilled cheese on the secret menu at Fiddlestix these guys think of everything.* Why can't they be gone gone?

Cara tries contacting support to request that they are taken down. Only, there is no support.

Instead, she is referred along a convoluted chain to community forums which are no help. These companies are harvesting data from a third of the world's population, and are precision enablers of Russian interference with democracies in the West; yet somehow, when you need to be rid of a person, *that* is beyond them?

And it makes no difference on this platform over here, because Heather or *Clare* or whoever she is is set to public and still appears in the browser when Cara is logged out. (Yes, she uses web apps, she's middle-aged.) If only there were a single block button for all the social media. (Whoever is working on that, please can they get a move on.)

It would be easier to delete Cara's accounts and start again, and she's not averse to the idea. But as soon as she tries extricating herself, Facebook turns monstrous like an abusive boyfriend who won't let her go.

Park that.

Decides she'll cleanse her mailboxes, because this she has at least some control over.

She needs to delete Heather from *in, sent, archived, deleted* (because when you're deleted you aren't really deleted); and a folder she made called *personal*, which is a mix of sensitive messages, reservations and saved newsletters; as well as *contacts*. That's when she realises she doesn't know how to set up *redirect to trash* rules.

Does more googles.

By the time Cara is reading another *FAQs* page, she's tired. Stupidly post-cancer-tired.

It is the middle of the afternoon, and sleepiness is dragging her down by the ankles. Caffeine and a brisk walk won't stave it off. It's all the inconvenience of drunkenness with none of the pleasure. There is nothing to do but give in.

She sets her alarm, acknowledging she probably won't hear it. Watches the flashcards in her mind's eye, which are neither sleeping nor awake.

[Heather with her hand in the mouth of a green man]

Cara's subconscious is alerting her to the fact that she ought to have moved the spare key by now. She's kept it in the same hiding place for years.

A job for tomorrow, she thinks, as it'll involve repositioning garden ornaments.

She puts the kettle on and eats a chocolate biscuit. Picks up her computer where she left off.

Suppose for a moment Cara purges her folders, and sets up blocks on all networks and devices: she couldn't stop Heather using a different email address to get round them. It's not as if Cara is able to redact her own contact details from the world. What is she going to do, take her profile down from the university website?

Heather might phone.

Or send a letter (no, she won't do that) or turn up out the blue (yes, she is capable of that). Is Cara going to change her numbers and move house just to be on the safe side?

And photos. Thousands.

Where does Cara even start with them? Decades of careful copying to external hard drives have come back to bite her on the bum. Being forced to choose between viewing each individual item to delete what's appropriate – or wiping everything. Even then they back up to the cloud. She can't stop them; the cloud is basically stealing her photos. When your photos are online, they're out of your hands. Phucking photos.

It's another reason she's mad at her. For being careless. For giving that much power away. Cara had the sexting talk with her, she may as well not have bothered.

Palpitation-cough.

So be it. Cara is not 'deleting' Heather mainly because it creates too much admin. Truer to say she is ignoring her. Unfortunately this means her parting shot will be *I am ignoring you now*, which doesn't have quite the same ring to it.

She will find the words to end it once and for all. Can start the message from scratch. *You are not my problem.*

Slams the laptop closed.

Unless Heather is the victim here.

The possibility she has a pimp or was trafficked somehow is

406

not one Cara has considered before. If Heather has been forced into this lifestyle against her will, then that changes everything. Then it's okay.

No, not 'okay'. But the onus is on Cara to be kind and understanding. Hasn't she read tabloid stories on this very subject? About respectable girls, who grew up riding ponies and playing the violin, being drawn into a seedy underworld of violence and addiction. How modern-day slavery is happening under our very noses in places like Cirencester and St Albans – never mind Las Vegas, where it's endemic. The grainy artwork of a waif on a bare mattress juxtaposed with a smaller picture of a blonde little girl in a tutu. They go into graphic detail, putting the reader in a state of anxiety. Then a belligerent feminist with a rich spouse explains what the solutions are in her column. It is at least conceivable that Heather could end up as *Daily Mail* fodder.

In some sense these 'awareness campaigns' must have worked on Cara, who pauses.

She hovers over the *Clare* avatar. Enlarges it.

Clare Pembroke is a mirror selfie of Heather's body from the neck down, her face obscured by her phone. It is her.

Even if the silhouette were not instantly recognisable, Cara can see Ruth's necklace and knows the handbag up close.

She inhales through the nose – a waft like bergamot. Suddenly feels a bit self-conscious. As though she were guilty of snooping.

Look, it isn't snooping when an algorithm pops up *friend* (verb) and *follow* (noun) suggestions. Cara blew past them multiple times – disregarded them as sex bots and background noise. Which in a way they were. Heather, blithely copying content from one account to the next, has only herself to blame. Reverse image searches are available to anybody.

She seems to be running several different identities, such as *@clarepem6roke* and *@cl_r__p_mbr_k_*, unable to settle on a definitive version. Probably keeps getting banned for violating terms of service, she thinks.

Another incarnation, *Clar Pemb (silent b)*, is the classic photographer's self-portrait, looking through a camera viewer back to herself.

This is the moment to stop.

Cara knows what she knows. She has read several unsavoury replies from appalling males already, and has acronyms in her browser history that she'd really rather weren't there. She's already uncovered things she can't unsee.

Dithers the mousepad.

What if Heather's posing like a page-three girl? What if she isn't and it's worse? What if she's *in flagrante* – if they're stylised misogynistic abuse – if they're self-hating cries for help?

Photo photo photo stretching back in a timeline. She daren't look directly at them.

Clicks a thumbnail at random.

Topless, as Cara feared. Although her nipples aren't showing. The photo has been taken coyly, in a polished rectangle that looks like part of a carved door.

Click.

Modelling lingerie in a baroque mirror, peering over the top of a peacock fan. That it's monochrome hardly makes it classy.

Click.

A picture of the back of her head, her phone raised in both hands like a source of power.

Click.

Heather from the neck down in underwear, in the morning light of a hotel-room window. A fuzzed-out shape behind her.

Click.

Heather's bare legs in shorts with slutty heels and a Bardot top. It's another selfie in a mirror, in a nightclub ladies' loo. Her hair is swept across her face; partygoers in the background; and a neon sign in reverse which says, *Thought is Free.*

Click.

Provocatively eating a banana, it fills her whole face – in public, on a travellator.

Click.

Finally, one that's not a selfie: it is a portrait of a woman, a soccer-mom type, wearing reflective sunglasses. Heather's features are distorted points in the lenses.

Click.

Taken in a ceiling mirror above a messy bed. Heather's arm shields her eyes.

Click.

Sandals, heels, flip-flops, boots, tennis shoes, sneakers, all piled up – including a child's shoes. Her bare feet with scrappy remnants of a pedicure.

Click.

Liquors in rows on a back bar and a glimpse of her waiting to be served.

Click.

An ailing motel and a man in a seahorse carnival mask. The photographer's shadow is visible on the tarmac.

Click.

Poolside knees.

Click.

A metal lampshade: canteen benches and windows are reflected in it, and the customers and staff are like a Lowry.

Click.

String bikini with a sunhat that blots out her face.

Click.

Sitting outside doing her make-up in a cosmetic mirror. The shady tangles of an overhanging plant criss-cross her.

Click.

A store window on a street. Heather grey and faint, drinking through a straw from an oversized cup. Spectral pedestrians pass by behind.

Click.

Red bodycon, red hair, red umbrella.

Click.

Heather lurks on the edge of the frame like the Woman in Black, the only soft shape in a retreating hallway of straight lines and sharp corners.

Click.

Eyes in rear-view mirror.

Click.

Escalators up and down between gold polished panels, and several smudgy figures standing on them.

Click.

She is completely bare, frowning through a gap wiped in the steam of a bathroom mirror.

Click.

A silhouette stretches along the ground in early evening, the city colours blend like marbling inks.

Click.

Changing-room selfie, wearing an elegant dress. Her reflection looks over her shoulder, joined to another view of her profile turned away.

Click.

Mirrors on opposite walls and a dotted line of tealights

create the impression of infinity. Casual Heathers, in jeans and vests and—

My sunglasses, Cara thinks.

Click.

Scruffy in patio doors, exhaling smoke like a medium. Concentrating on something the viewer can't see.

'Why didn't you tell me you're an artist?'

The treatment that saved Cara's life and that she is supposed to be grateful for has accelerated the ageing process. It is a menopausal moment. Suddenly Cara feels hot. She wets a piece of kitchen roll for her neck and cheeks, and when it doesn't work, struggles off her lounge top and throws open the back door, not caring if the neighbours see her mutilated chest.

Bright specks swimming. She leans, ears thumping with blood, sighs through the dizzy spell. Still they swim in her peripheral vision.

She stares at the aquarium and doubts her sanity.

Oliver has had a baby. A full-grown goldfish baby.

No, that's not it. Asexual reproduction: he has split off a clone. Nope? Maybe another goldfish climbed in through the window then.

Orange and white gold.

They mouth. Fan their pectoral fins. Hustle the glass.

Oh crap. What if Dr Brenner went to the pet shop herself, bought a second goldfish, put it in the tank with the first one, and totally forgot about it? Dementia? Blackout?

And yet count them. Hers and another. Two.

Unless they were both here all along and Cara didn't notice. Impossible.

9

Thermoreceptors

temperature

Heather

The shield has four lions passant guardant on red, and a closed book on an ermine cross.

Hinc lucem et pocula sacra.

From here, enlightenment and sacred quaffing.

If you're accepted, you are matriculated. Keep term within the university precincts. Then you bunder before you take the Tripos. Eat meals in dining halls with Masters' portraits, and hammerbeam roofs. Experience Cindy's like a local, Sex Club, and the nervous heat of Suicide Sunday. Feel at home in your college, thanks to the army of bedders, porters and stewards.

From freshers testing their slang to academics wearing gowns for degrees earned fifty years ago: make it here, and no one can deny you've made it.

But none of that is going to happen to you, Heather. Don't worry, your Cantabrigian life will be short.

She's in the Arid Lands glasshouse at the Botanic Garden where the heat is soaring, trying to figure out if she recognises any cacti from real life. They're in hard beds arranged with rocks, chubby limbs taller than she is, green globes fat on the ground, and hairy with needles.

She reads the labels. *Euphorbia horrida (African milk barrel)* and *Ferocactus pilosus (Mexican lime cactus)*. Likes them because they look the way you'd expect them to, like cartoons.

Can't see any she's familiar with. Not that she took much notice when she was out and about in the desert.

Heather focuses manually on a *golden barrel* with a fast shutter speed to eliminate shake. A pompom to the naked eye – zoom closer and it's covered with spines. Click. There is so much to look at in here, and she isn't put off by the heat.

Incoming text from Glenda. *U wondered of. Where r u?*

Heather sends *greenhouse*.

Immediately, *Which?!!!*

She tucks her phone in her pocket. Refocuses on a *mammillaria* as near as she dares to its specks spiralling outwards. '*Cacti spiral spikey-wikey*,' she mumbles as she clicks.

The phone pips again. She ignores it because she can see Glenda outside, fanning herself with a garden map.

Then Cara appears too.

Heather ducks behind a prickly pear with mean orange pimples. She's certain that tea at Glenda's house would've been good enough for them both. When Heather mentioned visiting the Botanic Garden, she was introducing a new topic entirely. She meant alone, so she could practise taking pictures ... But Glenda has assumed the role of mediator, and here they are.

Cara looks older and her posture is cowed. Less impressive than she was. She is wearing a printed dress with Menorcan sandals, and her hair is pixie short and smoky. She faces in another direction and shrugs her rounded shoulders.

Their lips move like a silent film, questioningly.

Cara shakes her head. Looks every which way but hers.

Heather points her camera. Grazes the shutter button without pressing.

Glenda carries on out of shot, and Cara doesn't follow her. She folds her arms, scrapes the parched ground with her foot. Turns away from the glasshouses.

Heather exits the desert.

Enters the tropical rainforest house, which smells of flowering vines and drenched leaves, humid and hotter.

Cara

Cara is sitting on a bench near the Glasshouse Range. She is within the sound of a fountain, by the bee borders in various shades of violet (Amethyst, Lubecca and Liquorice Blue) and palm trees. The bees zizz strangely in the heat. She cannot remember a day like it.

Grids of windows are full of greenery like giant display cabinets. Dense as jungle. Leaves as large as banners press against the glass, and creepers dangle like party streamers. Difficult to make out if anyone's in there.

(Increased blood flow to the fusiform face area (Brodmann area 37) tucked behind the ears.)

Cara lifts her hand to wave at the appropriate moment. Decides in advance it'll be a casual gesture to convey *no hurry*. Doesn't get the chance to use it, because Heather disappears into the vegetation without looking at her.

Perhaps it's not that hot. Perhaps it's only Cara's body on its menopausal journey of embarrassment. She's sweating through her underwear. Her face is on fire.

Minutes later, Glenda and Heather come out together. Glenda is carrying a map of the Botanic Garden like a theatre programme.

Heather looks as though she's gone up a dress size, has colour in her cheeks and deeper dimples, also the hint of a frown line. Wears a white T-shirt which looks too large for her, and pink shorts. Her hair is dusty pink. She has on a backpack, carries a bulky camera on a strap, and is wearing Cara's sunglasses.

'Doesn't she look well?' Glenda says.

Cara rolls her eyes. *She's* the one who looks well.

'I've been kicked out of bars and of hotels – even a country. But I've never been kicked out of a greenhouse before.'

'Doesn't she make you laugh?' Glenda says. 'It was absolutely roasting inside, it couldn't possibly be safe, and there she was snap-snap like it was normal. If I'd had to stay in there any longer, I swear I'd have fainted dead on the floor, you'd be carrying me out on a stretcher. They have to close it, though, because they don't want to get sued, you see.'

Heather twiddles her camera. 'I wasn't finished. Hey.'

'Hi.'

Glenda fans. 'It's like we're abroad. In some countries it's like this all the time, I don't know how they manage.'

'They have real Venus flytraps in there; they're smaller than I thought they'd be. Tiny, like this.' Heather shows the tip of her finger, compared to a macro photo on her camera of a deep, fleshy organism. 'There really were dead flies in it, how does it know? I'd love to see one land in its jaws and get eaten.'

'Are you all right, Cara Mia? Are you okay in this heat? I don't want you suffering in silence.'

'I'm fine.'

'Because if it's too hot today, we can always come back when there's less chance of heatstroke? She gets fatigue, you see, and then she'll be grumpy with you for hours on end, and you

419

won't know why – and afterwards she'll say it's because of the treatment she had way back when. Only by that time your whole outing is ruined.'

Heather rummages in her backpack.

'She's lost her energy,' Glenda continues. 'That I do understand, none of us is getting any younger. But I thought something like this was supposed to help a person see the world in a new light? Grow. Be appreciative. No offence, Cara, but it's become your excuse for everything.'

Heather takes out a red umbrella and gives it to Glenda. 'Here. Works great for the shade? You can go home if you like, and I'll stay and make sure she's okay?'

'I *am* okay.'

'As a parasol?' Glenda opens it with a flourish. 'I feel like a lady in a Jane Austen. Text me. Either of you.' She toddles down the path, scrunching with every step.

They watch her go.

Heather examines the visitor's map. 'Are you in any pain?'

'Of course not.'

She looks over her shoulder. 'We need to find the lake. D'you know where it is?'

'No, I'm afraid I don't. I haven't been here before.'

'You have. You must've done. Glenda said you had?'

'They might have brought me when I was a child. And I came to a recital ages ago, but it was dark.'

'We came here together, the three of us. You, me and Dad. We saw the lake. You got angsty because I was standing too close to the edge and I told you I couldn't swim.'

'I'm sorry, I still don't know where it is. Anyway, it's more of a pond ... Where did the map come from?'

'Woman on the front desk.'

'She didn't give me one.'

'Maybe she thinks you're a loser?' Heather stomps ahead.

Cara traipses after her. They don't stop to admire the roses. 'So: how are you getting on at Mother's?'

She replies without turning around, 'I love living with Glenda.'

'Living with, is that what you're doing?'

'Living? Staying? Either way, she's an easy roommate. She has a good heart. And she's not complicated, and I've lived with some total nightmares, mentioning no names.'

Cara shakes her head. 'Rather you than me.'

'She was crying last night,' Heather says simply.

'What on earth for?'

'Because she was upset maybe?'

'I can't think why. She hasn't said anything to me. Then again, I've hardly spoken to her lately.'

'Then you don't think you've done anything wrong? Interesting.'

Cara laughs. 'Have I? Do tell. I'd love to know.'

Heather stops in the middle of the pathway. Pushes the sunglasses up into her hair while she gets her bearings. 'Wait, we've gone wrong somewhere. This place is massive, who knew there were so many plants to look after?'

'I think it's a bit rich of her to come crying to you, I'm not impressed by that at all. Whatever it is.'

'Yep. I get it.'

Cara tuts. 'Do you?'

'Glenda's feelings don't count, because she got into the habit of hurting you without quite realising it. You probably tried to tell her that you were sick, only she didn't understand how serious it was. Then you took matters into your own hands because you're used to being independent. You told yourself there was nothing wrong with keeping it secret, because you were entitled

421

to do this your way. It was nobody else's business.'

'It's not "secrecy". They call it patient confidentiality for a reason. How is she still upset about that?'

'She isn't – she remembers with questions. It's not the same. It doesn't matter. The fact is, you're here and alive, and she is here for you now when you need her – and there's nothing else to add into the equation, is there? I put it in science speak for you.'

'Good. All's well that end's well.'

'Right?' Heather looks hard at her. 'No one needs to be upset, ever.'

'Are you upset?'

'I'm going to say no. Although, I do wonder how bad it would have to be for you to bother being honest with me. It's not like we weren't in contact or anything, you know, or was that bullshit?'

She snorts at the irony. 'Since we're talking about what we're talking about . . .'

Heather tilts her face. Pulls back some pink hair, as though it actually makes a difference as to whether or not she'll hear her. 'Yeah?'

Cara inhales, ready to make the speech she has prepared for precisely this moment. It strikes her that Heather, who used to be terrible at eye contact, is holding her gaze. That's good. She should be able to look at her like an equal. It makes it easier for the nuance to come through.

What is about to follow is nothing less than a researched statement. A gracious critique of the dangers she put herself in. Not confrontational: just firm and fair. Plus, a way forward, with reasonable conditions attached.

Cara flattens her magnanimous mouth. She has held her breath for several seconds. Says, 'I thought that thing you did with the fish was out of order.'

422

Heather blinks slowly. 'What fish?'

'Your little joke. It wasn't very mature of you.'

'What are you talking about? When did I make a fish joke?'

Oh no, Cara thinks, swinging back ever-so-slightly to having imagined it. 'Forget it.' If she pretends she isn't interested, then Heather is more likely to confess. 'I'm dead serious about the other thing, though. I don't see why I should feel guilty.'

'Because we had a pact.'

'That was if one of us got married.'

'But not if one of us gets cancer? Can you hear yourself?'

'Please, not this.'

'I don't understand *why* you think it's okay to keep something like that from me,' Heather screeches. 'I was available, wasn't I? I left the way open. You could have tried. I almost said to you – I knew there was something wrong, it was driving me crazy, and I never said, because *this* never occurred to me. Aunt Kathy knew before I did. What the hell is that about? Unless you truly believe, deep down, that I wasn't part of your life – and may I remind you I actually was, basically, for most of my childhood, and if things had worked out differently ... I cannot bear the thought of you going through this without me. Because if I had been here, I could've told you it wasn't your fault.'

She says quietly, 'I know it wasn't my fault.'

'Do you?'

'Of course. It was bad luck.' Cara suddenly feels dehydrated. 'These things happen randomly. I'm fine. Really. I had good cancer.' She adjusts the neckline of her dress, which has slipped down slightly. 'I hear what you're saying, though, and it's sweet of you to be concerned. It's in the past – not far enough in the past.'

'Is it? What if it comes back? Did you ever think of *that*?'

Honestly, does Cara ever think of that? No more than ten

times a day. 'I did what was right for me. How other people react is not my problem.'

'You are the stupidest professor I ever met. Don't let them hear you talk like this, or they'll take away your degrees.'

'I'm not a ... You're exhausting.'

'I'm keeping this,' Heather says, consulting the map again, 'this is my map. If you want one for yourself, you'll have to pick it up on the way out. Those trees are in the way.'

They follow a path through a forced woodland to an artificial stream flowing into the lake with stepping stones. It's clustered with lily pads, reeds, yellow irises, and the water is the colour of black tea, reflecting the trees and sky. Insects rest on surface tension. The flat stones lie above the waterline, baking in the sun.

'For what it's worth,' says Cara, 'I could have walked away from the chemo. That would have been a valid choice as well. But I was responsible, I knew what I was putting my body through, and I could handle it.'

Heather is folding the map and putting it in her rucksack, instead of giving it to her to hold. 'Yay you.'

Cara's expression hardens. 'Wasn't it you who said I was doing too much – that I should please myself more, and worry less about other people? I should be reducing my stress levels? Well, you were right. On this occasion, I agreed with you.'

'Yay me.'

'It was my tumour, and my agenda, Heather, and you know what else? If I want to put fake boobs on a real woman, I will get them done. I still have the option. Or perhaps I won't. I don't make decisions based on what other people think of me; not all of us are as wrapped up in our appearance as you are. And if I want tattoos to cover every centimetre of my skin – if I want to smoke eighty cigarettes a day for the rest of my life, or favour acupuncture over western medicine, or go skydiving, I can do that too. I may not be brilliant, and sometimes it occurs to me I'm not even clever, but I'm right about this – and you know I am. The day my hand is trapped in the rubble of a collapsed building and I cannot be rescued – give me a saw, and watch me amputate my own arm. I will do it. What's mine is mine. I will not apologise to anyone. Do I seriously need to convince you of all people?'

She adjusts her camera and exhales like a horse. 'Sorry. I stopped listening.'

Heather steps off. Walks across the stepping stones on the lake and stares at what's below the surface. Leans forwards. Points her camera down to the water.

Serves her right if she falls in.

Click.

(Will it be shallow, though, shallow and come up to her knees like a sitcom? Or is it deep, deeper than a mineshaft, and the water will cover her head as she sinks?)

Cara steps onto a rock, engaging what's left of her core strength to catch her mid-plunge. Will pull her out by the backpack if necessary.

Heather checks the display and grimaces. Tries again to take – something.

Cara sees what, nearly blurts it out—

Heather

'—I can hear you thinking it?' Heather says. 'They aren't selfies. They're self-portraits. There are rules.'

Cara is bent with her hands on her knees, as if her stepping stone is a ledge.

They both look to see what's beneath, where life is soft. A liquid system of slimy skins, stings and jelly. Knotted weeds. Squirmy critters. A grey bolt moves through webs of green.

Up here is the heavens to them.

'I'm not vain or jokey, what you said today is wrong. You're a snob, Cara . . . I can't do it with you looking?'

Cara retreats to dry land, hesitant.

Heather takes a few extra shots, murky in outline. 'The body is really weird. How it wants to go on. A lot depends on where you are at a given moment, what's within reach, and how, um, important the world is telling you you are. You take that into consideration. I do. I can understand why some people take the shortest route to stop their pain, but I'm not that way inclined. There's the thing – and then there's being isolated because of the thing. It is your body that really does the job of telling you to carry on. Because it's waiting for you to feel better. On some level it is sort of aware it's possible. And it fights for you! We are capable of change, you told me, and that is the truest thing anyone has ever said. But, and it is a big but, it needs . . .' She focuses on some ducks. 'Space. If you have a bit of leeway to feel into, then you will eventually be overall okay. On the inside, I mean. The space you usually let other people fill – and where you keep your expectations if you have any – you have to set it aside for yourself. It's harder than it sounds. And this is the space where ideas come from. Breakthroughs happen there, if it's not too overcrowded, and repairs too, I've seen it in other girls. Sometimes we are a safe person for someone else, and they share a tiny bit of what they can't handle on their own. We do that without fully understanding how it works. Yet we recognise it when it comes along. And when you can't explain what has happened, it might be a sign you need to leave it alone for longer. Feel, until the body has worked out what it needs to. Is caught up. It's always keeping a record, you see. I was fortunate, I had the option of stepping back. My body wanted me to, and so did I.'

'Are you okay?'

'I am something other than okay. I'm capable of more than being totally angry. Other voices come through, like yours. And I have a place to stay and rest – thanks to Glenda. Who doesn't tax my brain. I didn't have much stuff to lose. I backed up my photos. A gazillion photos, funnily enough.'

The garden looks like a picture book.

Cara says, 'Shall we find a pizza?'

'Yes, please.'

The restaurant has propped open its doors and positioned fans which push around the warm air.

Heather pulls apart a pizza as she talks. 'I have a job interview on Friday. It's care work. I'm not exactly qualified for it, but they reckon they can arrange training, and they sound kind of desperate to hire.'

'Is that wise?'

'Why not? What's wrong with it? Because you think care-giving isn't a proper skill? Because personal care for older people is icky?'

'No, nothing like that.' Cara has ordered the mushroom risotto instead of seafood linguine. Seems unhappy with her choice.

Heather asks how it is.

'*Così-così*,' she replies.

'It's not unskilled,' Heather continues. 'This may come as a surprise to you, but having a job is the line before scarcity for most people in real life? What you need to get by. Not everyone is privileged enough to have a career.'

'I'm growing tired of hearing how *privileged* I am,' Cara says, 'the implication being that I can't recognise what's grotesque when I see it.'

Heather frowns. 'I thought you gave up social media?'

'Accomplished women are soft targets, everyone agrees—'

'Excuse me, we were talking about me?'

Cara lays down her fork. 'Is this because of Ruth?'

'Nope. I don't think so.'

'Sometimes we make choices emotionally.'

'How else does a person make choices? I don't understand, how can a job interview be connected with Mum?'

'You're right. It isn't. It was just a thought. I mean, I'd like for you to do what interests you. That is all I've ever wanted for you. Do something with your abilities the way your friend Betty has.'

'I am.'

'Would you say caring is your passion then?'

'I'd say it's labour that society needs, and I might be okay at it.

I have a passion, I have a hoofing big camera, didn't you notice? My roommate gave it to me.'

'All right, I'll stop trying to make it better.' She takes a sip of water. 'Nice roommate?'

Heather nods. 'She meant well. I wonder if I'll ever see them again, everybody who was passing through? Wow, me too, now I come to think of it. They have a project for everything there: there was one I liked where I made friends, and that was cool.'

'Like a community?'

'More of a coven. They're wild for public speaking. I am not.'

'I don't know,' Cara says. 'Your video diary is pretty interesting.'

They eat in silence for a while. Heather browses on her phone in one hand, and holds a pizza slice in the other. Without glancing up, she says, 'I take it the boyfriend is long gone?'

'I was shocked every time I looked in the mirror and saw how much damage had been done. Maybe he was right to end the relationship when he did.'

'And if it was reversed, would you have broken up with him too?'

Cara looks forlorn. 'I don't feel sexy any more,' she whispers.

'Oh, but you will. Scars are even sexier than tattoos are. Loads of men would be into you, and your body, I can tell you that for a fact.'

'If I want dating advice, I'll ask for it.' She pushes risotto around her plate. 'What are you going to miss most?'

'Honestly, it has an – atmosphere. The shows, and colours – neon and natural, that I never got sick of – and fantasy buildings. Dreamers of all sizes in the same place, brushing against one another. Blowing on dice. Taking risks. Frittering away whatever they've got. The pop and fizz and clink of glasses. Festivals in the desert. Freelancers and moonlighters and dancers. It's only when you come out that you realise there is nothing to show for it.'

'Maybe you can go back someday?'

'I don't think they're going to let me in again.' Heather blows her pink fringe. 'I burnt my bridges.'

'I'm sure we could fix it,' Cara says uncertainly. 'Here, drink some water. Are you in trouble? Do you need money?'

'A change of scenery is not the worst thing for me right now.' Heather dabs herself with a napkin, and is sticking to the leather seat. Pretends to say to the near-empty restaurant, 'You're going to have to be less stingy about installing air con, guys?'

'Do you remember going to Great Yarmouth, the two of us, the day Ruth passed away?'

'Yes.'

'The idea of closure is vague to me, I don't know enough about it. But I do worry that I made things worse for you, without meaning to.'

'We don't have to talk about this, Cara.'

'True, it is too hot for serious discussions, and we're only drinking tap water ... I tried telling him you were old enough to choose your level of involvement. That you might cope better if we trusted your judgement more. I tried saying, as tactfully as possible, that no good would come of your having to sneak around. That you shouldn't miss out on anything.'

I knew you were on my side is what Heather might say if she didn't have a mouth full of pizza.

'I had no idea how fragile he was, and he didn't listen.' Cara shrugs. 'All my suggestions were wrong after that.'

'Have you been to Venice, Italy?'

'I haven't.'

'Why don't we go together this weekend?'

'We can't. You've got an interview on Friday.'

'Next weekend then? Are you free?'

'But what if they ask you to start straight away?'

'That will only be an issue if they offer it to me, and it won't be if they don't, so . . .' She nibbles the crust. 'Shall I come by yours afterwards and tell you how it went?'

'Okay, I'll cook something plant-based for dinner. I take it you can find your way?'

Heather gives a flicker of a smile. She produces the spare key from a zip compartment and places it in the middle of the table.

'You didn't consider waking me . . .?'

'Glenda said not to. It was an emergency. May-who-lives-next-door is downsizing and she was going to leave it behind, which is cruel. I swear, it wasn't a joke. You're saving a small shining life.'

Cara sighs. 'There's no rush,' she says, pushing the key back to Heather's side of the table. 'We could book Venice for Easter, you know, if you decide to stick around. I bet it's lovely in spring-time. And less crowded. Perhaps we can invite Glenda.'

'Will we still be allowed to go by then? Aren't they taking away our visiting rights? Are they making it up as they go along? You're the intellectual – you should do something about that.'

The intellectual rubs her forehead with her knuckles.

'Please be gentler to your skin,' she says, lifting away Cara's fingers.

'You should know better than to drop a goldfish in a new tank too quickly. You need to introduce the bag gradually, give it time to acclimatise first.'

'What makes you think I didn't?'

Cara   Heather

The Bridge of Sighs is a Victorian throwback to medieval times, and nothing whatever to do with the original (also named with Byronic licence). The covered bridge is riddled with Gothic tracery and has crenellations across the top. Foils, portcullis and fleur-de-lis are carved in the stonework. It is simply a pathway.

A punt of tourists slides underneath. The river is opaque.

She says, 'You aren't by yourself.'

'*Tak.*'

A blackbird projects from the trees, a low burr rising to a scattered woodnote, and a curt, squeaky end.

Acknowledgements

I wrote about Las Vegas and Cambridge as an outsider, and no doubt I have made errors. Any details I got right are due to the knowledge and kindness of many people. While I cannot thank everybody personally, a few names stand out.

In Las Vegas: Thank you to Prof Barb Brents, Prof Lynn Comella and especially Andrea Dassopoulos at University of Nevada, Las Vegas. Thanks also to: William Bruchert; and Matthew O'Brien. Unplanned conversations with hospitality workers, drivers, visitors and residents contributed to the world-building of 'my' Las Vegas. Most of all, thank you to Dr Jenny Heineman (now at University of Nebraska Omaha), I will be forever grateful.

In Cambridge: Thank you to Margaret Patterson for the quotidian details I was looking for. Thank you to CamBRAIN: The Cambridge Neuroscience Society, University of Cambridge. Likewise, thank you to New Directions in the Study of the Mind (2015–2017) at the Faculty of Philosophy, University of Cambridge. Unplanned conversations with a tour guide and an economist added colour to 'my' Cambridge. Most of all, thank you to Dr David Vogelsang (now at Leiden University), I will be forever grateful.

During my research I was privileged to meet several advocates for evidence-led policymaking who shaped my thinking in unexpected ways. A huge thank you to Niki Adams and Laura Watson at the English Collective of Prostitutes (ECP), a network of sex workers working both on the streets and indoors, campaigning for decriminalisation and safety. Likewise, a huge thank you to Prof Sarah Main at the Campaign for Science and Engineering (CaSE), the UK's leading independent advocacy group for the STEM sectors.

Thank you to Maddy Caulfield for the helpful conversation. Thank you to Isabella Carta for the helpful email.

I wouldn't flourish without a supportive creative writing community here in Suffolk. Thank you to Wolsey Writers for trusting, motivating and challenging me since 2015. Your journeys on the page, and beyond, are inspiring. Thank you to the talented English Team at University of Suffolk: Dr Jenny Amos, Dr Amanda Hodgkinson, Dr Darragh Martin, Dr Lindsey Scott and Dr Andrea Smith. Your excellence and positivity are reflected in the accomplishments of our students. Of the many local champions of culture and literature, I wish to highlight and express my thanks to: New Wolsey Theatre; Jon Wright, BBC Radio Suffolk; Gill Lowe, Suffolk Book League; Mai Black, Suffolk Writers Group; INK Festival; and Andrew Marsh, Dial Lane Books.

Of the festivals and book groups I have participated in since my debut, I remain especially grateful to the English Language Book Group, Maisons Laffitte/Le Mesnil le Roi, Paris; Milton Keynes Lit Fest; Elaine Newton: Critic's Choice, Artis – Naples, Florida; and Channel 4 TV Book Club.

To the authors I've met through published works, empathetic emails and in-person – you are a lifeline. Thank you to: Jessica

Cornwell; Jim Crace; Nicci French; Dr Ashley Hickson-Lovence; Dr Beatrice Hitchman; Dr Ed Hogan; Frankie Miren; Kate Sawyer; Eva Verde; and Kate Worsley.

Thank you to Bill Hamilton and the superb team at A. M. Heath Literary Agents. I'm incredibly lucky to have you on my side.

Thank you to Ursula Doyle at Fleet for giving *Pathways* a good home. You have understood my writing from the start. Thank you to the wonderful team at Little, Brown UK, especially Nithya Rae, Zoë Hood and Clare Smith.

This novel wouldn't exist had I not read the philosopher Mary Midgley's *Science and Poetry* (Routledge, 2001). Midgley uses a simile of the 'ill-lit aquarium' to describe 'our world, including ourselves' which must be viewed through its various windows to be better understood. Seeing Teller's magic trick *Silver Fish* live at the Rio in 2016 provided further inspiration.

My creative process was interrupted by breast cancer. Thank you to the loved ones who supported me throughout; and thank you to the brilliant NHS staff at Ipswich Hospital who saved my life. To my readers, thank you for your patience.

Finally, I would not be the author I am without the friendship and belief of Hilary Mantel. She understood our ephemeral and material lives better than anyone.